Available in from Mills &

THE BODYGUARD'S RETURN

"So, you're offering to...what? Be my personal bodyguard?"

"In an unofficial capacity," Joshua replied.

Savannah had managed to minimise the danger of last night since she'd awakened this morning, but his offer of bodyguard services put a new spin on things.

"Are you sure that's necessary?" she asked.

"No, I'm not sure about much of anything. But I've always thought it was better to be safe than sorry."

"If we're talking about my safety, then I like the way you think," she said with a touch of dry humour. She wasn't sure what made her more uncomfortable, the way her heart pounded at the thought that she might be in danger, or her heart's reaction to the thought of having Joshua at her side for the next couple of days.

INTIMATE ENEMY

"Can I help you with something?"

He stiffened and the air between them practically shimmered. The tightness in her gut warned her it was Russ before he glanced over his shoulder, but it didn't lessen the impact of coming face to face with him for the first time in months. It didn't make the derision in his blue eyes any easier to take.

Slowly he stood and she watched. His jeans fitted just as snugly and his T-shirt looked a luscious size too small. With his impressive muscles flexing, his dark hair cut really short and his jaw stubbled with beard, he looked too damn sexy for her own good.

"Sorry," he said in a tone that clearly said he wasn't. "I didn't hear the portals opening."

The portals of hell. She'd heard some of the names he called her.

She would have been amused by them if they'd come from someone else.

All the characters in this book have no existence outside the imagination of the author, and have no relation whatsoever to anyone bearing the same name or names. They are not even distantly inspired by any individual known or unknown to the author, and all the incidents are pure invention.

All Rights Reserved including the right of reproduction in whole or in part in any form. This edition is published by arrangement with Harlequin Enterprises II B.V./S.à.r.l. The text of this publication or any part thereof may not be reproduced or transmitted in any form or by any means, electronic or mechanical, including photocopying, recording, storage in an information retrieval system, or otherwise, without the written permission of the publisher.

This book is sold subject to the condition that it shall not, by way of trade or otherwise, be lent, resold, hired out or otherwise circulated without the prior consent of the publisher in any form of binding or cover other than that in which it is published and without a similar condition including this condition being imposed on the subsequent purchaser.

® and ™ are trademarks owned and used by the trademark owner and/or its licensee. Trademarks marked with ® are registered with the United Kingdom Patent Office and/or the Office for Harmonisation in the Internal Market and in other countries.

First published in Great Britain 2009
Harlequin Mills & Boon Limited,
Eton House, 18-24 Paradise Road, Richmond, Surrey TW9 1SR

The Bodyguard's Return © Carla Cassidy 2007
Intimate Enemy © Marilyn Pappano 2008

ISBN: 978 0 263 87346 7

46-1209

Harlequin Mills & Boon policy is to use papers that are natural, renewable and recyclable products and made from wood grown in sustainable forests. The logging and manufacturing processes conform to the legal environmental regulations of the country of origin.

Printed and bound in Spain
by Litografia Rosés S.A., Barcelona

THE BODYGUARD'S RETURN

BY
CARLA CASSIDY

INTIMATE ENEMY

BY
MARILYN PAPPANO

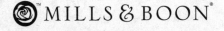

MILLS & BOON

THE BODYGUARD'S RETURN

BY
CARLA CASSIDY

Carla Cassidy is an award-winning author who has written over fifty novels. In 1995 she won Best Romance from *Romantic Times BOOKreviews*. In 1998 she also won a Career Achievement Award for Best Innovative Series from *Romantic Times BOOKreviews*.

Carla believes the only thing better than curling up with a good book to read is sitting down at the computer with a good story to write. She's looking forward to writing many more books and bringing hours of pleasure to readers.

Chapter 1

She'd never meant to make Cotter Creek, Oklahoma, her home. Savannah Marie Clarion had been on her way to nowhere when the transmission in her car had decided to go wonky. She'd managed to pull it into Mechanic's Mansion on Main Street before it had died completely.

She'd taken one look around the dusty small town and had decided Cotter Creek sure felt like nowhere to her.

That had been three months ago. She now hurried down Main Street toward the Sunny Side Up Café where she was meeting Meredith West for lunch. After that she had an interview to conduct for her job as a reporter for the *Cotter Creek Chronicle,* the daily newspaper.

"Good morning, Mr. Rhenquist." She smiled at the old man who sat in a chair in front of the barbershop. His deeply weathered face looked like the cracked Oklahoma earth as he scowled at her.

"Somebody eat the bottom of your britches?" he asked.

She flashed him a bright smile. "It's the latest style, Mr. Rhenquist. They're cropped short on purpose."

"Looks silly to me," he replied. "No place for fashion in Cotter Creek."

"If they ever ban grouchy old farts from Cotter Creek, you'd better pack your bags," she retorted. She instantly bit her lower lip and hurried on, trying not to feel self-conscious in the short gray pants, sleek black boots and pink sweater that clashed cheerfully with her bright red curly hair.

She could almost hear her mother's voice ringing in her ears as she hurried toward the café. "You're brash, Savannah Marie. You're outspoken and it's quite unbecoming."

She stuffed her mother's voice in the mental box where she kept all the unpleasantness of her life as she entered the Sunny Side Up Café. She was greeted by the lingering breakfast scents of fried bacon and strong coffee now being overwhelmed by burgers and onions and the lunchtime fare.

Immediately she spied Meredith at a booth near

the back of the busy café. At the sight of her friend, Savannah couldn't help the smile that curved her lips.

Meredith West had been one of the first people Savannah had met when she'd settled into the upstairs of a house owned by Ms. Winnie Halifax. Meredith had been visiting the sweet old lady when Savannah had been moving in.

On the surface Savannah and Meredith couldn't be more different. Meredith always looked like she'd dressed in the dark, pulling on whatever her hands managed to land on while still half-asleep. On the other hand, Savannah had been breast-fed fashion sense by a superficial mother who had believed physical beauty was the second most important thing to being rich.

"Don't you look spiffy," Meredith said as Savannah slid into the booth opposite her.

"Thanks. Rhenquist just asked me what happened to the bottom of my britches."

Meredith's full lips curved into a smile. "Rhenquist is an old boob."

A young waitress appeared at their table to take their order, interrupting their conversation momentarily. "So, what's up with you?" Savannah asked when the waitress had left their booth. "Are you off on another adventure?"

Meredith worked for the family business, Wild West Protective Services. Savannah had been intrigued when she'd learned her new friend worked as a bodyguard. "And when are you going to let me interview you for my column?"

"No, and never," Meredith replied. "I've decided to take some time off." She leaned forward, her green eyes sparkling. "My brother, Joshua is coming home. He should be here sometime today or tomorrow."

"You have too many brothers. Which one is Joshua?"

"The baby. He's been in New York for the past year and a half and we've all missed him desperately." Her affection for her younger sibling was obvious in her voice.

"Is this a visit?"

"No, he's decided to move back here. He says he's had enough of the big city. He'd probably love for you to interview him. Joshua has never shied away from attention."

"I'll keep that in mind," Savannah replied. "I'm interviewing Charlie Summit this afternoon."

"Now that should be interesting. I can't believe Cotter Creek's epitome of crazy as a loon is going to talk to you." Meredith shoved a strand of her long dark hair behind one ear.

"Actually, beneath his gruff exterior and eccentricities, Charlie is a very nice man. I sometimes go over to his place in the evenings and we play chess together. He's lonely and he was thrilled when I told him I wanted to talk to him for one of my 'People and Personality' columns."

"When we were kids he used to scare the hell out of us," Meredith said after the waitress had returned to serve their orders. "He lived all alone out there in the middle of nowhere and looked like Grizzly Adams on a bad day. There was a rumor that his root cellar was filled with children who had disobeyed their parents."

Savannah laughed. "I wonder who started that particular rumor?"

"Probably some parent with disobedient children."

Meredith paused to take a sip of her iced tea, then continued. "Actually, Joshua became good friends with him when Joshua was about fifteen years old. You know that weather vane that Charlie has stuck in the ground next to his house?"

"You mean that copper monstrosity with the rooster?"

Meredith nodded. "One night a bunch of Joshua's friends dared him to steal it. Joshua sneaked up and Charlie was waiting for him with a shotgun in hand."

"So, what happened?"

"Charlie made Joshua go inside the house and call my father. As punishment Joshua had to go over to Charlie's twice a week after school and work. I think he's kept in touch with Charlie even while he's been in New York."

"If your brother is his friend, that makes two friends for Charlie. I'm hoping my article on him will humanize him and make people look beyond the scruffy beard and gruff exterior."

"Oh, I almost forgot." Meredith opened her purse and pulled out a cream-colored envelope and handed it across the table to Savannah.

"What's this?"

"A wedding invitation. Clay and Libby are getting married a week from next Saturday."

"Wow, that's kind of fast, isn't it?" Savannah knew a little about the romance between Meredith's brother Clay and the beautiful blonde from Hollywood.

Clay had been sent to Hollywood to play bodyguard to Libby's daughter, Gracie, who was a little movie star and had been receiving threatening notes in the mail. Clay and Libby had fallen in love, and Libby and her daughter had moved to Cotter Creek a couple of weeks ago.

Meredith smiled, a touch of wistfulness in her eyes. "Yes, it's fast, but, according to Clay and Libby, when you know something is right you don't waste any time."

The two women continued to visit as they ate their lunch, then all too quickly it was time for Savannah to head to her interview with Charlie.

It was almost one o'clock as Savannah drove down Main Street, headed to the outskirts of town and the small ranch house where Charlie Summit lived.

Every morning for the past three months she had awakened and been vaguely surprised to discover herself for the most part content with her new life.

And content was something she couldn't ever remember feeling in her twenty-four years of life.

Savannah had awakened one morning in her beautiful bedroom in her parents' beautiful house and had realized if she didn't get away from the criticism and unrealistic expectations she'd never know who she was and what she was capable of being.

And so she'd headed for the biggest adventure of her life…finding her life.

It had been that faulty transmission that had brought her to Cotter Creek and a further stroke of luck that Raymond Buchannan, the owner of the local newspaper, was getting old and tired. When she'd approached him with her journalism degree in one hand and an idea for profiling the locals in a column each week in the other, he'd hired her.

In the time she'd been here, she'd grown to love Cotter Creek, but she'd begun to think something bad was happening here. There had been too many accidental deaths of local ranchers lately. On a whim she'd done some research and the results were troubling, to say the least.

She shoved away thoughts of those deaths and rolled down her window to allow in the crisp early-October air, so different from the desert heat in Scottsdale, Arizona, where she'd grown up.

She was looking forward to the interview with Charlie. All her teachers in her journalism classes had told her that she was particularly good at the art of interviewing.

She always managed to glean one little nugget of information that exposed the very center of a person. It was one of her strengths. Her mother had spent her lifetime cataloging Savannah's weaknesses.

Charlie Summit lived, as most of the ranchers in the area did, in the middle of nowhere. But, unlike most of the flat pastures of his neighbors, Charlie's little two-bedroom ranch house was surrounded by woods and a yard that hadn't seen the blade of a lawnmower in the past twenty years.

A rusted-out pickup truck body sat on cinder blocks on the east side of the house, surrounded by old scraps of tin and the infamous, huge, elaborate copper weather vane.

The junkyard collection, coupled with his hermit-like tendencies, certainly helped add to Charlie's reputation as an odd duck.

What was definitely odd was that, as Savannah pulled her car to a halt in front of the overgrown path that led to Charlie's front door, his two dogs, Judd and Jessie, were pacing the porch, obviously agitated.

Charlie never let the dogs stay out on their own. He'd always told her the two mutts were too dumb to know to scratch an itch unless he was sitting beside them telling them how to do it.

As she got out of her car, the two came running to her. They raced around her feet, releasing sharp whines. "What's the matter, boys?" she asked and knelt down to pet first the tall, mostly golden retriever then the smaller, mostly fox terrier. Savannah loved dogs, one of her many character flaws where her parents were concerned.

She stood and looked toward the house, where the front door was open, but no sound drifted outward. Odd. Charlie never left his door open. He'd always told her that an open door invited in trouble.

The curly red hairs on the nape of her neck sprang to attention as a sense of apprehension slithered through her,

"Charlie?" she called as she stepped closer to the porch. Judd and Jessie whined at her feet. "Charlie, it's me, Savannah."

She climbed the steps and paused at the front door as she caught a whiff of a scent that didn't belong. It smelled like a firecracker seconds after explosion. She rapped her knuckles on the screen door, then stepped inside.

"Charlie? Are you home?" She walked the short distance through the foyer, then took a single step into the living room.

Charlie was home. He sat in his favorite recliner in the cluttered living room, a handgun on the floor beside him and the pieces of his head decorating the wall in bloody splatters behind him.

Savannah froze, for a moment her mind refused to make sense of the scene before her. In that instant of immobility she was acutely conscious of the pitiful yowls of the dogs coming from the porch, the laughter of a live audience drifting from the televi-

sion and a mewling noise that she suddenly realized
was coming from her.

That moment of blessed denial passed, and the
horror struck her like a fist to the stomach. Charlie's
sightless blue eyes stared at her as she stumbled
backward, fighting the need to be sick, swallowing
against the scream that begged to be released.

Tears blurred her vision as she backed out the
screen door. She turned blindly, intent on getting to
her car, where her cell phone was in her purse on the
front seat.

The scream that had been trapped in the back of
her throat released itself as a pair of strong hands
grabbed her shoulders.

The red-haired, pink-clad woman nearly barreled
over Joshua West as he stepped up on the porch of
Charlie's house. The shriek she emitted as he caught
her by the shoulders nearly shattered his eardrums,
but the kick she delivered to his shin sent him
backward with a stream of cuss words that would
have daunted the devil.

"What in the hell is wrong with you, lady?" he exclaimed as he grabbed the porch rail to steady himself.

She stared up at him, whiskey-colored eyes wide
and filled with tears. Her mouth worked, opening
and closing, but it was as if the act of speech had left
her. Her skin appeared unnaturally pale, a smatter-
ing of freckles seeming to stand out a full inch from
her cheeks.

As he scowled at her she raised a hand and pointed a trembling finger toward the inside of the house. It was only then that Joshua realized it was fear and horror that rode her features.

He had no idea who she was or what she was doing here, but several other questions quickly filled his head. Why hadn't her ear-splitting scream brought Charlie careening out the door to see what was going on, and why were the dogs running loose?

He took a good, long look at the young woman, in case he had to describe her later, then he went into the house. He'd only taken a single step inside the tiny foyer when he noticed the acrid smell of gunpowder and his gut twisted with a sense of dread.

Smelling gunpowder inside a house was never a good sign. As he took a step into the living room his sense of dread exploded into something deeper, darker. As he stared at Charlie's body, disbelief fought with shock and a quick stab of grief.

It was obvious in a glance that the old man was dead. Joshua was smart enough to know not to disturb anything, although it looked like an open-and-shut case of suicide.

He needed to do something. He needed to call Sheriff Ramsey. Grief threatened to overwhelm the denial, but he shoved it back, knowing there were things that needed to be done.

What had happened here? How on earth had this happened? Dammit, what had made Charlie do such a thing? What had happened to make the man take his own life? Of all the men Joshua had known, he would have thought Charlie the last one who would do something like this.

It was only when he stepped back out of the house that he remembered the woman. She was crouched down next to her car, a hand on Jessie's furry back. As he walked down the steps to the path, she stood, a wary suspicion on her features.

"I called the sheriff," she said, obviously recovering her gift of speech. "He should be here any minute now. Don't come any closer." She held up a can of pepper spray.

Joshua stopped in his tracks. She would have looked quite menacing if the hand holding the spray can weren't shaking so badly.

Some of her color had returned to her face and the freckles now looked as if they belonged on her skin. It was obvious she didn't belong here, didn't belong in Cotter Creek.

She had the sheen of the big city on her, from the toe of her polished boots to the top of her short, curly gelled hair. She represented everything he'd left behind in New York City.

Her hair suited her small, delicate features. She wasn't beautiful, but she was striking. More importantly, there was no blood on her pink sweater or gray cropped slacks. No splatters on the tops of her polished boots.

"Who are you and what are you doing here?" he asked. What had happened in Charlie's house before he'd arrived, and what did she have to do with the old man's death?

"I could ask you the same," she replied, eyes narrowed and finger poised above the sprayer on the can.

"I'm Joshua West and I was just on my way home and decided to stop and say hello to Charlie."

Relief filled her amber-colored eyes and she lowered the can. "I heard they were expecting you either today or tomorrow."

"You didn't answer my questions. Who are you and what in the hell is going on here?" Anger swept through him, much more agreeable than the grief that clawed at his insides as he thought of Charlie.

The relief that had shone from her eyes was short-lived. A frown tugged her thin eyebrows closer together. "My name is Savannah Clarion and I don't know what the hell is going on. I got here about two minutes before you did, just long enough to go inside and find…" She bit her bottom lip as tears welled up.

The anger that had momentarily reared to life dissipated. "Why are you here? Charlie isn't…wasn't exactly the type who liked to entertain guests." And he couldn't imagine that a young woman like her would have an interest in visiting with the old man.

"I was going to interview him. I write a column for the *Cotter Creek Chronicle* called 'People and Personalities.'" Tears spilled onto her cheeks. "Why would he do something like this? I can't believe it."

Joshua raked a hand through his thick, dark hair and frowned. "I just spoke with him two days ago. He seemed fine, his usual self." Judd nuzzled Joshua's hand, seeking a reassuring pat on the head.

"What's going to happen to Judd and Jessie?" Savannah asked. "Who's going to take care of them?"

"I'll take them with me. They'll be well taken care of at Dad's."

"I don't understand this." She wrapped her arms around herself, as if chilled to the bone. "Seems like a drastic way to get out of an interview." She gulped in a deep breath.

He wondered if she was about to get hysterical on him. The last thing he wanted was a hysterical woman on his hands. He shoved his hands in his slacks pockets as he heard the wail of a siren in the distance.

The joyous homecoming he'd expected had transformed into something horrible, and he knew the full realization that Charlie was dead hadn't even struck him yet. What he couldn't yet comprehend was the fact that Charlie hadn't died in his sleep or suffered a heart attack, but, instead, from all indications Charlie had eaten the business end of his gun.

He said no more to Savannah as the sheriff's car pulled onto Charlie's property. *Things have changed,* he thought as he watched Sheriff Jim Ramsey lumber out of his car. The sheriff had put on a bit of weight in the year and a half that Joshua had been gone. His hair was more salt than pepper, and as his gaze fell on Savannah an expression of annoyance flashed on his features. What was that about?

The West family and Sheriff Ramsey had always shared a precarious tolerance for one another. A tolerance that often threatened to dissolve whenever the sheriff felt that the West work stepped on his toes.

Ramsey nodded to Savannah, then walked past her. "Joshua," he greeted with a touch of surprise. "Heard you were expected back here. Hell of a welcome home. Want to tell me what's going on?"

"I was on my way into town and decided to stop and say hello to Charlie. I stepped up on the porch as Ms. Clarion came crashing out the door. I went inside to see Charlie. It looks like he shot himself."

"I came out here to interview him for my column," Savannah said and stepped closer to the two men. "Something isn't right here. Charlie was excited about being interviewed. He would have never done something like this. I want a full investigation into his death."

Ramsey sighed audibly. "I'm going inside. I've already put in a call to Burke McReynolds."

"Burke McReynolds?" Joshua didn't know the name.

"You haven't met him. We hired him on a month ago as a part-time medical examiner. If I have any more questions for the two of you, I know where to find you both. There's no reason for you to hang around here."

It was an obvious dismissal, and Joshua was more than ready to leave this place of death. There was nothing he could do for Charlie, and more than anything he was eager to get home to his family.

"I'm not going anywhere," Savannah replied. Although her eyes still shone with tears, she raised her chin and looked at the sheriff defiantly. "I have a responsibility to my readers, a responsibility to Charlie."

The annoyance that had flashed momentarily across Ramsey's features appeared again. "Savannah, you write a gossip column and there's nothing you can do for Charlie. Now you go on and get out of here. We don't need you in the way as we go about our business."

If her face had lacked color before, it didn't now. A flush of red swept up her slender neck and took over her face, nearly matching the bright red of her hair.

"There's something rotten in this town, Sheriff Ramsey, and I'm not going to quit until I figure out what it is." She stomped to her car and got inside.

"What was that all about?" Joshua asked Ramsey as she pealed out and took off down the road.

"Who knows. Just spare me from Lois Lane wannabes." Jim sighed again. "I got work to do." As he headed for Charlie's front door, Joshua loaded Jessie and Judd into the backseat of his car, then got in behind the steering wheel.

As Ramsey disappeared into the house, Joshua

thought of Savannah Clarion's parting words. *"Something was rotten in Cotter Creek."*

What was she talking about? What in the hell had happened in his town in the time that he'd been gone?

Chapter 2

Savannah awakened with grief pressing thickly against her chest. The early-morning October sunshine drifted through the frilly lace curtains in her bedroom, and all she wanted to do was pull the pillow over her head and forget what had happened the day before.

Charlie was dead. The thought hit her in the stomach with the force of a blow. Other than Meredith and her landlady, Winnie, Charlie had been the only friend she'd made since coming to town. And now he was gone, dead in a way that made no sense whatsoever.

She'd never again see that slow, easy grin of his, never hear his acerbic sense of humor or match her wits against his in a game of chess.

"Charlie," she whispered, her voice nothing more than a hollow echo of itself.

She wanted to weep, but she'd spent most of her tears the night before. Besides, crying didn't change anything and neither did covering her face with a pillow and hiding in bed all day. She owed Charlie more than tears, more than denial.

She was a reporter, and even though her published work so far was nothing more than a couple of gossip columns and fluff pieces, as Sheriff Ramsey had characterized them, it was time she became an investigative reporter and found out the truth about what had happened to Charlie. She owed the old man that much.

Galvanized with a new determination, she showered, then dressed in a pair of black pencil-thin slacks and a lightweight lavender sweater. Even though it was only the first week of October, the weather had been unusually cool.

The scent of bacon and freshly brewed coffee greeted her as she stepped out of her room and headed downstairs. No matter what time Savannah got up in the morning, her elderly landlady was always up before her.

Winnie sat at the kitchen table, a cup of coffee in front of her. She smiled a greeting as Savannah entered the kitchen. "Coffee's on and the bacon is fried. All you need to tell me is how many eggs you want."

"None. I'm not hungry this morning." Savannah went to the cabinet that held the coffee mugs, then poured herself a cup of the brew and joined Winnie at the table.

She suspected the old woman hadn't rented the upstairs of her house to Savannah because she needed the money but rather because she wanted companionship and somebody to cook for. Winnie's husband had died three years before, and it was obvious she was lonely.

"How did you sleep?" Winnie asked, the wrinkles in her forehead deepening in concern. When Savannah had come home from Charlie's place the day before she'd told Winnie what had happened.

Savannah wrapped her hands around the warm coffee mug in an attempt to fight off a chill. "Terrible." She suddenly remembered the night-mares that had plagued her all night, visions of blood and death and poor Charlie.

Winnie shook her head. "I just don't understand it. I don't understand how anyone becomes so desperate they commit suicide." She paused a moment to take a sip of her coffee. "Why, I saw Charlie yesterday at the grocery store and he seemed just fine."

Savannah stared at Winnie. "You saw Charlie at the grocery store? What time?"

"I don't know, it must have been around noon. We met in the ice cream section and he told me how much he loves butter pecan and I told him I was quite partial to plain old chocolate."

"Did he buy ice cream?"

Winnie frowned. "I saw him get a gallon out of

the freezer, but I didn't see him when he left the store."

Savannah took a sip of her coffee, her brain burning up as it worked overtime. She knew how much Charlie had loved his butter pecan ice cream. Many evenings she'd shared a bowl with him as they had played a game of chess.

Did a man who planned to commit suicide buy groceries? Did a man who intended to take his own life buy a gallon of ice cream?

All through the night her gut instinct had told her that Charlie didn't commit suicide, and the fact that the old man had bought ice cream an hour or so before his death only deepened her gut instinct.

Winnie eyed her over the rim of her coffee cup. Despite being seventy-two years old, Winnie was still a sharp tack. "What's going on in that head of yours, Savannah?"

"I just don't believe that Charlie committed suicide. Aside from the fact that he bought ice cream a short time before his death, I know Charlie would have never done something like that, knowing I was coming to his house. He would have never wanted me to find him like that."

"Then what do you think happened?"

"I think Charlie was murdered. He was murdered and somebody made it look like a suicide and I intend to prove it."

"How are you going to do that?"

Savannah frowned thoughtfully. "I'm not sure.

One of the first things I need to do is talk to Sheriff Ramsey." She took a sip of her coffee, then shook her head. "There's been too many deaths around here lately." Strange falls off tractors and from haylofts, a gas heater explosion and other odd deaths. The citizens of Cotter Creek were either unusually unlucky or something more frightening was going on.

She suddenly thought of the handsome hunk she'd literally bumped into on Charlie's porch the night before. "What do you know about Joshua West?"

A smile curved Winnie's lips. "Before he left town I think every rancher in the area was locking up their daughters for safekeeping. He's a charmer, spoiled as a dozen eggs left out in the sun too long, but like all those West boys he's got a good heart."

Savannah didn't care if he was a charmer, or spoiled or had a good heart. His attraction as far as she was concerned was that he was a local who had been out of town for a while and might have some objectivity that could work to her advantage.

But, more importantly, she knew the West name carried weight in Cotter Creek and the sheriff would give more credence to Joshua than he ever would to her. She had a feeling if she wanted people to take her seriously about Charlie's death, then it wouldn't hurt to have Joshua West on her side.

"Are you sure you don't want something for breakfast?" Winnie asked. "You know a good break- fast is always the way to start a good day."

Savannah laughed. "My mother believed a protein shake and an hour on a StairMaster was the way to start each day."

"That's what happens to people when they got more money than sense," Winnie scoffed. "A couple of eggs?"

Savannah relented and nodded her head. She suspected Winnie didn't care so much about what she ate but wasn't quite ready for Savannah to fly out the door and leave her alone for the day.

It was after nine when Savannah left the house, her stomach full and a renewed burn of determination in her soul. Her first stop was at the sheriff's office, where she was disappointed to learn that Sheriff Ramsey wasn't in.

She left the office, got into her car and headed for the West ranch. She hoped she could enlist Joshua West's help in demanding a full investigation into Charlie's death. Charlie deserved at least that much, and, as far as Savannah was concerned, Sheriff Ramsey hadn't been too diligent in following up on other deaths in the small town.

The West ranch was a sprawl of pasture surrounding a huge rambling home with a long wooden porch that was perfect for sitting and watching the sunset in the evenings. On more than one occasion in the last couple of months she and Meredith had sat on the porch, talking while the sun went down.

Savannah had always found friendships difficult.

From the time she was young her mother had chosen her friends. They had to be beautiful, stylish and from privileged backgrounds. Savannah had never fit in and had found it difficult to trust females so different than her.

But Meredith West was another story. She certainly came from a family who had tons of money, but she suffered no airs, didn't judge people by their clothes or their looks. She was refreshingly normal after Savannah's years of being surrounded by superficiality.

It was Meredith who answered Savannah's knock. As usual the tall brunette was clad in a pair of jeans and a sweatshirt. Her long dark hair was in a careless ponytail. "Savannah." She opened the screen door, stepped out on the porch and drew Savannah into the warmth of an embrace. "I heard about Charlie. I'm so sorry."

A wave of grief swept over Savannah, but she shoved it aside. She had no time for grief. She was on a mission. "Thanks, I still can't believe it myself."

"I was going to call you this morning to see how you were doing."

"I'm doing okay. Actually, I'm here to see your brother."

Meredith frowned. "My brother? Which one?"

"Joshua. Is he home?"

"He's here, but he's out riding at the moment. Come on in. He should be back before too long." Meredith ushered her into the house and toward the kitchen.

Smokey Johnson, the West cook and the man who had helped raise the West children when their mother had been murdered, scowled as the two women entered the room he considered his exclusive domain.

"You be nice, Smokey," Meredith exclaimed. "Savannah is quite fragile this morning."

The old man snorted. "Red-haired girls aren't fragile. They're tough as nails, got to be to get through all the teasing they take when they're young."

Savannah was accustomed to Smokey, who was a cliché of a tough old coot with a heart of gold. "I'm not feeling fragile this morning. I'm feeling more than a little pissed off because I think somebody killed my friend and made it look like a suicide."

Smokey pointed a gnarled finger toward a chair at the table. "What are you talking about? According to what Joshua told us when he got home last night it was an open-and-shut case of suicide."

Meredith gazed at Savannah sympathetically. "Everyone knew how much Charlie missed his wife since her death eight years ago. Maybe he just got tired of waiting to join her in the hereafter."

Savannah shook her head vehemently. "After eight years? Give me a break. Sure, Charlie missed Rebecca and he was looking forward to the time when they would be together again, but he also believed that everyone went when it was time for them to go. After eight years of being alone why would he suddenly decide to end it all?"

Before anyone could reply, the back door opened and Joshua stepped into the kitchen. He stopped short at the sight of her and frowned. "What in the hell are you doing here?"

"Joshua!" Meredith shot her brother a dirty look. "Where are your manners?"

"I lost them when she kicked me in the shin hard enough to half cripple me yesterday."

Warmth swept up Savannah's neck as she remembered the kick she'd delivered to him. "I thought you'd killed Charlie."

She'd recognized in the brief time she'd seen him the day before that he was handsome, but his attractiveness today hit her like a kick from a horse.

She hadn't noticed yesterday just how thick and shiny his dark hair was, or the amazing green of his eyes. She hadn't paid attention to his raw masculinity that today screamed from him.

Clad in a pair of jeans and a long-sleeved knit shirt that pulled tautly across broad shoulders and a flat stomach, he was blatantly male and sexy as hell.

Winnie had said he was a charmer, but there was nothing charming in the look he shot her. He looked irritated and tense and just a whisper away from dangerous.

"If you'll excuse me, I'm heading to the shower," he said.

Savannah popped out of the chair. "Actually, I'm here to talk to you. Would it be possible for us to speak somewhere alone?"

"I can't imagine what we'd have to talk about."
He started out of the kitchen and with a glance of
apology to Meredith and Smokey, Savannah
followed Joshua.

"Of course we have things to talk about," she exclaimed, unable to help but notice that he had a
perfect butt for jeans. "We were both at a crime
scene. We should compare notes and see if we can
help the investigation."

His long strides carried him down the hallway
toward the master bathroom. "There's no notes to
compare. The investigation is over. I spoke to
Ramsey early this morning, and according to him
there's no reason not to think it's anything but a
suicide."

"Ramsey is an overweight, lazy, incompetent jerk
who is just biding time until his retirement at the end
of the year," she protested.

She jumped in surprise and stumbled a step
backward as he unexpectedly twisted around to face
her in the bathroom doorway.

"And he told me you were an overeager, conspiracy theorist who was desperate to find a story
that will take you away from writing silly gossip
columns and gain you some real respect." He yanked
his shirt over his head and threw it to the bathroom
floor behind him.

Savannah tried to maintain focus as she was pre-
sented a broad, bare, muscled chest that would make
most women weak in the knees. "That's not true.

Ramsey doesn't like me because I'm questioning his investigation skills."

Joshua's hands went to the waist of his jeans where they unfastened the first button on his fly. A lazy smile curved his lips upward. For just a moment there didn't seem to be enough oxygen in the area.

"Unless you want to discuss this while I scrub your back, I suggest you take a hike," he said.

For just a brief, insane moment the idea of this sexy man washing her back was infinitely appealing. But she reminded herself why she was here and why it was important to get Joshua West on her side.

"All right, I'll take a hike right now, but sooner or later you need to hear what I have to tell you. Something isn't right in this town, and somebody needs to do something about it." Hoping she sounded mysterious enough to pique his interest, she turned on her heel and stomped back to the kitchen.

Joshua walked toward the white tent that had been set up in the cemetery for Charlie Summit's funeral. When he'd parked, he'd been dismayed to see so few cars here. It appeared that Charlie was going to go out of this world much like he'd spent most of the past eight years of his life…alone.

Joshua knew all about feeling alone, although in the year and a half he'd spent in New York City, he'd rarely been alone.

He'd worked hard and had played even harder. He'd thrown himself into the Manhattan single lifestyle, serial-dating sharp, beautiful women with fascinating careers. But in spite of all that he'd never shaken a core sense of homesickness that had eaten at him day and night.

Failure. A little voice whispered in his head. He'd struck out on his own, determined to make a life separate from his family. He'd wanted to be his own man, but in the end he'd run back home like a wounded puppy.

Although he had been successful as a stockbroker, the shambles of his personal life had finally forced him to get out of town and head back to Cotter Creek.

His father, Red West, had just assumed Joshua would step back into the family business and work for Wild West Protection Services as a bodyguard, but Joshua had told his dad he was taking a little time off to decide what he wanted to do. Going to work for the family business felt like yet another failure.

He shoved these thoughts aside as he approached the tent, the scent of too-sweet flowers cloying in the air. Charlie had left a will with an account set up for his funeral. He'd wanted only a gravesite service and to be buried beside his beloved wife, Rebecca. Together in life, now together again in death.

As he entered the white structure, he stiffened at the sight of Savannah Clarion. She stood next to Winnie Halifax, Savannah's hair sparkling and appearing even more red against the black of her long-sleeved blouse and black slacks.

He nodded to the preacher, then took up a position

on the opposite side of the casket from Savannah, who had been an irritating pain in his ass over the past three days.

She'd left a message at the house every day, requesting that he call her back, but the last thing Joshua wanted was to get mixed up in any drama. He'd had enough of that before he'd left New York.

Within a few minutes others began to arrive. His sister, Meredith appeared with his dad and Smokey. Meredith hurried to Savannah's side, while his father and Smokey joined him.

Raymond Buchannan, the owner of the Cotter Creek newspaper, arrived, looking old and tired. Joshua realized the man must be close to eighty and wondered if he ever intended to retire.

Mayor Aaron Sharp also arrived, shaking everyone's hands as if he were at a political campaign instead of a funeral.

Finally the service began. As Reverend Baxter talked about life and death and redemption, Joshua found himself looking again and again at Savannah.

He hadn't thought her particularly pretty the day he'd seen her at Charlie's house, but there was something in her irregular features that was arresting.

The dark red curls suited her, complemented by her eyes, which were a mix of gold and copper. She had a killer figure, slender hips and long legs and was unusually busty for a slim woman.

Over the past three days Meredith had made it her job to extol the virtues of her friend to him. Witty and smart. Fun-loving and soft-hearted. Tenacious and outspoken. He'd heard more about Savannah Clarion than he'd ever wanted to know.

He had a feeling his sister was attempting to indulge in a little matchmaking, but Meredith didn't realize the last thing Joshua wanted in his life was any kind of a relationship with a woman.

Unlike his brothers, who seemed to have a knack when it came to the opposite sex, Joshua had failed miserably in that respect as well.

Grief for Charlie shoved every other thought out of his head. The old man had been a special friend to Joshua before he'd left Cotter Creek, and Joshua would miss him.

He was grateful when the service ended. He didn't hang around to make nice with the other funeral attendees, but rather slipped out of the tent the minute the service was complete.

Instead of walking to where his car was parked, he followed the path to another area of the cemetery, the place where his mother was buried.

The entire right corner of the cemetery contained the West plots. His mother was buried beneath a grand red maple tree whose leaves were just beginning to turn scarlet with autumn grandeur.

He stood before her headstone. Elizabeth West, beloved wife, beloved mother. Joshua had never known her. He'd been a baby when she'd gone to the grocery store one evening and later had been found dead beside her car on the side of the road. She'd been strangled, and her murderer had never been found.

Sometimes Joshua wondered what his life would have been like if he'd had a mother, if he'd been raised by a woman instead of by his father and the cantankerous Smokey, who had run the house like an army barrack.

He'd heard stories about his mother, a beautiful woman who had given up an acting career to marry his father and build a family here in Cotter Creek. But he knew her only from photos and didn't have a single memory of his own.

"Meredith told me about your mother's death."

Joshua stiffened at the sound of Savannah's voice. The woman was as tenacious as an Oklahoma tick on the back of a hound dog. He turned around to look at her, noting how the sunshine sparked in her hair. "What do you want from me?"

"I want you to listen to me, that's all. Just hear me out with an open mind. Did you know that Charlie went grocery shopping an hour before his death? Did you know that he bought a gallon of butter pecan ice cream? Why does a man who is suicidal buy groceries that nobody will eat?"

She talked fast, as if afraid she wouldn't get everything out before he walked away from her. "Joshua, Charlie knew I was coming to interview him. He would have never killed himself knowing that I was expected to be there, that I would be the one to find him like that. Charlie would have never done that to me."

As much as Joshua didn't want to get caught up in what he'd considered her drama, her words gave him pause. "Maybe he went shopping then got depressed. Maybe he wasn't suicidal until five minutes before he picked up his gun."

She shook her head, red curls bouncing. "At least three times a week I spent the evenings with Charlie. I'm telling you the man wasn't depressed. He wasn't suicidal. He had plans, big plans. He was going to plant a flower garden next spring, fill it with all the flowers his wife had loved. He was thinking about taking lessons to learn how to play bridge."

Joshua wished he had touched base with Charlie more often while he'd been in New York. He'd called every couple of weeks, but the calls had been brief, too brief.

"It's not just Charlie," Savannah continued. "There have been others deaths…too many."

He suddenly remembered her parting words to Ramsey the day of Charlie's death, that something was rotten in Cotter Creek and she intended to get to the bottom of it. "What deaths? What are you talking about?"

She glanced around, then looked back at him. "It's too complicated to go over all of it now."

"Why me? Why are you coming to me with all this?"

She frowned, the gesture wrinkling her freckled nose with charming appeal. "For two reasons. First of all you've been out of town for a while. I figure you'll be more objective about things than any of the other locals. Secondly, you're a West and that holds a lot of weight in this area of the country."

"Meredith is a West, why not enlist her help?" he countered. He tried not to notice her scent, a spicy musk that was intensely pleasant.

"I told you the other day that Sheriff Ramsey was lazy and incompetent. The man is also a raging sexist. He wouldn't pay any more attention to Meredith than he has to me."

Despite his reluctance to the contrary, he was intrigued. "Okay, I'm listening," he said.

She glanced over her shoulder to where Winnie stood in the distance, obviously waiting for her. "I can't go into it all now. Besides, I have some research at the newspaper office. I'd like you to see it."

He had a feeling she wasn't going to stop bothering him until he agreed at least to see what she thought she had. "Okay, just tell me when and where to meet you and I'll see what you've got."

Her features lit with relief. "We need to meet at the newspaper office, but I'd rather do it when Mr. Buchannan isn't there. He always leaves the office at around eight in the evenings. Could you meet me there tonight about nine?"

Somewhere deep inside him, he knew this was probably a mistake. But, since returning to Cotter Creek, he'd felt unsettled. He'd grown accustomed to the fast pace of the city, of having places to go and things to do. In truth, he was bored, and he told himself that was the only reason he was agreeing to meet her.

"All right, nine tonight at the newspaper office," he said.

She smiled. The look softened her features and transformed her from arresting into something close to beautiful. "I'll see you tonight. And Joshua, thanks." She turned and hurried toward Winnie.

Joshua stared after her, wishing he could take back his agreement to meet her. He had a feeling he'd made yet another mistake in a long string of mistakes that had been made in the past year and a half.

Chapter 3

The *Cotter Creek Chronicle* office was located on the bottom floor of a two-story brick building on Main Street. The front of the building was a large picture window, at the moment as dark as the night that surrounded Savannah as she parked her car in front.

It was eight-forty-five, and Main Street was completely deserted. Most of the shops and businesses closed their doors at eight-thirty. The only nightlife Cotter Creek had to offer was a couple of taverns on the edge of town.

She turned off her car engine and tapped a pale pink fingernail on her steering wheel, a surge of excitement filling her.

Finally, finally she had somebody who would

listen to her. She certainly hadn't been able to get her boss, Raymond Buchannan, interested in her theories. All he wanted from her were fluff pieces that would please a more feminine audience.

"I write the news fit to print," he'd told her the last time she'd broached him about the multitude of deaths in the Cotter Creek area. "I reported what happened in each of those deaths, and there's nothing left to report."

Nor had Sheriff Ramsey or Mayor Aaron Sharp been interested in what she'd had to say. This town definitely had a good old boy network and she had several strikes against her. First, she was a woman. Second, she was an outsider. And last, she had a feeling that most everyone in town thought she was here only to make a name for herself and have a body of work to take to a bigger newspaper job.

Nothing could be further from the truth. It had taken her only a week in this dusty Oklahoma town to fall in love with Cotter Creek. She had no intention of going anywhere. In fact, she had broached the topic of buying the paper from Raymond Buchannan when he decided to retire. If he ever decided to retire.

She had enough money in a savings account to be able to meet whatever price Buchannan settled on when he did decide to sell. Thankfully her parents had begun investing for her when she was a baby, and on her twenty-first birthday those funds had become available to her. Over the past four years she'd tried not to touch that money unless it was absolutely necessary, believing that it was her nest egg for the future.

At exactly nine o'clock a big black pickup pulled into the parking space next to hers. Joshua got out of the vehicle, and Savannah tried not to notice his physical attractiveness.

He was clad in a pair of black slacks, a black turtleneck and a worn leather bomber jacket. His hair was slightly tousled, as if he'd driven with the window down and the night breeze had blown through his dark locks.

The last thing she was looking for was to be attracted to any man, but especially one who had the reputation for being a player, at least before he'd left town. Besides, men who looked like Joshua West didn't date women who looked like her, and she'd do well to remember that.

She quickly got out of her car and smiled at him. "Thanks for coming. I really appreciate it."

He gave her a curt nod, his expression letting her know he would rather be anywhere but here at the moment. She pulled her keys from her purse and walked to the front door of the newspaper office.

"All I ask of you is to please keep an open mind when I show you everything I've compiled. It took a while and a lot of research before I finally started to make some horrifying connections." She was rambling. When she was nervous she always rambled and something about the silent man standing next to her made her nervous.

She sighed in relief as she got the door open. She stepped inside, flipped on the overhead lights, then walked across the wooden floor toward a small room in the back that served as her office.

She was conscious of Joshua close behind her, his loafers ringing on the floor. He had yet to say a word, and that only made her anxiety increase.

If he saw the material she'd gathered and judged her as some crazy conspiracy theorist looking for a story she didn't know what she'd do. She hadn't felt so right about anything since she'd been seventeen years old and told her mother that she absolutely, positively was not getting a breast reduction.

The office Buchannan had given her to work in was little more than the size of a storage closet. It was only large enough to contain her desk and office chair. She'd tried to dress up the small space, claim it as her own by placing things she liked on the scarred wooden desk.

There was a basket of her favorite candy bars, a stuffed frog that one of her friends had given her for luck when she'd left Scottsdale and, finally, there was a plaque that read, Live Well, Laugh Hard.

Joshua picked up one of the candy bars and gave her a wry look. "Guess you aren't into counting calories."

"Never," she replied and punched the button to boot up her computer. "My mother started counting my calories the day I was born. When I finally got out on my own I decided I was going to eat whatever the heck I wanted."

He nodded, a touch of amusement lightening his green eyes. "That's one of the things that drove me crazy about the women in New York. None of them eat. I'd take a lady out to dinner and it would have been just as easy to toss her a head of lettuce and call it a night."

Despite her nervous tension, Savannah laughed. "You take me out to dinner and I'll eat your money's worth," she exclaimed, then hurriedly added, "not that I think you'd ever take me out to dinner. I mean, not that I'd even want you to take me to dinner."

His amusement was even more evident as he simply stood there and watched as she dug a hole with her tongue. She flushed and bit her lip to stop her mouth from running away with her.

Thankfully at that moment the computer loaded up and she sat in the chair in front of it to retrieve the files she wanted him to see.

He moved behind her and she was intensely aware of his nearness. He smelled like the outdoors, a scent of fresh Oklahoma sunshine and night breeze and beneath that a clean cologne that tantalized her senses.

"I started all this because of what happened to Kate Sampson's father," she said as she finally found the file she wanted and opened it.

Kate Sampson's father, Gray, had been murdered three months before. It had been Joshua's brother Zack who had ridden to her rescue and helped her solve the murder. But the one thing the investigation hadn't yielded was a credible motive for his murder.

"I think maybe Zack's planning on running for

sheriff in November," Joshua said, his breath warm on the nape of her neck.

"I'm sure he'll do a far better job than Ramsey," she replied and hit the print button. "You might not know it, but Gray Sampson was killed by a ranch hand named Sonny Williams."

"I heard. My brother Clay told me about Gray's murder and Sonny's arrest."

She pulled up another file and began the print process, then turned around in the chair to face him. "But, did you know that Sonny Williams supposedly killed himself in jail? Did you know that before he died he said that Gray's death was just a part of a bigger plan?"

Joshua frowned. "I might have been told something about that, but I was a thousand miles away and to be honest had other things on my mind."

"Gray Sampson's death wasn't the beginning of things." She stood and grabbed the material from the printer. "Let's go back out to Raymond's desk."

The space in her office was too small for the two of them as far as she was concerned. Joshua was too tall, too male to share such a tiny space with her.

She breathed a sigh of relief as they returned to the main office area. At least in here she could breathe without smelling the scent of him.

She sat at Raymond's desk and motioned him into the chair on the opposite side of the desk. "Are you a wannabe true crime writer or what?" he asked.

The question irritated her. He knew nothing about

her but was already making judgments. "No, I'm not. When I took the job here I decided it was a good idea to read as many of the back issues of the paper as possible to familiarize myself with both the newspaper I'd be writing for and the town where I'd chosen to live."

"And why did you choose Cotter Creek?" His green gaze held hers intently, as if he were seeking answers to questions he hadn't yet spoken.

"To be perfectly honest, I feel as if Cotter Creek chose me." She broke eye contact with him, finding his direct gaze somewhat disconcerting. Instead she looked at the framed front page of the first copy of the *Cotter Creek Chronicle* that hung on the wall just behind him.

"I wasn't sure where I was going when I left Scottsdale and eventually made it to Cotter Creek where my car transmission blew. It took a couple of days to fix and, while I was waiting, I just fell in love with the town."

"And how did you meet Charlie?"

She looked at him again, fighting a wave of impatience. "I thought you were here to see the material I have, not to play a game of twenty questions."

He smiled, one that lifted only a corner of his mouth with sexy laziness. "I like to know a little bit about the people I deal with."

"Fine. I'm twenty-four years old. I love animals and candy bars, I hate superficiality and people who don't have a sense of humor."

She leaned forward, meeting his gaze directly. "I met Charlie on the first day I arrived in town. I'd just left my car at Mechanic's Mansion and was looking for a hotel or motel to stay in while the car was being fixed. There were a couple of teenagers on the corner and I asked them about accommodations, and they told me there was a nice bed-and-breakfast on the edge of town."

His eyes began to glitter with humor, obviously seeing where her story was leading. "Anyway," she continued, "one of the boys offered to drive me there. He took me to the entrance to Charlie's place and left me there."

"I'll bet you were horrified," he said.

She laughed. "When I broke through the trees and saw Charlie's place, I suspected I'd been had, but I wasn't one hundred percent sure so I marched up to Charlie's door and told him I'd heard he ran the best bed and breakfast in town."

She smiled at the memory of Charlie's face and a swift sharp grief pierced through her, stealing her smile and forcing the sting of tears to her eyes. She raised a hand to swipe them away.

"Sorry, I didn't mean to upset you." His voice was gentle and she saw real regret in his eyes.

She nodded. "I'm just going to miss him so much. Other than your sister and Winnie, Charlie was my only friend in town. We used to spend hours playing chess." She released a small laugh. "I never got a chance to beat him."

"I could never beat him either." For a long moment their gazes remained locked. It was a moment of connection, two people mourning for somebody they had both loved. This time he broke the eye contact and gestured to the papers in front of her. "Okay, show me what you've got."

She cleared her throat, stuffing her emotions for Charlie back deep inside. "I noticed when I was reading back issues of the paper that there seemed to be an unusual number of fatal accidents in the area."

"It's a ranching and farming community, there are always accidents."

"True, but Cotter Creek seemed to have more than its share, so two weeks ago I did some statistical analysis, comparing like-size ranching and farming communities. What I discovered was that the incidence of accidental deaths was three hundred times higher in Cotter Creek than anywhere else I compared it with."

Joshua raised a dark eyebrow and took the sheet of paper that held her data. She watched him as he studied it. She'd met most of his brothers, each more handsome than the next, but Joshua seemed to have gotten the West good-looking gene in spades.

Savannah had been raised among the beautiful people of Scottsdale and if they weren't beautiful by nature, then plastic surgery solved the problem. She'd been the anomaly, a busty redhead with a snub nose covered in freckles, who had no interest in bee-stung lips or liposuction.

about Savannah Clarion made him a little bit jumpy, made his thoughts race in directions they shouldn't be going.

As she'd talked to him, he'd found himself wondering if her red curls were soft and silky or wiry and coarse. He'd wondered if her full mouth would be soft and yielding beneath his or fierce and demanding?

Those kinds of thoughts irritated him. Hadn't he learned his lesson in New York? He focused his attention on the next piece of paper she shoved over in front of him.

"I made a list of all the people who have died. As you can see, all of them are men," she said.

He read the list of names, then looked back at her. "Look, this is all very interesting, but I don't see any big conspiracy here."

She frowned, her lower lip jutting out slightly in what appeared to be a small pout. "I'm not finished with all the investigating I intend to do," she said. "Help me, Joshua. Please help me find out exactly what happened to all these men. With two of us working together it will take half the time to get some answers."

He leaned back in his chair and swiped a hand through his hair. "I'm not sure what the questions are that need to be asked."

"We need to look at each individual incident and see if there are any anomalies, anything that doesn't fit with it being an accident. Like I said before, Gray Sampson's death would have been ruled an accident.

It wasn't until your brother picked up the rock where Gray had supposedly fallen off his horse and hit his head and saw blood on both sides that they realized the rock had been used to bludgeon him to death."

She paused to draw a deep breath and he tried not to notice the rise and fall of her breasts beneath the light lavender sweater she wore.

"As far as I'm concerned, Charlie buying ice cream an hour before he supposedly committed suicide is a huge red flag," she continued. "Joshua, you were his friend. You should know Charlie didn't have a suicidal bone in his body. Don't you want to know the truth? Isn't Charlie worth a little of your time?"

Joshua sighed. He had to admit that the fact that Charlie bought groceries then went home and blew his brains out, didn't make sense. Charlie's wife Rebecca had been gone a long time and Charlie seemed to have made peace with the fact that he would live out the rest of his years alone.

Surely if a man was going to commit suicide to be with his departed wife, he wouldn't wait eight long years. Charlie's suicide just didn't make sense, although any other scenario didn't make sense either.

What else do you have to do with your time, a little voice whispered inside his head? He didn't want to work the family business and he wasn't interested in continuing as a stockbroker, but had no idea what he really wanted to do. He had nothing but time on his hands at the moment.

"All right," he relented after a moment's hesitation. "I'll do some checking into these deaths. I'll get the accident reports and look them over."

"Thank you." She smiled and he felt a jolt of heat sweep through him. She had one hell of a smile. She grabbed a sheet of paper and scribbled something then handed it to him. "That's my phone number at Winnie's and my cell phone number."

He took them reluctantly, having no intention of calling her except to tell her he'd done as she'd requested. Something about her unsettled him and the less interaction she had with him the better he'd feel. "It should just take me a day or two." He stood, eager to be away from her with her sexy scent and heart-stopping smile.

She handed him the papers she'd printed off and he folded them and stuck them in his back pocket. "Why did you decide to come back to Cotter Creek?" she asked, also rising. "Meredith told me you'd been doing quite well in New York."

I ran back home like a dog with my tail tucked between my legs. I screwed up with a relationship that turned more than ugly. The thoughts flew through his head, bringing with him the sense of failure that had ridden his shoulders since he'd made the decision to return home.

"I missed my family. When you're used to being surrounded by people who care about you, a place like New York City can be pretty lonely."

She eyed him wryly. "I doubt if a man like you had too many lonely nights."

"There's a difference between being alone and being lonely." He gestured toward the door, uncomfortable with the personal turn of the conversation.

"Must be nice to have a loving family," she said as she gathered her papers, then joined him at the front door.

"You aren't close with your family?" he asked. She stood close enough to him that he could again smell her scent, a heady fragrance that put all his nerves on alert.

"It's just me and my parents," she replied. "I don't think my mother ever recovered from the shock of not birthing a perfect blond, beautiful miniature of herself, and my father was mostly absent while I was growing up. He had to work long hours to keep my mother in baubles and bling."

She turned out the light, locked the door and they stepped out of the building. Night had completely fallen, but the illumination from a full moon cascaded down, painting her features in a soft, becoming light.

"I can't thank you enough for meeting me here tonight and listening to me."

"Don't thank me yet," he warned. "You haven't convinced me that there's anything ominous going on."

She nodded, her curls dancing with the gesture. "How are Jessie and Judd?"

Joshua thought of the two dogs he'd brought home from Charlie's place. "Initially they were confused and seemed depressed, but they're begin-

ning to settle in just fine. Smokey wasn't thrilled that
I'd brought them home."

She laughed, a low throaty sound. "Is that man
ever happy about anything?"

He grinned. "Smokey's bark is definitely louder
than his bite. After my mother's death I'm not sure
my father could have coped with six small children
without Smokey's help."

"How did that happen? I mean, where did he
come from?"

"Smokey worked as a foreman on the ranch until
a terrible fall from a horse crushed his leg and left him
with permanent damage. He'd just about healed from
his wounds when my mother was murdered. Smokey
stepped into the house as if he were born to the job."

"I'd love to interview him for my column.
Actually, I'd love to interview you, you know, something about the return of the prodigal son."

"No way, I'm not interested in being interviewed. And good luck with Smokey," he added
drily. At that moment a loud bang resounded and
almost simultaneously the picture window just to
the right of them exploded.

Without thought, acting only on instinct, Joshua
dove toward Savannah and tackled her to the ground.

Chapter 4

Savannah hit the pavement hard, the back of her head connecting with the concrete with a dull whack that momentarily created whirling stars in her brain. Joshua's body covered hers as shards of glass rained down around them.

For a moment she was frozen, unable to think. The back of her head throbbed from the blow. She opened her eyes and winced. "What happened?" she asked as the initial shock began to wear off.

"Shh." He shushed her sharply. She could swear she felt his heart pounding against her chest, but then wasn't sure if it was his or her own beating so frantically.

In the moonlight she could see his features, taut

and dangerous-looking as he gazed at the darkness across the street.

What was he looking for? What had just happened? A dog barked in the distance, the only sound in the otherwise silent night. "What's going on? Do you see anything?" she whispered.

"Where are your keys to the office?" His voice was like hers, just a whisper.

She dug her hand into her pocket and withdrew the keys. He took them from her. For the first time since they'd fallen to the pavement, he looked down at her. "I'm going to open the office door and when I do, I want you to crawl inside. Whatever you do, don't stand up."

His eyes gleamed more silver than green in the moonlight. Dangerous. He looked so dangerous it frightened her. "What happened, Joshua?" she asked again, her fear evident in her voice. "What's going on?"

"Somebody just took a shot at us." His eyes narrowed as he once again looked across the street. "And I don't know if the shooter is still there waiting for us to make a move or not."

A shot? Somebody had shot at them? Fear swelled inside her. Her head throbbed with nauseating intensity. "I told you something was rotten in this town." Her voice rose in volume. Surely this was proof. "I must be onto something and now somebody is trying to shut me up."

"How about you shut up right now until we get inside and can call the sheriff."

She would have been offended by his words if she hadn't been so busy trying to process the fact that apparently somebody had just tried to kill them.

As he started to get off her, she had the crazy need to wrap her arms around his neck and keep him in place so close to her.

Don't go, she wanted to say. But, she didn't. She held her breath as he slowly eased up into a crouch and quickly made his way to the office door.

She tensed, waiting for another gun report, praying another bullet didn't come careening out of the night toward him. She released a sigh of relief as he reached the door, unlocked it and shoved it open.

"Keep low," he said.

Keep low? She'd crawl on her belly like a worm if it kept her alive. And that's exactly what she did. As she moved, she was aware of the grit of the sidewalk beneath her, the shards of glass that littered the way.

Tension made her feel like throwing up. Somebody had shot at her. Somebody had pointed a gun and pulled the trigger. Her head pounded with the horrifying knowledge. Apparently somebody wanted her dead.

She made it to the doorway and slid inside. Joshua sat on the floor next to Raymond Buchannan's desk, the phone to his ear. As she crawled up next to him he hung up. "The sheriff is on his way. Are you okay?"

"My head hurts and my clothes are ruined, but other than being positively terrified, I think I'm fine." But, she wasn't fine. A trembling shuddered through her as she thought of the window exploding and the bullet that had caused it.

He nodded, then rising to a crouch once again he moved away from the desk and to the edge of the broken window where he peered outside. "I don't think our shooter is out there now."

"How do you know that?" Even though she wasn't at all sure she liked Joshua West that much, what she wanted to do more than anything at the moment was curl up in his arms. There was no doubt in her mind that the bullet had been meant for her.

He turned from the window and glanced back at her, his eyes glittering darkly. "If the shooter was still out there, there's no way we would have been able to make it back inside to call the sheriff. He would have fired again to try to prevent us getting help."

"What more proof do you need that something is going on? Somebody just tried to kill me and it can only be because I'm digging into things somebody doesn't want uncovered."

"Don't jump to conclusions," he replied tersely. "And when the sheriff gets here let me do the talking. If you come off like a half-hysterical female, he won't listen to either one of us."

"I've never been a hysterical female in my life," she replied with more than a touch of irritation. Now that some of the fear was passing she found herself aggravated by his words. "Part of the problem in this town is that the men don't listen to the women."

Both Meredith and Winnie had extolled Joshua's charm, but so far Savannah had seen little evidence that the man possessed any at all.

As the sound of a siren filled the night, Joshua rose to his feet, apparently convinced that whoever had shot at them was gone.

He flipped on the light and gazed around the room. Savannah remained seated on the floor. She wasn't going to stand up until Sheriff Ramsey walked into the building.

"Whoever made that shot didn't intend to kill with it," Joshua said.

She frowned. "And how do you know that?"

"Too much damage for it to have been a single bullet. It looks like it might have been birdshot, a fairly ineffective way to try to kill somebody. It can sting like hell, but usually isn't deadly, especially at this distance."

"Then maybe it was done to scare me," she said thoughtfully. "And if that was the objective, then it succeeded." She brushed off tiny pieces of glass clinging to her jeans and tried to ignore the headache that was banging at the back of her head.

The siren came closer. "This might have nothing to do with you or what you're investigating."

"Okay, then who have you pissed off since you've been back in town?" she retorted.

He didn't reply and at that moment headlights flashed through the doorway, signaling that the sheriff had arrived.

Joshua rode his horse hard, enjoying the whip of early morning wind and the sunshine that spread warmth across his back and shoulders.

Riding was one of the things he'd missed while in New York City and each morning since being back he'd started his day with a ride.

This morning, however, his mind wasn't on the joy of the massive horse beneath him or the beauty of the morning but rather on the events of the night before.

He and Ramsey had sent Savannah home, then the two men had canvassed the area, looking for clues as to where the shooter might have been standing when the trigger had been pulled.

As he'd expected, they'd found nothing. The sheriff had thought it was possible that a couple of teenage boys were responsible. He'd told Joshua that last month two of them had gotten drunk on their daddy's beer and had shot out the windows of the café in the middle of the night with a load of birdshot.

"Damn fool kids got nothing to do in this town but cause mischief," he'd said. Still, he'd promised a full investigation.

Ramsey had called Raymond Buchannan, and

when the old man had arrived they'd all worked to cover the broken window with plywood.

Ramsey might think the culprits were a couple of kids, but Savannah had been convinced that the shooting was meant to scare her off her current path. She'd reiterated before she'd left to go home that somebody better wake up and smell the coffee before more people died.

Joshua wasn't convinced that the shooter had meant to harm or scare her. He wasn't convinced the shooting was about her at all. He thought it might have been about him and that worried him.

He pulled up on the reins as he approached the stables and saw with surprise that his brother Clay was standing next to the corral gate, obviously waiting for him.

Clay opened the gate and Joshua rode through the wooden fence and directly into the stable. He dismounted, then motioned to Bobby Walker, one of the stable boys. "Bobby, you want to unsaddle and brush her down for me?"

"Sure, boss." The young man hurried over to take the reins from Joshua.

Joshua swept his hat off his head and walked out to meet his brother. "Hey bro, what are you doing here instead of having breakfast with that gorgeous fiancée of yours?"

"Just figured it was time to check in with my baby brother. I've hardly seen you since you've been back," Clay replied.

The two fell into step side-by-side as they headed for the house. "How's the wedding plans coming?" Joshua asked.

Clay winced. "For some reason I had the stupid idea that all I needed to do was hire a preacher, find a place and say I do and it would be a done deal. But women seem to have their own ideas about what should be involved when it comes to weddings."

Joshua laughed. "Libby is great, Clay. I'm happy for you." He'd met his brother's fiancée a couple of nights before, along with her daughter, Gracie. "You're going to have your hands full with that little girl. Gracie is a smart cookie and as charming as can be."

Clay smiled, his affection for the child obvious. "Yeah, she's something else. She had Smokey curled around her finger in a matter of minutes, and Dad is an absolute fool over her."

For just a moment a sharp envy shot through Joshua. He'd seen the way both eight-year-old Gracie and the beautiful Libby looked at his brother. They looked at him as if he'd hung the moon and Joshua had no doubt that the life his brother was going to share with them would be filled with plenty of love.

The last thing Joshua had been looking for in his time in New York was marriage or even a committed relationship. But since returning home and seeing his brothers with their spouses and intended spouses, he'd found himself wondering what it would be like to have a special lady in his life.

As they reached the house, Clay motioned Joshua into one of the two chairs that sat on the porch. "Let's sit and talk a bit before we go inside."

"Okay." Joshua eased down into one of the chairs as Clay sat in the other.

"It's good to have you home, Joshua. We all missed you," Clay said. "It didn't seem right whenever the family got together and you weren't there."

"Yeah, it's good to be back."

Clay stared off in the distance, a thoughtful frown wrinkling his forehead. "Actually, Dad wanted me to talk to you. He's been worried about you since you've been home."

Joshua looked at Clay in surprise. "Worried? Why?"

His brother looked at him. "He says you haven't been yourself since returning to Cotter Creek. You're quieter, more withdrawn, and he doesn't understand why you seem so adamant against working for the business."

Joshua leaned back in the chair. "I'm not totally against it, I just told him I need some time to decide exactly what I want to do."

He knew his brothers loved working for the body-guard business and he didn't know how to explain to anyone that, for him, going back to work for that business felt like a failure.

No matter how inept, no matter how unskilled he might be, that was a job waiting for him simply by the mere accident of being born a West.

"Is there anything else going on? Anything bothering you?" Clay asked.

If Joshua was going to bare his heart to anyone in his family, it would be to Clay. The two brothers had always been close.

But the West men had never been big on soulbaring, and to be honest, Joshua was more than a little embarrassed by what had happened in New York to drive him back home. He wasn't ready to talk about it with anyone.

"I had a little excitement last night," he finally said. He explained to Clay about Savannah enlisting his aid in her quest for answers, then described the shooting that had taken place at the newspaper office.

"It was nothing but birdshot," Joshua explained.

"You think she's onto something?" Clay asked when Joshua had finished.

"I don't know," Joshua admitted thoughtfully. "It's possible what happened last night was nothing more than some kids looking for a little excitement." He released a deep sigh. "All I know for sure is that I had the feeling if I didn't agree to help her she was going to be a major pain in my ass. Have you met her?"

Clay smiled. "Yeah, Meredith introduced us to her. She seems really nice. Meredith certainly thinks the world of her."

Joshua scowled and leaned forward. "I have a feeling the woman can be stubborn as a mule, and she could definitely talk a man to death."

"Are you going to help her?"

"I told her I'd talk to Ramsey, get a copy of the reports of each incident and take a look at them for any red flags."

"You might want to talk to Zack. When Kate's father was murdered he did some investigating into some of the other deaths."

"Did he come to any conclusions?" Joshua asked.

"Apparently not."

"He told me he's thinking of running for sheriff in November."

Clay nodded. "Ramsey has said he intends to retire."

"According to Savannah he retired a long time ago and just didn't tell anyone."

Clay laughed, then sobered as he eyed his brother for a long moment. "You sure everything is all right?"

Joshua forced a grin to his lips. "You can officially report back to Dad that I'm fine. Just taking a little down time before deciding what I want to do."

Clay rose from the chair. "Don't forget you have a tuxedo fitting this afternoon. I can't have my best man looking anything but his best."

"Don't worry, I promise I won't embarrass you by turning up next weekend in anything but a well-fit tux."

Clay started for the front door. "You coming in?"

"No, I think I'll sit out here for a while."

Clay gave him a long, measured look, then went into the house, leaving Joshua alone with his thoughts.

Joshua leaned back and stared out at the pasture in the distance. He'd missed this view. It hadn't taken him long in New York City to recognize that he was a country kind of man at heart.

For a while the city had been exciting. The nightlife, the fast pace, so alien from what he'd known, had invigorated him. But, after the initial novelty had worn off, he'd missed home.

He'd missed the scent of fresh hay, of green grass and cattle. But, the view wasn't all that he had missed. He'd been homesick for his brothers and his sister. Maybe because there had been no mother around, the siblings had grown up being unusually close.

But things were changing. Three of his brothers were either married or getting married. His eldest brother, Tanner, had married a princess who had come to Wild West Protective Services when renegade forces had taken over her father's kingdom.

Zach had found love with the girl next door. Kate Sampson had captured his heart while he'd helped her investigate her father's death.

And now Clay was about to take the walk down the aisle with the Hollywood beauty he'd fallen in love with. Three down, three to go, Joshua thought. He frowned as his thoughts returned to Savannah.

He needed to know if she'd uncovered something that made somebody nervous enough to take that shot the night before. The thoughts that had plagued him on his ride returned. What worried him was that it might not be about her at all.

It might be about him. He feared his problem from New York had followed him to Cotter Creek.

And if that were the case, then it was possible that just by being with her he'd put Savannah in more danger than she could ever imagine.

Chapter 5

It was just after nine when Savannah drove toward the West ranch house. She was hoping to talk Smokey into allowing her to interview him for her column. The column was due the next day and she was running out of time. Of course, she'd much prefer interviewing Joshua, but he'd made it fairly clear he wasn't interested.

Despite the horror of the night before, she'd slept like a baby. She liked to think her peaceful sleep came from the fact that whoever had shot at them had used birdshot and Joshua had told her it was obvious it wasn't meant to kill. It didn't hurt that Sheriff Ramsey had mentioned that kids had done something like that in the past.

Still, she suspected her deep sleep had been because she no longer felt so alone. At least for the moment she had Joshua on her side.

Joshua. The man was definitely under her skin, and she wasn't sure why. Granted he was nice-looking, but it was more than that. She sensed something dark in the depths of his green eyes, a torment that piqued her reporter interest.

As the West ranch came into sight she thought of the family that lived inside the house. Joshua had told her that he'd returned to Cotter Creek because he'd missed his family.

Whenever she'd spent time at the house with Meredith, she'd felt surrounded by the love the house contained, something she'd never felt in her own home.

She'd long ago come to terms with the fact that her parents had been incapable of loving her the way children needed to be loved. But that didn't mean that sometimes in the dark silent moments of the night or in a reflective pause during the day it didn't hurt.

She found it hard to imagine what the West house must have been like when there had been six small children inside. Now there was just Joshua and Meredith living at home.

Tanner and his princess bride, Anna, had built a home on the West property. Zack had moved into the Sampson home with Kate. Clay and Libby had rented a house in town until their home could be built, also on the West property, and Dalton also rented a place in town.

She had a feeling it wouldn't be long before the house would be filled with grandchildren. Already there was Gracie, Libby's little girl, and Meredith had told Savannah the other day that she suspected Anna might be pregnant.

Savannah didn't think much about marriage or having children. Certainly she would love to have both those things someday in her future, but knew better than to pine for something that might never be.

"Find a job you love, Savannah Marie," her mother had often told her. "Because your job is probably all you're going to have to fill your life."

Shoving away her mother's voice, she parked in front of the sprawling ranch house and before she got out of the car she flipped the rearview mirror into position so she could see her reflection.

She finger-combed her curls and checked her lipstick, then, realizing she was primping just in case Joshua was home, she frowned with irritation and snapped the mirror back into place.

No amount of finger-combing could transform her red curls into lush blond waves. No amount of primping could erase the freckles that danced across her nose or make the shape of her nose more elegant, her cheekbones more pronounced.

"You're plain, Savannah Marie, and you might just as well accept the idea." Her mother's voice echoed in her ears.

She grabbed her pen and notepad and got out of the car to the raucous barks of Judd and Jessie. She took a moment to pet Charlie's dogs, then went up to the porch and knocked on the door.

Red West greeted her, a broad smile lighting his features. He was a tall man, still fit despite his age although Meredith had told her he suffered from arthritis. He had all but retired from the family business, leaving it in his eldest son Tanner's hands.

"Hi, Savannah. I'm afraid you've missed Meredith. She already left to go shopping for a dress to wear to Clay's wedding."

"Actually, I'm not here to see Meredith. I'd like to talk to Smokey."

Red's eyebrows danced upward in surprise as he gestured her inside the door. "You know where to find him."

"Thanks." She walked through the large living room and into the kitchen, where Smokey sat at the kitchen table reading the morning paper.

"Too late for breakfast and too early for lunch so I can't imagine what you're doing here," he said.

She sat at the table next to him and smiled brightly, hoping she could wheedle him into the interview. "How are you doing this morning, Smokey?"

"Same as I did yesterday morning, same as I probably will be doing tomorrow morning." Smokey turned the page on the newspaper.

"I see you're enjoying this morning's issue of the *Cotter Creek Chronicle*."

"Who says I'm enjoying it?" His grizzled eyebrows drew together in a frown.

If she hadn't spent so much time at the West house she might have gotten her feelings hurt by Smokey's cantankerous attitude. But she'd been around often enough to know he talked that way to almost everyone. He seemed to take perverse pleasure in being irascible.

"Actually, I'm here on behalf of the paper," she said. "I'd like to interview you for my column on notable people in Cotter Creek."

Smokey stared at her over the edge of the paper. "Now what in God's creation makes you think I'd be interested in such nonsense."

"Give her a break, Smokey." Joshua came into the kitchen and a ridiculous wave of pleasure swept through her. He took a seat at the table opposite Savannah. "She's had a rough couple of days."

She flashed him a surprised, but grateful smile and tried to ignore the way the sight of him made her heart dance. "Come on, Smokey. I promise I'll make it as painless as possible." She tried to focus on the old man and not on Joshua, but found it impossible not to shoot surreptitious glances at the attractive cowboy.

This morning he wore a pair of jeans and a navy-blue knit shirt that clung to him in all the right places. She willed her attention back to Smokey.

He huffed a sigh and set the paper aside. "All right, but if you think you're going to make me cry like Barbara Walters always makes people cry in her interviews, you've got another thing coming."

"Great." She pulled a miniature tape recorder from her purse. "Even though I take notes, I like to make a recording as well. Is that all right with you?"

Smokey eyed the tape recorder like it was a piece of smelly trash that had somehow made its way to the table, but he nodded his head in agreement.

Savannah opened her notepad and began the interview. Initially she felt self-conscious with Joshua seated at the table, watching her with his dark green eyes.

Within minutes she forgot his presence as she talked to the cook who was not just a wounded cowboy who had no longer been able to ride the range, but a man who had stepped in for a family who was desperately in need.

She'd instinctively known the old man's story would be a good one and as he talked about the special place he'd found for himself in the West family her heart was melting for the old rascal.

It took almost an hour to get what she needed and by that time Smokey was showing definite signs of impatience to be finished.

"Thanks, Smokey. I'll just get these notes typed up and next Sunday morning everyone in town will be reading about you."

He got up from the table with a grunt. "All I care about is getting you out of my kitchen so I can get to the business of making lunch."

"You're good at that," Joshua said, falling into step with her as she left the kitchen. "You got him to talk about stuff I didn't know about him."

She smiled, a wealth of warmth sweeping through her at his compliment. "Thanks, that's my job."

"What are your plans for the rest of the day?" he asked.

"My first order of business is to get to the office and get this interview turned in," she replied. "Why?"

They stepped out on the front porch. "I was thinking maybe I'd hang out with you. You know, get an idea of a day in the life of a reporter."

She eyed him with disbelief. "You're interested in maybe becoming a reporter?"

His gaze didn't meet hers, but instead shifted out to the pastures. "No, but I'm just back in town after being gone for a while. You're relatively new to town. I just thought it might be fun to hang out together."

For just a brief second a flutter of pure feminine pleasure swept through her, but it quickly vanished beneath a dose of harsh reality.

He thought it might be fun to hang out together? This from the man who hadn't even returned her phone calls in the first three days he'd been back in town. "That's the biggest bunch of crap I've ever heard," she said flatly.

His gaze shot to her, as if her unvarnished reply had surprised him. "There's some women in this town who would probably be flattered if I told them I wanted to spend time with them."

"Yeah, well I'm not some women and I know a load of crap when I hear it. Now, are you going to tell me what's going on?"

He leaned back against the porch railing and ripped a hand through his dark hair, a frown creasing his forehead. "I've just been thinking about what happened last night and I think maybe it wouldn't hurt for me to keep an eye on you until we figure out if the shooting really was an attempt to warn you off your current path."

"So, you're offering to what? Be my personal bodyguard?"

"In an unofficial capacity," he replied.

She'd managed to minimize the danger of last night since she'd awakened this morning, but his offer of bodyguard services put a new spin on things.

"Are you sure that's necessary?" she asked.

"No, I'm not sure about much of anything. But I've always thought it was better to be safe than sorry."

"If we're talking about my safety, then I like the way you think," she said with a touch of dry humor. She wasn't sure what made her more uncomfortable, the way her heart pounded at the thought that she might be in danger, or the beat of her heart as she thought of having Joshua at her side for the next couple of days.

"Okay then." He gave a curt nod of his head as if satisfied with this new turn of events. "If you'll just wait here, I'll get my keys and things and I'll follow you back into town."

As he went back into the house, Savannah leaned against the porch railing and drew several breaths in an attempt to gain control of her racing heart.

He might not want to work for the family business, but obviously the family business was in his blood. She had to remember that he hadn't offered to spend time with her because he found her witty and charming, but rather because he thought she might be in some kind of danger.

She'd risk her life to get her story, but she certainly wasn't fool enough to risk losing her heart to a man like Joshua West.

Joshua followed behind Savannah's car in his pickup. He wasn't thrilled by his decision to act as bodyguard to her, but his personal moral code made it impossible for him not to. If he had brought danger to her, then he was responsible for keeping her safe.

It was ironic that he suspected it was possible that just by being seen with her he might have made her a target. It still stunned him, that a jilted lover could become a psychotic danger not just to him, but to a woman whose only mistake had been to be seen in his company.

He wasn't sure if he was putting Savannah into more danger by continuing to be in her company, but he was concerned that the damage had already been done. If Lauren had followed him from New York and had seen him with Savannah, then she might be in danger anyway. By playing bodyguard Joshua might make things worse, or he might just be in the right place to keep danger away from Savannah.

He patted his jacket and felt the bulk of his shoulder holster and gun beneath. He hadn't worn a gun since he'd left Cotter Creek one and a half years before. His conceal-and-carry permit was still good, and it vaguely surprised him that the weapon felt as if it belonged resting against his body.

He frowned and tightened his fingers on the steering wheel. It would be so much easier to decide on his next course of action if he knew for sure who had shot at them last night and why.

After Clay had left that morning, Joshua had gotten on his cell phone and tried to call the woman who had made his last few weeks in New York a living hell. He'd wanted to make sure she was still in New York and that she hadn't followed him here to continue her reign of torment.

Unfortunately Lauren hadn't answered the call. That didn't necessarily mean she had left New York City. She might be at work, and, although he knew she'd been a paralegal, he didn't know what law firm she worked for. He'd have to try to call again that evening.

Until he could confirm that it hadn't been her that had shot at them last night, he intended to make sure Savannah stayed safe. She shouldn't have to pay the price for his bad judgment, for his botched relationship with a nut.

He thought he'd been clear in his intentions with Lauren. He'd thought she'd understood that he was just having a good time. He'd thought she was doing the same, but she'd taken their brief relationship to heart, had manufactured it into something that had nothing to do with reality.

Then she'd gone crazy and made a scene and now he wondered just what she might be capable of. Following him here to Cotter Creek and shooting at him or at Savannah, who she might assume was his new romantic interest?

He shoved thoughts of the beautiful Lauren Edwards out of his head and tromped on the gas as he realized Savannah drove almost as fast as she talked.

When they reached the newspaper office she pulled into a parking space in front of the building and he parked next to her car.

He got out and met her on the sidewalk, where the glass from the broken window had been swept up. A new window had been installed in the storefront of the office, although it lacked the lettering that announced the place as the *Cotter Creek Chronicle*.

"While you type up your interview and do your reporter thing, I've got a couple of things to take care of here in town," he said. "I'm headed to Ramsey's office to see if I can get copies of those accident reports, then I have a fitting for my tux for Clay and Libby's wedding."

"At Henry's?" she asked. "Maybe I could go with you to your fitting? I need to get a dress."

He frowned. Although he intended to keep an eye on her and remain close, he hadn't figured on shopping with her. She must have read his hesitation on his face. "I promise I'll be quick," she hurriedly said.

"All right. I'll head over to the sheriff's office and take care of that, then I'll check back in here with you. Don't leave this building without me. Don't go to lunch, don't take a walk, don't poke your nose outside for any reason."

"Aren't you being a little drastic?"

"As I told you this morning, I'd rather err on the side of caution."

"All right, then I guess I'll see you back here in a little while."

He watched until she disappeared inside the building, then he turned and headed down the sidewalk toward the Sheriff's office. He thought she'd be safe at work with Raymond Buchannan inside with her. Lauren was crazy, but it was a devious kind of crazy. She wouldn't want witnesses around if and when she went after Savannah.

"Joshua!" A feminine voice called to him and he turned to see an obviously pregnant Melinda Kelly hurrying down the sidewalk toward him. He and Melinda had dated a couple of times before he'd gone to New York.

"I heard you were back in town." She gave him a quick hug. "You look wonderful."

"So do you," he replied with an affectionate smile. He and Melinda had shared some fun times, but there had never been that special spark between them.

"Don't lie, I look fat." She placed a hand on her burgeoning belly.

"That doesn't look like fat," he countered. "That looks like your future."

She laughed. "This baby and my husband, Jimmy, are definitely my future."

"Jimmy? You mean Jimmy McCarthy?"

She nodded. "We got married ten months ago."

"He's a good man." Jimmy McCarthy was a year younger than Joshua, and when Joshua had left town he'd been working at Mechanic's Mansion.

"He's great," she agreed, her smile reflecting a happiness Joshua had never put on her face during the time they had hung out together.

"When are you due?"

"Three more months. I've got a doctor's appointment in ten minutes, so I've got to run. It was good seeing you again, Joshua," she said, then with a warm smile she turned and went back in the direction she'd come.

Joshua watched her go, then resumed his walk in the direction of the sheriff's office. He thought of Melinda. He was glad she'd found happiness. She was a nice girl and he was pleased that she'd found a future filled with love.

And what was his future? At the moment he

didn't have a job, didn't know what he wanted to do
with his life. He certainly had nobody special. He
had nobody who made him happy to wake up in the
morning and eager to go to bed with her at night.

Unbidden thoughts of Savannah jumped back
into his head. He'd never been particularly fond of
redheads, but there was something about the shade
of her hair that looked warm and invited a finger to
dance through the curls.

How was it possible a woman he hardly knew, a
woman who talked too fast and, he suspected, had a
stubborn streak a mile long had managed to get
under his skin more than just a little bit? A knot
formed in the pit of his stomach.

Maybe it was nothing more than he hadn't yet
found his place here in town. Like Savannah, he felt
like a newcomer without much of a support system
other than his family.

All thoughts of Savannah fled his mind as he
entered the sheriff's office. He recognized the deputy
who sat at the desk in the main office. "Morning,
Brody. Is Ramsey in?"

The young deputy nodded and gestured to the
door in the back. "You can go on in."

Joshua gave a sharp knock on the door, then
opened it to see Jim Ramsey seated at his desk, a
large mug of coffee in front of him.

"I figured you'd be checking in before the
morning was out," Ramsey said. "Want a cup of
coffee?"

"No, thanks." Joshua sat in the chair opposite his desk. "But I do have a request for you."

"Before you make it, I should let you know that I checked in with the Rasley twins' father this morning. They were the boys that shot up the storefronts about a month ago. Anyway, they were both home all night last night. Seems they've been grounded for the last four weeks."

Joshua nodded, the knot in his stomach twisting just a little tighter. He'd hoped that the shooting last night would have an easy answer, and two ornery teenagers with a penchant for birdshot would have been the easy answer.

"What I'd like from you is a copy of all the reports for some specific accidents that have occurred in the last two years." Joshua dug the list of names that Savannah had given him out of his pocket and handed it to the portly sheriff.

Ramsey took it from him, then leaned back in his chair and frowned. "Guess Savannah Clarion has been bending your ear. She's been driving me crazy for the last couple of weeks."

Joshua offered the sheriff a conspiratorial grin. "I'd say if anyone could bend an ear, she could."

"You got that right," Ramsey returned dryly. "I got to tell you, when she first started yammering at me I pulled all those reports and looked over them again, but I didn't see anything that would make me think a conspiracy of some sort was going on."

"Would you mind me looking at them again? If I

come up with the same conclusion that you did, then maybe I can get her off both our backs."

"It will take me about an hour to pull the files and make copies. You want to wait?"

Joshua was never one to sit and cool his heels. "Nah, I'll come back for them." He stood and Ramsey did as well.

"You might tell Savannah that I haven't closed Charlie's file yet. I'm conducting a full investigation into his death, but I've got to tell you, we're a small department and there isn't much to go on."

He frowned and ran a hand through his salt and pepper hair. "I know Savannah thinks I just sit at my desk and eat doughnuts, but if I thought something bad was going on in my town, I'd be on top of it."

A few minutes later as Joshua left the office, he thought of Ramsey's words. He had no doubt that Ramsey did the best job he could as sheriff of the small town, but Cotter Creek wasn't New York City, or even Tulsa.

Most of the crime in Cotter Creek consisted of bored teenagers getting into mischief or cowboys revved up on too much beer and not enough sense.

As sheriff, Jim Ramsey hadn't had to face too many complicated or heart-stopping crimes. Joshua and his family members were far more savvy when it came to real criminals and life and death situations.

In the couple of years that Joshua had worked for the family business, he'd protected the son of a senator in Washington, D.C., against a potential kidnapping plot. He'd also spent time in Florida on a job protecting an environmentalist who had received death threats.

Joshua had liked the work, but he'd never quite gotten over the feeling that he hadn't done anything to earn his place. That was one of the reasons he'd decided to continue his education and strike out on his own.

He left the sheriff's office and decided to stop in at the Wild West Protective Services office, which was just down the street. His brother Dalton would be manning the office, and Joshua hadn't really had much of a chance to visit with him since he'd returned home.

Dalton, at thirty-three years old, was the second eldest of the siblings. Like all of them he had the dark hair and green eyes that marked him as a West. He was a quiet man, not easily riled, but with a definite stubborn streak. He'd taken over the daily running of the office duties when Tanner, Joshua's eldest brother, had gotten married almost six months before.

Dalton sat behind the desk working a crossword puzzle. "Is that what you do to get paid the big bucks?" Joshua asked.

Dalton grinned and shoved the puzzle aside. "Things have been slow the last couple of days. Seems the world is sane, at least for the moment."

"I suppose it depends on who you talk to." Joshua plopped in one of the chairs and for the next hour visited with his brother. They caught up on town gossip, discussed world politics and laughed about old times.

Afterward, Joshua returned to the sheriff's office, where Ramsey had the paperwork ready for him. By that time it was almost noon. Joshua returned to the newspaper office to check in on Savannah.

"I'm so glad you're here," she exclaimed the moment he walked through the door. "I'm starving. How about we get some lunch, then head over to Henry's?"

The tension that always seemed to fill him when she was around kicked in once again. "Okay. Sunny Side Up Café?"

"As if there's any other choice in this town for lunch," she replied with one of those quicksilver grins that warmed her features.

As they walked down the sidewalk toward the café, Joshua kept an eye on their surroundings, noting the people on the streets, looking for a particular person who didn't belong.

It disturbed him that despite the scent of fall that rode the air he could smell Savannah's perfume, that intoxicating fragrance that seemed to permeate his entire head.

"I finished up the column on Smokey. I think it came out great," she said as they walked. "Thanks for helping me convince him to be interviewed."

He cast her a rueful smile. "I have a feeling he was secretly pleased. If he hadn't really wanted to be interviewed, then nothing you or I could say would have made him agree."

"Was Sheriff Ramsey cooperative when you spoke to him about getting those reports?"

He nodded. "I have them in my truck. I'll go over them this evening and let you know what I find."

"Why can't we go over them together this afternoon? I'm finished with my work for the day." She bobbed her head, red curls dancing. "Yes, I really think we should go over them together."

They entered the Sunny Side Up Café, and Joshua led her toward a booth in the back where he slid into the side facing the front door of the restaurant and she sat across from him.

It was almost noon and the place was quickly filling with the lunch crowd. He cast a quick, assessing glance around the room, noting that most all of the faces of the diners were familiar ones.

If it wasn't for the woman seated across from him he'd relax, but he was aware of her gaze on him as he reached for one of the two menus propped up on the side of the table.

"This place always smells yummy, doesn't it?" she said once they were settled. "Scottsdale has a hundred fine restaurants, but none of them smell as good as this café."

"I missed the food here almost as much as I missed Smokey's cooking," he replied.

"Don't you want to take your jacket off?" she asked. "It's pretty warm in here."

"I need to keep it on." He moved one side of the jacket aside so she could see the shoulder holster and gun beneath.

Her pretty eyes widened. "Is that really necessary?"

"I don't intend to get shot at again without having the potential to return fire if needed." He let the jacket fall back into place and stared down at the menu.

His thoughts filled with the woman he'd left behind in New York, a woman who had developed a fatal attraction for him. He'd seen what she was capable of, knew the bitter hatred that now burned in her heart for him.

If she'd followed him here to Cotter Creek and if she had gotten it into her head that Savannah meant anything to him, then Savannah was at risk. He touched his jacket and felt the reassuring bulk of the gun.

Was the gun necessary? What he feared was that it might be the only thing that stood between Savannah and danger, and he hoped if it came to that he'd be able to use the gun on a woman he'd slept with in order to save a woman he wasn't even sure he liked.

Chapter 6

It was during lunch that Savannah saw flashes of
the charm Winnie and Meredith had told her Joshua
possessed.

They swapped stories, her telling him a little
about her life in Scottsdale and him telling her
about New York City.

The conversation was light and easy, but something about him intrigued Savannah like no man had
intrigued her in a very long time.

When they'd finished lunch they went directly to
Henry's, where Joshua disappeared into a back room
to be fitted for his tux and she surfed the racks
looking for a perfect dress to wear to the wedding.

She found a buttercup-yellow dress with classic

lines and bought it off the rack. She'd done enough shopping to know what style looked best on her and what size to buy. By that time Joshua was finished with his fitting.

"Why don't we go to my place to go over the reports?" she said as they left Henry's.

"What's wrong with the newspaper office?"

"Mr. Buchannan doesn't exactly support my investigative efforts. I've got a little office at Winnie's. We can work there." His face radiated reluctance. "What's the matter Joshua, afraid I'll jump your bones if we're alone?"

He looked at her in surprise. "Why would I think that?"

"I'm sure a guy who looks like you is accustomed to women wanting to jump your bones, but I promise you I'll restrain any impulses in that direction."

He obviously recognized that she was teasing him, trying to keep things light between them. "And what makes you think I'd want you to restrain yourself?" he countered with a slow, sexy grin.

A rush of heat swept through her and she decided she liked him better when he was taciturn. That smile of his could definitely be dangerous for it made her think all kinds of inappropriate thoughts.

"Give me a break," she retorted, sorry she'd started the stupid conversation in the first place. "Shall we ride together to Winnie's or do you just want to follow me?"

"I'll follow you."

Minutes later as she drove toward Winnie's house, her thoughts filled with Joshua West. She couldn't seem to get a handle on him.

He'd been a pleasant lunch companion and yet there was a darkness that clung to him, a darkness that pulled her closer with a desire to understand.

She had the feeling he'd agreed to investigate the deaths of the area more in an effort to get her off his back than because he believed anything suspicious was going on in the town.

He'd definitely surprised her with his offer to act as personal bodyguard until they knew what was going on.

It gave her investigation more substance, as had the shooting the night before. She was eager to go over those reports.

She'd requested them from Sheriff Ramsey a little over a week ago but he'd put her off, telling her he didn't have the manpower for somebody to stand around and make copies all day long. Funny that he'd managed to get it done for a West.

But the thought of going through those reports wasn't what prompted the tingle that danced across her skin or the wave of heat that warmed her insides like a jigger of whiskey swallowed in one gulp. Those particular physical sensations came strictly from the thought of spending more time with Joshua.

For just a moment she'd flirted with him with her comment about restraining herself from jumping his bones. But he'd flirted back, and from that point on she'd had difficulty concentrating on anything except the memory of that sexy grin that had curved his lips.

By nature she'd never been a flirt, but something about Joshua made her wish she were adept at a little harmless feminine flirtation. She could get used to that smile of his.

She pulled into Winnie's driveway and parked, aware of Joshua's pickup pulling in behind her. *Stay focused on the business,* she commanded herself.

His darkly lashed green eyes or his handsome chiseled features couldn't distract her. She couldn't allow herself to dwell on the sexy curve of his mouth or that lingering vision of him shirtless. She knew to indulge in any of these kinds of thoughts where Joshua West was concerned was to invite in certain heartache. And she was a champion at guarding her heart.

Together they went into the attractive two-story house where Winnie had lived with her late husband for forty years. Winnie greeted them in the living room, where she was seated in her favorite chair with her quilting frame in front of her.

She stood and smiled at Joshua, obviously delighted to see him. "Joshua West," she exclaimed and walked over to give him a hug.

"If it isn't the most beautiful lady in Cotter Creek," he said as he released her.

Winnie slapped his chest playfully and giggled with uncharacteristic girlish delight. "Of all you West boys, you were always the one most full of charmer beans. I'm glad to see New York City didn't change that."

"I've got to admit, it's good to be home," he said.

"I'll bet your family is glad to have you back. I know your daddy worried about you all the time while you were gone."

A slight frown creased his brow. "He had nothing to worry about. I'm capable of taking care of myself."

"Well, of course you are," Winnie agreed.

"We've got some work to do," Savannah explained to Winnie. "I thought we could work in the office upstairs, if that's all right with you."

"That upstairs is your home, honey. You don't have to get my permission to have a man up there," Winnie said. "In fact, I'd say it's high time. It's not right, a nice girl like you not having any male callers."

A warmth of embarrassment swept into Savannah's cheeks. Without glancing toward Joshua, she started for the staircase. "Let's get to work," she said briskly.

The upstairs of Winnie's house consisted of three bedrooms and a bath. When Savannah had moved in one of the bedrooms had been empty and it was that room she had set up as a home office.

The desk was actually an old square table that Winnie had stored in her basement. Savannah's laptop sat on top, along with a silver frame containing a photo of her parents and a crystal bowl holding a couple of candy bars.

"It's not much, but at least we'll have room to spread out those reports," she said and motioned him to one of the two straight-back chairs that were at the table. She moved her laptop and the other items off the table and to the floor next to her.

He eased down into one of the chairs and gazed at her with a raised dark eyebrow. "Cotter Creek is full of lonely cowboys. You've been in town several months and I'm the first man you've had here? Why is that?"

She sat across from him and returned his gaze. "Let's face it, Joshua. I'm not the prettiest crayon in the box. My mother told me it was important that I compensate for that fact by being well-groomed, sweet-natured and a good listener. I got the good grooming part down, but I'm not particularly sweet-natured. I talk too much, I'm abrasive, aggressive and I think I scare the hell out of most of the lonely cowboys in this town."

Amusement lit his eyes and he grinned that lazy smile. "You don't scare me a bit."

Oh, but he scared her. He scared her with his bedroom eyes and the deep languid tone of his voice when he was teasing. He scared her because he made her wish she were something other than what she was.

"Let's get to work," she exclaimed, irritated with him but even more irritated with herself.

For the next three hours they pored over the

reports, looking for anything that might support her theory that the deaths ruled as accidents weren't what they appeared to be.

Tension made her shoulders ache and a faint headache pounded just behind her eyes. She knew that Joshua's assessment would determine whether she was written off as a nut or taken seriously.

He said little as he read each of the reports carefully, occasionally reaching for a pen and underlining a sentence. She had to bite her bottom lip to keep from asking him what he was underlining, what was he thinking? She had a feeling the more questions she asked, the less likely he would be to see things her way.

Already she sensed he was not a man who was easily pushed, and she knew if he made up his mind that she was wasting his time, then she'd get no other opportunity to sway him differently.

The scents of dinner wafted up the stairs when Joshua finally set the last report aside and leaned back in his chair with a sigh.

"I don't know," he said slowly. "You're right, there are some small red flags, but nothing that absolutely jumps out and screams foul."

A wave of disappointment swept over her. "So, you think I'm just a nut." She reached down beside her chair and grabbed one of her candy bars. She offered it to him, but when he declined she ripped the paper off with a vengeance and took a bite.

He grinned. "Yeah, I think you're probably a nut,

but I also think there's enough questions that I'd like to dig into these accidents a little further."

She flashed him a smile of relief, hoping she didn't have gooey chocolate decorating her teeth. "For real?"

"Don't get too excited," he warned her as he stood. "I'm still not convinced that there's anything here." He glanced at his watch, then back at her. "What are your plans for the rest of the evening?"

"Probably the same as they are for most nights. Winnie and I will probably play a couple of games of rummy, then I'll work a little bit on a couple of stories for the paper."

"Until we have a handle on why we got shot at, I'd prefer you not go out anywhere alone."

"Okay," she agreed. Although she didn't like curtailing her freedom, she also didn't intend to be stupid enough not to heed his warning.

Together they walked down the stairs. Winnie had apparently abandoned her sewing for dinner preparations and the scents emanating from the kitchen were heavenly.

"You want to stay for dinner?" she asked. "Winnie always makes plenty."

He shook his head. "Thanks, but I need to get back to the ranch. What time are you planning on going into the office tomorrow?" he asked as they stepped out on the front porch.

"Actually, I hadn't planned on going in until the afternoon. Mrs. Miller is having a breakfast for her garden party in the morning and I'm supposed to attend and write up the affair. Garden parties, funerals, weddings, whenever there's a social affair, I'm the reporter on record."

"And you're satisfied with that?" he asked.

"Of course not," she replied honestly. "But, it's enough for now. My real goal is to get Buchannan to sell me the paper when he decides to retire."

He smiled. "You think he'll really sell?"

She shrugged, acutely aware of his nearness on the small porch. "He says he might be interested in retiring by next spring and we might be able to work out a deal."

"Then you intend to still be in town next spring?" He moved a step closer to her, so close she could smell his scent, feel the heat of his body.

"Don't listen to the rumors you hear about me trying to make some kind of a name for myself here then going to a bigger city, a bigger newspaper. I could have stayed in Scottsdale and gotten a job there, but that wasn't what I wanted." She was rambling again, nervous by his nearness, disturbed by it.

"And what do you want?" he asked in a low voice.

You. The word jumped into her mind. Just for a minute. No, just for a night. A long night of crazy lovemaking, of total abandonment. God, what was wrong with her?

"I guess I want what everyone wants," she said quickly. "Happiness and a sense of purpose. Good health and friends I can count on." She sounded lame. "What about you? What do you want, Joshua?"

"At the moment I can just think of one thing I want." He stared at her mouth for a long moment, then leaned in and captured it with his.

He didn't know why in the hell he'd decided to kiss her, other than the fact that she had looked so damned kissable. Her lips were soft and yielding and her mouth tasted of just a hint of chocolate.

She leaned into him, her full breasts pressing against his chest and the contact shot a fierce wave of heat through him. What he wanted was to wrap his arms around her and pull her tight against him. What he wanted was to take her clothes off and see if the rest of her tasted as sweet as her mouth.

He broke the kiss and stepped back from her, irritated by his own actions.

"I didn't mean to do that." He glared at her, finding her personally responsible for his own lapse in judgement.

She returned his gaze coolly. "Don't worry, it will be our little secret. I won't tell anyone you kissed the plain conspiracy theorist who has been driving everyone crazy with questions." She released a sigh. "So what happens now, and I'm not talking about after a kiss. What happens in our investigation? What's our next step?"

He wanted to say something to take the sting out

of her words. He wanted to tell her she wasn't plain at all, but he had a feeling saying anything like that would only complicate the whole situation. "We'll talk about it tomorrow. What time is your breakfast thing?" All he wanted was to get away from her with her sexy smell and kissable lips.

"Nine."

"Then I'll pick you up around eight-thirty." With these final words he turned and left the porch.

Minutes later as he headed back to the family ranch, he wondered again why he'd kissed her. Maybe it was because he'd spent the last several hours cooped up in a small room with her.

He'd been intensely aware of her physical presence, the scent of her, the soft sighs that occasionally escaped her while reading those reports. More than once he'd watched her run a finger across her lower lip when she was concentrating, a gesture he found both enticing and irritating.

He had no idea how she could really consider herself plain. Plain was boring and there was nothing remotely boring about the way that Savannah Clarion looked.

Okay, so he'd made a mistake and kissed her. No harm. No foul. He just needed to make sure he didn't do it again. The last thing he wanted to do was repeat the mistakes of his past. He didn't want her to mistake a single, stupid kiss for something more.

He shoved thoughts of the kiss aside and instead thought about the reports he'd read throughout the afternoon. He didn't know if Savannah was really onto something or if somehow she'd managed to suck him into her delusion.

He remembered Clay mentioning that Zack and Kate had done some investigating when Kate's father had been murdered and decided to swing by the Sampson ranch on his way home.

As he pulled up in front of the ranch house he saw his brother and Kate seated on the front porch swing. Zack stood up as Joshua got out of his truck.

"Well, well, look what the wind blew in," he said.

"Hi, Zack, Kate." He smiled at his pretty sister-in-law. "You two got a few minutes?"

"Sure, come on in," Kate said. "I was just about to fix us some coffee."

Together the three of them went inside and to the kitchen, where Zack and Joshua sat at the table and Kate made the coffee.

"So, when are you coming back to work for the agency?" Zack asked the minute they got settled in the chairs.

Joshua frowned, tamping down an edge of irritation. "Why does everyone keep asking me that? Why does everyone just assume that's what I'm going to do?"

Zack leaned back in his chair and eyed his brother in surprise. "I never understood why you wanted to do anything else. You might have been a good stock-broker, but you were a terrific bodyguard."

Joshua waved his hand as if to physically dismiss the compliment. That's what family did, told you that you were good no matter what the truth was. "Actually, what I wanted to talk to you about was the investigation you did when Gray was killed."

Kate carried coffee to the table and set a cup in front of each of the men, then slid into a chair next to Zack. "What do you want to know?" she asked.

She was a pretty woman, with long reddish-brown hair. The red shades of her hair reminded him of Savannah and that damned kiss they had shared. He shoved the memory of that brief but hot kiss aside to focus on the questions he wanted to ask.

Briefly he told them about Savannah's suspicions and the shooting at the newspaper office. When he was finished, a deep frown cut across Zack's forehead.

"After Gray's death we found out that not only had Sonny Williams killed Gray, but he'd also tried several times to kill Katie." He reached over and took his wife's hand in his as if to assure himself that she was fine.

She flashed Zack a quick smile, then looked at Joshua. "We also found out that a deposit of a hundred thousand dollars had been deposited in Sonny's bank account on the day my dad was killed."

Joshua released a small whistle. "That's not exactly chicken feed."

Zack nodded. "We tried to chase down the source of the money, but we hit dead ends everywhere we turned."

"When Sonny was arrested and before he was led away to jail he told us that my father's death wasn't anything personal, that it was strictly business," Kate said. "We've tried to follow up on what he meant, what it all means, but like Zack said, we've hit nothing but dead ends."

Joshua wrapped his hands around the coffee mug. "But what you've told me definitely lends credence to Savannah's notion that something is going on in this town."

Zack and Kate exchanged glances and Zack nodded. "We've felt the same way, but we haven't been able to get to the bottom of things."

"Besides, we've been pretty busy here at the ranch," Kate added. "When Dad died the ranch was in a bad financial state. Things had been neglected and it's taken all of our time and energy to get things back into shape." Once again she reached for Zack's hand. "We're slowly getting things back to what they once were, but it's been a struggle."

"After Gray's death and Sonny's arrest I talked to Jim Ramsey about my concerns and left it at that," Zack explained.

Joshua sipped his coffee, his thoughts racing in half a dozen directions. Was Savannah right? Was she really onto something? A plot that had somebody killing the ranchers in Cotter Creek and making the deaths look like accidents? It sounded plumb crazy.

Had somebody killed Charlie and made it look like the old man had eaten his gun? But why? Why would anyone do such things?

"So, you never figured out why Sonny killed Gray?" he asked.

Kate shook her head. "That's been one of the most difficult things of all, not knowing why Dad was killed or why Sonny tried to kill me."

"Maybe it's time somebody gets to the bottom of all this," Joshua said thoughtfully.

"Let us know if there's anything we can do to help." A hardness swept into Zack's green eyes. "There's nothing we'd like more than to find out who was really responsible for Gray's death. We know Sonny did the actual murder, but somebody paid him a lot of money to do the deed. That's the person I want."

Joshua nodded, finished his coffee, then stood. "I'd better get out of here and let you two enjoy the rest of your evening."

"I'll walk you out." Zack rose as well and the two men walked back outside.

Of all the brothers, Zack and Joshua were the most alike in temperament. Zack was impulsive, quick to anger but equally quick to forgive. He was passionate about things he cared about, passionate about his convictions.

Zack walked with him to the pickup. "There's been a lot of speculation that you're going to run for sheriff in the fall," Joshua said.

"It's not speculation, it's fact. Ramsey intends to retire and I'd like to take over his job."

"So, you'll quit working for Wild West Protective Services?"

Zack hesitated a moment, then nodded. "I feel like I've got more to offer to this town as sheriff than I'm willing to offer to the business." He glanced back toward the house. "I loved working as a bodyguard, but I'm not willing to travel anymore. My life now is here with Katie."

There was a quiet happiness in Zack's voice that shot an unexpected wave of envy through Joshua. "I think you'll make a great sheriff."

Zack grinned. "Thanks, brother. I appreciate the vote of confidence."

As Joshua drove home he thought about that unexpected emotion. What was it about seeing his brothers' happiness with their wives that made him wish he had something like that in his own life?

Why now? When his life was so unsettled, when he had no real direction, when he was confused by who he was, separate and apart from being a West?

As he pulled up in front of the West ranch house he consciously willed his disturbing thoughts about relationships and his brothers away.

He wasn't ready for a relationship with any woman. If he had learned nothing else in New York, he'd learned that he didn't know how to handle women.

All he had to figure out was how to get through this investigation with Savannah, keep her safe from harm and not do anything stupid that would only complicate his life.

Chapter 7

Savannah stood in front of her bathroom mirror and stared at her reflection. The yellow dress she'd bought for Clay and Libby's wedding had been a good choice. It fit her figure as if it had been specifically made for her and the color complemented both her skin tone and her red curls.

Joshua should be here within the next fifteen minutes or so to pick her up and take her to the wedding. This afternoon Clay would marry the woman he loved and another of the West men would be permanently off the dating market.

Joshua. She turned away from the mirror and returned to the bedroom where she sat on the edge of her bed.

Joshua. The past week spent in his company had been both the most exhilarating and the most frustrating she'd ever spent in her life.

Exhilarating because something about him made her heart beat just a little bit faster, made her breath come with a little more difficulty. His slow, sexy smiles didn't come frequently, but when he gifted her with one, it sizzled through her.

She'd learned many things about Joshua West. He didn't like to talk about himself. He had a self-confidence that at times bordered arrogance, and sometimes when he looked at her he made her forget that she wasn't beautiful.

They'd argued politics, talked about movies and shared a fondness for apple pie and ice cream. She knew him better after the short time than she'd ever known another man in her life, and yet there were parts of him that were definitely a mystery.

She'd asked him several times to let her interview him for her column. She believed everyone would find him an interesting profile as many of the people of Cotter Creek would never get close to living in a big city like New York. But he continued to refuse.

They had spent the week digging further into the accidental deaths that had plagued the area for the past two years, but they had come up with nothing to sink their teeth in.

She felt as if somehow they were missing something, overlooking a fact that would make everything make sense. But for the life of her she couldn't figure out what that might be.

She was frustrated with their failure to make any progress on the investigation but her real frustration came from the fact that each moment they were together she felt a tension that neared explosive proportions.

She wanted him. Whenever she was with him her desire for him made it difficult for her to think of anything else. She wanted him and she knew nothing good could come from it.

It had been over a week and nothing more had happened to make her think she might be in any danger. She'd definitely begun to believe that the shooting that night at the newspaper office was either the work of a drunk or bored kids looking for a little excitement.

After the wedding this afternoon she intended to tell Joshua that his bodyguard responsibilities weren't needed any longer. It was getting more and more difficult to spend time around him and not think about that kiss.

That kiss. That brief, unexpected kiss that had rocked her world, weakened her knees and made her want more from him than he would ever be willing to give to her.

Yes, it was time she gained some distance from him and she intended to tell him. Glancing at her dainty gold wristwatch she realized it was time for him to arrive.

"Don't you look beautiful," Winnie exclaimed as Savannah came down the stairs.

"Thanks. You look very nice, too." Winnie was clad in a light blue dress with lacy accents. She was riding to the wedding with her best friend, Lillian Walker, who worked as the Cotter Creek city clerk. "I think everyone in town has been invited," she said as she grabbed a matching beaded blue purse from the coffee table.

"Are you all going to the reception afterward?" Savannah asked. The wedding was taking place at two, and at four there was to be a huge reception at the West ranch.

"I wouldn't miss it," Winnie said. "Red and Smokey know how to throw a party." A honk from the driveway interrupted their conversation. Winnie looked out the window. "That's Lillian."

"Go on, I'll lock up," Savannah assured her. "We'll see you at the church."

She watched as Winnie joined Lillian in the car and they pulled out of the driveway and disappeared down the street. At the same time Joshua's pickup appeared and pulled into the driveway.

She didn't wait for him to get out of the truck, but instead grabbed her purse, locked the door and ran out to meet him.

The minute she saw him in the black tux with the cranberry-colored cummerbund and matching bow tie, the same crazy tension that had been present all week long renewed itself.

She'd seen him in jeans and knit shirts, she'd seen him in dress slacks and sports jackets, but nothing had prepared her for Joshua West in a tux.

"You look gorgeous," she blurted out as he backed out of the driveway.

"Thanks, you look pretty hot yourself," he returned with an easy grin.

Of course, she knew it was a lie, but she appreciated the effort on his part. "It's a gorgeous day for a wedding," she said. "Of course, as far as I'm concerned there isn't a bad day for a wedding."

"Is that what you're waiting for? A wedding day?"

"Sure, someday I'd like to get married and have a family, but I'm not looking to make it happen anytime soon. I'm young and I'm not in a hurry. In fact, that's the last thing on my mind these days. What about you?"

"Definitely not in the market for either." He said the words fiercely, as if to let her know exactly where he stood on the matter. "There are some guys meant for happily ever after. I'm not one of them, at least not at this point in my life."

"Don't worry, Joshua. You aren't my type anyway," she said lightly. "When I decide to get married, I'd like the bride to be prettier than the groom and in our case that just doesn't work."

He cast her a sideways glance. "Why do you do that?"

"Do what?"

"Why do you put yourself down like that?"

She flushed slightly. "I'm not putting myself down, I just don't suffer any illusions about myself. I know who I am and what I have to offer. I know my strengths and my weaknesses." She definitely knew her weaknesses, having them cataloged by her mother from the time she was a child.

He pulled into the church parking lot. He said nothing until he'd parked the truck and turned off the engine, then he turned and looked at her, his gaze enigmatic. "You want to know what I think? I think somebody definitely did a number on you and you don't have a clue what your strengths are."

He didn't wait for her reply, but got out of the truck and slammed the door with more force than necessary. Moody. Definitely, the man was moody.

As they walked toward the front of the church Savannah found herself wondering about the darkness she sensed in Joshua.

There were times when his eyes were shadowed with emotion she didn't understand, and it surprised her that she wanted to know the root of that darkness. It surprised her that she was as attracted to the inner man as she was to his outward appearance.

She found a seat in one of the back pews as Joshua disappeared to find the rest of the wedding party. She'd meet up with him again after the ceremony and they'd go together back to the West ranch for the reception.

As she waited for things to begin, she pulled out

a small notepad and made notes that would become an article for the paper.

White and burgundy roses bedecked the church, their beauty so intense it created a small ache inside her. Scented candles were lit, their flickering glows completing the romantic ambience.

When the men took their places near the minister and the traditional music began to play, a swell of emotion filled her.

Weddings always made her cry and the tears began the minute Libby's daughter, Gracie, began her walk down the aisle as flower girl. She looked like a miniature fairy princess in a billowing white dress and with her pale blond hair falling in ringlets down her back. As she walked and dropped rose petals, she smiled at the man who would be her official daddy when the ceremony was finished.

Clay stood at the front of the church, his brothers beside him as groomsmen. Her gaze lingered on Joshua, who looked slightly ill at ease but handsome as the devil. Clay smiled at the little flower girl, and she hurried her footsteps, almost skipping toward him.

As the bridesmaids began their march down the aisle her throat closed up as her tears increased. Meredith was first, looking more lovely and put together than Savannah had ever seen her. Then came Kate and Anna and another woman Savannah didn't recognize. One more lovely than the next in their cranberry-colored dresses and with flowers decorating their hair.

By the time Libby appeared in a stunning wedding gown and made her regal walk toward Clay, Savannah dug into her purse for a tissue.

Clay's face lit at the sight of his bride, his gaze filled with such love it was palpable in the air.

It was at that moment Savannah knew she'd lied to Joshua. She'd basically told him that love and marriage wasn't important to her, but that wasn't true.

There was a deep core of loneliness inside her, one that had ached inside her for as long as she could remember. She wanted somebody in her life, somebody who would listen to her dreams and share her desire.

She was filled with the need to love, with the desire to be loved. And her greatest fear was that she'd never find her lonely cowboy, she'd never get the opportunity to see a man look at her as Clay looked at Libby.

Her greatest fear was that her mother had been right when she'd told Savannah that she'd better learn to be content alone because a happily-ever-after probably wasn't in her future.

The white canopy shielded the wedding guests from the late afternoon sun. Beneath the canopy were tables and chairs and enough food to feed two townships.

Joshua stood near one of the food tables, a soft drink in his hand, his bow tie dangling loose. It appeared that the whole town was here. Mayor Aaron Sharp was holding court at one of the tables, talking to several other members of the city council. Jim Ramsey sat with a couple of his deputies, looking relaxed and definitely off duty.

Red and Smokey bustled between the kitchen and the tables, making sure the platters of food remained heaping and everyone got their fill.

A local band provided the music and a wooden dance floor had been laid out on the grass. A dozen couples occupied the space, two-stepping to a Garth Brooks tune. One of those couples was his brother Dalton and Savannah.

She looked like a bright yellow daisy, warm and vibrant amid the other people on the dance floor. Yellow was definitely a good color on her.

He narrowed his gaze as he watched them dance. It was obvious Savannah didn't know how to two-step and each time she messed up she raised her head to look at Dalton and laughed.

Heat coiled in Joshua's stomach, a familiar heat that he felt each time he looked at her. If only he hadn't kissed her. The kiss had been a momentary lapse of judgment he'd paid for ever since with a heightened sense of sexual desire for her.

Over the last week he'd learned several things about Savannah Clarion. She was smart and confident when she was working. She was good with people and had a sense of humor most people would envy.

But, even though she had a bravado about her, he sensed her insecurity as a woman. She obviously had no idea that she possessed an earthy sexiness that was far more interesting than traditional beauty.

She seemed to have no idea that when she smiled she lit from within and that whoever was gifted with that smile felt special. More than once she'd repeated something her mother had said to her and Joshua wouldn't have minded taking her mother out and horse-whipping her for the insecurities she'd put in Savannah's head.

Damn the woman anyway. He turned his back on the dance floor and instead eyed the faces of the crowd, seeking one who didn't belong, one who might have hatred in her heart.

For the past week he'd tried to connect with Lauren, to assure himself that she was still in New York City and not someplace in Cotter Creek.

Unfortunately, he'd been unable to get in touch with her. Her answering machine picked up at her house no matter what time he'd tried to call. She was either not home or not taking calls.

He'd also made several calls to mutual friends they had shared, but none of those friends had been able to tell him where she was or what she might be doing. Nobody had seen her at the usual places for the past week.

It had been a frustrating week on all levels as far as Joshua was concerned. He'd not only fought against his own desire for Savannah and failed at finding out what Lauren might be up to, but their investigation had stalled as well.

They had spent the week getting in touch with family members of the victims of the accidental deaths. Most had moved away, others weren't interested in rehashing the tragedies and nothing they had learned had indicated there was foul play at hand.

And yet despite that they'd hit nothing but dead ends, over the past week Joshua's instincts had begun to whisper that maybe Savannah was right. Maybe something bad was happening in the town he loved.

It was Charlie's death that made him believe something wasn't right. As the week had progressed and he'd gained some emotional distance from the trauma of finding Charlie dead, he'd found it hard to believe that Charlie would have done such a thing under his own volition.

Although his logic battled with his instinct, he'd decided to go with his instinct for the moment. He glanced back at Savannah, who had changed partners and was now dancing with Joe Steward, a middle-aged widower with four kids at home.

Joshua thought about cutting in, but the idea of holding Savannah in his arms, feeling her lush curves against him sent an uncomfortable shot of desire through him.

"Heard you're moving."

Joshua turned and smiled at his brother Zack. "Yeah, I've decided to move into the cabin." The cabin was a little two-bedroom place down the lane from the big house. At one time or another almost all the brothers had lived there. Zack had been the last and had left to move in with Kate.

"Any reason why you decided to make the move?"

"Nothing in particular. I just got used to having my own space while I was in New York." Certainly that was part of the reason he'd decided to move, but not the main one.

Each time his father looked at him Joshua felt a silent pressure to bend to his father's will, to agree to go back into the family business.

"You need help moving your things?" Zack asked.

"Nah, it's just a matter of taking a couple of suitcases to the cabin." At that moment Kate joined them.

"Hey, Joshua, you look as handsome as ever," she said. "All you Wests look fine in a tux."

Zack tugged at his collar. "Personally, I can't wait to get out of this monkey suit."

"I couldn't agree more," Joshua said with a laugh.

"If you'll excuse us, I believe my husband has promised me at least one spin around the dance floor." Kate grabbed Zack's hand, who moaned loudly but allowed his wife to pull him to the dance floor.

Once again his attention was captured by Savannah, who was twirling on the arm of yet another man. Didn't the woman ever take a break? She'd been dancing nonstop almost since the moment the band had begun playing.

"Nice party."

Joshua turned to see a familiar face. "Hi, Ms. Burnwell," he said to the flashy-dressed woman who worked as a Realtor in Cotter Creek.

"It's Wadsworth now, Sheila Wadsworth." She smiled. "While you were in New York I went and got myself married."

"Congratulations," Joshua replied. "Have you retired from the real estate business?"

"Heavens, no, I'm busier than I've ever been. Thomas, that's my husband, he's always complaining that the only way he can get any attention from me is if he wears a For Sale sign around his neck. And speaking of Thomas, I'd better go find him. That man has an unusual fondness for the spiked punch."

As she hurried off Joshua stared after her. So, the real estate business was booming in Cotter Creek. He frowned, a thought niggling at the back of his head. As the thought took full form, he looked around for Savannah.

He spied her on the dance floor with yet another partner, a young man he didn't recognize. Her cheeks were flushed with color and she looked at Joshua in surprise as he tapped her partner on the shoulder. "I'm taking your partner," he said to the young man.

He frowned, but stepped back. Joshua grabbed Savannah's hand and led her off the dance floor. "What are you doing?" she asked.

"I've thought of something and we need to check it out." He pulled her away from the party and toward his truck.

"What? What did you think of? Where are we going?" She hurried to keep up with his long strides.

"We need to find a plat of the area. I have a hunch."

"I have a plat in my office at Winnie's."

He got into the truck and started the engine as she scrambled into the seat next to him. "What's your hunch?" she asked as they pulled away from the West ranch.

"I'll tell you when we get that plat." He might be wrong. He needed to visually see on paper what was in his mind at the moment. "You looked like you were having fun." He cast a quick glance at her, noting that her cheeks still held a flush of color and her eyes sparkled brightly.

"I love to dance. I'm not terrific at it, but I love it. The wedding was wonderful, wasn't it? Libby looked like a fairy princess."

As they drove to Winnie's place she continued to chatter about the wedding, talking about how cute Gracie had looked, the decorations in the church and how happy the bride and groom had appeared.

He thought he heard a wistful note in her voice but told himself all women got a little silly when it came to weddings and babies.

By the time they reached Winnie's, he was as tense as he'd ever been. He told himself it had nothing to do with Savannah, that he was anxious to see if his suppositions were right. If what he believed was correct, then Savannah wasn't crazy and there was something wicked going on in Cotter Creek.

Savannah unlocked the front door, then led him up the staircase. He followed behind her, trying not to notice the sway of her shapely bottom mere inches in front of his face as they climbed the stairs.

Once they were in the room she used as an office, he stood in the doorway and watched as she dug through a pile of papers stacked in one corner.

"I know I've got one somewhere," she said as she flipped through the stack. "I got one from Lillian down at City Hall when I first arrived in town. It made it easier for me to know where everyone lived when I needed to conduct interviews. Ah, here it is."

She straightened and unfolded the large plat and laid it on the table. Joshua walked over and looked at the map that detailed the lots and land of Cotter Creek and the immediate surrounding area.

As he focused on the map, he tried not to notice the disturbing scent of her, a fragrance that smelled clean and fresh with just a hint of vanilla and musk. He grabbed a pen, then looked at her. "Who was the first person who died in a suspicious accident?"

"George Townsend. A kerosene heater exploded and his place burned down, him with it."

Joshua looked at the plat and placed a big *X* on the Townsend property. "Who's next?"

"Roy Nesmith. He fell out of his hayloft."

Joshua identified the Nesmith property and placed a large *X* there. One by one they went through the names and marked the property, with Charlie's land being the last on their list.

"Oh, my God," Savannah said softly as they both stared at the plat. The marked areas formed a disturbing pattern. All the accidental deaths took place on the west side of town.

"What do you think the odds of something like this happening are?" he asked. "That all the accidents would happen to men who lived in the same area?"

Savannah's eyes were wide as she held his gaze. "It's about the land, isn't it?" She looked down at the plat, then back at him, her breasts rising and falling with quickened breaths.

"It has to be about the land." Without warning she threw her arms around his neck. "You did it! I knew you could help me figure it out."

The moment her arms curled around his neck, the instant her breasts made contact with his chest, he lost the ability to figure out anything. All he knew was that she was warm in his arms and that since the last time he'd kissed her all he'd thought about was when he might kiss her again.

She must have seen something in his eyes, something that should have made her dance away from him, but instead she pressed closer into him and parted her lips as if in invitation.

He couldn't help but respond. He'd been on the verge of an explosion for the past week. As he crashed his mouth down to hers, he allowed the explosion to consume him.

Chapter 8

Savannah felt as if she'd waited a lifetime for his kiss. There was a hot, hungry demand in his lips that forced all thoughts of crazy conspiracies and land schemes out of her mind.

His strong arms wrapped her tight, pulling her as intimately against him as she could get. He was all hard muscle and she relished the feel of him against her, boldly aroused and taut with desire.

His tongue swirled with hers, evoking a want in her that she'd never experienced before. The hunger she tasted in his mouth clawed inside of her, made her weak and needy in a way that only he could sate.

As the kiss continued, his hands swept first up her

back, then down to cup her buttocks through the silky material of her dress.

His touch filled her with heat. She wanted him in her bedroom, in her bed, his naked body against hers. She wound her arms around his waist beneath the tuxedo jacket and unfastened the cummerbund.

As it fell to the floor, he stepped back from her, his eyes blazing and his chest heaving. "This isn't a good idea." His voice was husky as his gaze swept slowly down the length of her, then back up to meet hers.

His lips might be saying one thing, but the heat of his gaze said quite another. He wanted her. The knowledge torched fire through her, making her think that following through on what they had begun was a very good idea.

"Why not? We're both single and consenting adults." She reached out, took his hand and pulled him out of the office and into her bedroom. He came willingly, although once they were in the bedroom he pulled his hand from hers, his gaze tormented.

"If you don't want me, then I certainly don't want to make you do anything you don't want to," she said, as if it didn't matter to her. But it did. Her heart hammered in her chest. There was no doubt in her mind what she wanted. Him.

"I want you," he replied, his voice thick. He took a step toward her. "I haven't been able to think about much of anything else except how much I want you."

His words made her heart beat faster. He took

another step that brought him to within inches of her. He reached out and ran his fingers through her hair, as if unable to stop himself. "I definitely want you."

"Then what's stopping you?" She felt his hesitation and it was killing her.

He dropped his hand, his eyes darkening with the shadows that often filled them. "Because if we're going to do this, then you have to understand that it isn't any kind of a commitment on my part. This isn't a promise of a relationship, it doesn't mean we owe each other anything."

"And you tell me that I talk too much," she said teasingly.

His cheeks flushed slightly with color and he smiled back at her. "I just want things to be completely clear between us. I don't want there to be any kind of misunderstandings on either side."

"What makes you think I want anything else from you except a hot roll in the hay? Joshua, why don't you just shut up now and kiss me," she demanded.

His eyes flared and he did. It was as if the brief conversation had unleashed something wild inside him. Still kissing her he shrugged out of the tuxedo jacket and removed his shoulder holster and gun.

He then once again wrapped her in his arms and as his fingers worked to lower the zipper at the back of her dress, hers unfastened his shirt buttons.

She wanted to feel the expanse of muscled chest that had taunted her since she'd seen it naked when he'd been on his way to the shower. She wanted to curl her fingers into the dark springy hair that decorated the center of his broad chest.

When her dress zipper was lowered, he slid the garment off her shoulders and it fell to the floor, leaving her clad in her bra, her pantyhose and panties.

He ripped the tie from around his neck and finished unbuttoning his shirt. He shrugged it off, exposing the naked chest that had caused so many fantasies in her mind.

He grabbed his wallet from his back pocket and removed a foil wrapper. He placed it on the nightstand, then reached for her once again.

Within seconds the rest of their clothes quickly joined her dress on the floor and when they were both naked, they fell together on the double bed, a tangle of arms and legs and hunger.

As his mouth took possession of hers, his hands covered her breasts, filling her with a heat that burned all thought from her head.

His mouth left hers and trailed down her neck and across her collarbone, causing sweet sensations of pleasure to shiver through her. She raked her hands down his warm, smooth back, loving the play of muscles beneath the skin.

The golden dusk of twilight filtered through her bedroom curtains and played on his features with a soft illumination. He raised his head to look at her, his eyes gleaming with a breathtaking intensity.

Her heart thundered and desire crashed inside her

as he dipped his head and took one of her nipples in his mouth. She gripped the back of his head, his hair thick and soft beneath her fingers.

Mindless pleasure swept through her as he nipped and licked at her breast and she wanted to give him the same kind of mindless pleasure.

She ran her hand down the hard expanse of his chest, over the washboard muscles of his stomach then curled her fingers around the hard length of him. He moaned, a deep low growl that only increased her need for him.

For the next few minutes they explored each other's body, touching and tasting as the tension in Savannah spiked higher and higher.

It seemed that he could indulge in the foreplay forever, but it didn't take long for her to feel as if she might explode if he didn't take her completely.

"Joshua," she moaned his name. "Make love to me."

He turned over on his side and grabbed the condom from the nightstand. She took it from him, ripped open the package then rolled it onto him. By the time she was finished, he was trembling with his own need.

As he moved on top of her, she opened her legs to welcome him. He entered her, filling her up and at the same time his mouth took hers in a breathless kiss.

For a long moment neither of them moved. He ended the kiss and held her gaze as he moved his hips, withdrawing slightly, then stroking back into her.

The primitive yearning that had possessed her during their foreplay now exploded into something bigger, something so intense she felt as if at any moment she might fragment into a million little pieces.

She met his hips thrust for thrust in a rhythm that grew more frenzied. Her senses were filled with him, his scent, his touch and the sound of his rapid breaths and low moans. His features were taut, lips pulled tight and eyes smoky as he moved faster and faster.

Her release crashed through her and she clung to him, half-crying, half-laughing as waves of sensation washed over her. It was as if he'd only waited for her before allowing himself to let go. He stiffened against her, crying out her name as he shuddered, then collapsed on top of her.

As they waited for normal breathing to resume, for heartbeats to slow, she stroked her hands down his back, loving the feel of his warm skin. She was grateful he didn't immediately jump out of the bed, eager to be away from her now that they'd sated themselves.

He finally rolled to her side, but gathered her in his arms. "That was amazing," he said.

She smiled and placed her hand on the side of his face where she could feel the faint stubble of whiskers. "I think I've wanted to do this from the minute you took off your shirt and offered to scrub my back in your shower."

He didn't give her a responding smile, but instead

a frown furrowed his forehead. She could almost see the wheels turning in his head and she sighed impatiently. "Honestly, Joshua, if you're worried that somehow I'm going to get all mushy and romantic on you, don't."

A flash of relief shone from his eyes. She propped herself up on one elbow, vaguely irritated. "Other women might think you're all that, but this was just a hormone call as far as I'm concerned."

He propped himself up on his elbow, his face mere inches from hers. "Do you get these hormone calls often?"

She knew he was really asking about past relationships. "It's been over a year since I've been with anyone."

"Why is that?" He reached out and swept a curl away from her eyes.

He confused her. He'd been so intent in making sure she understood this meant nothing to him. Yet he was exhibiting a gentleness that pulled her toward him and a curiosity about her that seemed in direct conflict to his earlier words.

"I don't know. Relationships aren't a priority for me." There was no way she intended to confess to him that relationships had always been difficult for her, that she'd never found a man who loved her, flaws and all. "What about you? Did you leave a trail of broken hearts back in New York?"

"Not me. I tried to make sure hearts didn't get involved."

Somehow that didn't surprise her. "It must have been rough growing up without a mother," she said, changing the subject.

The shadows that had momentarily drifted across his eyes lifted and he shrugged. "It's hard to miss what you never knew. I was just a baby when she was killed. I have no memories of her at all."

"And they never found out who killed her?"

"I think it's the only unsolved homicide that's ever happened in Cotter Creek," he replied.

"Sometimes I wish I had less memories of my mother," she said drily.

"I gather from little things you've said about her that she was difficult."

She smiled ruefully. "There are some people who are just not cut out to be parents. My mother and father were two of those people. Sometimes I think it would have been easier to be raised by a pack of wolves."

"Is that why you left Scottsdale?"

"I left because it was time for me to leave. It was time for me to figure out who I was separate from my parents." Funny, they'd spent the entire week together but this was the first real conversation of substance they'd shared.

"I can understand that." Once again a darkness filled his eyes. "That was why I decided to head to New York, because I needed to know who I was aside from being a member of the West family."

She wanted to ask him more, wanted to know

about the thoughts that caused those shadows, but knew she had no right. This night was supposed to mean nothing and that meant she had no ownership of his inner thoughts.

"When are you going to let me interview you for my column?" she asked.

He grinned. "You never give up, do you?"

She curled her fingers into his chest hair. "I just think you'd be an interesting subject."

"Trust me, it would be the most boring interview you've ever conducted."

She sighed. "So, what happens now in our investigation?"

He sat up and swiped a hand through his hair. "We need to find out what happened to the land, if it was sold, if it went to heirs, whatever."

"What made you think of it? How did you put it all together?" She sat up, too, clutching the sheet to her chest.

"Sheila Wadsworth. I had a brief conversation with her at the reception and something just clicked in my head." He swung his legs over the side of the bed and reached for his slacks. "I'll be right back." He held his pants in front of him as he left the room and a moment later she heard the click of the bathroom door.

She lay back against her pillow and closed her eyes, for a moment allowing herself to replay each and every kiss, each and every caress they had shared. It had been more than amazing. And it didn't mean anything. She couldn't allow it to mean anything.

You'd better get used to being alone, Savannah Marie. You don't have many assets to offer a man.

"Thanks, Mother," Savannah said softly and forcefully shoved her mother's words to the back of her head. She suddenly remembered Joshua's words when they had arrived at the wedding.

He'd said that somebody had done a number on her. Of course, he was right. For as long as she could remember, her mother had pointed out all her flaws, both physical and character ones.

The main reason Savannah had left Scottsdale was to figure out who she was and what she had to offer to other people without the constant negativity from her parents. She'd needed to get away from the constant hurt that her parents could inflict on her.

She opened her eyes as she heard the bathroom door open. Joshua came back into the bedroom clad in his slacks. "You want to get dressed and I'll take you back to the party?" he asked as he grabbed his shirt from the floor. "It will probably go on until the wee hours of the morning."

There was a part of her that wanted to go back to the party. It would be fun to get Joshua out on the dance floor with her, fun to drink too much champagne and laugh with him. But, there was another part of her that wanted to remain in the bed that smelled of him, that retained his warmth.

"No, I think I'll stay right here," she replied. She

wanted to just stay in bed and savor the memory of their lovemaking. "Besides, I imagine it won't be long before Winnie gets home."

"What are your plans for tomorrow?" He fastened his cummerbund around his waist, then reached for the bow tie.

"Most Sundays I just hang around here. Take the day off, Joshua." Once again she sat up. "In fact, I was going to talk to you about this bodyguarding business. Nothing has happened to make us think I'm in any danger since that shooting at the newspaper office. Maybe that really didn't have anything to do with me. Maybe you playing bodyguard is just a waste of your time."

He frowned and put on his holster. "Next week we're going to start asking some questions that might make somebody uncomfortable. I'd feel better if we just leave things the way they are for now, at least until we know more about what's going on."

She wasn't sure why, but she was pleased that he didn't want to take the easy out that she had offered him. Although she certainly wasn't going to get all silly over him, she was glad to have him by her side.

"You know, Sheila Wadsworth has been not-so-subtly indicating to me that she would love to be interviewed for my column. Maybe I should call her tomorrow and set up a time for Monday. If anyone knows who owns those places now, she'd know."

"Great idea. You have a piece of paper and a pen? I'm going to be in and out tomorrow and I'll give you my cell phone number and you can call and let me know what you've set up for Monday."

She reached into her nightstand and pulled out a small notepad and pen. He took them from her, wrote his number, then placed it on the nightstand. He grabbed his shoulder holster and gun and put them on, then pulled on his tux jacket. "Sure you don't want to go back to the reception?"

She snuggled back beneath the sheets. "Sure you don't want to stay here?"

His eyes flashed with heat. "Don't tempt me."

Oh, but she wanted to tempt him. She'd love nothing more than to invite him back into her bed and make love with him until the sun came up in the morning. But, her desire for that frightened her just a little bit.

"Get back to the party and I'll call you tomorrow," she said.

When he left he seemed to take all the energy in the room with him. Night was falling outside the window and she almost wished she'd gotten up and returned to the party with him.

She could imagine the tent lit against the darkness, laughter spilling out as the band played and people danced and celebrated the joy of Clay and Libby's union. But, making love with Joshua had shaken her up more than she cared to admit.

By nature she was cautious, especially when it came to sex. Jumping into bed with Joshua after knowing him only a little over a week had definitely

been out of character for her. But, the enforced closeness that they had shared over the past week and a
half had built up not only an intense desire but also
a strange sense of intimacy.

She rolled over on her side as a small wave of
irritation niggled at her. It was definitely egotisti-
cal of him to worry that somehow by going to bed
with her she'd expect something more from him.
Why didn't he worry about wanting something
more from her?

He was probably accustomed to women
throwing themselves at him, but she didn't intend
to be one of the lovesick masses who wished Joshua
West could commit.

She sighed and closed her eyes and within
minutes fell into a deep, dreamless sleep.

She had no idea what awakened her, whether it
was a noise in the room or something else. But, the
moment sleep fell away she sensed that she was no
longer alone in the room.

Suddenly the blanket was yanked over her head
and a weight fell on top of her. Any fogginess of
residual sleep fell away. Claustrophobia closed her
throat as she fought to be released from the cocoon
of blankets that held her captive.

"Hey," she cried, wondering if Joshua had
returned and was playing some kind of a sick joke
on her. "This isn't funny."

Her heart hammered as she increased her efforts
to get free. Whoever held the blankets held them

tight, keeping her captive and unable to see what was going on. "Let me up," she cried, kicking her feet and flailing her arms in an effort to get free.

The first blow caught her in the stomach, a vicious punch that knocked the air from her lungs and assured her that whatever was happening certainly wasn't a joke.

Frantically she kicked out and fought, her throat closing as terror possessed her. As terrifying as the blow to her midsection had been, equally as horrifying was her inability to see her attacker.

A second punch to the stomach forced a rising nausea. When another blow struck her hip, she gave up all efforts to get free of the blankets and instead rolled onto her side and pulled herself into a fetal ball in order to protect herself from the blows that rained down on her.

A hit to her jaw stunned her and stars swam in her head. Tears filled her eyes as she realized she was about to get beaten to death in her own bed. With a cry of rage, she renewed her fight to free herself from the blankets.

She managed to get a leg free and kicked wildly. She connected with something and heard a sharp moan. Sobbing, she kicked again and again.

"Savannah. Are you home, dear?" Winnie's voice came from the downstairs.

Savannah froze. Oh, God. No. Fear for her elderly landlady sizzled through her. "Winnie! Run! Run, Winnie," she screamed.

As she frantically fought the blankets, she heard the thud of footsteps racing down the stairs, then Winnie's high-pitched scream.

Chapter 9

It had been a huge mistake. As Joshua drove back toward the West ranch, the weight of his mistake hung heavy in his heart.

He'd been on a slow simmer where Savannah was concerned. He had no idea why she'd affected him so intensely, but someplace in the back of his mind he'd hoped that by sating his desire for her once, it would be done and over.

Unfortunately, it hadn't worked out that way. Rather than being done, just thinking about what they'd just shared made him want to share it again. He'd been so tempted to forget returning to the reception and instead crawl back into bed with her.

At least he didn't have to worry about her getting

emotionally involved. She seemed less inclined to form a commitment with anyone than he did.

In fact, she'd made it pretty clear to him that he'd been nothing but a booty call. It was an odd feeling for him and one he was surprised to discover didn't feel altogether terrific.

He tightened his grip on the steering wheel as if symbolically getting a grip on himself. Despite the fact that the sex with Savannah had been unbelievably hot, in spite of the fact that she could make him laugh and at times pulled forth a protectiveness inside him, he wasn't looking for any kind of a real hookup at this point in his life.

Still, the thought of Savannah's warm curves in his arms, the fire that had been in her kiss and her total giving to him as they'd made love couldn't easily be dismissed from his mind.

He was halfway between the ranch and town when he saw the sheriff's car racing toward him, the cherry light on top flashing against the darkness of the night.

Most everyone in town was at the West ranch. Where could Jim be heading? With an odd, sick premonition, Joshua flashed his lights a couple of times and Ramsey pulled to a halt next to Joshua's truck.

He rolled down his window and Joshua did the same. "Something happened at Winnie Halifax's place," he said.

The premonition exploded into fear. "I just left there a few minutes ago," Joshua said. "What happened?"

"Apparently somebody attacked the women."

The words were scarcely out of Ramsey's mouth before Joshua pulled a U-turn and roared back the way he'd come. He was vaguely conscious of the lights of the sheriff's car following close behind as he sped back to Winnie's.

Somebody attacked the women. Somebody attacked the women. The words played and replayed in his head in a sick echo.

What exactly had happened? How badly was she hurt? Dammit, he should have never left her alone. What in the hell had he been thinking, and who had made the call to Jim? He held the steering wheel so tightly he felt as if his fingers might break.

How had they gotten inside the house? He'd locked the front door when he'd left Winnie's, knowing Savannah was still snuggled down in bed. Had the attacker broken in or had Savannah let somebody in?

Savannah might have opened the door to an attractive woman, not knowing the danger. Lauren could charm her way past a palace guard if she wanted inside badly enough.

He should have told somebody about Lauren. He should have swallowed his pride and told his family, told Savannah about the danger Lauren might pose.

Attacked. Dammit, what did that mean? Had she been raped? Stabbed? Shot? Had Winnie gotten home and found Savannah dead in her bed? Was Savannah lying in a pool of her own blood as Winnie had frantically called the sheriff?

"Jesus," he whispered. Emotion clawed up his throat as he pulled to a halt in front of the Halifax two-story house.

It looked as if every light in the house was on. Joshua pulled his gun as he left the truck and raced toward the front door.

He burst inside and nearly fell to his knees in relief as he saw Winnie and Savannah sitting on the sofa, their arms wound around each other. Whatever had happened, at least they were both alive.

"Joshua." Savannah stood and launched herself into his arms as deep, wrenching sobs shook her body. She wore a thin blue cotton robe and as he held her, he was aware that she had nothing on beneath it. But, more importantly, she was wonderfully alive in his arms.

Her tears only lasted a minute, then she stepped back from him and wiped her cheeks. Joshua's stomach knotted as he noticed for the first time the redness of her lower jaw. He reached out and gently touched the spot. "What happened?" he asked.

At that moment Ramsey flew through the door.

Savannah resumed her seat next to Winnie, who looked shaken and frail. "After you left, I decided to go to bed," Savannah said with a meaningful glance at him. She obviously didn't want them to know that the two of them had been in bed together and that's where Joshua had left her.

She crossed her arms in front of her chest and hugged herself. "I fell asleep and the next thing I knew somebody was on top of me, punching me.

Whoever it was had me trapped beneath the blankets and they kept hitting me."

Her terror radiated from her eyes and Joshua wanted to hit somebody, punish whoever was responsible for that fear, for her pain. "They kept hitting me and hitting me and I couldn't get free of the covers."

She reached up and touched her jaw and winced slightly. "I think they would have beaten me to death if Winnie hadn't arrived home when she did." She grabbed the older woman's hand.

"I unlocked the front door and stepped inside," Winnie said, her voice faint and trembling. "Then I called up to Savannah. The next thing I knew somebody came crashing down the stairs, knocked me clear over and flew out the front door."

"Did you get a look at the intruder?" Ramsey asked.

Winnie shook her head, her pale blue eyes filling with tears. "It all happened so fast. I wasn't expecting it. Whoever it was had on all black and maybe a ski mask. All I saw was black, then I was on the floor and he was gone."

Joshua had an incredible need to pull Savannah back into his arms, to assure himself that she was really all right. He told himself the need had nothing to do with her as a person but rather because he was supposed to protect her, and he'd failed.

"I'm going to take a look outside," Jim said.

"I'll look around in here and see if I can tell how

they got inside," Joshua replied. Jim nodded and the men parted ways, leaving Winnie and Savannah seated side-by-side on the sofa.

It took him only a step into the kitchen to see how the intruder had gained access to the house. The window beside the kitchen table was broken, the screen torn away to provide an easy entry.

Cold rage swept over him as he thought of Savannah's reddened jaw, how she'd been trapped in the blankets while somebody had pummeled her. What would have happened had Winnie not come home when she had? The thought sent a new wave of rage through him.

Had it been Lauren? Certainly he suspected she was capable of such an attack. At one time he'd believed he was a good judge of character, but his experience with Lauren had shaken that belief right out of him.

He left the kitchen and checked the rest of the house. He touched nothing in Savannah's bedroom, but looked for clues as to the identity of the intruder. Unfortunately, if the person had worn a ski mask, the odds of finding a hair or any other evidence were minimal.

Sheriff Ramsey joined him in the bedroom, a frown tugging his graying eyebrows together. "I didn't see anything outside. Saw the window in the kitchen so I guess we know how they got inside." He looked around the room in obvious frustration. "Who in the hell would do such a thing?"

"That's what I was just asking myself. It's the craziest thing I've ever heard."

Joshua stood by the door while Ramsey wandered around the room, obviously looking for the same things Joshua had looked for…clues as to who might have been in the room beating up Savannah.

"I don't think you'll find anything useful," Joshua said. "If what Savannah and Winnie believe is true, that the perp was wearing all black and a ski mask, then I imagine he or she was also wearing gloves."

"I think you're probably right," Sheriff Ramsey agreed. He looked at Joshua in speculation. "You think this has something to do with all the questions Savannah has been asking around town?"

"I think anything is possible." He told Sheriff Ramsey the latest information he and Savannah had come up with as to the location of the land and the coinciding accidental deaths. With each word he spoke, Jim Ramsey's frown grew increasingly deeper.

"I'd like us to work together on this, Joshua. I want to get to the bottom of this as quickly as possible."

Joshua nodded. "I think she's right, Jim. I think there's something going on here."

A hard light gleamed from Ramsey's eyes. "Until I decide to retire, this is still my town and I'll be damned if I'll just sit by and allow some sort of criminal activity to take place right under my nose. I'm going to take statements from the women, then go get my fingerprint kit and see what I can find.

Who knows, maybe we'll get lucky and the perp left a print behind."

While Jim took down the official statements, Joshua went out to Winnie's garage and found a piece of plywood to temporarily cover the broken kitchen window.

It was after eleven when Jim finally left the house. "I'm going to bed," Winnie said. "It's been a trying night and I'm exhausted." She got up from the sofa, her weariness evident in her sagging shoulders.

Savannah stood as well and gave the woman a hug. "I'm so sorry, Winnie."

"You don't have anything to be sorry about, child."

"Are you sure you're all right?" Savannah asked.

Winnie smiled tiredly. "I'm fine, dear. It takes a lot more than a masked man to get me down."

As Winnie went down the hallway toward the bedroom, Savannah looked at Joshua, her eyes still retaining the fear of what she'd experienced. Never had a woman looked as if she needed a hug as much as Savannah did at that moment.

But, before he could decide if that was a good idea or not, she seemed to find some source of inner strength. She straightened her shoulders, tilted her chin up and smiled.

"Well, this has been interesting. How about I make some coffee and we talk about it," she said.

Nothing she had done or said over the past week earned as much of his respect as she did at that moment. With her eyes shining overly bright and her lower lip trembling slightly, she nevertheless displayed a core of strength he couldn't help but admire.

"Coffee sounds great," he said. He had a feeling she wasn't ready for him to leave, but she couldn't know he didn't intend to go anywhere, at least not until after he told her about Lauren. She had a right to know what his past might have brought into her life.

He sat at the table and watched silently as she busied herself making a short pot of coffee. When it began to drip into the glass carafe, she turned and looked at him, her eyes less haunted than they'd been moments before.

"The redness in your jaw is fading," he observed. "I don't think you're going to bruise."

She reached up and touched the spot, then dropped her arm to her side. "I've got to tell you, even though the attack lasted only a couple of minutes, they were the scariest minutes of my life. At first I thought maybe it was you, that you'd decided to come back. When the covers were pulled up over my head, I thought you were playing some sort of a joke on me."

Again a fierce protectiveness filled Joshua, along with a healthy dose of anger. "I'm sorry, Savannah. I'm sorry I left you alone and vulnerable."

"It's not your fault." Her eyes darkened as she looked at the board covering the broken window.

"You think you're safe locked in your own home, then something like this happens and it shakes up any sense of safety you have."

She turned back to the coffeepot and poured them each a cup of the fresh brew. She set his cup in front of him, then joined him at the table and curled her fingers around her cup. "I guess I should be grateful that Winnie arrived home when she did and that whoever attacked me used fists instead of a knife."

The visual picture of her trapped in the sheets while somebody stabbed her over and over caused Joshua's heart to stutter in his chest. This night could have ended so differently. It could have ended in tragedy.

"Could you tell if your attacker was a male or female?" he asked.

She sat back in her chair and looked at him in surprise. "I just assumed it was a man." She frowned thoughtfully. "Why would you think it might have been a woman?"

He took a sip of his coffee, then drew a deep breath. "You asked me after the night of the shooting who I might have pissed off since returning home to Cotter Creek. As far as I know I haven't made anyone mad since I've been back home, but I left somebody in New York who would love to hurt me and whoever she thinks I might care about."

Savannah's frown deepened. "And you think that person might have come here to Cotter Creek? That she might be the one who attacked me tonight? My

God, Joshua, what did you do to her to inspire such hatred?"

He sighed. *Failure*, a little voice whispered in his head. "Her name is Lauren Edwards. I met her at a club one night. She was gorgeous and smart. She told me she worked at a law firm as a paralegal and was considering going to law school to become an attorney."

He scooted his chair back and stood, too restless to sit as he thought of how badly he'd screwed up. "Anyway, we hooked up that first night and I thought we were both on the same page. I thought she understood that I wasn't looking for anything permanent. I thought we were both wanting the same things, just a little bit of fun and nothing serious."

"But she wanted more?"

"Apparently." He began to pace the small confines of the kitchen, his mind going back over the last couple of weeks he'd spent in New York. "Anyway, we saw each other for about a month and I thought everything was cool. We hadn't talked about an exclusive relationship. Hell, we hadn't talked about a relationship at all. We weren't seeing each other on any regular basis."

"But she thought of it as something more than it was?" Savannah asked.

"She started planning a wedding and that's when I called a halt to things. I tried to be nice and let her down gently, but I sure as hell wasn't prepared to marry her after a month."

"I'm guessing she took it badly?"

"That's an understatement. A couple of nights after I broke it off with her, I met a female coworker for dinner. We were in the middle of our meal when Lauren burst into the restaurant like some crazy person."

He stopped his pacing and leaned with his back against the refrigerator. That night had been the most embarrassing that Joshua had ever experienced in his life. "She came in screaming about how I'd betrayed her. She called the woman I was with a slut and tried to fight her. She was escorted out of the restaurant, but when my coworker went to leave, she discovered that the windows in her car had all been broken out."

He began to pace again. "Then the next day while I was at work, my apartment was broken into." He still remembered the stunned shock he'd felt when he'd stepped into his apartment. "Everything was destroyed, slashed with a knife, smashed beyond repair. It took a tremendous amount of rage to do the kind of damage that was done."

"She wasn't arrested?" A tiny frown raced across Savannah's forehead.

"I knew she did it. The police questioned her, but unfortunately one of her girlfriends provided an alibi."

"And you think maybe this Lauren followed you here? That she might have been the person who tried to beat me up tonight?"

He returned to the table before answering. "I think it's possible," he said. "I've been trying to get in touch with Lauren ever since the night of the shooting, but she's not answering her home phone. I couldn't remember what law firm she worked for, but I finally got a hold of a mutual friend who told me. The receptionist at the law firm where she worked said she'd taken some vacation time, but I don't know if she's still in New York or not."

"Isn't there somebody you can call to see if she's still in town?" Savannah asked.

"I tried. I spoke with several of our mutual friends and nobody has seen her for the past week or so."

"But that doesn't mean she isn't still in New York."

Joshua shrugged. "True. But I figured it was best I tell you about her, just in case."

"So, basically I should watch my back for a love-crazed New Yorker who has claimed you as her man."

The lightness of her tone irritated him. Didn't she understand that he'd somehow screwed up? That he'd misjudged the entire situation?

"It's not funny," he said with a scowl. "I don't know what this woman is capable of, I don't know how dangerous she might be."

Her eyes darkened once again and one slender hand reached up to touch her jaw. "I guess she's dangerous enough if she's the one who attacked me tonight." She finished her coffee, then got up and carried her cup to the sink.

She rinsed out the cup then turned to face him.

"I'll keep an eye out for women I don't know, but you realize it's equally as possible that whoever attacked me tonight did so because we're making somebody nervous with all our questions about those deaths."

"How many people have you talked to about your suspicions?" he asked.

Her cheeks pinkened slightly. "You should know by now I like to talk. I told anyone and everyone who would listen that I thought something bad was happening. I talked to waitresses and sales clerks, the mayor and members of the city council."

He also took his cup to the sink, rinsed it then turned to her. She looked tired and although her jaw wasn't as red as it had been, it still held a touch of color. He reached out and placed his fingers against the redness. "Are you sure you're all right? Were you hurt anywhere else?"

She leaned toward him as if to welcome his touch. "I took a punch to the stomach and a few to the back, but I'm okay. I was terrified when it was happening, but the moment you walked in here I knew it was all going to be okay."

Her words both touched and concerned him. He didn't want her depending on him. He obviously didn't have the tools to judge people and their intentions, which was an integral part of being in the personal protection business.

He dropped his hand from her face and stepped back, needing to distance himself from her. "We just need to be smart and understand that for whatever reason you're at risk."

She nodded and wrapped her arms around herself. She looked small and vulnerable. "I'm sorry you missed the rest of the party."

He smiled. "There will be other parties. You need to go to bed. It's late."

"And I'm beyond exhausted." She glanced over to the boarded-up window, then back at him, her gaze holding a dark whisper of fear. "You don't think the attacker will come back again tonight, do you?"

"If it would make you feel better, I'll sleep here on the sofa for tonight."

"I hate to ask you to do that, but it would make me feel better." She flashed a tight smile. "I'll bet you're sorry you ever got involved in all this," she said as they left the kitchen.

"If it's Lauren, then I'm sorry I got you involved," he replied. It had been easier to tell her about Lauren than he'd thought it would be. In fact, he had a feeling he could talk to Savannah about anything.

"I'll just get you a pillow and some blankets," she said as they moved into the living room. She disappeared down the hallway and returned a moment later with the bedding in her arms. "Are you sure you don't mind staying here?" Her brow wrinkled with worry.

"It's fine," he reassured her. "I wouldn't have offered if I minded." He took the bedding from her arms. "Now, you'd better get some sleep."

She reached up on her tiptoes and kissed his cheek. The imprint of her lips shot heat straight to his heart. He backed away from her, confused by his reaction, vaguely irritated by a quick whip of desire that swept through him.

"Goodnight, Joshua." She walked to the stairway but before she took a step up she turned back to look at him. "The thing with Lauren, at least you know you managed to inspire tremendous passion in somebody. That's something I don't expect to do in my lifetime." She didn't wait for his reply, but instead climbed the stairs.

He watched her until she disappeared from his sight, then he unfolded the blankets and made his bed for the night on the sofa. Whatever he'd inspired in Lauren, he didn't believe it had anything to do with real passion. It had everything to do with sick obsession.

As he placed his gun on the coffee table in easy reach, he thought of what she'd said about his being sorry he'd gotten involved.

The truth was he felt more alive, more vital than he had since he'd left Cotter Creek almost one and a half years before. The problem was he didn't know if it was the woman or the potential danger that had his blood pumping and his adrenaline flowing.

Chapter 10

"Don't forget the security code if you get home before me this afternoon," Winnie said over breakfast Monday morning. "I'm having my hair and nails done today."

Winnie had arranged for a security system to be installed the day before, insisting that she should have done it years ago when her husband had first passed away and left her all alone.

Savannah had to confess, the new alarm system definitely gave her a sense of security that had been stripped from her with the attack. "I won't be home until later this evening. First thing this morning Joshua and I are heading to City Hall to see Lillian. We want to find out who owns the property of the ranchers who died. Then, I have an early dinner date with Sheila Wadsworth."

Winnie wrinkled her nose. "Now that's a woman who doesn't know the meaning of subtle."

Savannah laughed, thinking of Sheila's penchant for glitter and sequins. "She certainly hasn't been subtle about wanting me to interview her for my column."

"Sheila will do almost anything for attention or money," Winnie said. "She's been like that all her life. Rumor has it that she met her husband when she joined some dating service. Of course, I try not to listen to rumor." Winnie smiled slyly.

Once again Savannah laughed and carried her breakfast dishes to the sink. "This town runs on gossip. It's the favorite pasttime of everyone."

Winnie's smile increased. "And I know the latest piece of gossip that's making the rounds."

Savannah rinsed off her dishes, placed them in the dishwasher, then turned and looked at her landlady. "And what would that be?"

"Everyone is talking about how quickly you managed to snap up the most eligible bachelor in town."

"I didn't snap him up. We're just working together, that's all," Savannah exclaimed, her cheeks warming with a blush.

Winnie raised an eyebrow. "You two might just be working together, but that doesn't account for the sparks that fly in the air whenever the two of you are in the same room."

"Nonsense," Savannah scoffed as she felt her blush deepen, spilling heat into her cheeks. "There is absolutely nothing personal going on between Joshua and me."

Except she hadn't been able to forget what it felt like to be held in his arms, to be kissed with his lips, to feel his body taking hers. "And speaking of Joshua, he should be here anytime. I'm going to run upstairs and grab my purse and notebook."

Alone in her room, she sat on the edge of the bed and thought about what Winnie had said. If there were any sparks in the air between her and Joshua it was only because of the physical attraction she felt for him and nothing else.

It had been almost impossible for her to fall asleep Saturday night knowing he was downstairs on the sofa. She'd wanted nothing more than to go downstairs and get him and bring him into her bed.

She'd wanted his strong, warm arms holding her through the remainder of the night. Her desire was so intense it had frightened her. She told herself it was because of the trauma she'd suffered, but she suspected it was something deeper and more profound than that.

He'd left the next morning after the alarm system had been installed and they had only spoken on the phone once during the day to set up a time for him to pick her up this morning.

Despite that she had known him less than two weeks, in spite of the fact that they'd made love only

once, he was getting beneath her defenses, making
her wish for things she'd never wished for before.

"Savannah Marie, get a hold of yourself," she
said aloud. She had sworn to Joshua that she wasn't
going to get all mushy and romantic where he was
concerned and she was determined to keep her word.

She grabbed her purse and notebook and left the
bedroom. She'd just hit the bottom of the stairs when
the doorbell rang.

It was Joshua. She tried to ignore the expanse of
her heart at the sight of him. Clad in a pair of jeans,
with a blue and gray sports shirt and dark gray sports
coat, he threatened to take her breath away.

"All set?" he asked.

She nodded. "Winnie, we're leaving," she yelled
toward the kitchen.

Within minutes Savannah and Joshua were in his
truck and headed toward City Hall. She drew a deep
breath, enjoying the scent of him, that wonderful
blend of sunshine and clean male.

"What happens if we don't see anything suspicious about the sale of those properties?" she asked.

"Then I guess you just have to suffer through an
interview with Sheila and write a column about her."
He flashed a quick glance at her, his eyes lit with
humor.

She smiled. "I guess that's not the worst thing
in the world. So, what did you do on your day off
yesterday?"

"I moved."

She looked at him in surprise. "You moved? Where?"

"There's a little two-bedroom cottage down the lane from the big house. It used to be used by a variety of ranch managers, but for the past several years Zack lived there. Since he and Katie got married, the place has been empty."

"Is there a reason for the move?" She couldn't imagine leaving the love and support that brimmed to the top at the West ranch for isolation in a cabin.

He hesitated a long moment before answering. "I just got used to being alone in New York and prefer to be by myself."

She didn't believe him. There was something more to it than that. It surprised her how much she wanted to know everything about him, all his thoughts, his worries, his dreams.

She told herself it was only because she was a reporter and he was an intriguing man from a powerful family, but she knew she was only fooling herself. She was beginning to care about Joshua West, and that scared the hell out of her.

Maybe she was just feeling unusually emotional because of the attack and it was only natural she'd turn to Joshua for comfort and support. She had nobody else to turn to.

A wave of loneliness suddenly overtook her. She had parents who had never really bonded with her, a friend who had either committed suicide or been murdered and a man who had slept with her but had made it clear he wanted nothing more from her than a booty call. If she thought about it for too long she'd get downright depressed.

"It's not like you to be so quiet," he observed, breaking into her somber thoughts.

"Are you implying that I normally talk your ear off?"

He grinned. "Yeah, that's pretty much what I'm saying." He pulled into a parking place in front of the brick one-story city hall. He cut the engine, then turned to face her, the smile gone. "Are you okay? Did you sleep all right last night?"

"I slept fine," she assured him. "It's amazing how much a little thing like a state-of-the-art alarm system can do for your peace of mind." She unfastened her seat belt. "And now let's go inside and see how many cages we can rattle today."

She'd just stepped out of the truck when a male voice called her name. She whirled around to see Larry Davidson hurrying toward her. She smiled at the rugged cowhand who wore his black hat at a jaunty angle.

"Hi, Larry. How's life treating you?"

"Not bad." He shot a glance at Joshua.

"Do you two know each other?" She looked from Joshua to Larry.

"Haven't had the pleasure," Larry said and held out a hand.

The men made their introductions, then Larry

faced Savannah once again. "Could I talk to you alone for a moment?" he asked.

"I'll wait right over there," Joshua said and walked several feet away.

Larry swept his hat off his head, revealing a head of unruly dark blond hair. He worried the brim of his hat between his thick callused fingers. "I was just wondering if maybe you'd like to have dinner with me sometime."

Savannah took a step back from him, surprised by the invitation. Perhaps if she hadn't met Joshua she might have considered accepting his offer. But it didn't seem right to sleep with one man and have dinner with another. Besides, there was absolutely no sparks where Larry was concerned.

"Thanks, Larry, but right now I'm really busy with work." He looked crestfallen. "Maybe you could check back with me in a couple of weeks," she added, not wanting to hurt his feelings.

"I'll do that," he said and plopped his hat back on his head, then turned and headed down the sidewalk.

Savannah rejoined Joshua, who stood near the front door of the city hall building. He scowled. "How do you know that guy?"

"One of the first people I profiled when I started my column was Mayor Sharp. Larry works on the Mayor's ranch, and while I was out there he showed me around the place."

"What did he want?" The scowl showed no sign of lifting.

"He wanted to ask me out to dinner," she said, then added, "not that it's any of your business."

"I hope you turned him down. He's definitely not your type."

She looked at him in surprise. "And just what is my type?"

The scowl finally vanished, replaced by a knowing glint in his eyes. "He has to be strong, otherwise you'd ride ripshod all over him. And he has to have money." His gaze slowly slid down the length of her. "Because you are definitely a high maintenance kind of woman."

"I have my own money, thank you very much," she replied.

"Oh, and he'll have to be the silent type because the odds are good he'll rarely get a word in edgewise."

"Ha, ha, I bet you think you're funny." She grabbed him by the arm and steered him toward the door. "Come on, let's see if you can exude some of that Joshua charm on Lillian so she won't take all day getting the records we want to see."

Cotter Creek City Hall was a study in opulence for a Midwest cow town. The floor was imported gray marble with pale pink veins, more befitting a plush hotel than a government building.

Several years ago Aaron Sharp had pushed for major renovations for City Hall, resulting in mahogany counters, gleaming brass fixtures and the latest in computer technology.

One thing that hadn't changed was Lillian. She

sat at a desk behind the counter, the same place she had sat five days a week for the past ten years.

She got up from her desk as they came in, a smile of welcome on her wrinkled face. "You must not be here to pay taxes because you don't look mad."

"Actually, we're here for some information," Savannah said. "We'd like to find out who owns some of the property in the area."

"Should be easy enough," Lillian said. She took the list of properties that Savannah had prepared. "It's going to take me a few minutes."

"We'll wait," Joshua said.

As Lillian returned to her desk and her computer, Savannah tried to still her racing heart. She was anxious to find out what information Lillian might be able to give them, but she suspected her quick heartbeat might also be because as crazy as it sounded, Joshua had acted like a jealous suitor for a moment.

She glanced over to where he stood leaning against the counter. *Don't be ridiculous, Savannah Marie. A man who looks like Joshua might sleep with you because you're convenient, but when it comes time for him to settle down, it won't be with a woman like you.*

"Shut up, Mother," Savannah muttered.

"Excuse me?" Joshua eyed her curiously.

"Nothing, I was just talking to myself."

He grinned, that easy, lazy smile that never failed to warm her. "It's nice to know you don't need anyone else around to fulfill your need for meaning-less chatter."

She might have been offended by his words if it hadn't been for a soft, indulgent light that filled the green of his eyes.

"I spent most of my childhood talking to myself," she said lightly. "I'm used to it."

His smile faltered and instead he gazed at her for a long, somber moment. "I'm sorry about that."

There was something soft, something gentle in his voice that pierced through the protective barrier she kept so firmly around her heart. For just a moment as she looked into his eyes hope buoyed inside her, a fragile hope that she was afraid to hang onto. She feared that if she grasped it too tightly, she'd be shattered when she discovered her mother had been right about her after all.

"This is odd," Lillian said as she handed Joshua the information they'd been seeking. "All of those properties are listed to two men who have the same address in Boston. Isn't that odd?" Lillian looked from Joshua to Savannah.

"It's more than odd," Joshua said as he exchanged a meaningful glance with Savannah. "Come on, we've got more work to do."

"I was right, wasn't I, Joshua?" Savannah said as they left City Hall. "This is proof, isn't it?" Her cheeks flushed becomingly. "I knew I wasn't crazy. I might be a lot of things, but I'm not crazy." She followed him down the sidewalk. "Where are we going? What happens now?"

"We're going to see if we can find out who these two men are and why they have the same Boston address. Dalton should be in the office and with his help maybe we can get some answers before your dinner date with Sheila."

A hard knot pressed inside his chest. Savannah had been right. There was something evil happening in the town he loved. Somebody was buying up all the land, land that had belonged to men who had died in what now seemed like damned suspicious accidents.

He'd worried that somehow Lauren had found him and set her sights on Savannah. He'd believed that the attacks on her had been from the woman he'd left behind in New York City. Now he wasn't so sure.

If this was as big as he thought it might be, then it might just be big enough for Savannah's questions to be making somebody very nervous. He fought an impulse to reach out and take her hand in his, as if to assure himself that at least for the moment she was safe.

The Wild West Protective Services wooden sign creaked on its hinges in the midmorning breeze as he and Savannah approached the front door.

Inside Dalton sat at the desk, looking bored and with a computer game pulled up in front of him. "Hey, what's up?" He greeted them and closed down the game.

"We need some answers and I'm hoping you can get them off the Internet," Joshua said. He handed

Dalton the sheet of paper Lillian had printed out for them with the names and addresses of the men who owned the properties.

"I want to know who these men are and why they're buying up land in Cotter Creek," Joshua said, then went on to explain what he and Savannah had been investigating.

"Strange," Dalton said when he'd finished. "Why would a couple of Boston men want anything to do with Cotter Creek?"

"That's what I'm hoping you can find out," Joshua replied.

"This may take a little while," Dalton said.

Joshua looked at Savannah. "Want to grab a quick cup of coffee at the café while we wait?"

"Sounds good to me," she replied.

"We'll be back in twenty minutes or so," Joshua said to his brother, who nodded absently, his attention totally focused on his task.

There was no way Joshua felt like just sitting and waiting in the office. He knew Dalton would work better if he didn't have the distraction of him and Savannah standing over him.

"What does all this mean, Joshua?" Savannah asked him a few minutes later as they sat at a back booth in the café. "Why would those men be buying land here?"

"I don't know. Maybe Dalton will come up with some answers that will make sense."

She frowned thoughtfully. "You think those men

are responsible for all those ranchers' deaths? Do you think one of those men killed Charlie?"

"Who knows? To be perfectly honest, I don't know what to think." He took a sip of the strong, hot coffee, then continued. "Cotter Creek is such a small town. I do find it difficult to believe that there are strangers running around killing people then buying up their land. People around here notice strangers."

Savannah's pretty eyes gazed at him somberly. "Then that means probably somebody here in town is killing those people. Somebody we know. Maybe somebody we trust."

Once again the knot in his chest constricted tighter. "Hopefully when we get back to the office Dalton will have some answers for us."

Savannah wrapped her slender fingers around her coffee cup and stared out the nearby window. As she looked outside, he found himself staring at her.

She was right. She wasn't beautiful in the traditional sense. But she was pretty, and when she smiled she exuded a warmth that was entrancing.

Today she was dressed in a pair of navy slacks and a pink and navy striped sweater that intimately hugged her curves. As he stared at her, desire struck him like a punch to the gut.

He liked her. The sudden knowledge surprised him. In the time they had spent together he'd definitely come to admire her intelligence, he enjoyed her sense of humor and sensed they shared the same moral standards.

He'd even grown to like the fact that she'd never met a silence she couldn't fill and had come to realize that her stubbornness was actually a fierce determination to do what she thought was right.

There was a soft vulnerability in her that touched him. Even though she often joked about her mother and the ugly things she'd been told about herself, he sensed she carried deep scars from her childhood and it surprised him that there was a part of him that wanted to heal those scars.

He wanted her again. Right here. Right now. He wanted to strip that sweater over her head and kiss the freckles on her shoulders. He needed to hear her soft sighs as he caressed her skin.

She looked at him then and a small gasp escaped her. A blush worked up her neck and swept to her cheeks…as if she were privy to his innermost thoughts, as if his desire was raw and bare in his gaze.

"What are you thinking?" she asked, her voice a husky whisper.

"I was just thinking that maybe after we see what Dalton finds, you'd like me to fix you some lunch at my place." Of course, that hadn't been what he'd been thinking. His thoughts hadn't been of food, but rather of her.

"I'd like that," she said simply, her eyes simmering with unspoken words.

"Don't you want to know if I can cook or not?" he asked.

Her smile heightened the tension and made him glad he was seated at a booth. "I don't care if you can cook or not."

Her reply let him know she was aware of what would happen if she came to his place, she was not only aware of it but apparently wanted him as much as he wanted her.

She cleared her throat and sat back in the seat. "So, you still think it's possible Lauren is after me?"

Thoughts of their lunch date instantly disappeared from his head. "I don't know. I still haven't been able to make contact with her and I have to admit that worries me a little."

He took another sip of his coffee and frowned thoughtfully. "I can't believe how badly I screwed that up."

"From what you told me about the situation, you didn't screw up. It sounds to me like Lauren had some major problems to start with." Savannah leaned forward. "I've never understood those kind of women who smash car windows or rip up clothing or stalk a man because of unrequited love. If a man doesn't want me, then I certainly don't want to be with him. Life is too short for that kind of drama."

"Yeah, but I should have seen that Lauren wasn't right. Somehow I missed the signals, I misjudged her. Reading people and situations is part of what I was trained to do as a bodyguard." Frustration edged through him at thoughts of Lauren.

She reached across the table and touched the back

of one of his hands. "Joshua, stop beating yourself up. If disturbed or evil people were so easy to pick out then we'd know who in this town was responsible for those deaths just by looking at his face. Besides, as far as I'm concerned you're a terrific bodyguard. You saved me from getting a butt full of birdshot, didn't you?"

He turned his hand and grabbed hers as he thought of that moment when Jim Ramsey had told him somebody had been attacked at Winnie's place. "Yeah, but somebody almost beat you to death in your bed and I was nowhere around."

"You aren't to blame for that. Who knew that anyone would break into Winnie's. You can't be with me every minute of the day and night." She released his hand. "Joshua, if I had to handpick a bodyguard, you'd be who I'd choose."

"Why? Because I'm a West?"

"I wouldn't care if your name was Mud." She leaned back in the booth and eyed him intently. "I've seen the way you are when we're out in public, the way you look at everything and everyone, how you measure the safety of the place and the people around me. I'd hire you because whenever I'm with you I feel safe."

Her words dug deeply into him, touching him more than he wanted her to know. "Thanks, and personally I'm glad my name isn't Mud."

She smiled. "You think we should head back over to the office?"

"Yeah, let's go see if Dalton has managed to get us some answers."

Together they left the café and walked the short distance back to the Wild West Protective Services office. Dalton was waiting for them, a frown etched across his forehead.

"I have something for you, but it isn't much," he said. "I can't find anything on the two men, but the address comes back with a listing for a MoTwin Corporation."

"Did you find out anything about the corporation?"

Dalton shook his head. "All I've managed to learn so far is that it's a privately owned corporation. It's going to take me longer than twenty minutes to get more information. It looks like it might be some sort of dummy corporation."

"Keep digging, would you?" Joshua asked.

"Definitely. I'll keep you posted on what I find out."

Once again Joshua and Savannah stepped outside into the late morning sunshine. "So, what do you want to do now?" he asked Savannah. "Do you need to check in at the newspaper office or anything?"

She shook her head, her hair glinting like fire in the sunlight. She looked at him, her amber eyes blazing more gold than brown. "How about that lunch you offered me? I'm suddenly ravenous."

Chapter 11

Not a word was spoken as Joshua sped to the West ranch. Savannah knew they were going to his cabin for one reason and one reason alone.

To make love.

The air between them snapped and crackled with their intent, with their desire for one another. It was as if the electricity was so big, so intense it left no room for talk or thought.

Even though she knew there was no future with him, even though she knew she'd never be anything but a momentary diversion in his life, no doubts entered her mind, her heart. She would take whatever pieces Joshua was willing to give her of himself.

She'd take from him until he tired of her then she

would go quietly away. No drama, no tears. She was the queen of reality, and she had never questioned that her future would ultimately be a lonely one.

They flew by the West ranch house and down a pasture lane, eventually stopping in front of a small cabin half hidden by lush trees and overgrown brush. The place held a rustic charm that wasn't lost on her. It looked like the perfect place for a private midday rendezvous.

Savannah's body nearly sang with anticipation as they got out of the truck and she followed Joshua across the small porch and to the front door.

She'd barely gotten inside the door when he grabbed her and crashed his mouth to hers. The kiss felt half-angry, demanding and all-consuming.

She returned it with the same emotions. She was half-angry with him because she knew that he wanted nothing more from her than to sate a physical desire. She demanded that he give her all he was capable of giving because she was at least worth that much.

They'd entered into the kitchen and the force of the kiss drove her back against the refrigerator. Joshua leaned into her, trapping her between the cool enamel of the fridge and his hot, hard body.

"What are you doing to me?" he asked, his voice a half growl.

"I don't know, but you're doing the same thing to me," she replied breathlessly.

He slammed his mouth back to hers and ground

his hips against hers. She ground back, loving the
feel of his arousal hard against her. It frightened her
more than a little, the ease that he could sweep all
thoughts out of her mind, how easily he drove her
half-crazy with desire.

The kiss ended and he stepped back from her, his
chest heaving with deep breaths, his green eyes
glowing with a primal energy.

"You make me crazy," he said, his voice a husky
whisper. "I can't remember ever wanting a woman
like I want you right now."

The admission from him simply fanned the
flames that burned inside her. "Joshua, I want you
so much it's all I can think about."

He took her mouth again with his, his tongue
battling hers in a sensual war. Savannah wound her
arms around his neck, melting against him as the
heat of his kiss weakened her knees.

This time when the kiss finally ended he grabbed
the bottom of her sweater and with one smooth
action pulled it up and over her head. He tossed the
garment toward a small wooden dining table, then
grabbed her hand and pulled her into the bedroom.

She had no opportunity to pay attention to the surroundings. There was only Joshua and her desire for
him. She was blinded to anything else.

It took only moments for them to undress and get
beneath the sheets that smelled of him. They moved
together in a frenzy, the lovemaking fast and furious,
and when they were finished they remained in the

bed, the afternoon sunshine streaming through the window.

For the first time since arriving Savannah took note of the room. Navy curtains hung at the window, matching the navy bedspread that had been thrown off at some point. A wooden dresser sat against one wall, a photo of the West family on top.

She turned over on her side and looked at Joshua, who was on his back, staring up at the ceiling with a frown cutting across his forehead. "What are you thinking?" she asked softly. She placed a hand on his chest, the thump of his heartbeat against her palm.

The frown disappeared as he gazed at her. "Nothing. At least nothing important."

She held his gaze for a long moment. "Do you miss New York City?"

"Not at all." His reply came quickly. He placed an arm around her shoulder and pulled her closer to him. She snuggled into him, savoring the quiet intimacy of not just their physical closeness but also a momentary emotional one as well.

He released a deep sigh. "Going to New York was a mistake. I realize that now. I want my life to be here, in Cotter Creek. At the time I moved to New York I had a need to get away from here, find a place, an identity that was all my own. It's great having a big family, but I needed to get off by myself."

"I can't imagine having everything you have here and choosing to leave it all," she replied. "It has to be amazing to know how much you're loved by everyone around you, to have such wonderful support from your family."

"It is wonderful," he agreed easily, "but it's one thing for your family to think you're terrific. I needed to find out what kind of a person I was separate from my family."

He frowned once again. "Everyone in my family told me how smart I was, how competent, but the only job I'd worked was as a bodyguard for a business my father owned. I needed to find out if I was worth anything besides being a West and working for Wild West Protective Services."

"And did you find what you were looking for?"

"The verdict is still out."

"It's funny, you had to leave your family because you had too much love and support and I had to leave mine for just the opposite reasons." As always, a tiny rivulet of pain fluttered through her as she thought of her parents.

He tightened his arm around her. "Tell me about your mother and father. You've mentioned before that they weren't cut out to be parents."

She ran her hand across the muscled expanse of his chest, enjoying the feel of his chest hair beneath her fingertips. "They aren't bad people. To be honest, I hardly know my father. He worked a lot and when he was home he was completely caught up in my mother. There wasn't time for me in his life."

"And your mother?" His hand rubbed her back in

a gentle swirling motion that was both erotic yet soothing at the same time.

Savannah sighed. Thoughts of her mother always confused her. "I love my mother, but I don't like her very much." She propped herself up on an elbow and gazed at Joshua. "My mother is an absolutely stunning woman. Her life before she met my father had been beauty pageants. By the time she was ten years old she'd won over a hundred contests, but I think that world made her worship beauty above all else and unfortunately I didn't fit into her world. Nothing worse for a beauty queen than to have a red-headed, freckle-faced, outspoken, lacking-of-poise daughter."

Joshua smiled and touched the tip of her nose. "I like your freckles." His smile faded as his fingers slid down her cheek, and he caressed the length of her neck.

He leaned forward and kissed her, a kiss of infinite tenderness and quiet passion. Savannah pressed herself against him, returning his kiss with a tenderness and passion of her own.

She wanted him again and it was obvious from his arousal that he wanted her, too. As his hands moved down the length of her, they didn't move with the white-hot fever that they had earlier, but rather this time it was a slow burn that slowly consumed her.

He touched her everywhere with his hands, with his mouth, caressing and tasting and bringing her again and again to the brink of release then denying her with a low wicked laugh.

She returned the favor, loving the fact that when

she touched him low across his belly he groaned and when she licked across that same skin, he gripped her shoulders and groaned her name like a plea.

When he finally entered her, it was a slow, smooth glide into magic. They made love as if they had all the time in the world, as if they knew each other so intimately there was no need to be adventurous or exploratory. They simply moved together in perfect rhythm, giving and taking as naturally as breathing.

As he kissed her, a deep, soulful kiss, she felt the rise of intense emotions filling her. It was so intense tears stung her eyes. Her heart felt too big for her chest and it was in that moment that she realized she'd only been fooling herself.

She'd believed that she could spend almost every waking hour with Joshua and have sex with him and not get her heart involved. She'd thought she was strong enough not to fall victim to his charm. She'd thought she could know the man inside and not care about him, but she'd been wrong.

The truth was, she was falling in love with Joshua West. He liked her freckles. How could she not fall in love with a man who told her he liked her freckles.

Unfortunately, she knew as surely as she was breathing that she was headed for heartache.

Joshua listened to the sounds of the shower coming from the bathroom. He'd taken a quick shower minutes before and now sat at the kitchen table and waited for Savannah to shower and dress.

He had never felt so confused in his life…confused about himself, confused about Savannah. After they'd had sex the second time he'd looked at her and wondered how anyone could ever even imagine that she wasn't beautiful.

And that had scared the hell out of him. She was creeping in where no other woman had ever been…into his head, into his heart.

At the moment all he felt was a need to run, to escape her with her charming chatter and innate warmth. He needed to distance himself not only from his desire for her on a physical level, but also an emotional level as well.

Despite her background with her family, he thought she was the most together woman he'd ever met. She seemed to know exactly who she was and what she wanted from life and he envied her that.

She'd shown him some of the scars that had been left by her mother and as the youngest son of a loving family, he'd ached for her pain, a pain he'd never known.

He tensed as he heard the shower water shut off. He looked at his watch, surprised to realize how late it had gotten. They had spent the entire afternoon in bed.

There was a part of him that wished they could just grab a bite to eat from the refrigerator, then tumble back into each other's arms and sleep together through the night. But there was a bigger part of him that needed to get away from her.

She was supposed to interview Sheila in less than an hour. He'd take her to the café for the interview, then take her home and tomorrow he'd be stronger where she was concerned.

He had to get control of his feelings, because until he knew where he was going with his life, he had no intention of taking anyone along with him.

He was still seated at the table when she came out of the bedroom. Despite his need to control his emotions, he couldn't help the way his heart leaped as she gifted him with one of her wide smiles.

"I can't believe you don't have a hair dryer," she said as she finger-combed her curly, damp hair.

"Yeah, well, that's because I discourage female visitors," he said.

She stopped in her tracks and stared at him. "Oh, forgive me, I didn't realize you were discouraging my presence here when you were driving ninety miles an hour to get me here."

"You're right. I guess I just want to make sure that you understand that nothing has changed as far as I'm concerned." He knew he was being an ass, but he couldn't stop himself. She scared him, his feelings for her scared him and he needed to gain a safe distance. "I just don't want another Lauren situation on my hands."

Her eyes narrowed. "You're some piece of work, Joshua West. How dare you even think I'd be capable of being a 'Lauren situation.'" Her words were clipped and curt with anger.

Her eyes blazed as she stalked across the room to the front door. "You might be all that and a bag of chips to most of the girls you sleep with, but I told you from the very beginning that all I was looking for was a little fun. You're so worried about me wanting more from you, but what makes you think you're so great that I'd want anything more from you?"

She opened the front door, stepped out then slammed the door behind her. Joshua hurriedly followed, instant regret weighing heavily on his shoulders.

As Savannah started walking, short angry strides taking her past his truck, he called after her. "If you're planning on walking back to town you're going to be late for your interview with Sheila."

She paused, whirled to face him, then walked back to his truck and got in. He slid behind the wheel, then turned to face her. "I'm sorry," he said. "I shouldn't have said that."

She looked at him and in the depths of her eyes he thought he saw a whisper of hurt, but she raised her chin in a show of defiance. "Just get me back to town. I have a job to do." She averted her gaze out the passenger window as if to dismiss him.

He started the engine and pulled away from the cabin, sorry that he'd said anything, sorry that he'd obviously hurt her feelings.

They rode for a few minutes in silence, a taut silence that deepened his regret.

"Savannah, I didn't mean for it to sound like I thought you might be like Lauren," he said after several minutes of the impossibly strained silence. "I just don't want there to be any complications, I wanted to make sure you know where I stood with you."

"You've made that crystal clear," she said with marked coolness in her voice. She turned to face him once again. "Look, Joshua, things have somehow gotten out of control between us, with the bodyguard thing maybe we're spending way too much time together. You know what they say about familiarity breeding contempt."

Once again she turned her head and looked out the passenger window. Her breasts heaved with a deep sigh. "I think maybe we need a break from each other. I appreciate the fact that there might be some sort of threat against me, but I'm a big girl. We have the alarm system now at the house and I know to watch my back."

"We're in the middle of an investigation," he protested. "I'm not sure now is the time to change things." He pulled up and parked in front of the café. He cut the engine, then turned to face her. "We're both running a little high on emotion here. Why don't we wait and see what we find out from Sheila before we make any rash decisions?"

"Fine," she replied, and without another word got out of the truck and slammed the door.

Chapter 12

Savannah knew she'd probably overreacted, but the fact that he'd reminded her that he really wanted nothing from her on any level other than a physical one echoed with old hurts from her past.

For just a moment, with her newly realized love for him aching in her heart, she'd hoped for something more from him. She'd hoped that the gentleness of his lovemaking had indicated a depth of feeling for her, that the passion he'd shown her had sprung from someplace other than his groin.

Don't expect too much from men, Savannah Marie, her mother's voice rang in her ear. *You just aren't the type of woman that men get all gushy and soft about. I'm only telling you this for your own*

*good. I wouldn't want you to hope for anything that
you might never have.*

Her mother's words followed her from the truck
inside the café where she picked a booth near the
back and slid in. A moment later Joshua sat across
from her, his forehead wrinkled with a frown.

"Savannah, I didn't mean to make you mad."
There was a plea in his deep green eyes.

How she wanted to hang on to some anger, how she
longed to raise her anger like a shield against her
feelings for him. But, as hard as she tried, she couldn't
sustain her irritation. How could she be angry with him
for simply reiterating his rules for their relationship?

She sighed, a new burst of love for him swelling
in her chest. "I'm not mad. Let's just forget it, okay?"
She glanced at her wristwatch. "Sheila should be
here any minute and I need to gather my thoughts
for my interview."

She felt incredibly vulnerable and desperately
needed some time alone, but she knew he wanted to
be here when she spoke with Sheila.

The waitress arrived at the table and both of them
ordered only drinks, knowing that they would be
eating when Sheila arrived. As they waited for the
Realtor to arrive, the silence between them grew un-
comfortably taut.

For the first time in her life Savannah felt no
desire to fill the silence with talk. Instead she
wrapped it around her like a defense against her own
feelings.

The café was quickly filling with people as dinnertime approached. Laughter rang in the air, along with the clatter of cutlery and the buzz of conversations.

Normally Savannah would find these kinds of surroundings invigorating, but at the moment a headache began a slight pound across her forehead and she just wanted to get this day finished.

She pulled a notepad from her purse and spent the next few minutes making notes concerning the questions she wanted to ask Sheila.

She wasn't really angry with Joshua, she was angry with herself. She had momentarily forgotten what had been drilled into her from the time she could understand language. Joshua hadn't done anything wrong. She had. She'd fallen in love with a man who was emotionally unavailable.

She looked up to see him staring out the window, and she thought of what he'd told her earlier, about what had driven him away from his family and off to New York to find himself.

It was strange how two people as different as them, as different as their backgrounds had been, could share a common goal to discover themselves amid strangers.

Whatever Joshua had needed, he hadn't found it in New York and she had a feeling until he found whatever it was he needed, he had nothing to offer any woman. In any case he'd made it clear he had nothing more to offer her.

She sat up straighter in the booth as she saw Sheila's luxury car pull up in front of the café. It was the first time she could remember actually looking forward to talking with the abrasive, pushy woman.

"Here she comes," Joshua said as Sheila burst through the front door of the café. Savannah breathed a sigh of relief. It was time to focus on what was important, on what she did best. It was time to interview a woman who might know something about what was going on in this town. At least this was something she did well.

"Savannah, darling, I'm so excited to be here," Sheila said as she reached the booth. "And Joshua, I'm really not surprised to see you as well. The gossip mill has been working overtime about the fact that you two have been joined at the hip since you came home."

Joshua stood and indicated that Sheila slide into the booth opposite Savannah where he had been sitting. "Savannah and I don't pay much attention to the gossip mill," he said.

Savannah thought he might move to another booth or table and leave her alone with Sheila, but instead he slid in beside Savannah, his warm thigh pressing against hers. He obviously intended to be present during the interview.

"I'm just so excited to be here," Sheila said again as she got settled in the booth. "I just love your column and can't believe you're going to write about little old me." As she talked, her long dangling earrings bounced against the shoulder of her rhinestone-bedecked red jacket.

"Shall we order some dinner before we officially begin?" Savannah asked.

Sheila winked at her. "There's two things I love, closing on a great real estate deal and eating." She raised a hand to gesture for the waitress.

As they waited for their orders Savannah and Sheila small-talked about upcoming events in town while Joshua sat silently, invading Savannah's thoughts with his mere presence.

"Lovely wedding the other day, wasn't it? Imagine Clay going all the way to Hollywood to find a bride," Sheila said.

"Yes, it was a lovely wedding," Savannah agreed. She tried not to remember that it had been the day of the wedding that she and Joshua had first fallen into bed together.

The small talk continued as they ate, and it was only when their dishes had been cleared and fresh coffee poured that Savannah got down to business.

She opened her notepad, pen ready. "I always like to start an interview by asking, what are the two things you'd like the people of this town to know about you that they might not already know?"

Sheila frowned and reached up to twirl a strand of her bleached blond hair. "Oh my, I never thought about it before. I suppose I'd like everyone to know that everything I've achieved in my life has been from damned hard work and long hours. And the other thing is that I know I dress flashy and gaudy, but when I was poor and growing up I always said when I got money I'd dress to please myself, and there's nothing I love better than gaudy flash."

"Tell me about your childhood. You grew up right here in Cotter Creek, didn't you?" Savannah asked.

"Right out there on Route 10."

As Sheila launched into the story of her past as one of four children of a dirt-poor rancher, Savannah tried to keep her attention focused on the interview and not on the man beside her or the questions she really wanted to ask Sheila.

There was no point in thinking about Joshua, and it was far too early in the interview for her to start hitting Sheila with hard questions.

People stopping at their booth to greet them interrupted them more than once, but the visits were brief as the visitors realized Savannah was conducting official newspaper business. If there was any doubt about what she was doing, Sheila was quick to inform everyone that she was being interviewed for Savannah's column.

As the questions and answers went on, Savannah felt Joshua's growing impatience and knew he wanted her to get where he wanted her to go. But, Savannah knew the importance of building trust and she wasn't going to allow Joshua's impatience to make her rush things with Sheila.

By the time Savannah decided to heat things up, her headache had fully blossomed, squeezing across her forehead like a vise.

"You ever go to bed hungry?" Sheila asked.

Savannah nodded and she continued. "I went to bed hungry almost every night as a child and I decided then that I was going to make something of myself, make sure I never spent a hungry moment in the rest of my life."

"The real estate business seems to be booming right now in Cotter Creek," Savannah observed, and she felt Joshua tense as if coming to attention.

"I keep busy, that's for sure," Sheila agreed.

"I'd say you've been more than busy." Savannah flipped through her notes. "According to my research, in the last eighteen months you've sold the Townsend and Nesmith places, the Wainfield and Cochran ranch." Savannah named the other ranches that had been sold due to the deaths of the owners.

Sheila's eyes narrowed slightly. "Well, yes, I was the agent for all those places. Whenever any property in this town is ready to market, I try to be there to get an exclusive."

"Did you ever find it odd that all those men died in accidents?"

Sheila blinked once, twice…three times. "I guess I never thought about it before."

She was lying. Savannah knew it in her gut. The rapid blink of her eyelids and the fact that she averted her gaze from Savannah let her know Sheila was definitely lying.

"Then think about it now," Savannah said. "I find it very odd that all those men died in strange accidents, and you were the agent there to sell their property."

Sheila looked at her once again, a hard glitter in her eyes. "All I do is sell land. That's all I do. When I heard each of those men was dead, I talked to their remaining family members and told them I'd get them the best offer if they wanted to sell. All of them wanted to sell. Nothing strange about it."

Joshua had been quiet throughout the interview process, but he now leaned forward. "Sheila, if you know something about those deaths, you need to tell us now."

"I don't know what you're talking about." Her hand rose to her throat, and once again she blinked rapidly. "I told you, I'm just a real estate agent. All I did was sell those properties. I haven't done anything wrong."

"What is MoTwin?" Joshua asked.

Sheila's face paled, and she looked at Savannah with accusing eyes. "I thought this interview was for your column. You got me here on false pretenses." She grabbed her purse from the booth. "I'm leaving. This interview is over." She slid out of the booth. "I don't know anything and I want you both to leave me alone."

"Sheila, men have died and we think they've been murdered. If you know anything, please tell us," Savannah exclaimed.

The older woman shook her head, then hurried away from the booth but not before Savannah saw a flicker of fear in the depths of her eyes.

"She knows something," Savannah said, frustration making her headache intensify. "She knows something and she's scared." She wondered if she'd have managed to get something out of Sheila if Joshua hadn't been there. Maybe his presence had intimidated her.

"Yeah, well, I don't think either one of us is going to get her to talk. Maybe Ramsey can get something out of her. I'll let him know what we've found out."

Now that Sheila was gone, Savannah was acutely aware of Joshua so close to her side. All she wanted was to escape both the noise of the café and Joshua.

"I need to go home," she said and rubbed a hand across her forehead. "I have a headache and I'm tired."

Joshua scooted out of the booth and she did the same. As they walked to his truck a deep weariness swept over her. It had been a day of sheer emotion.

First the unbelievable thrill of making love to Joshua, then the crash down to earth as he reminded her that basically she meant little to him and finally the tense interview with Sheila.

What she wanted more than anything at the moment was a cup of hot tea and meaningless conversation with Winnie, then the privacy and comfort of her bed.

Once again silence reigned as they drove toward Winnie's place, and once again she had no desire to try to break the silence. The vulnerability she'd felt earlier was back, and she was afraid that if she said anything she might make the mistake of showing Joshua just how deeply she cared for him.

It was he who finally broke the silence as he pulled into Winnie's driveway. He put the truck in Park, then turned to look at her. "I'll contact the sheriff first thing in the morning and let him know everything that we've found out."

She nodded wearily. "I still don't think it's necessary for us to be together every waking hour."

He frowned. "We showed our hand to Sheila. Now isn't the time to make changes."

"No more than I've showed my hand before. I've been ranting and raving about a conspiracy for the last couple of weeks. I'll be fine on my own."

She was determined to get some space from him. "Look, all I plan to do for the next couple of days is go into the newspaper office then back home again. You've gone above and beyond for me and I appreciate it. But, let's be real, we have no idea when we'll have some answers about what's been going on and I certainly don't expect you to be my bodyguard for the rest of my life." She certainly knew better than to expect him to be anything to her for the rest of his life.

"You're right," he said after a moment of hesitation.

She sighed in relief. If he'd fought her on her decision to halt his bodyguard duties she wasn't sure she'd have been strong enough to hold her ground.

"You'll let me know if Dalton discovers anything else?" she asked.

"Of course," he agreed.

She opened the truck door and started to step out,

but paused as he softly said her name. "If you get nervous or scared or something doesn't feel safe to you, you know I'm just a phone call away."

"I know that," she said, then slipped from the truck, wanting to be away from him before she said or did anything stupid.

Joshua watched her until she disappeared through Winnie's front door, then he backed out of the driveway and headed home.

He felt bad. He felt really bad. He knew he'd broken something between them and that no matter what happened in the future nothing would ever be the same where the two of them were concerned.

The closer he got to home, the heavier the weight of depression descended upon him. No matter how much he told himself Savannah meant nothing to him, that she'd been a diversion from reality, he knew he was lying to himself.

The sex between them had been amazing, but that wasn't the only thing that drew him to her. She was intelligent and funny and had a warmth about her that drew people to her. But, he wasn't ready for somebody like her in his life. He wasn't ready for any woman in his life.

As he turned onto the West property, he thought about going back to the cabin. He knew the place would smell like her, that her scent would linger in the bedroom, amid the sheets.

Damn, he couldn't remember the last time he felt

so confused, so unsure of his actions and emotions.
She'd twisted him up inside in a way nobody had ever
done.

Instead of driving by to get to his cabin, he pulled
up out front of the big house and parked. For the first
time since he'd returned from New York, he didn't
feel like being alone. Judd and Jessie greeted him
like old friends, following close at his heels as he
went up the porch.

He entered the house and headed directly toward
the kitchen where he found Smokey seated at the
table, a ranching magazine opened before him.

"Hey, Joshua. What are you up to?" The old man
closed the magazine and leaned back in his chair.

"Not much. Where's everyone else?" Joshua sat
in the chair opposite Smokey.

"Your dad decided to call it an early night and has
already gone to his room, and I think Meredith went
out to the stables. You want something to eat? I've
got plenty of leftovers from dinner."

"No, thanks. I ate at the café a little while ago."

"Where's your sidekick?"

"I left her at Winnie's."

"So, what's on your mind, son? You got that look
in your eyes like you need to talk."

Joshua smiled and shook his head. Smokey knew
him better than anyone, just like Smokey knew all the
West kids inside and out. He'd always been able to
tell if one of them needed to talk, had always known
if one of them had burdens that needed to be shared.

"How about a drink?" Smokey got up and went to one of the cabinets and pulled down a bottle of whiskey. He poured them each a healthy splash of the liquor, then added a couple of ice cubes to each glass and rejoined Joshua at the table.

"Thanks." Joshua wrapped his hands around the glass. "I'm thinking about working again for the business."

"It's about damn time," Smokey exclaimed. "I don't know what took you so long to make up your mind."

"I don't know. I guess I needed to sort things out in my head."

"It's in your blood, Joshua. You were born to work for Wild West Protective Services."

Smokey's words shot right to the heart of Joshua's insecurities. "That's what bothers me," he confessed after a moment of hesitation. "The idea that the job is there for me because I was born a West, because it's what the West boys do and it has nothing to do with my capabilities."

Smokey stared at him for a long moment, then took a drink and set the glass back down. "What's the matter with you? Do you really think your father would encourage you to come back to the business if you weren't capable?"

"Maybe," Joshua replied faintly, the single word deepening Smokey's scowl.

"Hell, he loves that business almost as much as he loves you kids. Do you really think he'd jeopardize the company reputation by putting you in position as a bodyguard when you aren't qualified?"

Smokey got up and grabbed the bottle of whiskey from the countertop and carried it back to the table. "Damn boy, what did that time in the city do to you?"

He poured himself another shot of the drink and eyed Joshua intently. "If your daddy had any question about your ability as a bodyguard, he'd put you to work as a bookkeeper or a ranch hand. He would never risk anyone's life by assigning a bodyguard who was inadequately trained, or physically and mentally unprepared."

Smokey's words found the tightness that had been in Joshua's chest for the past couple of weeks and eased it. In his heart Joshua knew the old man was right.

Wild West Protective Services had a stellar reputation. His father had worked most of his life to build a company that was known not only in the United States but worldwide for its security and capability.

Smokey was right. If Joshua wasn't good enough, he'd be the last man his father would want working for him, no matter how thick the blood they shared.

Joshua stared down into his glass. "It feels like failure, coming back here, coming back into the family fold. But I missed you all more than I thought I would." He hadn't realized how heavy the burden of feeling like a failure weighed on him until he'd spoken the words out loud.

"Since when is it a failure for a man to know where he wants to spend his life and who he wants around him? Hell, Joshua, it isn't a weakness to need the people you love. It isn't a weakness to surround yourself with people who love you."

Smokey held his gaze intently. "Does this have something to do with that red-haired chatter box?" Smokey asked. "She got you twisted up inside and doubting yourself?"

"No, it has nothing to do with her." He couldn't help but smile at Smokey's characterization of Savannah. He took a sip of his whiskey and relished the slow burn down to the pit of his stomach, then continued. "It's just that everything has always come easy for me. I don't feel like I've ever had to really prove myself or my worth."

Smokey grinned, the gesture lifting his white grisly eyebrows. "You're right. You were plumb spoiled by everyone and that's a fact. All of us catered to you, you being the youngest and all. You didn't have to work real hard to feel special." Smokey took another swallow of his drink. "Maybe we should have made it a little harder on you, but I suppose there's worse things than being surrounded by people who dote on you."

"Yeah, like having nobody who dotes on you." Once again his thoughts turned to Savannah. What would it have been like to be raised by people who never spoke of your worth, who never made you feel special?

He suspected in most cases it could destroy a

person, but in Savannah he sensed a deep well of strength, a core of identity that nothing and nobody could shake. He respected that in her.

He was also surprised to realize that it bothered him more than a little bit that she so easily had dismissed him, that she'd seemed perfectly content in keeping their relationship nothing more than a mutual lustfest.

"What else is on your mind?" Smokey asked, breaking into his thoughts.

There was no way in hell Joshua was going to confess that a woman he'd known only two short weeks was messing with his mind. Instead he found himself telling Smokey everything they had learned that afternoon and about their interview with Sheila.

"Have you talked to Ramsey about all of this?" Smokey asked, his grizzled eyebrows pulled together in a deep frown.

"Some of it, not all of it. I plan on meeting him first thing in the morning to fill him in on everything." Joshua finished the last of his whiskey, then leaned back in the chair. "Whatever this is about, Sheila Wadsworth is in it up to her neck."

"Sheila Wadsworth doesn't have the imagination or the guts to orchestrate what you think has been happening here," Smokey scoffed. "She might be in on it, but I'd bet you my good leg that she's only a grunt. Somebody else is in charge. Somebody here in town."

"And that's who I want. I want the man who is responsible for Charlie's death, for all the deaths that resulted in the sale of that land." A hard knot formed in his chest. "I'm hoping Dalton can find out something about the MoTwin Corporation. I want to know who's running it and what they intend to do with the land."

"If what you believe is true and all those men were murdered, then I'd guess this job is too big for Ramsey, too big for any of the local people to handle. Maybe it's time to get in touch with the FBI."

Joshua sighed. "You're right about this being too big for the local law. Unfortunately, right now all we have is supposition where those deaths are concerned. Knowing what's happening and proving it are two different things. And it's not against the law for a corporation to buy land. Until we have some sort of proof, I doubt if we could get the FBI interested."

"Maybe not officially, but you know we've got some contacts there we could call, some markers that could be cashed in," Smokey reminded him.

Joshua nodded and stood. Certainly over the years of working a variety of bodyguard duties, they had all run into FBI agents. In fact, Dalton had become particularly close to one, a man named Alex Bailey.

"I'll give it a couple of days and see what Dalton can find out about MoTwin, then I'll talk to him about him speaking to that buddy of his in the FBI."

"Sounds like a plan," Smokey replied.

"I guess I'll head back to the cabin. Thanks for the drink and the conversation, especially the conversation."

Smokey grinned. "Hell, boy, I didn't tell you anything you didn't know deep in your heart. I'll let you tell your daddy that you're coming back into the fold."

Joshua nodded, then turned and left. A few minutes later he unlocked his cabin door and went inside, instantly assailed by the scent of Savannah that lingered in the air.

It was a good thing that she'd released him from his bodyguard duties, he told himself. She'd been right. It might take some time to get to the bottom of things and he couldn't spend every minute of every day for the rest of his life in her company.

He wasn't even sure the two attacks were related to what was happening in Cotter Creek. If what they suspected was true and men had been murdered to get to their land, then why had the person who'd attacked Savannah in her bedroom not killed her?

Why had she just been beaten up rather than shot or stabbed? While the thought made his blood chill, it also gave him pause. If the attacker had been part of the land deal, then certainly another murder wouldn't have made much difference in the grand scheme of things.

He sat at the table and pulled his cell phone from his pocket. As he had almost every evening for the past week, he punched in Lauren's phone number. He still couldn't quite let go of the possibility that Lauren was here in town, that she was behind the attacks.

It rang three times, then she answered. He was so stunned by the sound of her voice, for a moment he couldn't find his own voice.

"Hello? Is somebody there?" she asked.

"Lauren, it's me, Joshua." He sat up straighter in his chair. So, she was still in New York. But had she been there on the night that Savannah had been attacked? Or had she been here in Cotter Creek, exacting some sort of sick revenge on him?

"Well, well, a voice from the not-so-distant past. What do you want, Joshua?"

"I've been trying to call you for the past week."

"I took a week-long cruise, went to the Bahamas and basked on the beaches. The best thing I ever did for myself. Why have you been trying to reach me? Are you still out there in Oklahoma?"

He couldn't very well tell her he'd suspected that she might have followed him to Cotter Creek and terrorized Savannah. "Yeah, I'm still here. I just wanted to check in and make sure you were okay. The last time I saw you things got pretty ugly."

There was a long silence, then she sighed. "I'd like nothing better than to forget that night at the restaurant. I'm not proud of the way I acted, Joshua. All I can say now is that I'm sorry and I wish you the best of everything."

He believed her. He had no real reason to, but he believed that she'd been on a cruise and the only thing she wanted was to forget her bad behavior, forget him. He suddenly realized that maybe she wasn't the only one who needed to apologize.

"Lauren, I'm sorry for the way things worked out."

Again there was another moment of silence before she spoke. "It's not your fault you didn't fall in love with me," she replied softly. "But, let me give you a little unsolicited advice, Joshua. Don't sleep with a woman and before you're even out of her bed tell her how much she doesn't mean to you. It makes her feel stupid and worthless, and no woman in the world deserves to feel that way."

A vision of Savannah exploded in his head. Was that how he'd made her feel when he'd reiterated that he wanted nothing from her moments after they had made love?

"Thanks for the advice," he said aloud.

"Goodbye, Joshua. Please don't call me again. I'm moving on with my life."

Before he could reply she'd hung up. He replaced the phone in the cradle thoughtfully. He wasn't sure what bothered him more, the fact that he might have made Savannah feel worthless and stupid, or the knowledge that Lauren wasn't responsible for the attacks on her.

Chapter 13

It was just after nine when Savannah decided to call it a night and go to bed. Winnie had retired a half hour earlier, and for the past thirty minutes Savannah had been sitting alone at the kitchen table.

The sharpness of her heartache surprised her. She'd never expected anything from Joshua and the fact that he'd really offered her nothing shouldn't be so painful. But it was.

Falling in love with him had been the last thing she'd expected, the last thing she'd wanted. But he'd snuck into her heart when she hadn't been looking.

She should have known the moment she met him that he was trouble. She should have never enlisted his aid in her investigation. And yet she knew if she hadn't they wouldn't have discovered everything they had.

She got up from the table and moved to the kitchen window and stared outside. It was an unusually dark night with no moonlight piercing through thick clouds. The darkness mirrored her mood.

The ring of the phone made her jump. She hurried to answer before the blaring noise disturbed Winnie.

"Savannah, it's Sheila…Sheila Wadsworth."

Any weariness Savannah might have felt shot away. "Sheila, what's up?" she asked.

"We need to talk. Just the two of us." Tension was evident in the woman's voice.

Savannah clutched the phone more tightly against her ear. "Just tell me when and where."

"In thirty minutes at Big K's Truck Stop out off old Highway 10. You know the place?"

"Yes," Savannah replied.

"Please, come alone and don't tell anyone you're meeting me. I'm putting myself at risk. I trust you, Savannah, but I don't trust anyone else and you shouldn't either."

"Okay, I'll see you in thirty minutes," Savannah confirmed.

Sheila hung up before Savannah could say another word. Savannah quickly grabbed her purse and her car keys and after scribbling a quick note to Winnie to let her know she'd gone out, Savannah left the house.

It would take her all of the thirty minutes to get

to Big K's Truck Stop, which was a good twenty or thirty miles south of Cotter Creek.

As she backed out of the driveway, she thought about calling Joshua but decided to wait and call him after she heard what Sheila had to say. She knew if she called Joshua and let him know what was going on, he'd insist on coming with her and Sheila had made it clear she wasn't going to talk if Savannah wasn't alone.

Driving out of Cotter Creek, she kept a careful eye on her rearview mirror, making sure that she wasn't followed. She'd told Joshua she knew how to take care of herself, but there was a little part of her that was uneasy meeting Sheila alone.

Still, the important thing was that she suspected Sheila was going to tell her something that would break the investigation wide open. She couldn't risk not agreeing to Sheila's terms.

Besides, she felt somewhat confident in meeting Sheila away from Cotter Creek and any prying eyes that might see them together for this secret meeting. Big K's was a busy truck stop. There would be plenty of people around.

When she got to Big K's, if she didn't like what she saw, she wouldn't even get out of her car. She wasn't stupid and wasn't about to walk into any kind of a trap.

As she drove she couldn't help the fact that her thoughts returned to Joshua. She'd been right to tell him that she didn't want him guarding her anymore.

Her heart couldn't stand the thought of spending each and every day with him by her side.

She didn't want to fall deeper and deeper in love with him, knowing that there was no future for the two of them. Whatever his personal demons, he didn't seem inclined to have any kind of meaningful relationship with any woman.

She still was surprised that in such a short span of time a man could get so into her heart. But Joshua had managed to burrow deep inside her soul, and the length of time she'd known him had nothing to do with the strength of her feelings for him.

She consciously willed thoughts of him away as she drew closer and closer to Big K's. Old Highway 10 was nothing more than a dark two-lane road that was little traveled going from Cotter Creek south. Most of the traffic the truck stop saw came from the north, off a freeway exit.

Adrenaline filled her as she anticipated the meeting with Sheila. Maybe finally she was going to get some answers. Maybe finally she'd know the truth about Charlie's death. "I'm going to get to the bottom of things, Charlie," she said aloud. At least his death had sparked a real investigation.

Big K's Truck Stop sported a huge neon sign announcing hot showers and other amenities for truckers. The parking lot was full of eighteen-wheelers, along with several cars parked in front of the large structure.

Savannah was comforted by the fact that there

were plenty of other people around. What she didn't see as she parked in front of the building was Sheila's luxury car. She shut off her engine, then checked her watch. Nine forty-five. Unless Sheila had changed her mind, then she should be arriving at any minute.

As she waited, she tapped her fingernails on the steering wheel and stared inside the windows to make sure she saw nobody from Cotter Creek seated inside.

She saw nobody familiar and that made her relax slightly. If she'd seen anyone from Cotter Creek inside, she would have had second thoughts about going in. Instead she would have turned her car around and headed back to Cotter Creek.

What was Sheila going to tell her? How many questions could Sheila answer about what had been happening? She checked her watch again, hoping that Sheila hadn't chickened out.

Ten long minutes later she saw Sheila's big shiny car pulling into a parking space two slots over from where she was parked. Sheila was alone and didn't appear to notice Savannah as she got out of her car.

Savannah remained in her car and watched as Sheila went inside. She walked with her head down, her steps short and hurried. Once inside she was seated at a booth, then looked at her watch.

Savannah waited several long minutes, watching the people who came and went, checking out the general area for anything or anyone who looked suspicious.

Only then, when Savannah was certain that Sheila was truly alone and nothing looked dangerous, did she get out of her car and go inside.

The place smelled like fried onions and strong coffee and had an underlying scent of motor oil. Most of the occupants were men with tired eyes and stiff shoulders who barely glanced her way as she walked toward the back where Sheila was seated.

"I'm glad you came," Sheila said as Savannah slid into the seat across from her. "I was beginning to think you might not come."

"I wanted to make sure you weren't followed," Savannah said honestly. "What's going on, Sheila?" She pulled her notepad from her purse.

"No, no notes," Sheila protested, her eyes dark and worried. "Please, I just want to talk…off the record or whatever. I need to talk to somebody and I don't know who else to go to."

Savannah put her notepad back in her purse. "All right, off the record," she agreed.

At that moment a waitress arrived at their table. They both ordered coffee, then waited until they were served before continuing.

Sheila wrapped her hands around her coffee cup and for a long moment stared out the nearby window. When she finally looked back at Savannah her eyes were filled with stark fear. "It wasn't supposed to be like this," she said softly. "It wasn't supposed to be like this at all. People weren't supposed to die."

Savannah didn't say anything. She sensed that Sheila needed to tell her whatever was on her mind without prompting. Patience, she told herself. Patience was always a virtue when conducting an interview.

Sheila raised her cup to her lips, her hand trembling slightly. She took a sip, then carefully placed the cup back on the table.

"I'm scared, Savannah."

"Tell me," she urged. "Talk to me, Sheila. We can get through this together." Savannah felt electrified by the fear that wafted from Sheila.

Sheila released a deep sigh. "It started almost two years ago. I got a phone call from a man named Joe Black. He said he and his partner, Harold Willington were part of a corporation that was looking to buy some land in the area."

Joe Black and Harold Willington were the two names listed as owners of the property. "MoTwin," Savannah said.

Sheila nodded. "All he wanted from me was to compile a list of properties that were owned either by men who lived alone or who might be interested in selling out for a decent price. He promised that along with my usual Realtor cut, I'd receive an additional twenty-five thousand dollars for each piece of property the corporation obtained. He told me to go ahead and approach the people I thought might sell, and I did. I talked to Nesmith and Wainfield and most of the others, but none of them were interested in selling despite the fact that ranch life was a struggle."

"So, what happened next?"

"When Joe Black contacted me again I told him the ranchers weren't interested. He told me to keep trying and he gave me a cell phone number to call. He said I should give the list of names to the person who answered the cell phone."

Savannah's head whirled with the information. "So, you called the cell phone?"

Sheila nodded her head. "I just figured maybe they were going to try a little high-pressure effort. But, soon after that was when they started to die."

Once again Sheila's eyes were filled with fear and she reached for her coffee cup, as if needing the warmth to erase a bone chill. "When George Townsend's place blew up with him in it, I thought it was just what it was reported to be, a tragic accident with a kerosene heater. Then Roy Nesmith supposedly fell to his death from his hay loft, and that's when I started to get a bad feeling."

Once again she raised the cup to her mouth and took a sip. "Then more accidents happened, and I knew something bad was happening, something real bad and that somehow I had become a part of it."

"Why do they want the land?" Savannah asked. "What do they plan to do with it?"

"Build a community of luxury condos and homes. According to what Joe Black told me, it's a multi-million-dollar deal. They already have a waiting list of people from both coasts who want to buy when construction begins."

"And who shows up for closing on these deals?"

"Both Joe Black and Harold have shown up for the closings. They fly in, close the deal, then leave town." Sheila replied.

"Do you think he's doing the killing?"

Sheila shook her head. "No. I think there is somebody else working in Cotter Creek. A local, somebody who knew those men, somebody those men trusted and that's the person who has committed the killings."

Savannah leaned back in the booth, her head working overtime to process everything Sheila was telling her. "Do you have any idea who that person might be?"

Once again Sheila shook her head. "I have no idea. I will tell you this, not only is there a cold-blooded killer somewhere in Cotter Creek, there's also people who know what's been going on, people who are in on this whole deal and hoping to cash in big-time. Joe Black was courted by somebody here in town. He didn't just pull the town of Cotter Creek, Oklahoma, out of a hat."

For a long moment the two were silent. Sheila stared back out the window, her features sagging and looking older than she had when Savannah had first arrived.

A sense of euphoria filled Savannah as she realized she had the answers she'd sought. She'd been right about a conspiracy. She'd been right about the deaths not being accidents. But, the euphoria was tempered by the knowledge that good men had died in the name of turning a profit.

"You know you need to go to the sheriff," Savannah said.

Sheila looked back at her once again, her gaze filled with torment. "What if he's part of it?"

Savannah frowned. Sheila was right. There was no way of knowing if Ramsey might be part of the conspiracy or not. She leaned forward. "I'll tell you what, I'll talk to Joshua and maybe he'll know who you need to talk to, who would be safe to talk to."

Sheila worried a paper napkin between her fingers, tearing it into tiny pieces that littered the top of the table. "I'm going to jail, aren't I?"

"I don't know," Savannah answered truthfully. "Maybe you can cut some sort of deal and avoid any real jail time."

"I swear to God, I never knew this was what would happen. When I realized the men were dying, I didn't know who to tell. I didn't know who I could trust. I was afraid to talk to anyone."

"Joshua will know," Savannah replied.

Sheila nodded. "I've got to get home. I need to talk to my husband about what I've done." She motioned for the waitress to bring them their tab.

"I'll take care of it," Savannah said. "And I'll call you as soon as I speak with Joshua. We'll figure it out, Sheila. You did the right thing, coming to me."

"I should have told somebody after George

Townsend died." Sheila stood and grabbed her purse from the booth next to her. "You can't tell anyone except Joshua that we talked. These people are ruthless, and I don't want to be the victim of a fatal accident."

"I'll call you as soon as I have a plan," Savannah said, then watched as Sheila left.

Savannah remained seated after Sheila had gone. She grabbed her notepad from her purse and made notes about what Sheila had told her.

She'd keep her promise to Sheila and wouldn't write a story, but the notes were for herself, to make sure she forgot nothing. This was huge, bigger than she'd even suspected. So many deaths for luxury condos. It made her sick to think that this might be why Charlie had died.

It was just after eleven when she got back into her car to return to Cotter Creek. She'd been so eager to arrive to meet Sheila she hadn't noticed how little traveled old Highway 10 was. She met no cars as she drove the two-lane road.

Joe Black and Harold Willington. The two names went around and around in her head. Had those two businessmen known that they were acquiring their property through death, through murder? Or had they been ignorant of how their contact in Cotter Creek was getting results?

One thing was sure. If Sheriff Ramsey wasn't in on it, it was far too big for him to handle. They were going to have to get outside help. Joshua would know where to go from here, who needed to be brought in to get the guilty people behind bars.

She slowed and pulled her cell phone from her purse, eager to speak to Joshua about what she'd learned. She punched in his cell number and listened as it rang once then went directly to voice mail.

"Joshua, it's me, Savannah. I just met with Sheila Wadsworth at Big K's Truck Stop off old Highway 10. She told me everything. They want the land for luxury condos. I just left the truck stop and am now headed back to Cotter Creek. Call me as soon as you get this message."

She clicked off and threw the phone on the seat next to her, hoping he'd call back soon. Glancing up to her rearview mirror she saw in the distance the headlights of a car coming up behind her.

The car was approaching fast and she moved over to the right shoulder to give the driver plenty of room to pass her. She frowned and squinted against the glare of bright lights reflected in her mirror.

Her phone rang and she grabbed it from the seat.

"Savannah, what in the hell are you doing?" Joshua's voice rang harshly in her ear. "You should have never gone to meet Sheila without me. What were you thinking?"

"It's okay. I'm fine. I'm on my way home now." She squinted into her rearview mirror. "Dammit," she muttered.

"What? What's wrong?"

"Some jerk is behind me with his brights on,"

she replied. The words were barely out of her mouth when the vehicle slammed into the back of hers, the force of the impact wrenching the steering wheel out of her hand.

She screamed and dropped the cell phone, then grabbed the wheel with both hands in an attempt to keep her car on the road. But, once again she was struck from behind with tremendous force.

The steering wheel spun wildly and her car left the road. In horror she had a flash of trees just ahead and knew she was going to hit them.

The last thing she heard before impact was Joshua screaming her name over the cell phone.

Then nothing.

Joshua heard the splintering sound of an impact. He shouted her name several more times and when she didn't answer he hung up and called Sheriff Ramsey.

As he quickly told Ramsey where Savannah was and that she was in trouble, he raced to his truck. Within moments he roared away from the West property and headed for Big K's Truck Stop.

His heart beat so hard, so fast it felt as if it might explode from his chest at any moment. He'd heard the sound of crunching metal, the sound of breaking glass and he knew she'd hit something.

Right now she could be bleeding to death on the side of a road where it might be minutes, or an hour before another car passed her. Fear sizzled through him, making him feel sick with impotence, sick with torment.

He tightened his grip on the steering wheel, a cold chill seeping through him. She'd seen headlights behind her. Some jerk with his bright lights on. That's what she'd said.

He tromped his foot on the gas pedal, wishing he had wings to fly to her. Damn her for going off on her own to meet Sheila, but double damn whoever might have caused her harm.

As he drove he punched in her cell phone number, hoping, praying she'd answer, but it went directly to her voice mail. The fact that she wouldn't or couldn't answer sent a new chill coursing through him.

When he reached old Highway 10 he slowed down, his gaze shooting left and right of the two-lane road, seeking any sign of her car.

It was about a twenty-mile stretch between where he was now and Big K's Truck Stop. He had no idea where Savannah had been on this road when she'd made the phone call to him.

Emotion clawed up his throat, tasting like grief, but he told himself there was nothing to grieve about. She was okay. She had to be okay. Somehow she'd had a fender bender and now her phone wasn't working. He just had to find her and she'd be all right.

The stretch of highway was so dark, with no streetlights, no light of the moon cascading down from the cloudy night sky. "Where are you,

Savannah?" he muttered, his gaze flying first to the left, then to the right of the road.

He felt ill, more ill than he'd ever felt in his life. As he tried to find her along the dark, lonely road his mind filled with visions of her.

Her charming freckles, her beautiful smile, the warmth of her curves in his arms, each was a haunting memory that ripped at his heart.

As he gazed into his rearview mirror he saw a flash of cherry red lights illuminating the dark and knew that Ramsey was coming up fast behind him. Ramsey must have jumped in his car the moment Joshua had called. Thank God for that. Surely with two of them searching they'd find her more quickly.

When he looked back at the road he saw her car. It was on the right side, about a hundred feet off the road. The front end was smashed against a tree trunk, the interior light on as the driver door hung open.

Joshua yanked his truck to the side of the road, slammed it into Park and left the cab at a run. He was vaguely conscious of Ramsey pulling to a stop just behind his truck as he raced to the wrecked vehicle.

"Savannah!" Her name tore from his throat as he reached her car. It took only a moment's glance to realize she wasn't in the driver's seat. The windshield had shattered, raining glass on the dash, and the airbag had deployed, but there was no sign of Savannah in the car.

"She's not here," Joshua said to Ramsey as the

sheriff hurried toward him. The fear that had sizzled through him before now exploded into unmitigated terror.

"Maybe she tried to walk to get help?" Ramsey suggested.

Joshua looked around wildly. "Savannah!" He yelled her name with all the power in his lungs. Was she wandering around in the dark? Stunned or injured?

His chest tightened as a frantic sob threatened to erupt. Headlights in the distance appproached at a quick pace, but Joshua paid little attention as he yelled her name again and again. The grass beside the driver door was matted down, as if something had either fallen or been dragged.

The car that had approached pulled up behind the Sheriff's, and Bill Cleaver, a rancher from nearby stalked over to where Ramsey stood next to the wrecked car.

"Somebody hurt here?" he asked.

"We don't know, but it looks like it," Ramsey replied.

"Sheriff, that damn fool Larry Davidson just now practically ran me off the road," he exclaimed, then pointed to Savannah's car. "As reckless as he was driving, he probably made this happen, too. He had to have been either drunk or high. I don't give a damn if he works for the mayor or not, he's a menace on the road."

Joshua stared at Bill. Larry Davidson. Wasn't that the cowboy who had stopped them before they'd gone into City Hall? The man who'd asked Savannah out to dinner?

Had he wanted dinner, or had he simply wanted to get Savannah alone? Was he part of the conspiracy going on in town?

The idea of Savannah wandering around in the dark dazed and hurt was bad enough, but the possibility that she had been forcefully taken from the car was terrifying. The matted grass next to the driver door suddenly took on an ominous tone.

"How long ago did he pass you?" Joshua asked tersely.

"About ten miles down the road, was driving like a bat out of hell in that big blue pickup of his."

The words were barely out of Bill's mouth before Joshua was on the run to his truck. Somehow in his heart, in every fiber of his being, he knew that Savannah was in that blue pickup. Now, all he had to do was find her.

Chapter 14

Pain splintered through her head, a pain so intense she felt like throwing up. Her face hurt, too. As if she'd been burned. With her eyes still closed, Savannah started to raise a hand to her throbbing forehead, only to realize her hand wouldn't move.

She frowned, confusion filtering through the pain. What was happening? Where was she? She opened her eyes and stared down at her hands in her lap. Silver duct tape wrapped around her wrists. What? Why was there duct tape there? It didn't make sense.

As the fog of pain momentarily lifted she realized she was in a vehicle, and she turned her head to the left to see Larry Davidson behind the wheel.

She quickly closed her eyes again, feigning unconsciousness as her brain worked to figure out what had happened, how she'd come to be in a truck with Larry, with her wrists bound.

She'd been at Winnie's and the phone had rung. Sheila. She'd had a meeting with Sheila, then she'd been driving home. She gasped as she remembered the bright lights behind her, the crash into the back end of her car and the out-of-control veer off the road.

"Ah, you're awake," Larry said. He'd obviously heard her gasp as her memory had returned.

She thought about pretending to still be out of it but knew there was no point. Instead she opened her eyes once again and looked at him, trying to work past the pain in her head. "Larry, what's going on? Why did you duct-tape my wrists?"

He glanced at her, then back at the dark road ahead. "Ah, Savannah, this all would have been so much easier if you'd just stayed unconscious. I like you, I like you a lot. I tried to warn you off, tried to get you to stop snooping around."

Savannah frowned, the pain in her head making it difficult for her to think, to process what he was saying. "What do you mean? You tried to warn me off?"

"That birdshot that night at the newspaper office? That was me. I thought maybe I could scare you, but you didn't scare easy."

"Was it you who got into my bedroom and beat me up?" Savannah worked her wrists, trying to get the tape to loosen up.

"Yeah, that was me. I hated to do it, but you were

running your mouth to too many people and making somebody uncomfortable. I was told to shut you up. I was hoping that would do it, but you're one stubborn woman, Savannah."

At the moment she wasn't stubborn as much as she was afraid. Fear whispered just under the surface and she tried maintain control of it, knowing that to give it free rein would make it impossible for her to think. And she had to figure out a way out of this.

"We knew that stupid Sheila might be a weak link so I followed her tonight," he continued. "What did she tell you with that big mouth of hers?"

"I was interviewing her for my column, that's all."

He backhanded her. The blow was completely unexpected and caught her on the side of her jaw. "Don't lie to me. I might be nothing but a cowhand, but I'm not stupid."

Tears sprang to her eyes and she realized she was in trouble…big trouble. Her fear unleashed itself, whipping through her.

"I imagine she told you about the plans for those high-dollar condos and townhouses. Cotter Creek is going to become the place for the wealthy, a playground in the middle of the country for the beautiful people."

"I don't know what you're talking about," she replied.

He snorted. "Too late to pretend, Savannah. This is the best thing that could ever happen to Cotter

Creek. Whether you know it or not, that town is dying. This deal with MoTwin will put money in everyone's pockets. New businesses will come in and the economy will boom."

"Who's in charge in Cotter Creek? Who is your boss?" she asked, working her hands more frantically in an effort to get free. He was talking to her too freely, and that didn't bode well for her.

"Don't know and don't care. I get a phone call telling me to do a job. I do it and I get a nice cash payment deposited in a Swiss account."

"What kind of jobs?" Savannah asked. Keep him talking, that was her goal. Keep him talking until she could get her hands free or come up with a plan to get away from him.

She'd been on the phone with Joshua when her car had struck that tree. If she could just keep Larry talking long enough maybe Joshua would find her.

"All those accidents you've been investigating, they were my work." As he began to tell her about how he'd committed each "accident," Savannah realized there was no way he was going to let her live.

He was confessing to the murders of half a dozen men, pride deepening his voice as he explained how he had set each one up to look like an accident.

Savannah closed her eyes against the burn of tears, a horrible resignation sweeping through her. Her head still ached with nauseating intensity, she couldn't get her hands free no matter how hard she tried, and she knew Larry was driving her to her grave.

"You won't get away with this, Larry. Sheriff Ramsey will figure it out," she said.

He laughed. "Ramsey is a buffoon, too stupid to know what's going on in his own town."

"So, he's not in on it?"

He laughed again. "Ramsey would be the last person they'd bring into this."

They were out in the middle of nowhere and as he turned off the highway and crossed a cattle guard into a large pasture, she knew that it was possible her body would never even be found.

"Old Charlie, he was a tough one," Larry continued. "We knew no matter how much money he was offered he'd never sell. He cursed me with his last breath."

Savannah's chest ached as she thought of Charlie, as she thought of Joshua and everything that was lost to her. She would never know what it felt like to be loved wonderfully, desperately by a man. She would never know what it felt like to look into a man's eyes and see her own soul reflected back to her.

According to her mother, she hadn't been worth much in life and she certainly wouldn't be worth much in death. Suddenly she was angry. Her mother's words had been poison, making Savannah accept less all her life because she hadn't believed she was worth more. She'd always gotten what she'd expected, because she'd never expected more for herself.

Even though she'd always told herself her mother's criticism had fallen on deaf ears, she recognized now the depths that the cuts of those words had made to her soul.

Damn her mother for teaching her not to expect anything from life, and damn herself for taking those perverse lessons to heart.

The weary resignation that had momentarily gripped her was shoved aside by a rage, the likes of which she'd never known.

Dammit, she was worth something, worth far more than she'd gotten from life so far. She wasn't about to just allow this murdering cowhand to take her off somewhere and destroy not only her life but also any dreams she might have harbored for her future.

She couldn't let that happen. Frantically she worked her hands, rubbing them against each other, pulling in an effort to break the tape. She couldn't wait for Joshua, who might never find her. She couldn't wait for anyone to ride to her rescue.

She wanted to survive and promised herself that if she did she would expect more, demand more from life because she was worth it all.

When there was no give to the duct tape, and she knew there was no way she was going to break the bonds, she realized there was only one thing she could do.

Although he was moving across the pasture at a high rate of speed, she knew she had only one chance. Twisting her body, she gripped the door handle, yanked it open and bailed out.

"Hey!"

She heard Larry's outcry just before her body made contact with the ground. She bounced and skidded, pain ripping through her as the air left her lungs and she finally slammed one last time onto the hard earth.

For a brief moment she lay on the ground, trying to find her breath, knowing that if she didn't move she'd be dead. She hurt. Oh God, she hurt so badly. Every bone in her body, every muscle screamed with the abuse they had just received.

As Larry pulled his truck to a stop in the distance, she rose unsteadily to her hands and knees, fighting past the pain. She had to get away. She had to move! She crawled forward, her movements awkward with the duct tape still on her wrists. Sobs ripped through her.

His truck was parked in the opposite direction, the lights beaming away from her. As she moved across the pasture, she prayed the cloudy night would work to her benefit and Larry wouldn't see her.

"You might as well give it up, Savannah." His boots rang against the hard ground. "As much as I like you, I can't let you leave here alive. I got my orders."

She heard the unmistakable click of a bullet being chambered. She swallowed her sobs, afraid the sound would draw him to her. She didn't know whether to lie flat and hope the grass might hide her or keep crawling, knowing that a moving target was harder to hit than a still one.

It was a game of hide and seek in the dark, a game with deadly consequences. If he found her she would die. There was absolutely no way she could talk him into sparing her, no way he'd allow her to live.

She brought her hands up to her mouth and frantically tore at the duct tape with her teeth. Crazy hope filled her as she ripped and gnawed at the tape, finally getting it off her wrists.

At that moment the clouds parted and a shimmering shaft of moonlight drifted down, giving her a perfect view of Larry. And Larry a perfect view of her.

The light glimmered off the gun that he raised, pointing it right at her. A wrenching sob escaped her as she said a quick prayer.

The roar of an engine filled the air and twin headlights bounced into view. Larry spun around and pointed the gun at the approaching vehicle. He fired and glass shattered. He only got off one shot before the truck struck him.

There was a sickening smack, then his body flew into the air. The truck engine stopped at the same time Larry's body hit the ground.

Silence.

Savannah stared at the silent, familiar black pickup. Joshua. With every ounce of strength she had left she struggled to her feet at the same time the driver door opened and Joshua stepped out.

"Savannah! Thank God." He ran to her and wrapped her in his arms. She felt the tremble of his body against hers and the sobs she'd held back in an effort to save her own life exploded out of her.

"Shh, it's all right now. You're all right," he soothed her. He was still holding her when Sheriff Ramsey arrived moments later.

Joshua insisted he take her to the hospital, that any questions Ramsey had for them could wait until Savannah got medical treatment.

But, Savannah refused to leave until she'd told Sheriff Ramsey everything that she'd learned from Sheila and everything Larry had told her. She needed to tell them all of it, while it was still so fresh, so horrifying in her mind.

She held herself together for the telling, although more than once as she shared the details the press of tears burned hot at her eyes.

By the time she'd finished talking to the sheriff one of his deputies had arrived and it was he who drove Savannah to the hospital while Joshua remained behind to answer questions about Larry Davidson's death.

It was only when she was safe in the deputy's car that the full horror of what had just happened descended on her once again.

She wept silent tears, tears for Charlie and for all the other ranchers who had fallen victim to Larry and the crazy land scheme. She cried for Joshua, who had killed a man to save her life.

Finally she cried for herself, because somehow in those moments of facing death she knew she'd been forever changed, and she didn't know whether to weep for what she'd lost or celebrate what she'd gained.

It was just after three in the morning when Savannah sat in the emergency room exam room waiting to be released. She'd been checked over head to toe and had suffered a mild concussion, some facial abrasions from the air bag deployment and a variety of bumps and bruises, but thankfully nothing more serious.

Even though her injuries were minor, her entire body ached from the jolt it had taken when she'd jumped out of Larry's pickup. She was beyond exhaustion and just wanted to go home.

She looked up as the curtain moved aside and Joshua came into the small examining cubicle. He looked as exhausted as she felt with his eyes dark and hollow.

"Hey," he said.

"Hey yourself."

"The doctor told me you're going to be okay," he said.

She forced a smile to her lips. "It takes more than a murderous cowhand to get me down."

"It's not funny," he exclaimed, his forehead wrinkled with a scowl. "When I think about how close you came to being killed, it makes me crazy."

He swiped a hand through his hair, his gaze intent on her. "Have you heard about Sheila?"

"No." Savannah held his gaze and knew. "She's dead, isn't she?"

He nodded. "Ramsey got word that her car was found parked behind Big K's. She'd been shot once in the head."

The news didn't surprise Savannah, although she was sorry to hear that Sheila had been killed in such a brutal manner. "Do they think Larry did it?"

"Right now Ramsey doesn't think so. He doesn't think Larry would have had time to take care of Sheila then come after you."

"So, there's another murderer running loose around town."

"We're calling in the FBI. With the information Larry told you, Ramsey has agreed that he needs more resources than his department has to offer."

"That's good. Maybe finally somebody can get to the bottom of all this." She slid off the table and stood, wanting nothing more than to go home and put this night behind her.

Joshua took two steps toward her and wrapped his arms around her, his heartbeat strong and sure against her own. He didn't speak for several long moments, but simply held her tightly.

She leaned her head against his chest, welcoming the embrace that helped to banish the last of the horror that had clung to her.

"When I saw your car on the side of the road, I

thought I'd die." He stiffened his arms around her, pulling her even more tightly against him.

"I don't even remember hitting the tree," she murmured into his chest. "The last thing I remember is your voice screaming my name from my cell phone."

"Come home with me, Savannah. Let me take you to my place. I want to hold you through the rest of the night." His words were soft in her ear, words that should have brought her a flush of happiness, but they didn't. Rather they caused her pain.

She knew what he was offering. He was asking her for just another single night, a night of him holding her and them making love and then he'd let her go once again.

She might have been tempted before to indulge herself in accepting what little he offered. But, she wasn't tempted now.

She clung to him another moment longer, breathing in the scent of him, allowing her heart to fill with the love she felt for him, then reluctantly stepped back out of his embrace.

"I can't do that, Joshua. I can't do it anymore." She consciously willed away the sting of tears that burned in her eyes as she looked at him. "I've made the very foolish mistake of falling in love with you, and I can't pretend anymore that what you're offering me is enough."

She stepped back and leaned against the examining table, weary beyond words but praying for the strength to do what needed to be done where Joshua was concerned. "Before tonight it was enough. I was willing to fall into your bed whenever you wanted me and not expect more because I didn't think I deserved more. But something happened tonight when I thought I was going to be killed. I realized I'm worth having it all."

Emotion pressed tightly against her chest and she realized there had been a little bit of hope inside her, a piece of her that longed for him to take her back in his arms and tell her he loved her, too. She'd wanted him to say that tonight had changed him as well and now he recognized her worth and wanted more than anything to commit to her. But, he remained silent, his expression inscrutable.

"I deserve to have it all," she continued, fighting the growing need to cry. "I'll find me a lonely cowboy who loves me passionately, who is willing to commit his life to me. He'll love me not in spite of the fact that I talk too much and have freckles and am stubborn, but because of those things."

Joshua shoved his hands in his pockets, his gaze holding hers intently. "You're right. You deserve all that and more. And I hope you find it."

Those words broke what little sliver of hope she had inside her. He was letting her go and even though it let her know her decision had been the right one, it didn't make it hurt any less. At that moment the nurse appeared with her discharge papers.

"You need a ride home?" Joshua asked.

"No, thanks, I'll be fine." She had no idea how she'd get home, but she didn't want to spend another minute with him. Her heartache was too intense and she didn't want to cry in front of him.

He paused a long moment, his gaze intent on her, then he turned on his heels and left the examining room, taking a piece of her heart with him.

"What did you do? Let the dog chew on your hair?" Joshua stared at his sister across the kitchen table. He'd stopped into the big house that morning because he'd found the silence, the loneliness of the cabin oppressive.

Meredith shot a hand up to her dark crooked bangs. "I just trimmed it up a bit." She narrowed her eyes. "My bangs will grow out, but what is it going to take to get you out of your foul mood?"

"I'm not in a foul mood," Joshua replied with a scowl.

"You've been cranky and hard to live with for the past week," Meredith countered.

Joshua knew she was right, and he could identify the exact moment when his bad mood had descended. It had been exactly six days ago when Savannah had told him she was through with him.

It had been a busy six days. The town was buzzing with the news of Sheila's death, the near death of Savannah and the conspiracy of the land scheme. The rumor mill had been working overtime as people speculated on who might be involved in the whole mess.

Ramsey had contacted the FBI and was awaiting the arrival of agents to take over the investigation. Savannah had been responsible for hard-hitting news stories in the paper, and Joshua had told his father to put him back on the roster for the family business.

"I'll feel better when I have someplace to go and something to do," he now said to his sister.

"Things have been slow," Meredith agreed. "We've got half a dozen men out working, but nothing new has come in for weeks."

Joshua finished his coffee and stood, too restless to sit at the table and make small talk. "I think I'll head into town, maybe visit a bit with Clay and Libby." The newlyweds had returned from their honeymoon the day before.

"Tell them I said hi and I hope they had a wonderful time," Meredith said, then grinned. "If I ever get married I'm not sure I want my honeymoon to take place at Walt Disney World."

For the first time in days Joshua smiled. "I'm sure that choice was more for Gracie's benefit than for Libby and Clay."

Meredith smiled, a misty kind of wistful smile. "Libby and Clay would be happy anywhere as long as they were together. I hope I find something like they have some day." She looked at him for a long moment. "Joshua, I don't know what happened between you and Savannah, but I know she hasn't been the same the past week."

He frowned and tried not to remember Savannah's infectious laughter, her penchant for speaking whatever thought crossed her mind. "She'll be okay. She went through a traumatic event. That always changes a person."

"There's a sadness about her that wasn't there before." Meredith studied him. "There's a sadness about you, too."

"I'm not sad, I'm bored," Joshua replied. "I'll see you later. Tell Smokey and Dad I'll stop by later this evening."

Minutes later as he headed into town he tried not to think about what Meredith had said, but the thought of Savannah being sad killed him.

She was a woman born to laugh, a woman who deserved all the happiness life could offer. "She's not your problem," he said aloud.

With all the publicity concerning the imminent arrival of the FBI, he had no real concerns about Savannah's safety. Too many people now knew what had been going on for her to be at risk.

She no longer needed a bodyguard and that's all he'd really agreed to be to her. Meredith was wrong, he wasn't sad that their relationship had ended. He told himself he was relieved that he didn't have to listen to her anymore, that he didn't feel responsible for her.

Still, by the time he pulled up and parked in front

of Libby and Clay's two-story house, his foul mood had returned.

Savannah sat in her little cubicle of an office, typing furiously on the computer. She was writing her column on Sheila. It would be printed posthumously, but Savannah thought it was important that people see not only the bad side of Sheila but the good as well.

Sheila had sold out her neighbors, her town, but Savannah truly believed the Realtor hadn't been a bad woman at heart. She'd merely gotten caught up in something bad and evil because of greed.

Ray Buchannan poked his head in her door and she stopped typing. "I'm going to grab some lunch over at the café. You'll be here to answer the phone?"

"I'll be here," Savannah replied. In the past week she'd spent all her time either in her cubicle working or at Winnie's.

She had little desire to go much of anywhere in town where she might run into Joshua. She knew just seeing him again would bring back all the pain of loss.

The good news was that since the terrifying night out in that pasture her mother's criticizing voice had been silent in her head. Never again would Savannah hear that voice telling her she wasn't worthy, she didn't deserve true happiness and love.

Eventually she'd find what she was looking for, and in the meantime there was her work to keep her satisfied.

As she heard the front door of the newspaper office open, then close with Ray's departure, she leaned back in her chair and grabbed a candy bar from the bowl on the desk.

She unwrapped it and took a bite, deciding that whoever had said that chocolate was as good as sex was a liar. Chocolate couldn't substitute for the feel of Joshua's skin against hers, the taste of his mouth or the sweet joy of making love with him.

No, not making love, she corrected mentally. She had made love. He'd had sex.

It had been Sheriff Ramsey who had taken her home from the hospital that night, and she'd managed to hold herself together until she was in her bed. It was only then that the tears had come.

She'd told herself that the tears had been those of a woman who'd suffered a horrifying event, that they were the aftermath of fear. But, she knew in her heart that those tears had been for Joshua and her decision to halt whatever relationship they'd had.

Even now whenever she thought of him, she felt a swell of emotion in her chest, a wistful longing that things might have been different.

She now finished the candy bar, tossed the wrapper in the trash, then stared blankly at her computer screen. She had to forget him. She had to stop allowing thoughts of him to consume her.

The biggest news stories of her life were happening right under her nose. As a reporter this should be the most exciting time of her life.

Who would have thought a small town like Cotter Creek, Oklahoma, could be such a hotbed of intrigue and murder? Things could only heat up more once the FBI arrived.

The door to the office *whooshed* open and closed. Savannah stood, intent on going to see who had come in, but before she could move from behind her desk, Joshua filled the doorway of her small cubicle.

For a moment she stared at him in shock, wondering if she'd conjured up his image by her mere thoughts alone.

"Savannah." He spoke her name softly.

"Joshua, what are you doing here?" Her heart squeezed painfully at the sight of him. What could he be doing here? What could he possibly want?

"I want you to interview me."

She stared at him in surprise. "What?"

"You've asked me a dozen times for an interview and now I'm agreeing to it." Tension rolled off him and the air between them snapped with energy.

"I don't think I can use an interview now. There's news happening every day. I'm sure you've heard the FBI is going to be taking over the investigation and Sheriff Ramsey has officially announced his upcoming retirement. I've got more stories than I can use at the moment." She was aware that she was rambling and couldn't seem to stop herself.

He was killing her, looking so fine in his tight, worn jeans and navy knit shirt pulled tautly across his broad chest. He was killing her with a softness that radiated from his beautiful green eyes, a softness she didn't understand and was afraid to trust.

"Stop chattering and get out one of those notepads of yours because I want you to take notes," he commanded.

She grabbed a pad and a pen, wondering if something else had happened in town that he was here to report. She sat back down at her desk, then gazed at him expectantly.

"Now, ask me what's in my heart," he said. She looked at him in surprise, the pen poised above the pad. "Go on, ask me."

Her mouth was suddenly unaccountably dry and her heart banged an unsteady rhythm. "What's in your heart, Joshua?" The words came out in a mere whisper.

"You told me once that you'd probably never have a man be passionate about you. Well, you were wrong." His gaze burned into hers. "I feel passionately about you, and love for you is what's in my heart."

She stared at him, wondering if somehow she'd only imagined the words that had just come out of his mouth. The pen fell from her fingers and rolled off the desk to the floor.

"I've spent the last miserable, lonely week trying to forget all about you, trying to ignore what I really felt," he continued, his voice thick with emotion. "The problem was never if you deserved me, but if I deserved you. I came home from New York feeling like a failure, believing that I didn't deserve anything good."

"You aren't hearing my mother's voice whispering in your ear, are you?" She couldn't help it, she had to say something to ease the darkness that momentarily swept into his eyes.

He grinned then, that slow, sexy smile she loved. "No, I'm not hearing your mother. And over the course of the last week I've realized that I'm worth your love and I'm worth the happiness that you give me. I realized that I'm the lonely cowboy who wants to wake up with you every morning, who wants to go to sleep at night with you in my arms. And if you don't get up from that desk and jump into my arms right now, I'll be the most miserable man in the world."

She jumped up from the desk and threw herself at him, her heart so full she couldn't speak for a moment. His arms enfolded her and as she looked up at him, his lips took hers in a kiss that held not just her love, but his.

"This is the best interview I've ever conducted," she said when the kiss ended.

He laughed and pulled her closer. "I love you, Savannah Clarion. I think you're the most beautiful woman in the world. I love your freckles and your chatter. I want you in my life for as long as you'll have me."

"Did anyone ever tell you that you talk too much,

Joshua?" she teased. "Why don't you just be quiet and kiss me again."

"I'm happy to oblige," he replied, and he did and in that kiss Savannah realized all her hopes, all her dreams for a future filled with passion and with love.

* * * * *

INTIMATE ENEMY

BY
MARILYN PAPPANO

Marilyn Pappano brings impeccable credentials to her career – a lifelong habit of gazing out windows, not paying attention in class, daydreaming and spinning tales for her own entertainment. The sale of her first book brought great relief to her family, proving that she wasn't crazy but was, instead, creative. Since then, she's sold more than forty books to various publishers and even a film production company.

She writes in an office nestled among the oaks that surround her home. In winter she stays inside with her husband and their four dogs, and in summer she spends her free time mowing the yard that never stops growing and daydreams about grass that never gets taller than two inches. You can write to her at PO Box 643, Sapulpa, OK 74067-0643, USA.

For the Smart Women of Romance Writers Ink, the best writers, support and friends ever. You guys rule!

Chapter 1

In a small town like Copper Lake, Georgia, there were benefits to having an office right on the square, Jamie Munroe thought as she gazed out the window behind her desk. These days, there were bigger benefits being on the corner just off the square. Namely, the mega-construction project going on across the street, turning a shabby, rundown apartment building back into the gracious pre-war gem it had once been.

Okay, so the noise and traffic could be a hassle, but the workers…

"I swear, the best-looking guys in the county are on this crew," she murmured.

A few feet away, Lys Paxton, paralegal, computer wiz and friend, *uh-huh*ed with her feet propped on the credenza, her gaze locked on a pair of the smoothest, tannest, strongest, sexiest backs—and backsides—Jamie had ever seen. Both men wore jeans, faded, snug and caked with the usual residue of construction work, and both had stripped off their shirts in deference to the morning heat. They were unloading lumber from the bed of a pickup, and they were definitely ogle-worthy.

Lys sighed, her hands clasped loosely around a cold can of diet pop. "Don't you love it when the lumberyard can't make deliveries on short notice?"

"Hmm. Remind me to send the owner my thanks."

It was ten-thirty on Wednesday morning, and Jamie and Lys were officially on a coffee break. Up until a few weeks ago they'd actually locked up the office and walked over to the coffee shop on the square to spend ten bucks and fifteen minutes relaxing. Then the work had started on the mansion, and they'd begun taking their breaks in the office, chairs turned to the window, feet up, savoring.

It was the only male-female relationship of any sort in Jamie's life these days. Pathetic.

"When was the last time you went on a date?" Lys asked.

"I don't remember."

"Me, either." Another sigh. "I need one. Bad."

Jamie hadn't *needed* a man in a long time, not since law school, and she didn't intend to let it happen again. Oh, she wasn't giving them up or anything. She could want and have. She could use and discard. She could have a perfectly normal relationship. She would just never let herself *need* a man.

Men were dangerous to a woman's health. Every woman she knew had gotten her heart broken, her faith shaken and her self-esteem smacked. A couple of them had lost all their money to the rat bastards, as well.

Using, enjoying, not trusting, not needing. That was the way to go.

"I call the guy on the right with the rip in his jeans beneath his truly impressive butt," Lys said.

"You're welcome to him. I'll take the one on the left. I like a man who saves his revealing clothes for just me."

"Okay, it's time for them to turn around. The mystery faces revealed. Think we know either of them?"

"If I do, I haven't seen them like that before." Not that she made a particular habit of looking at men's butts.

When the last board was in place, both men did turn, Lys's first. He was as hot from the front as from the back, and unfamiliar to them both. Jamie's pick was slower. He bent to retrieve a bottle of water from the cooler next to his booted feet before straightening, giving them an oblique view as he tipped his head back and drained half the water at once. Watching his fingers grip the bottle, his throat work to swallow, his muscles ripple from the relief of the cold water, Jamie suddenly felt as if her own temperature had redlined. She was groping for her pop on the desk and found it just as he turned to face the window head-on.

The pop fell over, dripping off the desk to puddle on the mat. Lys choked, coughing until she sputtered, and Jamie turned to pure ice inside, too frozen to move or think.

Russ Calloway, owner of Calloway Construction. Brother to her good friend, Robbie. Respondent in the first divorce case she'd handled after coming to town. Sworn enemy. Former lover.

"Son of a bitch." Lys grabbed a handful of tissues to blot the desk pad, then mop up the cola on the floor. Catching Jamie's chair, she spun it around so her back was to the street. "There should be a warning."

Jamie managed a faint smile. "The signs on all those trucks over there do say Calloway Construction. So does the big fancy sign the bank put up at the corner." *This Calloway Construction Project Is Funded By Fidelity Mutual Of Copper Lake.*

"Yeah, but he's the freakin' boss. He's not supposed to be over there."

He was a hands-on boss, by all accounts. Just because they hadn't seen him before didn't mean he wouldn't show up. The crew had been working for only two weeks, doing basic demolition. She'd known he would be on site eventually. She'd been prepared for it. Eventually.

"It's not like I don't ever see him around town," she said, reassuring herself as much as Lys. "A woman can get lost pretty easily among twenty-thousand people, but there's always that chance."

"Yeah, but you don't drool over him if you catch a glimpse of him at the grocery store, do you?"

"Of course not," Jamie said. Truth was, she did. She couldn't remember a single time in her life when she hadn't felt at least a faint stirring of lust for Russ. Not when he'd broken up with her, not when he'd broken her heart, not when he'd sat in the conference room with her and his soon-to-be ex looking as if he despised them both.

It was his loss, Robbie had told her the one time she'd cried on his shoulder. Russ was being an ass—and Robbie knew, being the undisputed official ass of the Calloway family.

If it was his loss, why did it hurt *her?*

"Stop it!" Lys admonished. "I can tell by the look in your eyes, you're still thinking about him."

"Actually, I was thinking about that contract I have to negotiate with Robbie in ten minutes," she lied, forcing herself to really think about it. "He's such a phony—makes everyone think he's lazy and shallow and doesn't care about anything but fun, when he's a damn good lawyer."

"Which doesn't negate the fact that he really is lazy and shallow." Lys separated the Andersen folder from the stack on

Jamie's desk and handed it to her. "He's a classic Calloway. They're all worthless with the exception of Sara, and she wasn't born into the family. She only married into it and had the sense to stick around and enjoy the benefits after her scum husband died."

Jamie slid the folder into her bag, easily mistaken for an attaché. What could she say? She loved big purses. She was prepared for anything.

Except finding out that the man she was lusting over was Russ.

"Your meeting with Robbie is at the country club at eleven," Lys said, "and then you're supposed to see the shrink in Augusta about Laurie Stinson. He's expecting you at two. And since he charges by the hour, he'll probably be quite wordy, so you should go on home when you get back. I'll close up here."

"Robbie switched lunch to that new little place on the river—Chantal's. Says he's had all the country-club food he can stomach for a while." Jamie slipped off her sweater and folded it over her arm. The restaurant would probably be cold, but the four-block walk over wouldn't. "And I'll be back. I'll want to make notes on this afternoon's interview. But don't you wait around. I may have dinner in Augusta first."

Halfway to the door, she turned back. "Thanks a bunch, Lys. I don't know what I'd do without you."

"You'd probably still be sharing office space with Robbie and getting nothing done." Lys went into the outer office and settled in at her desk. "Have fun, boss."

Jamie went out the door and into the foyer. She was not, was *not* going to look across the street when she stepped out. She would turn left, walk the fifty feet to the corner, then turn left again. That was all.

She opened the door, stepped outside into the muggy May heat and her gaze zinged in on the construction site so fast that her vision went blurry. Lys's hunk was still there, and so was Russ. He leaned against the lowered tailgate of the truck, legs stretched out, ankles crossed, and they were talking. If she tried, she could hear his voice. The street wasn't that wide, the midday noises not that loud.

But she didn't try. She put on a pair of oversized sunglasses that hid half her face, turned left, bypassed her car and reached the corner without really being aware of the journey. Once she'd turned and solid limestone blocked the site from view, she sighed, her shoulders relaxing.

She'd known it wouldn't be easy living in the town Russ's family had founded and still pretty much owned two hundred years later. She hadn't expected easy. She just hadn't known it could be this hard.

Copper Lake was a lovely town, designed with aesthetics in mind. The entire downtown was on the historic register, where codes were rigid, and even new construction in town was closely monitored. The newest neighborhoods were almost as charming as the oldest, and even the shopping mall fit into the town planners' view for it.

She passed the square, site of war monuments, political rallies and summer-evening concerts. After crossing River Road, she took a few steps down into Calloway Construction's recently completed riverside retail complex. It was beautiful, looked as if it had been there a hundred years, and was already at full occupancy only a month after opening. Idly she wondered how much was Russ's vision and how much had come from his architects and designers. It was hard to think of him and *charming* in the same thought. Even before he'd hated her, he hadn't been exactly charming. Blunt, forthright, not charming.

She located Chantal's in the corner, and the hostess showed her to a covered deck with paddle fans cooling the air. Robbie was seated at a table near the river, gazing out as if he'd rather be out there fishing in his john boat than working.

She nudged his shoulder before setting her sweater and bag in the seat across from him. He wore jeans, honest-to-God pressed and creased, deck shoes and a polo shirt in bright lemon-yellow. Every other lawyer in town wore suits to work, but not him. He didn't even wear them to court unless he was feeling generous. Clothes didn't make a bad case good or turn a good one bad, he said. It didn't hurt that he was a Calloway, and a good lawyer.

"Hey, babe." He stood and kissed her cheek, then held the chair for her. "You walked over here, didn't you? If you'd called, I would have picked you up."

"If I'd wanted a ride, I would have driven. How are you?"

"Anticipating my vacation. Tomorrow morning, six-fifteen, I'm on a plane to Miami."

She'd heard all about the trip. A leisurely drive halfway through the Keys, then seven days on one of the charter fishing boats owned by a law school classmate. A fishing pole, beer and sun—all a Calloway needed to be happy. "Have fun."

"It's not too late for you to join me."

He'd made the offer before; she declined again. "Fishing isn't my idea of a vacation."

"Your loss. Anything new on—?" He shrugged.

She smiled politely at the waitress who set a glass of ice water in front of her, then made a face at Robbie. "I managed to forget it all morning, and now you bring it up."

His scowl reminded her of his brothers, any and all of them. Gerald Calloway had had four sons, three with his wife and one with a girlfriend. Rick, Russ and Robbie, along with

Mitch Lassiter, second in the lineup, all bore a very strong resemblance. Dark hair, dark skin, startlingly blue eyes, voices that sounded similar and matching scowls. Rick was the handsomest, Jamie had long ago decided, Mitch the most mysterious, Robbie the most charming and Russ the sexiest.

"You've got a freakin' stalker, Jamie. You shouldn't be forgetting it."

His words chased away what little ease she'd recovered after seeing Russ. *Stalker*—it sounded so ugly that she avoided using the word to describe the mystery man who'd come into her life a few weeks earlier. Secret admirer sounded so much more harmless. Less deadly.

Less likely, logic forced her to admit. But she'd lived through a nightmare before. She preferred the state of denial at this point.

"The flowers were the last thing." A dozen apricot roses—her favorite—waiting in a vase on her steps when she'd gotten home Monday evening.

"What the hell kind of guy sends apricot roses?" Robbie asked. "Red, yellow, pink—those are guy roses. You can't even buy apricot roses in Copper Lake. They're a special order thing."

She smiled faintly. "You called the florists, too?"

"Of course. And none of them had gotten an order for apricot roses in months. Did you call the police?"

"And say what? Someone sent me flowers? Left a note on my windshield? Had a box of chocolates delivered to my office? It's a little creepy, Robbie, but the guy hasn't crossed the line."

"Yet."

"Gee, thanks. That makes me feel better."

"Jamie—"

She pulled the file from her bag. "I've got to be in Augusta in a few hours. We should work while we eat."

He looked as if he wanted to protest, but after a moment his mouth flattened. "Okay. But next thing that happens, if you don't call the police, I do. Agreed?"

Jamie knew he wasn't kidding. His best bud was a detective with the Copper Lake Police Department, Rick worked for the Georgia Bureau of Investigation and Mitch worked for the state BI in Mississippi.

"Agreed."

Not that anything else was going to happen. Her admirer was shy but harmless. She wanted to believe that. Needed to, for her own peace of mind.

When his cell phone rang, Russ Calloway seriously considered not answering. He received about fifty calls a day, and at least forty-nine of them were complaints. He wasn't betting that this one would be the exception.

Still, he fished the phone from his pocket and flipped it open. "This is Calloway."

"Hey, so is this." Robbie, kid brother, company lawyer and eternal pain in the butt.

"What's up?" Russ asked absently, phone braced between his ear and shoulder while he examined the framing around a third-floor door.

"The price of gas. The price of a good time."

"You've been talking to Mitch." Those were their older brother's stock answers to the question. "How is he?"

"Anxious for this kid to be born."

"Jessica still turning on a dime?"

"If she's not puking, she's bitching. Mitch is pretty much afraid to be around her. Seems like the morning sickness and the hormones are all his fault."

"The joys of impending fatherhood," Russ said dryly. The

segment of trim was nearly five feet long and looked in good enough shape to survive the prying experience, once he got the nails loosened. "Hang on," he muttered, then sorted through the tools on the worktable until he found a hammer, a screwdriver and pry bars of varying sizes.

"Jeez, you can't even stop for two minutes for a phone call?" Robbie complained.

See? Russ had known this call wasn't going to be the exception. "Some of us work for a living."

"Yeah, but you overdo it. I bet you haven't even taken a break for lunch, have you?"

Russ glanced at his watch. It was nearly two. "Not yet. And I bet you have. A couple of hours. With a pretty woman."

"It was a working lunch, and it didn't come close to two hours. But you're right about the woman. She's gorgeous."

Hearing about the women in his brothers' lives was about as close to a relationship as Russ got these days. Considering that Rick and Mitch were both married, that left only Robbie for any real variety. Good thing he didn't limit himself to a type. "Who is this living, breathing goddess?"

"Jamie."

Robbie said more—he always did—but Russ quit listening. His gut clenched, and his jaw tightened until he felt real pain. Jamie Munroe was the one sore point between him and his brother. Robbie thought she was the perfect woman, and Russ wouldn't piss on her if she was on fire. He'd spent a lot of time wishing she would disappear off the face of the earth.

But she'd made herself at home in his hometown and showed no signs of leaving, so he'd learned to ignore her. It worked pretty well until he caught a glimpse of her on the sidewalk or going into the courthouse or browsing through the fruit at the farmer's market. When he wasn't prepared to see her, it was always a surprise. Recognition, an instant of normalcy, remembering old friends, law school, getting married. Then came the scorn.

Pry bar resting two inches under the molding, Russ realized Robbie was waiting for him to say something. His fingers throbbed from holding the tool so tightly, never a good sign when working with two-hundred-year-old wood, so he set it aside. Holding the phone in one hand, he tilted his head the other way to rub the ache in his neck. "What'd you say?"

"I said even you can't argue the fact that she's pretty."

Jamie? Pretty? Brown hair, light gold skin, a few freckles, blue eyes. Yeah, he supposed she was pretty, if a man liked the backstabbing viper type.

"Of course I can argue," he replied. "Don't forget, I've seen her with her fangs and cape."

"Aw, come on, bubba. It's been three years. Quit holding a grudge because the better lawyer won."

Correction: There was more than one sore point between them. Robbie thought the divorce was something Russ should have put behind him the day it was over. He thought Russ should acknowledge that he'd been an idiot to represent himself, that Jamie was better and get on with life.

Hell, he knew she was a better lawyer than him. He'd gone through school with the knowledge that he wasn't ever going to practice; once he'd taken and passed the bar, that was the end of it for him. She damn well should be better.

And he knew he'd been an idiot to represent himself, law degree or no. Robbie had wanted to take over, had all but bounced in the air, shouting, "Let me, let me!" And his brother wouldn't have let anything get in the way of getting the best deal for his client. Melinda might have been his sister-in-law and Jamie his best friend, but he would have trampled them both into the dirt to win.

Russ's marriage had been the most important thing in his life. Facing a divorce had been bad enough. Finding out about Melinda's affairs, her scorn for him and her lies had been damn near unbearable. Add to that, Jamie, once his own friend, allowing—encouraging?—Melinda's deceit... He'd gone from love for one and friendship with the other to despising them both.

He was over the divorce. He'd gotten on with his life. But he wasn't the forgive-and-forget type. His motto was: live and learn, and never give 'em a chance to screw you twice.

"Did you call for a reason?" he asked testily. "Because I've got about four more hours of work before I get out of here, and shooting the breeze with you isn't getting it done."

"Man, you need to get laid. You're getting pissier every day. I did call for a reason. Mom's been trying to get hold of you, but she keeps getting your voice mail. Rick and Amanda are coming over Saturday, and she wants you there for dinner. Seven o'clock, no grubby work clothes, and if you want to bring a date, she wouldn't object."

"Yeah, Saturday at seven. I'll be there." Before Robbie could say anything else, Russ hung up.

If he wanted to bring a date... He hadn't been out on a date in more than six years, since he'd married Melinda, and hadn't had sex in about three years, since she'd thrown him out. His brothers could understand his not dating—they'd all gotten screwed over at some point—but no sex... Hell, even his mother would wonder about that.

It wasn't that he wasn't interested. It was the intimacy he didn't want, and he'd forgotten how to separate the two. He'd once known—in high school, in college and law school. He'd always had a girlfriend or two, and while the sex had been fun, it had never really meant anything.

Finding out that sex meant nothing to the wife he'd loved had somehow made it mean too much to him. Was that twisted or what?

Frustrated, he walked to one of the arched windows that faced west in what had been the third-floor ballroom of River's Edge, a classic Greek Revival plantation home. It had once reigned over eight thousand acres until a long-gone Calloway had decided it was the perfect place to build his legacy. He'd bought the property, torn down everything except the house itself and made it his home while building the town around it. He'd decreed that no building between the house and the river could be higher than two stories to preserve the view from the third floor. Russ could see the Gullah River, a hundred yards wide at this point, as well as a dozen or more of his projects, old and new.

He'd always wanted to go into construction, even though Calloway men were lawyers whether they practiced or not. Rick had been the first to break tradition, getting his degree in criminal justice instead. Russ hadn't followed his lead, but had gone to the University of Georgia School of Law like a good Calloway son. It would make the family happy, he'd figured, and with his entire life ahead of him, a few years in law school couldn't hurt, right?

Yeah, right. He'd met Jamie there, which had led to meeting Melinda. The bloodsucker and the bitch.

Speak of the devil, or, at least, one of them…Jamie came out of her office across the street. Her hair was pulled back and clipped up in kind of a mess on the back of her head. She wore a red-and-white print dress that didn't reach her knees, with a sweater that was more for looks than warmth, and she carried a briefcase and a bottle of water. Huge dark glasses covered her eyes, but he could tell she never looked toward the house before she slid behind the wheel of her character-free black convertible.

He watched her back out from the space in front of her office, then drive off to the south. If he had any luck, she would keep driving south until she wound up somewhere deep in the Gulf of Mexico. But at the end of the block, she turned, jogged over to River Road, then headed north.

"Staring out the window doesn't get the work done."

He turned to find J. D. Stinson standing at the top of what had once been elegant stairs. They'd been chopped up along with the rest of the house sometime in the fifties, turning the place into cheap apartment rentals.

J.D. was a relative, too; his mother was Russ's father's youngest sister. He was an assistant vice president at Fidelity and oversaw all of Russ's construction loans. Nothing like keeping it in the family.

"I always finish ahead of schedule and under budget," Russ said mildly.

"And you usually have bonuses for doing so written into your contract."

Russ shrugged. He had a reputation for doing good work at a fair price. If people were willing to pay him extra for doing it quickly, as well, why not? "What are you doing out of the office and on the site on a warm day like today?"

It was a family joke that J.D. had gone into banking not because his father was president and it was expected of him, but because it meant an air-conditioned job wearing nice clothes. Casual for him was khakis and a polo shirt. He owned more suits than all the undertakers in the county combined, and the only thing he thought worth sweating over was his girlfriend of the month.

"I had some business to take care of across the street."

Russ resisted the urge to shift his gaze to the whitewashed-brick building that housed Jamie's office.

"What business do you have with Satan?"

J.D. scowled. "You know, if I was half as ticked off with Jamie as you are—"

"I'm not ticked off at Jamie. I don't like her. Under the circumstances, you shouldn't be dealing with her, either." Russ wasn't talking about his divorce, though family loyalty, with the exception of Robbie, should count for something. No, having won a damn fine settlement against one Calloway, Jamie was after another, representing J.D.'s wife, Laurie, in their split.

"I'm not dealing with her. That's why I waited until I knew she would be gone to come over this way."

Russ did look down at the building then. There were two good-sized windows, one in reception and one in the office. And through the first, he could see Lys Paxton sitting at her desk, using the computer. Her black hair concealed the buds that were usually plugged into her ears, but her head was bobbing, her entire body moving to music only she could hear.

He looked back at his cousin. "Lys Paxton? Give me a break."

His cousin bristled. "Lys and I used to date. There's nothing wrong with her."

"Yeah, right." She was young, more than a little freaky and didn't like Calloways. Plus she worked for Jamie and she'd once dated J.D. That was five strikes Russ could come up with in ten seconds.

"Besides, I haven't even talked to her today. Jamie hadn't left yet, so I came up here."

"Yeah, well, she's gone now."

"Watching her, were you?" J.D. asked with a smirk.

Russ pushed away from the window, returned to the door where he'd been working when his first interruption had come along and crouched, pry bar in hand. "You know, J.D., going out with your estranged wife's lawyer's paralegal might rank as one of the stupidest ideas you've ever come up with."

J.D. went to the window, no doubt watching Lys. "Knock it off, Russ. You're not my father, my brother, my lawyer, my priest or my boss. You don't get to tell me what to do."

"Someone needs to."

"Yeah, someone needs to set you straight, too, but I don't see you taking advice from anyone."

Russ scowled hard, focusing his irritation inward so he didn't inadvertently damage the piece of trim he was removing. "My life is fine."

"Yeah, you've got your work, your work and, oh, yeah, your work."

"Yeah, well, I don't have Jamie Munroe after my ass."

"Anymore. At least I'm smart enough to hire Robbie."

The pry bar slipped, leaving a mark in the plaster as well as the back of Russ's hand. He swore silently. "Dracula has gone out, and the bloodsucker-in-training is alone in their lair. You wanna make life harder for yourself, go ahead. Have at it. Just get the hell out of here and let me work."

J.D.'s smile was tight and hard, bearing an eerie resemblance to the only enduring memory Russ had of his father, who'd died when he was seven. "Yeah, well, like I said, you've got your work."

Russ listened until his footsteps were drowned out by the other workers in the house, then heaved a deep breath. Damn straight, he had his work.

And it was all he wanted.

* * *

The office of the psychologist Jamie had come to Augusta to see was located in a small enclave of similar offices near the Medical College of Georgia. She'd spent two hours listening to him assure her beyond a shadow of a doubt that her client had suffered egregiously at the hands of her husband. Now what she needed was an expert witness for her expert witness, because she was pretty convinced that Laurie and the doctor had cooked up a scheme to wring big bucks out of J. D. Stinson.

"He's a Calloway, you know," the doctor had mentioned near the end of the conversation.

What the hell did that mean? Jamie wondered as she unlocked her car with the remote, then opened the door to let the heat escape. Were all Calloway men genetically inclined to dole out abuse to their wives? Did all Calloways share some sense of entitlement that made them above the law? Were all Calloways rich enough to pay off disgruntled ex-wives whether the wives deserved payment?

She set her bag on the passenger seat, then peeled off her sweater. The doctor's office had been cold; the warm leather felt wonderful against her skin. Once the chill had seeped away, she stuck the key in the ignition and turned and…nothing. Another try, another nonresponse.

Grabbing her cell phone, she climbed out again and walked to the nearest shade under a lace-canopied tree. She knew nothing about mechanical things; popping the trunk told her as much about the engine as popping the hood did. So she did what she usually did when she was stuck: she called Lys. Within thirty sweltering minutes, a tow truck arrived to transport her car to the garage and soon after that, a car rental agency delivered a replacement. Jamie gratefully signed the paperwork, then slid inside, where the air conditioner was blasting on frigid.

Deciding to forego dinner alone, she headed back to Copper Lake. It was a lovely drive, quick on the interstate, peaceful on the two-lane state road. She'd never heard of the town until she'd met Russ and Robbie in law school and had visited only three weekends with Russ before he got married. Still, when she'd been looking for someplace to run away to after life had gone to hell in Macon and Robbie had suggested Copper Lake, it had seemed *right*. Immediately she'd felt as if she belonged. She'd borrowed office space from Robbie until she'd had enough clients to justify her own place, and she'd bought a house, made a few friends—and a few enemies, but at least they weren't the type to try to kill her.

She hoped.

Robbie was worried that her mystery man might be just that type. She hoped he was being overly protective. Everything the guy had done so far had been innocent. A vase of gorgeous flowers. A box of to-die-for chocolate liqueur candies. A scrawled note after a verdict that read *Congratulations. The best lawyer won.*

Innocent. Even if there was something inherently creepy about it. Even if it did rouse old memories, old discomforts.

It was after six-thirty when she drove into Copper Lake. She went downtown and turned at the east corner of the square to pull into a space right in front of her office. She would want to make notes on the interview with Dr. Sleaze, she'd told Lys. It wouldn't take long, then she could head home for dinner alone in front of the TV.

One thing she couldn't blame her admirer for: she didn't like being alone in the building. She'd been alone in the office in Macon when her former client's father had paid a visit.

She'd forced herself to deal with the fear that night had created—not conquer it, but cope with it. She made herself come in here once every week or two, even when the work, like tonight, could be done just as easily at home. She forced herself to be brave, or at least pretend.

Everything was quiet. She locked the entrance behind her, then locked the reception door. Lys always left a few lamps burning, and they were on now, lighting her way into her office. The blinds were drawn, per Lys's routine. No need to advertise that Jamie was there.

As if the car parked out front wasn't advertisement enough.

Jamie got comfortable at the computer, aware of the window behind her, opened a document file and began typing. She didn't like the idea of calling Laurie Stinson's psychologist to testify. She found the guy a little too smug, too condemning of J.D. and his family when he'd never met any of them. Just like everyone else, there were good Calloways and bad ones. Not wanting to be married to Laurie anymore didn't automatically make J.D. one of the bad ones.

Outside a car door thudded, stilling Jamie's fingers on the keyboard. She wasn't the only one downtown tonight, she reminded herself. The restaurant on the other side of the square was open until eight, the coffee shop until nine. Sophy Marchand, who owned the quilt store next door, lived upstairs; the street was the only place for her and her visitors to park.

Still, Jamie typed faster, leaving the typos to fix later. As soon as she finished, she saved the file, shut off the computer and, with a rush of relief, headed for the door.

The outer hallway was exactly the way she'd left it—lights on, stairs empty, door locked. She paused in the foyer to locate the keys for the rental, and movement outside caught her attention. A man crouched beside her car, next to the driver's door, and he was fiddling with something.

Her first impulse was to run into the bathroom in her office, locking every door behind her, and call for help. Her second was to take a deep breath. The street was well-lit, and there were people in the square. And this was Copper Lake, her office, her sidewalk. She was safe there.

She stepped outside as the man leaned closer to the car. The door swung shut with a soft whoosh, and she quietly turned the key in the lock before taking a step toward him. "Can I help you with something?"

He stiffened, and the air between them practically shimmered. The tightness in her gut warned her it was Russ before he glanced over his shoulder, but it didn't lessen the impact of coming face-to-face with him for the first time in months. It didn't make the derision in his blue eyes any easier to take.

Slowly he stood, and she watched. His jeans, cleaner than what he'd worn earlier, fitted just as snugly, and his T-shirt looked a luscious size too small. With his impressive muscles flexing, his dark hair cut really short and his jaw stubbled with beard, he looked too damn sexy for her own good.

"Sorry," he said in a tone that clearly said he wasn't. "I didn't hear the portals opening."

The portals of hell. She'd heard some of the names he called her—bloodsucker, Satan, queen of the dark. She would have been amused by them, maybe even proud of them, if they'd come from someone else.

"What are you doing to my car?"

His gaze dropped to the object in his hands. He turned it over a time or two, then held it out. "This was wedged behind the tire. I pulled it out."

When she didn't reach for it, he laid it on the hood of the

car. It was a thin piece of wood, maybe six inches long, with nails hammered through, their points extending several inches on the other side.

"Is that one of those strips used to hold carpet in place?"

"Not with 20d nails. It must have fallen out of the Dumpster when they emptied it this afternoon."

"Yeah, and the wind just blew it behind my tire." And backing out over it would have surely flattened the tire.

Apparently the same thought occurred to him. His scowl deepened and turned about ten degrees colder. "If I wanted your tire flat, there are quicker ways to do it that don't leave evidence behind. Like this." He slipped a knife from his pocket and unfolded the blade with ease, then twirled it between his fingers.

Blood rushed, echoing in her ears, and for a moment, just a moment, her chest grew too tight to allow any but the smallest of breaths. She took a step back, then forced herself to hold her ground, to breathe, to swallow the knot of fear in her throat, as she struggled to concentrate on his words.

"I didn't even know this was your car, and I don't give a damn whether you get a flat."

Her gaze locked on his face. He wasn't someone to fear. He might hate her, but he wouldn't hurt her. And she had no doubt he was being truthful. He had no interest whatsoever in her, beyond the fact that her existence annoyed him.

But the wood hadn't just magically appeared underneath her car, wedged, as he'd said, against the tire. It hadn't been there when she parked, or the tire would have already lost its air.

Maybe the mystery guy had left it. Better yet, maybe someone walking along the street had kicked it. Maybe a passing vehicle had caught the edge of it and sent it spinning, or some juvenile delinquent had put it there deliberately.

"You always look under neighboring cars before you get in your own?" she asked, edging forward enough to pick up the wood without getting close to him.

His mouth flattened, and one side quirked downward. "I opened the passenger door to get a flashlight and some papers fell out."

She could believe that. In law school, she'd never gone anywhere with him that he hadn't had to clear papers, books and other detritus to make room for her.

"I should thank you, I suppose, for not leaving it there to ruin the tire."

His mouth thinned even more. "Like I said, I didn't know it was your car." Closing the knife with a snap, he returned it to his pocket, took a heavy-duty flashlight from the bed of the truck and started across the street.

She watched until he disappeared into the shadows of a live oak before she unlocked the car door. She tossed her bag on the passenger seat and the wood strip in the floorboard, and was about to slide inside when a familiar car turned the corner.

Lys slowed to a stop behind her and rolled the passenger window down, looking from Jamie to the pickup truck beside her before frowning. "You see Prince Charmless?" she asked sourly.

"Yeah, I did. What are you doing out?"

"Picking up a pizza."

"You know, Luigi's delivers."

"Yeah, but this way I get to anticipate that first bite all the way home. Want to come over and share?"

Jamie shook her head. "It's been a long day. I just want to get home."

"You'll regret it when you're looking in your freezer at nothing but boxed dinners. I'll see you tomorrow."

"Yeah. Be careful."

"Always," Lys replied with a grin before driving away.

Jamie got into the car, started the engine on the first try and headed home. Her house was little more than a mile from downtown, in a neighborhood where the yards were big, the houses were old and the trees were older. The house was white siding above dusty red-brick, with the shutters painted black. The steps leading to the front door were brick, as well, and arched out from the foundation in half-round tiers, each anchored by pots of brightly blooming flowers.

She pulled into the driveway, stopping even with the sidewalk. She unlocked the gleaming black door, an elegant contrast to the brass kick plate, then braced herself before opening the door. Mischa, best friend, companion and confidant, rocketed into her with enough force to knock her against the jamb, then abruptly the dog dropped to her haunches, eyes wide, just the tip of her broad pink tongue showing. It was as close to a smile as a dog could get.

"Hey, sweetie, I've missed you, too. Do you know I turned down Luigi's Pizza just so I could come home and be with you?"

Mischa's ears perked at the magic word. She loved Jamie, pizza, an old red shoe and snuggling when she slept—not necessarily in that order.

"Don't you drool on my rug," Jamie admonished as she set her bag down at the foot of the stairs, then kicked off her shoes. "I said I turned down the *p-i-z-z-a*. We'll have to make do with what's in the kitchen."

Still looking hopeful, Mischa followed her down the hall and into the kitchen. A lone light burned above the sink, showing clean counters, gleaming pots hanging from a rack and a cooktop that looked as if it had come straight from the factory. Jamie wasn't much of a cook; the only appliance she used with any regularity was the microwave.

And Lys was right: she did regret turning down the pizza when she faced the stacks of frozen dinners in the freezer. Disappointed by her chicken-and-pasta choice, Mischa padded over to her food dish and munched on dry nuggets.

"Another exciting night," Jamie murmured as she punched the microwave buttons. "You and me alone."

Mischa looked at her, then went back to crunching.

Dull and alone were okay, Jamie reminded herself. She'd had excitement for a time, and it had almost killed her. She could handle dull and alone. She could even handle seeing Russ twice in one day.

Though, if that became the rule rather than the exception, it just might kill her, too.

Chapter 2

Predawn wasn't an unusual time for Russ to be out and about. He could get a good deal of work done before the crews or the office staff showed up. Getting up that early for Robbie, slumped in the passenger seat beside him, was apparently cruel and unusual punishment. His head tilted against the window, his eyes were closed and his snore was quiet. The guy could stay up until 5:00 a.m. partying, but ask him to get up then for a purpose, and he barely managed.

"Hey." Russ poked Robbie's shoulder as he merged onto the Bobby Jones Expressway in Augusta. "We're almost there."

One eye opened. "Almost where?"

"The airport. Remember? The Keys? Fishing? Catching the big one?"

"I'll do that tomorrow. Need sleep."

"You can sleep on the plane."

"I could sleep right here if you'd shut up."

"Hey, I'm not the one who wanted the first flight out this morning. You should be damn grateful that I offered to drive you."

Robbie straightened in the seat, looking as if he was coming off the end of a three-day drunk. "I should have scheduled a noon flight."

"You lazy bum. You give the rest of us a bad name."

"With the old man gone, someone's gotta do it." Robbie rubbed his eyes, then combed his fingers through his hair. Once he got around the other passengers and the flight crew, especially if any of them were female and pretty, he would shake off his fatigue and act like the TV bunny, going and going. It was easy for him.

Not so for Russ. Oh, he had the energy. He just didn't like expending it on people.

Bush Field was coming to life as employees prepared for another start of business. Russ pulled to the curb near one of the entrances and faced his brother. "Have fun."

"I always do." Robbie opened the door and slid halfway out, then turned back. "Listen, if you don't mind…keep an eye on things, would you?"

He sounded serious—a rare enough occurrence in Russ's experience. "What things?"

"Just…things. If anything seems strange or wrong, tell Tommy about it."

Tommy Maricci's father had been a shift foreman in the Calloway logging operation for years, and Tommy, Russ and Robbie had raised a lot of hell before they'd all gone off to college. Now a detective with the Copper Lake police, Tommy was still raising hell with Robbie.

"What kind of things, Rob?" Russ asked again. "Are you in trouble?"

"No. But someone I know might be."

Someone he knew would include the whole damn town of Copper Lake. Narrowing down which one of them would take more energy and interest than Russ possessed.

Robbie got out, heaved his bags from the pickup bed, then grinned. "Give my best to Amanda Saturday."

Russ snorted. "I'll give *my* best to her. I don't want to get punched for mentioning your name. Have fun. Bring back some fish."

"Will do." Robbie slammed the door, picked up his bags and headed inside the terminal. Before he even reached the entrance, he'd fallen into step beside a pretty flight attendant and said something to make her flash a million-watt smile.

Grinning, Russ pulled into the lane and headed back toward the expressway and home. It was a long drive back to Copper Lake, the sun slowly rising on the horizon behind him, his schedule for the day playing through his mind. An inspection at the Forsythia Drive address, a problem with the tilers at the new clinic on the highway out of town, an appointment with the interior designer, the kitchen designer and the lighting designer at the condo project on the west side of the river, a stop by the accountant's office. If he was lucky, he might squeeze in an hour or two to work at River's Edge.

And if his luck ran the way it usually did, he'd run into Satan while he was there. At least he knew what car to look for this time. Idly he wondered if her car was in the garage and why she'd been working late last night. Whether he knew the person whose life she would be ruining next. How that piece of wood had gotten wedged behind her tire.

And the wind just blew it over, she'd said sarcastically. Not likely. Now that he took the time to consider it, neither was his theory that it had fallen from the Dumpster. The wood had been set securely behind the tire, nails up, a flat waiting to happen.

Was Jamie the friend of Robbie's who was in trouble? Understandable. Russ surely wasn't the first or last person she'd pissed off. But, knowing how he felt about her, would Robbie ask him, even in a roundabout way, to keep an eye on her?

Russ's grin was flat. Yeah. He would.

The road into Copper Lake took him past the turns for his mother's house, his grandparents' place, his own place. Granddad had given each of the grandchildren five acres—one thing Melinda hadn't been able to touch in the divorce. He had built a house there after she was gone, way back in the woods, damn near impossible to find. Old logging roads crisscrossed the hillsides, most of them leading nowhere. With the nearest house belonging to Rick and Amanda—a weekend place—and few visitors, Russ liked the isolation.

Once he reached town, he stopped at the mom-and-pop doughnut shop for a cinnamon roll and a cup of coffee, then considered which project to check first. The house on Walton Way was closest—ninety years old, a complete remodel from inside out, nothing special or challenging about it.

Except that it was directly across the street from Jamie's house. He'd known that when he accepted the job and hadn't given a damn…but he also hadn't been over there before she left for work or after she'd likely be home for the day. Coincidence? Or subconscious decision?

He would like to say coincidence. He would like to believe it, too.

"Hey, Russ." Smelling of sweat and tobacco, Tommy Maricci slid into the chair opposite him. He wore shorts, a T-shirt and running shoes, and his skin was damp, his black hair sticking to his head. A pack of cigarettes showed in the breast pocket of the shirt, and his plate held two jelly doughnuts.

"You're the only person I know who jogs across town to get doughnuts and has a smoke on the way," Russ commented.

"I'm down to five cigarettes a day. Don't screw with me."

"How's crime?"

"Booming. You take Robbie to the airport?"

"Yeah. If he wasn't snoring, he was bitching about the time." Russ thought again of Robbie's request as he washed down a chunk of roll with coffee. "Is there anything going on with him that I should know about? Is he in trouble?"

Tommy raised his brows. "Robbie? In trouble?"

Only since he was old enough to walk and follow Russ and Rick on their adventures. Their family name was the only thing that had kept the three of them out of the legal system when they were teenagers, and the courtesy had extended to Tommy on more than one occasion. Not that they'd been *bad*. Just high-spirited, their mom said.

"What about one of his friends? Someone, maybe a female, who might drag him into her problems?"

Tommy shrugged. "You'd have to ask him about that. Or her. You have a particular female in mind?" After a moment, he grinned. "Of course you do. Only one woman still in town gives you that look."

Russ scowled. "Let her take half of everything *you* own, and see how warm and fuzzy she makes you feel."

"She didn't take it, man. Judge Whitley did."

"Based on the crap she let Melinda tell him."

"Come on. Everybody knows you didn't run around on Melinda, and everybody damn well knows you never mis-treated her."

Not everyone, Russ thought, his muscles tightening until

he felt a headache coming on. A lot of people had listened to Melinda's lies, and they'd assumed the worst of him. Clearly, the judge had believed them. Why else would he have rewarded Melinda so richly for being an unfaithful wife?

"Back to the subject," he said, knowing he sounded stiff and not caring. "Is Robbie involved in anything even remotely that could cause trouble for him?"

"He's a lawyer. He's friendly with everybody. He's a Calloway. Of course he could get into trouble. But that's nothing new."

If trouble doesn't find you, you go looking for it, their mother used to say. Was that after they'd gotten caught painting all the high-school windows in the school colors of blue and gold? Or maybe when Rick had gotten his nose broken in a fight after football practice and Russ and Robbie, despite being younger and smaller, had jumped in to help him. They'd held their own, too. Or the time they'd gotten caught racing for pink slips. Or…

"Why are you worried about him?" Tommy asked. "Did he say something?"

"Just to let you know if anything strange happened while he's gone."

Tommy considered it while he ate the last of his doughnut, then shrugged again. "If he's got a problem and he hasn't talked about it with you or me, how serious can it be?"

Good point. Robbie wasn't the sort to keep things to himself. If he had a thought on something, and he always did, he shared it. He wasn't a secretive sort of guy.

Tommy wadded up his napkin, then stuffed it into the empty coffee cup. "If anything strange does happen, you know how to find me. Otherwise, I'll see you around."

"Yeah," Russ agreed absently. "I'll see you."

* * *

"How was your frozen dinner last night?"

Jamie looked up to find Lys standing in the doorway, a bag slung over her shoulder and two boxes in hand. One bore the green and red of the Krispy Kreme doughnut shop down the block; the other was from Luigi's Pizza, no doubt bearing leftovers from Lys's own dinner the night before.

"Very good. Grilled chicken, bowtie pasta and fire-roasted veggies in a low-fat cream sauce. Yum."

"Uh-huh." Coming closer, Lys set both boxes on the desk, then pulled two cans of diet pop from her bag. "Sounds better than it tasted, I bet. Any word on your car?"

"I'm supposed to call the garage later today to get the bad news." Jamie opened the pizza box and lifted out a slice heavy with toppings. "I love cold pizza for breakfast."

"I know." Lys chose a glazed doughnut from the other box, holding it over a napkin, and settled into one of the two client chairs. Her slim sheath and three-inch heels were black and, with her sleek black hair and porcelain-delicate skin, should have looked stark, but it worked for her. It made Jamie, in khaki trousers and pale blue shirt, feel dumpy.

"How long were you here last night?" Lys asked.

"Not long. Half an hour, maybe."

"Any trouble?"

Immediately Russ popped into Jamie's mind. In anyone's book, he was trouble with a capital *T,* but not, she was pretty sure, what Lys was referring to.

"Anything new from your secret admirer?" Lys clarified.

After another bite of pizza, Jamie told her about the nail-studded wood.

As she'd feared, Lys looked concerned. "You think he wanted your tire to go flat so he could...play the white knight for you? Offer to change it? Give you a ride home? Jeez, Jamie…"

"It could have been an accident." She'd been telling herself that every time the incident came to mind, but she hadn't managed to convince herself yet. "It could have just been kids being brats."

"Or it could have been a setup to get you in this guy's debt— or into his car, alone somewhere. Did you call the police?"

"No." It seemed so petty. After all, no damage had been done, and the motive was purely speculation.

"Do you still have the wood?"

"It's in the car."

Lys laid down the doughnut and held out her hand. "Give me your keys. I'll put it in the vault for safekeeping. The police may want it later."

Jamie gave her the keys, then picked up the pizza again. Cold cheese, peppers, Canadian bacon and extra onions on a thin crust were particularly comforting this morning. She polished off that piece and made a good start on the next by the time Lys returned, wood strip in hand. She disappeared into the file room—an honest-to-God vault from the days when the building had housed a savings-and-loan—then returned to pick up her doughnut. "How did you find it?"

"I didn't. Russ did."

That made Lys sit straighter, alerting the way Mischa did to a squirrel intrusion. "Russ Calloway? He was poking around your car when this crap suddenly appeared?"

"Russ wouldn't have flattened my tire or changed it or offered me a ride home. He doesn't want my gratitude, and I'm the last person in the world he would play white knight for." Saying the words stirred an ache in Jamie's gut. There had been a time when they'd meant so much to each other, when she'd had such hopes for their future. Now he felt nothing but hostility for her. How had they come to this?

Well, for starters, representing his ex in their divorce hadn't been the best way to stay on good terms with him. But *someone* had had to take Melinda's case. The marriage was beyond saving, and Jamie had been new to town, looking for clients to build her practice. And Robbie had assured her it was okay. Russ was a lawyer himself. He would understand that it was just business.

Yeah, right.

"White knight, giving you a ride—those would have been secret admirer motives," Lys said. "Russ Calloway wouldn't have secret admirer motives."

Another twinge of pain. "And what kind of motives would he have?"

"Stalker motives. Vandalism. Harassment. Pure meanness. He doesn't like you, Jamie. He says horrible things about you. Maybe he wants to punish you. Maybe he wants to hurt you."

The pizza felt heavy and unwelcome in Jamie's stomach. She set the remains of the second slice down and took a cautious drink of pop, grateful when it stayed down. "Not Russ. He's a decent guy—"

"Who's mad as hell at you." Lys leaned forward, her dark eyes troubled. "Who happened to be right there when the wood showed up. Who has access to wood and nails on the job site. You said he found it and was removing it when you came out. What if he was really putting it there? He'd have no choice but to take it out again or be caught."

Jamie pictured the scene from the night before in her mind—the dusky evening, the man crouched beside her car, his back to her. She hadn't even recognized him until an instant before he'd turned; she certainly hadn't seen exactly what he was doing. Had he been removing the wood strip…or wedging it in place?

Common sense waved its little fingers for her attention. For God's sake, this was Russ they were talking about. His feelings for her aside, he was a good guy, respected in business, adored by his family, admired by his crews. Hell, she'd *loved* him. He wasn't the type who would vandalize a woman's car, not even hers. He wouldn't harass her, would never hurt her.

"Not Russ," she said aloud, and she believed it. "Okay, so he's holding a grudge—"

"A grudge? It's been three years, and he still calls you Satan."

The pang was smaller this time, barely a discomfort. "A little displaced anger isn't uncommon in a nasty divorce. Melinda left town. I'm the only one left to hate."

"Oh, yeah, sure. Every person who gets divorced feels that way toward the opposing counsel. It's a wonder that any lawyer will even take on a divorce case these days, isn't it?"

Lys's sarcasm made Jamie smile a little. "You've noticed that I've cut way back on divorces, haven't you?" While she'd practiced criminal law in Macon, it was tough to specialize in Copper Lake. Like the other lawyers in town, she did a little bit of everything, from criminal trials to estate planning to contract negotiation. While she would prefer to never handle another divorce, she still took on a few. It was part of practicing law in a small town.

"Jamie—"

"Lys, it was probably just kids who found the wood at the construction site and thought it'd be funny to flatten someone's tire. Until Russ showed up, my car was the only one on the block. I got picked by default."

Lys was reluctant to accept that version of events; it was clear in her grudging expression and tone. "You think so?"

"I do." And if she kept saying it, before long she would believe it. Not a stalker. Not a threat. Just kids, or really bad luck.

As the digital clock on the wall rolled over to 9:00 a.m., the phone began ringing, first the main line, then the rollover. Rising, Lys put both calls on hold, then gazed at Jamie a moment. "You be careful anyway."

The warmth of affection rushed through Jamie. Lys had been a good friend from the moment they'd met on Jamie's second full day in town. She'd applied for the job of paralegal and secretary, and had provided support, laughter and plenty of shoulders to lean on when Jamie needed them. She hoped she'd been as good a friend in return.

The morning was busy, but they still made time for their construction-watching break, though with more care this time. Jamie scanned all the vehicles parked along the streets, looking for the 1972 Chevrolet Cheyenne pickup that was Russ's baby—one piece of property Melinda had desperately wanted but failed to gain ownership of—and she studied every guy with dark hair, broad shoulders and a long, lean body. Ogling a site full of hard bodies to find one hard body in particular: nice work if you could get it, she thought wryly as she relaxed.

"Remember I said I need a date bad?" Lys murmured as she slid her feet back into her heels, then stood, about to return to work. "J.D. asked me out yesterday."

"J. D. Stinson? The Calloway cousin? Our client's soon-to-be ex-husband?"

"I didn't say yes." Lys gave her a chiding look. "I understand conflict of interest. But…we used to date. Before you came to town. For a while."

"What happened? Did you break his heart?"

Lys's smile was broad and extraordinarily white against the

crimson slash of her lipstick. "You've got to care about someone besides yourself before you can get your heart broken. We just lost interest. He met someone else, and so did I."

Lys hadn't been in a serious relationship in the three years Jamie had known her. She didn't ask how it had worked out with her someone else. The answer was pretty clear.

"He and Laurie have been separated six weeks, and he's already dating again?"

"He never *stopped* dating. A lot of what Laurie says may be bull, but the infidelity stuff—that's all true."

"So he's not too broken up by the divorce."

"Like I said, you have to care about someone besides yourself." With a wide-eyed shrug, Lys left the office for her own desk.

Jamie couldn't imagine it as she turned back to her desk and slid the computer keyboard closer. Marriage was a big deal. A person should go into it with hopes, dreams and commitment. Of course no one was guaranteed happily ever after, but if that wasn't your goal, if you weren't willing to work and compromise, why bother marrying at all?

If she ever got married, it would be with the intention of striving for the till-death-do-us-part. If divorce became inevitable, she would be heartbroken, but she would know she'd done everything possible to avoid it.

Like Russ. Even Melinda had admitted in an unguarded moment that none of it was his fault. He'd tried to work with her, had compromised and given in, had even been willing to go to marriage counseling. But all she'd wanted was out, with as many of their assets as she could get.

And Jamie had helped her get them. If she could somehow return to the past and undo her involvement in a particular case, that one would be at the top of the list.

Then she rubbed the spot low on her ribcage that still ached at times, though the wound was long since healed, and amended the thought: Russ's divorce would be second on the list.

She worked through the rest of the morning, hardly noticing the passage of time until her stomach growled. It was after one o'clock, and the satisfaction from morning pizza was long gone. Rising from her chair, she slung the strap of her purse over one shoulder and went into the outer office. "I'm hungry. Want to get a sandwich at the deli?"

Lys looked up from the fax machine she was feeding. "Sure. Why don't you go on over and order, and I'll be there as soon as I finish sending the Thompkins stuff to his new lawyer in Miami. I'll have a vegetarian wrap."

"With ranch dressing, baked veggie chips and bottled water."

Lys gave her a thumbs-up before turning back to the machine.

It was another warm day with only the thinnest of clouds in the sky. Humidity hung heavy, trapping the fragrance of the flowers that bordered the square close to the ground. Jamie loved the mix of smells: flowers, greenery, dampness, tasty aromas from Krispy Kreme, the coffee shop and the restaurants along the block. She fancied she could even catch a whiff of fresh-sawn lumber from the River's Edge project—which, she congratulated herself, she hadn't so much as glanced at since stepping outside.

Ellie's Deli occupied prime corner-of-the-square real estate, an old building that had begun life as a general store. Broad steps led to a porch, and a few items there harked back to its past: metal advertising signs mounted on the walls, a checkerboard balanced atop an old wooden barrel and rockers, silvered with age.

Jamie placed their order, took a number and went looking for a table in her favorite section, a long narrow enclosure that had once been a back porch. Screens had been replaced by windows that looked out on Ellie Chase's kitchen garden.

Her favorite table was empty. Setting down her bag, she slid
into the chair and tension she'd hardly noticed eased away. It
was a lovely place, with exposed brick walls and a well-worn
brick floor, with all the glass and light and ceiling fans lazily
stirring the air. The noise from the main dining room was muted,
and the proximity to the kitchen allowed the fragrance of hot
bread to seep into the space, along with hints of desserts baking.

She was so lost in *noticing* that she didn't realize she wasn't
alone until a pair of boots came into view through the glass
tabletop. Work boots, spattered with paint and mud. Faded
jeans, also spattered. A snug-fitting T-shirt with a coat of
chalky dust overlaying its crimson hue.

And a world-class scowl.

The muscles in her neck knotted and her jaw clamped
together hard. This wasn't fair. No more surprise sightings.
No more sightings at all if he was going to look at her as if
she were something nasty in need of squishing.

Russ rested one hand on the back of her chair and bent
closer. "I thought I saw blood oozing from the brick." Unin-
vited, he sat down in the chair to her left.

She forced a smile. "Watch it, or I might turn the sky
dark, too."

Coincidentally, the sun disappeared behind a cloud,
shadow falling over the garden. She resisted the urge to laugh
at the timing. He clearly felt no such urge.

"Have you dragged my brother into something he can't
handle?"

Jamie kept her gaze even, unflinching. Russ didn't even
make the list of people Robbie might have discussed her
admirer-stalker with. He and Jamie occupied distinctly
separate areas of Robbie's life. If he'd tattled to anyone, it
would have been Tommy Maricci or his cop brothers.

"Offhand, I can't think of anything Robbie can't handle."
Then she slyly asked, "We are talking about Robbie, aren't
we? You're not accusing me of impropriety with Rick or
Mitch, are you?"

His response was a snort, but it said enough. His older
brothers wouldn't be interested. She wasn't pretty enough,
sexy enough, to tempt them away from their wives, but no
woman was. Fidelity might not have meant much to all Calloways—J. D. Stinson came to mind—but it was important
to these four brothers.

And Melinda had taken such pleasure in publicly airing all
the dirty details of her extramarital affairs. A broken heart,
wounded pride and a bruised ego—Russ had hit the trifecta.

"What's going on?" His voice was deep, tautly controlled,
a lot like Robbie's, except she could count the number of times
she'd heard anger in Robbie's voice on one hand. It was all
she'd heard from Russ for three years.

"Maybe you should ask him."

"I did. All he would say was that someone he knows is
in trouble."

"And you automatically assume it's me?"

"Who else is as deserving?"

Her first inclination was to ignore the tiny ache in her
chest. As her number was called over the intercom, she
decided to go with her second. Rising, she put one hand on
the back of his chair, leaned close enough to smell sunshine,
sweat and dust and softly said, "Bite me, Russ."

She made it halfway to the hall that led to the main dining
room before he caught up with her. "If something's going on,
leave Robbie the hell out of it."

She didn't slow her pace. "Robbie's a big boy. He can
make decisions for himself."

"I'm not kidding."

She gave the girl behind the counter a tight smile as she claimed the trays that held her and Lys's lunches, then faced him again. "Give it up, Russ. I've been threatened by people way scarier than you. If you have enough energy to worry about someone's life, make it your own. You're way more screwed up than Robbie will ever be."

"You don't know what the hell—"

The bell over the door dinged, announcing a new arrival. Russ looked that way, and so did Jamie. Lys's gaze locked on them, and she charged forward like an overprotective bulldog in puppy's clothing.

Jamie shoved Lys's tray into her hands, then bared her teeth at Russ in a parody of a smile. "It's been fun talking to you. What do you say we wait another three years to do it again?"

Color stained his dark skin crimson, and his gaze turned stormy. She didn't wait to hear what he might say, but took Lys's arm and steered her toward the back. It wasn't until they'd turned the corner into the glassed-in porch that Lys spoke.

"Good show. Now would you please let go of my arm so the blood can start flowing again?"

Contritely Jamie did so. "I'm sorry. It's just…"

"I know. It's just Russ."

He'd been the reason for a lot of emotions in her life—happiness, giddiness, need, desire, lust, satisfaction, affection, love, anger, betrayal, headache, heartache and every other kind of ache. He'd been the best part of her life for a time, and the worst.

One of these days, he wasn't going to be any part. She promised herself that.

Just as soon as she figured out how to perform magic.

Chapter 3

In less than a day and a half, three people had offered criticism of Russ's life. He hadn't asked for advice, hadn't given a clue that he was open to suggestions, so why the hell couldn't they keep their opinions to themselves?

And after three years of pretty decent avoidance, why the hell did he have to keep running into Jamie?

"Because God doesn't like you," he muttered as he walked into the kitchen.

It was after eight o'clock. The sun had set, darkness had settled in, and he was still on the job. The day had turned into the day from hell—too many appointments, too much work, too little time—and his run-in with Jamie at lunch had only made it worse. He'd walked out of the deli with a pounding headache, and the aspirin tablets he'd taken were eating a hole in his stomach. He should have gotten something to eat before

the last dose, but anything he ate right now would just aggra-
vate the burning in his gut.

But this Walton Way job was his last stop, and then he was
heading home. A night's sleep would make everything
better—and no matter what else was going on in his life, he
always slept like a baby. He was lucky that way.

The work on this remodel was slow going. The house was
old, and they kept running into unforeseen problems, like
wiring that wasn't up to code and pipes that had to be
replaced. Another few weeks, and he could scratch this one
off his list.

Another few weeks, and he wouldn't have to come back
into Jamie's neighborhood until someone else hired him.

He shouldn't have spoken to her at the deli. He should have
just walked past as if she were a total stranger. She was right:
Robbie *was* grown. He didn't always make the smartest decisions—his continued friendship with Jamie proved that—but
he was old enough to face the consequences.

The next time Russ saw her, he *would* ignore her. He didn't
want anything to do with her; she didn't want anything to do
with him. Simple solution. They would act like strangers, and
before long they would really be strangers.

He finished his walk-through of the house, then let himself
out the front door, yawning as he locked the deadbolt. The
homeowners were staying with the husband's parents during the
remodel, and the wife called every other day wanting to know
when she could move home again. Russ, his secretary, his subs
and everyone on his crew who'd had to deal with the woman
would be as happy when that day came as she would be.

He was walking to his truck in the driveway when a
familiar voice across the street caught his attention. "Mischa?
Mi-i-i-scha."

The call was distant, coming from the back of Jamie's house. A sissy name for a pet. Probably a sissy cat.

Jamie's outside lights came on, then the front door opened. He refused to let his gaze linger; the instant she stepped outside, he focused narrowly on unlocking his pickup, on opening the door and tossing the clipboard he carried into the passenger seat. He was about to slide behind the wheel when her voice sounded again, this time only slightly calmer than a scream.

"Mischa! Oh my God!"

He couldn't stop himself from looking, even if it was just a damn cat. The lights on either side of her door shone down on a large form, and Jamie, damn near prostrate over it. Had she fallen? Was she hurt?

None of his business. If she had a problem, let her call someone for help. She had friends besides Robbie—freaky Lys Paxton, for starters—and the police were duty bound to come if she called. His head hurt. His stomach hurt. He'd dealt with enough for one day. He was going home.

But when he moved, it wasn't to step up into the truck. Swearing with every step, he stalked down the driveway, across the deserted street and into her yard. As he drew closer, he could see that the form was a dog, huge, black and tan, lying motionless on the top step. Shivers rippled through Jamie, and her words were frantic.

"It's okay, Mischa, you're okay, baby. Wake up. Come on now, open your eyes. You can't be…Mischa, you can't…"

Tears. Jamie Munroe was crying. He wouldn't have thought her capable of it.

He took the steps two at a time and crouched beside the dog. It could have been asleep, except no one could sleep through the shaking Jamie was giving it. "What happened?"

She looked up, startled, and swiped at her tears with one hand. "I don't know. I let her out a few minutes ago, like I do every night, and she didn't come back."

The dog was breathing, slow and easy. Running his hands over its body, at least on the side he had access to, didn't reveal any signs of obvious injury, but when he lifted its head, something crackled beneath his fingers. Heavyweight paper, index card-size, tied to the dog's collar with a ribbon.

He worked it out from beneath the dog, read the message neatly printed on it, then lifted his gaze to Jamie. "What the hell…?"

I can get to you as easily as I got to Mischa.

She stared at the words as if they made no sense, then a great shudder jerked her gaze back to the dog. "Oh my God, Mischa…"

Russ ripped off the note and slid it into his hip pocket. "Get your car keys. We've got to get him to the vet."

She scrambled to her feet and disappeared into the house, returning seconds later with her keys and purse. While she unlocked the car and opened the rear door, he heaved ninety pounds of limp animal into his arms, gritting his teeth with the effort. Getting the dog into the backseat of the rental wasn't any easier. It took both of them, supporting, tugging and pushing, and he was out of breath by the time they were done.

He held out his hand, and she slapped the keys into his palm, then wiggled into the back with the dog. He adjusted the seat for his legs, backed out of the long drive and headed out of the neighborhood. Sliding his cell phone from the clip on his belt, he offered it to her. "Call Yancy and tell him we're on our way. His number's in the phone book."

What the hell was he doing getting involved with this? He

didn't like animals. Didn't like Jamie. Didn't care what had happened to the dog or who had left that note on its collar or whether Jamie was in danger. With Robbie out of the state for the time being, he didn't give a damn about anything.

But there was no way she could move the dog on her own, and his mother, Rick, Mitch—all of them would have kicked his ass if he'd gone on home and left her there to deal with it. A Calloway—at least, their particular branch of the family—didn't walk away from someone in need, regardless of his opinion of her.

Yancy Yates's vet clinic was on the east side of town, a large cinder block building dating back to the 1920s. He was married to Russ's aunt Diane and lived in the rambling farm-house next door.

Yancy had already unlocked the door and turned on the lights. Looking surprised to see Russ, he helped him unload the dog and place it on a stretcher, then together they carried it into the back room of the clinic. Yancy checked the dog's breathing, listened to its heart and examined it thoroughly, keeping up a quiet murmur to Mischa, still out, and to himself.

"I'll draw some blood and send it to the lab," he said at last, "but my best guess is that she's been drugged."

Jamie's color was ashen under the florescent lights, and her voice was little more than a whisper. "With what?"

"I'll have to see the tox screen to know for sure. It could be something as simple as a sleeping pill or a sedative." Yancy looked from her to Russ and back again. "Why would anyone want to drug Mischa? I thought Russ here was your only enemy in town, and he would never harm an animal."

Russ's face warmed. Jeez, did everyone in Copper Lake know how much he resented Jamie? It wasn't as if he advertised the fact. Until lately, he hardly ever saw her, and other than a few outbursts three years ago, he never talked about her with anyone outside of a small group of friends and relatives.

Who apparently talked to everyone else.

Jamie didn't seem to notice the comment about him. "I don't know," she murmured, clearly not intending to mention the note. When she bent to stroke the dog's fur, Mischa breathed heavily, then rested her big head against Jamie's neck, as if seeking familiar comfort.

"Have you called the police?" Yancy asked.

"I didn't think about it."

"You should. Anyone who would drug someone's pet is obviously up to no good." Yancy rubbed one weathered hand over the dog's spine. "All we can do now is watch her. Odds are she'll get a good night's sleep, nothing else. I'll keep her here, and we'll have the results of the tox screen by noon tomorrow. Russ, you want to help me put her in that kennel over there?"

After they settled Mischa in the kennel, Jamie knelt beside it, stroking the dog, whispering to her. She didn't look so much like Satan at that moment.

Finally, she got to her feet. "Thanks, Dr. Yates. You'll call me?"

"I've got your numbers. I'll keep you updated."

They left Yancy there, making notes on a chart, and walked outside into the muggy night. Still looking pale, Jamie waited in silence for him to unlock the car doors, but instead he faced her over the roof of the car.

"What the hell is going on?"

In the past thirty minutes, Jamie had gone from pleasantly tired to exhausted. Her jaw hurt, her nerves were on edge, and the last thing she wanted to do was talk. She just wanted to curl up someplace safe. But where was safe? Not her house. Not after what had happened to Mischa right outside her door.

What kind of lowlife would threaten her dog? Mischa wouldn't hurt a fly, though she might chase it around the room a few times. She wasn't a guard dog, would never attack. If someone broke into the house, she would hide under the bed, eyes closed and whimpering. She loved everyone.

But apparently not everyone loved her.

The bulk of the lights went off inside the clinic, throwing them into shadow. She gestured impatiently toward the car door and Russ unlocked it. She slid into the seat and fastened the seat belt, but she didn't kid herself that she'd escaped his questions. She couldn't be that lucky.

The first thing she smelled inside the car was the earthy fragrance Mischa always wore when she'd been outside. The instant Russ slid into the driver's seat, it was replaced by *his* scents—sweat, hard work, a faint hint of cologne, *him*. Familiar smells. Comforting.

Even though Russ Calloway was the last person on earth she could take comfort from.

Through the plate-glass window, she caught a glimpse of Dr. Yates, still in the back room, no doubt checking on the other animals spending the night in his care. He was a good vet. Mischa would be safe with him.

Russ started the engine, powerful enough, but it had nothing on his own growl. "Well?"

"Someone wanted me to know that Mischa's vulnerable."

"No, someone wanted you to know that *you're* vulnerable. Someone who knows where you live, who knows your dog's name. Who?"

"I don't know."

"Oh, come on."

"I don't! If I did, I'd have his ass hauled off to jail for messing with Mischa." Threatening her was one thing. Threatening her dog... That was cold.

"What else has happened?"

She stared out the side window, hardly noticing the buildings they passed. "He's sent me flowers. Candy. A note."

Russ snorted. "Yeah, I saw the note."

The reminder of the message attached to Mischa's collar sent a shiver down her spine, and she hugged herself to contain it. "Another note. Congratulating me on a case."

"Why haven't you called the police?"

"I didn't think it was necessary." Couldn't *admit* it was necessary. Not again.

Hearing a rustle of movement, she glanced his way as he retrieved his cell and flipped it open. Feeling fairly certain he was looking up Tommy Maricci's number, she closed her eyes and rested her head against the seat.

Russ's conversation with Tommy was short. He shut the phone and set it in the cup holder. "Tommy's going to meet us at your house." He didn't look at her but kept his gaze locked on the road ahead. Both hands were on the wheel, and the muscles in his jaw were taut. He radiated tension.

But she was still glad to have him there. How would she have gotten Mischa to the vet's by herself? How would she have held herself together alone?

"Robbie knows about this."

It wasn't a question, but she answered anyway. "Yes."

"So you *are* the one dragging him into trouble."

There was no reason to feel guilty. She hadn't lied to him at the deli. She simply hadn't answered him at all, and that was her right. It wasn't as if they were friends, as if he had a stake in anything happening in her life. "I told him about it, but I didn't 'drag' him into anything. We just talked."

"And what did he think?"

"He said I should call the police. He thought it was weird."

He signaled for the turn off River Road onto her street. "What idiot wouldn't think it was weird?"

"I just hoped…" She'd convinced herself it was harmless weird. She'd fought too hard to get back a normal life; she hadn't wanted to surrender it without concrete evidence. She had that now.

The neighborhood was quiet as they drove through. She'd loved the area since the first time she'd seen it—the huge lots, the old charm of the houses, the trees, the privacy and the sense of *home*. In the two and a half years she'd lived there, she'd always looked forward to coming home. She'd always felt welcomed.

Until tonight.

Russ's truck was still parked in the Petrovskis' driveway, five hundred feet from her front door. How loudly had she shrieked when she'd found Mischa unresponsive on the steps?

Loudly enough to get his attention. To appeal to the decency that was inside him under all that hostility, to bring him to Mischa's aid. If he stayed angry with her for the rest of their lives, she would always be grateful for that.

He parked in her usual spot and shut off the engine. She got out and, still close to the security of the car, looked around. Neither of the houses to the side could be seen from her vantage point; tall hedges of azaleas and red-tip shrubs hid them. The Petrovski house across the street had a few dim lights burning, and lights were on at their closest neighbor's, but much of the yards were in shadow.

Was he out there somewhere, watching? He'd come close

to her house to reach Mischa; the dog never left the yard when she made her postdinner trips outside. Jamie had been inside, the television on, the dryer running, a book open on the arm of her favorite chair, blissfully unaware that someone had invaded her property. How easily could he have gained access to the house? She wouldn't have given a second thought to a noise at the back door; she would have assumed it was Mischa, unlocked the door and opened it without looking to let the dog in.

She shuddered.

Russ circled the car and started along the sidewalk toward the steps. The more distance he put between them, the more vulnerable she felt. Exactly what the mystery man wanted.

She caught up within a few steps, took the keys he offered and unlocked the door, but she hesitated at going inside. What if the stalker was in there, waiting for her?

Then he'd be disappointed to find Russ with her—and Tommy Maricci, who was turning into the driveway, followed by two officers in a marked car. Her comfort level eased up a notch or two.

"Any way this nutcase could have gotten inside the house?" Tommy asked as a greeting.

Jamie glanced down the long hallway. From the doorway, everything appeared as she'd left it, but that didn't mean anything. Had she locked the back door after futilely calling Mischa? Was the lock sturdy enough to keep him out? Had he broken a window somewhere in the shadows?

Her silence was answer enough. Tommy directed one of the men to check outside the house, the other to search inside. As soon as they went off in opposite directions, he gestured toward the door. "Let's go in the living room and talk."

It was harder stepping through the door than Jamie had expected. Damn it, she wouldn't let some pervert rob her of the comfort of her home. Squaring her shoulders, she walked into the hallway, then turned into the living room on the right.

Tommy didn't waste any time as he settled in an armchair. "I called Robbie on the way over here. He told me about the other incidents." A pause for effect. "He also told me about what happened in Macon. Is this a garden-variety stalker or could there be a connection?"

Russ, looking at the photographs on the fireplace mantel, turned around. "What happened in Macon?"

She'd decided to stand, but just the sharp edge of his gaze made her rethink and sink onto the sofa at the nearest end. "If there's a connection, I can't see it. Shan Davis and his father are in prison. His mother left town before Shan's trial even started. There were no brothers or sisters, no relatives who came to the trial or visited him in jail."

Russ moved forward, no more than a foot or so, but the distance between them seemed to shrink immeasurably. She could feel the annoyance radiating from him. "Trial for what? In prison for what?"

Tommy was quiet, leaving her to answer. In a monotone, she did. "Nearly four years ago, I defended Shan Davis on murder charges. He'd confessed, then recanted, but there were witnesses, fingerprints, DNA. The best I was hoping for was a life sentence, but he received the death penalty. He was nineteen, an only child. His mother accepted that he was guilty and left town. His father never accepted it. He blamed me for the verdict, and he came to my office one night when I was working late. Fortunately, I'd ordered out for pizza, and the delivery guy scared him away."

Russ stared at her, his blue gaze so intent that she felt it, hot and damn near vibrating along her skin. "He didn't go to prison for visiting you at your office."

"No," she agreed. "He went to prison for stabbing me four times. Obviously, none of the wounds were fatal." Painful, yes, and terrifying. She'd been utterly certain she was going to die, and she hadn't been prepared. She'd prayed harder that night than ever before.

Who'd known prayers could be answered in the form of a Domino's delivery guy?

Russ's entire body stiffened, and his expression shifted from annoyance to anger. Was he regretting that Harlan Davis hadn't succeeded at killing her? Then someone else could have represented Melinda. Someone else could have been on the receiving end of his hostility for the past three years.

He opened his mouth, but before he gave voice to any words, Tommy spoke. "Why the hell didn't we hear anything about this?"

"I guess it wasn't big news outside of Macon." Actually, the story had been picked up by the media outside the city— one of those little filler pieces that took a few seconds' airtime or an inch or so of column space, heard or read and forgotten immediately.

"Robbie knew."

Jamie smiled faintly. There was an accusing undertone to Tommy's voice, like a child left out of the secret his friends shared. "So did Lys. I asked them not to tell anyone."

Robbie had been in Atlanta the night it happened; he'd gone straight to Macon from there, or he surely would have told someone in his family first. She'd been a mess—weak, in pain, terrified and filled with self-recriminations. She shouldn't have worked late at the office, shouldn't have dismissed Harlan Davis as just another angry parent, shouldn't have taken his son's case to begin with. She should have fought harder, should have been stronger both before and after, should have resisted being such a victim. She'd been ashamed of herself and hadn't wanted anyone to know.

Hadn't wanted Russ to know. He'd been married, after all, and happily, as far as she knew. He'd long since stopped caring about her.

"So that was why you came to Copper Lake. To feel safer."

"To make a new start." Then she shrugged. "And to feel safer."

"If this guy was part of that," Russ said, drawing her gaze to him, "why send the flowers and the candy? Why make it look like he's interested?"

"To throw us off," Tommy replied. "If we're looking for a wannabe boyfriend, we're not gonna be looking at the guy who tried to kill her. Are those the flowers?"

She nodded. The vase sat on the coffee table that separated sofa and chairs. A bit of the bloom was off the roses, their color not quite so vivid, their petals not quite so fresh.

"No tag, no card, no delivery info?"

"No. And there's nothing special about the vase. I have three or four just like it under the kitchen sink."

"But there was a card tonight."

Russ pulled the note from his pocket, dangling it by the ribbon, as one of the officers came into the room. Tommy directed him to bag the note. "You'll find Russ's fingerprints all over it," he said with good-natured sarcasm.

"There's something else at the office," Jamie said, then told him about the wood strip. "I can get it for you tonight or in the morning. And you'll find Russ's, Lys's and my fingerprints all over *it*."

"If we get you amateurs out of the way, we might have a chance at ID'ing this guy," Tommy grumbled. "I'll pick it up

in the morning. In the meantime, you're not gonna stay here
for the next few days, are you?"

Her chest tightened. Part of her wanted to. This was her
home, her sanctuary. But the mere thought of the men leaving,
of being there alone, of locking the doors and turning off the
lights and knowing that she wasn't safe, was enough to make
her knees weak.

"You can move in with Lys, can't you?" Tommy suggested.

"No. If I've got some psycho after me, there's no way I'm
going near any of my friends' houses. I won't put them at risk.
I can go to a motel." It wasn't a great choice. Once she
checked in, she would still be alone. Would still be afraid.

Then, in a day filled with surprises, she got another.

Russ folded his arms across his chest, looking as distant and
cold as ever and, in a hard voice, said, "You can stay with me."

It wasn't the worst idea Russ had ever had. That was
marrying Melinda. But it wasn't the most sane, either,
judging by the looks Jamie and Tommy were giving him. He
shrugged off their surprise. "We're not friends, and I can
take care of myself."

There was that protective streak his mother had instilled in
him and his brothers. He didn't like the idea of any bastard
menacing a woman, not even Jamie, and damned if he would
stand by and do nothing. It wasn't a big deal. His house was
difficult to find, and the bedrooms were at opposite ends. He
usually left before sunrise and got back long after sunset. And
the last six months of his marriage had proven that he could
share a house with a woman without crossing paths with her.

"Okay," Tommy said at last. "Get what you need, Jamie.
We'll wait."

Russ expected her to argue, to insist on doing things her

way. She looked as if she wanted to, but in the end, she just nodded, then went upstairs.

"You know, if she disappears out there, you'll be our prime suspect." Tommy was grinning. He damn well knew that Russ wasn't a danger to Jamie and was amused by it. "Man, Robbie's right. You *are* freakin' irrational where she's concerned."

Russ's only response was to leave the room and wait impatiently just outside the front door. That didn't stop Tommy from joining him. This time, though, he was dead serious.

"Don't make the mistake she did of thinking this is no big deal," he said quietly. "A nutcase who hurts animals will have no problem hurting people, especially the guy who gets between him and the woman he's obsessing over. Don't confuse isolation with security, and keep a weapon handy just in case. Stalkers don't always kill, but a lot of the time they do. Don't get caught unprepared."

Russ held his gaze, long and steady, for a time before nodding. He wasn't just offering Jamie a bed. He was offering to do exactly what Tommy had said: get between her and whoever was after her. It was one hell of a responsibility, but he didn't back down.

"Leave her car here," Tommy continued. "I don't want her driving those logging roads by herself. Too many places for an ambush. And she shouldn't tell anyone where she's staying, not even Lys. Anyone has to get hold of her outside the office, they can call her cell phone. Keep your eyes open, and if anything at all looks or even feels wrong, call 911 and tell them to call me."

Russ nodded again, then dug his keys from his pocket. "I'll get my truck."

If he'd left the Petrovski house five minutes earlier, he would have been home by now, would have eaten dinner and been kicked back in front of the television or the computer. Jamie and her overgrown dog wouldn't have been his problem. She would be going to a motel, where she would spend the night alone, worrying about her dog, worrying about her stalker and whether he'd followed her and, if not, how hard it would be for him to find her.

And remembering what had happened when her client's father had found her.

Moving stiffly, he unlocked the truck's passenger door and transferred the papers, files and mail from the seat into a box kept behind it just for that purpose, then brushed dried clumps of drywall mud from the seat out the open door. After circling the truck, he slid behind the wheel, started the engine, backed out of the long driveway and pulled into Jamie's drive as she came out of the house.

Tommy took a suitcase and garment bag, leaving her to carry a laptop case and another small bag. Russ watched them approach, Jamie listening earnestly to what Tommy had to say, stress bracketing her mouth, giving her a jittery look. Russ had never seen much real fear, but he recognized it now. That was why she was going with him without protest. Better to stay with her enemy than to face her fear alone.

Tommy hefted her bags into the truck bed while she climbed into the seat. Instantly Russ caught a whiff of perfume, something light, more exotic than sweet. It was the same fragrance she'd worn back in law school. His sheets had smelled of it, his clothes, but he couldn't recall the name of it. Couldn't say that he'd ever paid enough attention to know.

After rolling down the passenger window, Tommy closed the door, then fixed his gaze on each of them in turn. "This isn't a game, okay? You both take it seriously. Damned if I'm gonna tell Robbie something happened to either of you while he was gone."

Russ was feeling pretty damn serious. Jamie looked it, too, in spite of her shaky smile. "He would be unbearable, wouldn't he?"

"You know it. I'll come by your office in the morning."

"I'll be there."

Tommy stepped back with a grim nod, and Russ backed out of the driveway into the street. Jamie fastened her seat belt, crossed her legs and folded her hands in her lap. Her expression, illuminated by the streetlights they passed, was grim, her jaw taut. As he turned north, she finally spoke. "I appreciate this."

His impulse was to respond flippantly, but he gestured in dismissal instead. He was sure she did appreciate his offer. She might not have taken the stalker seriously to start— though who could blame her for preferring flattery over fear? But she was a smart woman. Now that she knew the bastard was worthy of fear, she wouldn't take any stupid chances.

A smart woman who'd already survived one attempt on her life.

He couldn't believe that Robbie hadn't told him about the murder attempt, or that he hadn't heard gossip through some mutual old friend or classmate. But Robbie was nothing if not honorable; if he gave his word that he wouldn't tell anyone, he wouldn't. As for old friends and classmates, Russ hadn't stayed in regular touch with anyone outside of family. He hadn't done much of anything in the past three years besides work and resent the hell out of Jamie and Melinda.

"I don't even know where you live."

He glanced at her, seeing only the back of her head as she stared out the side window. "Not many people do."

"And you like it that way."

"Yeah." Russ liked his privacy, even if it did seem damn lonely at times.

A mile or so passed before he spoke again. "What happened in Macon…" Tommy had used the same phrase. It sounded innocent and harmless. So much better than *getting stabbed four times by a lunatic who wanted you dead.* "Why did you hide it?"

Finally she glanced at him, but her gaze shifted away quickly. "I didn't hide it. I just didn't call attention to it. I didn't want pity. I didn't want people to look at me and see a victim."

I wasn't just "people," he wanted to point out. They'd been friends. Hell, they'd slept together for all of one semester and half of the next. They'd still been friends when it happened, until she'd come to Copper Lake and agreed to represent Melinda—and *mis*represent him—in the divorce.

"You don't give people much credit, do you?"

"I didn't leave Macon right away. I went through physical therapy and rehabilitation. I even went back to work in the same firm in the same office. I saw the curiosity and the sympathy and the pity. I answered the endless questions. I gave all the gory details until I just couldn't give them anymore. When I moved here, I wanted to forget. I wanted to be normal again."

Could you forget almost dying in your own office? And if she'd been attacked at night in her office there, why the hell did she work nights in her office here?

To prove to herself that she could. That Shan Davis's father couldn't change the way she lived. He admired it at the same time he thought it was stupid. No one in Copper Lake gave a damn whether she worked late alone in her office. No one would think less of her, even without knowing her history, for refusing to do so.

Two and a half miles past the turnoff for his mother's house, Russ slowed, then checked the rearview mirror. His was the only vehicle on the road and had been since leaving the city limits. No one had followed them, and no one could possibly know to be waiting along the dirt roads that led to his house. Some of the tension gathered in his neck eased as he turned off the highway.

When he was a kid, the trees had grown in straight lines, evenly spaced, and the undergrowth had been kept relatively cleared. But Granddad had quit logging this section twenty years ago, letting it return to its natural state. It was a good place to hike and hunt, and Russ had spent plenty of hours doing just that. He knew every rise, every clearing and thicket, and could follow the banks of Holigan Creek blindfolded. He might get a little lonely, but living out there was worth it. This was where he felt at home.

The logging roads had been laid out in a grid, originally wide enough for two trucks to pass. They were narrower now, the forest encroaching, tree branches forming a canopy overhead in places. The roads they passed were mostly unused, though any number of them would get a person to his house if he knew where it was. It was Russ's goal for them to grow over entirely, disappearing, surrounding him with forest.

For a long time, it had been his goal to disappear himself. To shut out everyone and everything until nothing could touch him again. But his family hadn't let that happen. They were stubborn when they set their minds to something.

"Every intersection looks the same." Across the cab, Jamie gestured as they crossed yet another road. "How does anyone find their way around?"

"They're not the same. You just have to know what to look for."

"It's a little spooky out here. The road getting narrower and overgrown. The trees. No lights. No neighbors."

"That's why people move to the country. To get away from the lights and the people."

She gave a little sniff. "I like neighbors, thank you."

"They weren't of any help to you tonight, were they?"

The dim lights from the dash shadowed her face as her expression darkened. He wished he hadn't said anything. Relieved by the distraction, he made the last turn, negotiated a bumpy hundred yards, then rounded a curve. His house sat in the clearing ahead, illuminated by his headlights and a lone lamp next to the garage.

"Oh, it's pretty."

Her surprise irritated him. "Everything I build looks good. That's part of the job."

She gave him an admonishing look. "I didn't mean that. It just looks like the perfect family home. A yard, flowers, a porch swing."

And he wasn't the family type. Not anymore.

Scowling, he parked in front of the garage, then got out and circled the truck to unload her bags from the back. He normally entered through the garage, but this time he followed the stone path to the porch, fished the house key from the ring and unlocked the front door, then stepped back so she could enter first.

The only light burning was a lamp in the family room, straight ahead at the back of the house. It was enough to see that the place was neat and clean, that he hadn't left castoff clothes or dishes lying around as he often did. Not that it mattered. Jamie wasn't a guest. He wasn't looking to impress her.

He was just trying to keep her safe.

Chapter 4

The house wasn't overly large or ostentatious, though Russ could easily afford both, but it was lovely. Jamie set her bags on the stone floor of the entry, then moved farther into the family room. Rough-hewn beams arched overhead, the shape echoed in the stone fireplace that dominated one wall. The floors past the foyer were wood, broad planks that looked a hundred years old, and the walls were painted a bold hunter-green. Tall windows flanked the fireplace, looking out into the dark night, and soapstone lined the counters and the island that marked the kitchen to the right.

The chairs and sofa were distressed leather, the tables solid oak, the rugs homey and showing the signs of heavy wear. Family heirlooms, she'd bet, passed down through generations of Calloways.

It was a good thing he'd waited until Melinda was gone to build the house, or she would have done her best to get it, too.

Not that the house she'd been given in the divorce and immediately sold had been any too shabby. She had just been
greedy. She'd wanted it all.

Jamie had wanted it all, too, though her definition had varied
tremendously. A husband, kids, a home. Melinda's husband,
to be exact. And now here she was, a guest in his home.

She might have been safer at a motel.

He set her bigger bags next to the small ones, then went
past her and into the kitchen, switching on lights as he went.
"Have you eaten?"

"Yes." Another frozen dinner that had made Mischa turn
up her nose. Thought of the dog made her stomach clench. She
pulled her cell phone from her purse and was scrolling through
the directory for the vet's number when Russ spoke again.

"Cell service out here is hit-or-miss. There's a phone on
the desk."

The cell's power signal was at its lowest. With a nod, she
crossed to the desk at the far end of the room from the kitchen.
It was massive, oak with brass pulls, and bore the signs of a
long life of hard work. She remembered it well—one of only
a few pieces of furniture in his house in Athens that had made
the trip from home with him. It had belonged to Cyrus
Calloway, his ancestor who'd founded Copper Lake two
hundred years ago. She sat in the wooden chair with its leather
cushion and dialed the vet's number while the mouthwater-
ing aromas of sweet onions sizzling and ground beef grilling
filled the air.

Dr. Yates couldn't tell her anything new—just that Mischa
was okay and still sleeping. She thanked him, hung up, then
swiveled the chair so she could stand. Instead, she sat a
moment, watching Russ. He moved around the kitchen with
the familiarity of someone who spent a good deal of time

there. Back when they were together, he'd been even less adept at cooking than she was. He'd stored beer in his refrigerator, cookies and chips in the cabinets and had the take-out menus for every restaurant in town. Later, Melinda hadn't liked eating at home. She'd married one of the town's favored sons, and she reminded people of it every chance she got. They'd been regulars at the country club and every other decent restaurant in town.

Jamie hadn't cared about prestige or flaunting her catch. She'd just wanted Russ, while Melinda had wanted what he could give her. And he'd wanted Melinda. It wasn't fair.

If she hadn't learned that life wasn't fair a hundred times over growing up, she would have figured it out when Russ dumped her for Melinda, or when Harlan Davis attacked her.

Because watching him wasn't the best thing for her mental health, she rose from the chair and shifted her attention to the fireplace. A rugged beam served as mantel, and above it hung a family portrait, taken sometime after Gerald Calloway's death. Sara sat in the middle, surrounded by her sons and Mitch, wearing a smile of utter contentment. It was the same smile Mitch's wife, Jessica, wore, the same as Rick's wife, Amanda's, but for very different reasons.

"She never looked that happy when the old man was alive." Russ stopped a few yards away, munching on a napkin-wrapped burger. He liked them rare, Jamie recalled. With sauteed onions, mustard, pickles and ketchup, while she preferred hers well-done. Like shoe leather, he'd teased.

"An awful lot of people are happier without their spouse than with," she said carefully, watching peripherally for his reaction.

Any change in his expression was too guarded to catch. It wasn't necessary anyway. She knew he wasn't one of those. He'd loved his wife. In some ways, he probably still did.

"The guest rooms are this way." He led the way past the desk and into a hallway that ran front to back, opening into the foyer at the opposite end. There was a bedroom in front and another in back with a bathroom in between. The rooms were similar, one painted taupe, one pale green, each filled with mismatched antiques and large windows that let in the night.

Ordinarily she didn't mind such openness. The three sets of French doors that led to her patio were covered with only the filmiest of curtains, offering no privacy at all when the lights were on inside. But this was as far from an ordinary night as she'd seen in three and a half years. At least these windows, unlike the family room, had blinds she could lower and close so she could cower without any chance of curious eyes seeing.

The thought of someone out there in the darkness made her shiver, but she masked it with a shrug as she chose the rear room. The green on the walls was soothing, and the old-fashioned bed, high off the floor and piled with pillows, reminded her of her grandmother's guest room where she'd spent many a night as a kid. Everything had always been perfect at Gran's, and she could use a little of that illusion tonight.

"Where is your room?" she asked as she headed for the foyer to get her bags. It was going to feel weird enough staying the night in a strange house, even weirder knowing it was Russ's house. It would help to know where he would be if she got up in the night.

If she needed his protection.

He looked as if the thought had occurred to him, as well. "On the other side of the kitchen."

"You can go ahead and finish your dinner. I'll get my bags and, uh, get ready for bed." Easing past him, she took the hall in long strides. She was pretty sure he stood there near the door and watched until she was out of sight, but when she returned a moment later, laden with her bags, he was gone.

She hung the garment bag in the closet and set out the few toiletries she would need tonight in the bathroom, but left everything else in the bags. It wasn't as if she was staying more than a day or two. She couldn't imagine Russ's generosity or her own nerves lasting any longer than that. After washing the makeup from her face, she changed into her pajamas—cotton shorts and a tank top—then returned to the bedroom.

With the blinds lowered and twisted tightly shut, the room seemed cozier. It smelled faintly of hazelnut, though not from any source within the room. It was coffee brewing in the kitchen, perfuming the air. She didn't drink coffee herself, though she'd developed a taste for Russ's postcoffee kisses. Back when she'd been young and hopeful and he hadn't broken her heart and no one had tried to kill her.

Pretending it was any normal night, she snuggled into bed, fat pillows behind her and a puffy comforter pulled to her waist, and opened the magazine she'd grabbed from her night table. Usually, she'd had such a day that a few articles were enough to put her to sleep. Not tonight. Oh, she read the articles. She just couldn't focus. Couldn't make sense of the words. She wasn't even sure she was seeing the right words, partly because her eyes were watering, partly because her hands were trembling. Hell, her whole body was trembling.

Shoving back the covers, she slid from the bed. She knew this antsy feeling. Sometimes it grabbed hold of her just before the verdict was announced in a particularly important case. The first time she'd walked back into her Macon office after the attack, she'd been so anxious that she'd forgotten to breathe.

The first time she'd faced Russ as Melinda's lawyer, she'd been sick from the inside out. There was nothing to do but wait it out, though activity did usually help. If she were home, she'd hit the treadmill in the guest room. If Robbie were home, she'd call him to go for a walk along the river with her. He would complain, but he would do it. If things were different with Russ, she'd jump his bones. That would make her forget.

Stifling a bitter laugh, she opened the door and listened. The living room was dimly lit. There were no sounds, no television, no utensils against dishes, and the fragrance of the hazelnut was fading. Russ had probably gone to his room, maybe to bed. He'd always been an early riser.

Arms hugging her middle, she eased around the corner, saw that the room was empty, with only one lamp burning, and walked farther in. The wood floor was cool beneath her feet as she moved along the perimeter of the room.

Paintings of serious value—more family heirlooms—hung on two walls, while photographs of his family and friends filled in the spaces between. A set of six-foot-tall glass-fronted barrister bookcases, the shelves packed with books, marked the end of the display area, then the kitchen proper began. The cabinets were oak, the pulls antiqued brass. With the soap-stone counters and…

The sound of running water stopped her mid-ramble. Russ was in the shower. There was an image she didn't need, one she'd seen often enough before he'd met Melinda. Water hot enough to steam, smooth tanned flesh, hair sleek against his head, muscles flexing, skin glistening… Just the memory had the power to make her hot, to dry her mouth and make her hungry.

Abruptly the water shut off. She imagined him stepping out, reaching for a towel, dripping on the rug beneath his feet. Swallowing hard, she forced herself to move. But instead of rushing back to her room, she went to the cabinets, searching for a glass. She needed cold water before she ignited inside.

"What are you looking for?"

Her hand stilled, her fingers closing around the pull on the third cabinet door. There was no way he'd dried off and dressed that fast. Granted, his hair was so short that it needed just a swipe or two with a towel to soak up the excess water, but still… "Glasses," she managed to answer without sounding strangled.

"Next door over. There's pop, beer and bottled water in the refrigerator."

She shook her head. "I just need a drink." After taking a glass from the bottom shelf, she closed the door, then steeled herself to turn.

She'd been right. He hadn't had time to dry off and get dressed. He wore a thick towel knotted around his waist, and drops of water dampened his shoulders, arms and chest. She dropped her gaze to the floor—safer territory—and saw that his feet were still damp, too.

She had to pass him to get to the refrigerator. There was plenty of room, but it felt much too confined. She hadn't been with a man in a long time, hadn't been with this man in a very long time, and this wasn't a normal night. She needed activity. Distraction.

He rinsed his coffee cup, then set it in the dishwasher while she filled the glass with ice, then water. For her own protection—or was it his?—she went to stand on the opposite side of the island, sipping the water before commenting. "You're the only person I know who can drink a cup of coffee and be asleep in five minutes."

He shrugged, skin rippling. "Caffeine never has kept me awake."

"You still sleep like a rock?"

"Yeah."

Her smile was unsteady. "I'll remember that. If I have to scream, I'll scream loudly."

He didn't return the smile. "No one followed us here."

She nodded. She'd seen him watching the rearview mirrors all the way from her house.

"This is the last place anyone would expect you to go. They'd check the motels first, then maybe Lys's."

"Should I warn her?" All this time she'd been worried about Mischa, about herself, and hadn't given any thought to Lys's safety. Everyone in town knew they were best friends, and a stranger could find out easily enough. Lys lived alone in her half of a duplex, though the other half was shared by two of Copper Lake's hunkiest firemen. If they were off duty, they would come running at the first hint of trouble. *If* they were off duty.

Russ shrugged. "Call her if you want. But block the number, and don't tell her where you are."

"Why not?"

"Because Tommy said not to. Hiding isn't hiding once you start telling people where you are."

"But Lys—"

He shrugged again, clearly not caring.

Jamie took another drink of water, shivering as the icy liquid hit the back of her throat, then went to the desk. She had to look in the phone book for instructions on how to block the number. She was a regular person. She didn't try to hide from people.

She was halfway through a message when Lys picked up. Jamie kept the conversation intentionally vague, though it was hard, especially when Lys asked the inevitable question. "Where are you?"

Especially with Russ watching. "I—I can't say."

There was stunned silence on the line before Lys found her voice. "You can't—Jamie, this is *me*. Associate, employee, *friend*? What do you mean, you can't say?"

"Tommy Maricci told me not to."

Lys snorted scornfully. "Tommy Maricci never would have *made* detective if it wasn't for his friendship with the Calloways. Hell, if it wasn't for them, he would be *in* jail instead of trying to put other people there."

That wasn't true—Tommy was a good cop—but Jamie didn't argue with her. Keeping her voice steady, she said, "I'll be in the office in the morning, as usual. Just…be careful. If anything weird happens tonight, call the police." Before Lys could protest, she hung up.

"There's a bottle of aspirin in the top left drawer," Russ said.

"I don't have a headache."

"Lys always gives people a pain somewhere."

Pushing to her feet, Jamie returned to the island. "You don't like her much, do you?"

"I don't like her at all."

"Did you used to date her?" Jamie had always assumed a good deal of Lys's antagonism toward Russ was based on her own rocky relationship with him, but that was arrogant. He and Lys had grown up in the same town, though he was six or eight years older than her. She could have had plenty of contact with him before Jamie came to town, could have come by that antagonism completely on her own.

"Yeah, right, me and freaky Lys." He moved to lean against the counter, ankles crossed. "I never dated anyone seriously until Melinda."

Jamie's breath caught in her chest, and the floor seemed to sink out from under her. Feeling sore inside, she took one last drink of water, grateful she didn't choke on it, then eased the glass onto the counter. "I think I'll go to bed now."

Moving carefully and quietly, she returned to the guest room, closed the door and sat down on the edge of the bed. It was so high that only her toes touched the floor, pressing against the braided rug there.

She'd been in love with Russ six years ago, and she'd thought that he might have loved her, too. At the least, she'd believed he cared about her. Oh, she knew he'd gotten over her. He'd married Melinda, after all, and had been obscenely happy with her in the beginning. But he'd cared about Jamie first. He'd maybe-loved Jamie first. She'd found some comfort in that.

But she'd been wrong. He'd never even been serious about her. She'd just been a way to pass the time while he waited for the real love of his life to come along. He'd used her, fooled her, never cared about her at all.

She sat there a long time, not moving, not seeing, not thinking, until finally exhaustion claimed her. Sliding under the covers, warmed with her own body heat, she wondered if it was possible to not feel.

She damn sure intended to try.

Russ woke before six to the aroma of dark Colombian coffee brewing in the next room. He pulled on a T-shirt over his boxers, then headed for the kitchen for a jolt of caffeine and a toaster pastry.

The first thing he saw when he rounded the corner by the refrigerator was a pair of long bare legs. He damn near skidded to a stop, abruptly remembering. The dog, the stalker, Jamie. She was standing at the near end of the island, a book open in front of her—an old yearbook—and a bottle of water beside her. She still wore her pajamas, shorts and a top that were damn near indecent, and her hair fell in a tangle past her shoulders. No makeup, hardly any clothes and not even a finger-comb through her hair, and she still looked… How had Robbie described her the other day? As a living, breathing goddess?

No, those were *his* words, before he'd known who they were talking about. But pretty damn accurate all the same. Her legs were long, lean, and her ass, jutted out as she bent over the island, was damn fine. Nice waist, better-than-nice breasts, a few freckles dotting her cheeks and nose…

Aw, jeez, this was *Jamie*. Satan. Queen of the damned. The last thing in the world he wanted was to feel anything even remotely positive toward her.

No, the *last* thing he wanted was for anything to happen to her. Especially if he could prevent it.

She was reaching for a section of peeled orange from the napkin next to her water when he finally forced one foot forward, then the other. She glanced at him, her expression utterly blank, said a polite good morning, then turned her attention back to the yearbook.

He got his coffee, added milk and sugar and put two sugar-frosted Danish in the toaster before finally gesturing to the book with his mug. "You like looking at old pictures?"

She straightened. Too bad. "I like seeing how people have changed."

He didn't want to think about how he'd changed since high school. He'd been naive back then. With the exception of his loser father, life had been pretty good, and he'd stupidly thought it would always be that way.

"Robbie still looks the same."

He moved close enough to see the picture she was pointing at. Robbie, sophomore class president, wearing the grin that got him both into and out of more trouble than any three kids combined.

"So do you." She flipped back through the pages, past the junior class, to the beginning of the senior class pictures, tapping his photo. Her fingers were long and slim, the nails rounded and polished.

He hardly glanced at the photograph. "It's been a lot of years."

"Only fourteen."

"In calendar time. Not in real time." He'd aged a lot more than fourteen years since that picture had been taken, most of it in the past three years. Disillusionment had a way of doing that to people.

Using the toaster as an excuse to back off, he retreated to the other end of the kitchen, fishing out the hot pastries, dropping each piece on a saucer. Had *she* been disillusioned when her client's father tried to kill her? A thing like that could make a person go into seclusion, could make it damn near impossible to trust anyone again.

But she hadn't. She'd moved to a whole new place, where she knew only him and Robbie. She'd started over. She'd made friends. She hadn't turned her house into a fortified camp. Hadn't started carrying a gun or been afraid to move about.

Four stab wounds, Jamie had said. Picturing her clearly even though his back was to her, he wondered where. He hadn't seen any scars, not that he'd gotten to look as closely as he'd have liked. Given her history, it was a wonder she hadn't turned tail and run the other night when…

His face went scarlet, and he choked down the food in his mouth before turning. "When I pulled out that knife Wednesday night…I didn't know…I didn't mean… Jeez."

She shrugged as if the incident hadn't bothered her at all. "I knew you would never use it on me."

Knew how? His behavior since the divorce had been crappy. On the few occasions in the beginning, when she'd tried to be friendly, he hadn't even managed civil. He'd been so damn angry. How could she *know* anything about what he would or wouldn't have done?

Still, the conviction in her voice made him feel less of a bastard.

A little less.

"What time do you usually go to work?" he asked, pulling out a barstool at the end of the island and sitting down with his coffee and breakfast.

"The office opens at nine, but any time's okay. What time do you usually go?"

"I'm already on my way most days." But most days he didn't have an overnight guest. In fact, she was the first person to stay over in this house.

She polished off the last of the orange and wiped her hands on the napkin. "I can be ready in fifteen minutes."

"You don't have to—"

"The earlier you drop me off, the less likely anyone will see us." She returned the yearbook to the bottom shelf of the bookcase and lowered the glass door. He got one look of snug-fitting cotton stretched across her butt as she bent, and dropped his gaze to his breakfast. Suddenly it seemed too hot for steaming coffee and pastry, though in reality both had cooled to little more than warm.

Hell.

He finished the first pastry, then returned to the bedroom to pull on jeans and boots. After brushing his teeth, he tucked his shirt in, then zipped up. He was back at the island, finishing the second pastry, when she returned.

She wore snug-fitting gray pants and darker gray heels

that made her legs look a mile long, with a light-purple top and a matching sweater. Her hair was pulled back in a ponytail, then clipped up on her head, leaving the ends to fall back down, and she'd put on makeup. She didn't need it. She was pretty enough without it.

Grinding his teeth at the thought, he poured his coffee into a travel mug, grabbed his cell phone from the charger and clipped it to his belt. He was halfway to the door when he reversed, returning to his bedroom. When he came back with a zippered padded case in hand, Jamie's gaze fixed on it for a moment. The attack on her might not have made her hyper-cautious, but she recognized the gun rug for what it was. She didn't comment on it, though, and neither did he.

The morning was cool, the humidity high. It promised to be another muggy, hot day, not ideal for outdoor work, but better than an office anytime.

As Russ stopped to lock the double-keyed dead bolt, Jamie walked to the edge of the porch. "Do you ever sit outside and just enjoy the day?"

He glanced at the swing on one side of the door, the oak rockers on the other side, and shook his head. "I don't have time." His house was his refuge…but he suspected it wouldn't feel quite so good if he spent too much time there. It would give him too many chances to think about how different life was supposed to have been. So he worked instead. A lot.

The drive into town was silent. He drank his coffee and watched the traffic, and she sat motionless in the passenger seat, staring off into the distance. There were few cars on the highway, and not many more once they reached town. Morning rush hour in Copper Lake lasted all of five minutes, so there were no early commuters.

"Do you have a key to the back door of your building?" Russ asked as he turned at the square.

Jamie glanced at him blankly, then dug her keys from her purse. "Yes."

He drove to the end of the block, turned right toward the tiny parking lot carved out behind her building. He parked in the space nearest her door and climbed out. She didn't protest as she got out.

"I never park back here," she commented. "The only time the sun hits it is high noon, and at night it's downright creepy."

"Good place for a stalker to hide."

She cut him a look, then wiggled the key into the lock and twisted it. The door opened with a spook-house creak into a narrow space, where another door opened into the foyer. He followed her to her office, into reception, then into her private office. Everything was quiet. Normal, judging by her actions.

Russ pulled a business card from his hip pocket and offered it to her. His phone numbers—cell, office and home—were on it. "Call me when freaky Lys leaves this evening."

Again, she didn't protest, though she looked like she wanted to this time. Instead, she tucked the business card under the edge of the desk pad and absently said, "Don't call her that."

He stood near the door, ready to leave but feeling as if he should say something. But what? *Be careful?* She knew that. *Watch your back?* She knew that now, too. Instead, he shrugged and left, locking the doors behind him as he went.

At eight-thirty, fifteen minutes before her usual time, Lys blew into the office like a hurricane. She was clearly upset, but not too upset to make her usual stop for doughnuts and diet pop. Before she set the box and the cans on the desk, she demanded, "Are you all right?"

"I'm fine."

"And Mischa?"

"She's fine, too." Jamie had called Dr. Yates as soon as Russ left and gotten a good report. He was waiting on the tox screen, but Mischa had slept comfortably all night, had already made a trip outside and had been settling down to breakfast as they spoke. Whatever drug she'd been given, she seemed to be suffering no ill effects.

Ignoring the doughnuts once she'd opened the box, Lys sat back and crossed her legs, then her arms. Today she was dressed all in white—a slim-fitting sheath that stopped midthigh with four-inch strappy heels. White wasn't an obvious choice for her coloring, but somehow, like the solid black from the day before, she made it look good, even with the deep-red-with-purple-undertones lipstick that matched her nails.

"I didn't see the rental outside. How did you get to work this morning?"

Jamie stuffed half a glazed doughnut in her mouth, then lifted her shoulders in a shrug.

"I bet Maricci brought you. Where did you stay last night?"

Still using the food as an excuse, Jamie shrugged again.

"Come and stay with me. I know, you don't want to put me in any danger, but that's not a problem. I'm not afraid of this guy, whoever he is. You and I together will kick his ass."

Finally Jamie had no choice but to swallow. "I can't, Lys. It's too risky. And you *should* be afraid. You know Mischa. What kind of scum would hurt her?" Before Lys could say anything, she rushed on. "I appreciate the offer, really, I do. But we're both safer if no one knows where I am. You can always reach me on my cell phone." Service might not be reliable out in the woods, but she could use Russ's phone to check for voice mails.

"But, Jamie—"

Hating her tone, part pout, part plea, Jamie interrupted. "The garage in Augusta called after we left last night. My car's ready. Would it be possible for you to return the rental and pick it up today? I'd go, but I don't think Tommy would approve."

Lys sat in silence for a moment, then grudgingly nodded. "For once, I'd agree with him. Too many places between here and Augusta for something to go wrong."

"You're right. Forget I asked you. I'll find someone else—"

"No one's going to mistake me for you. Beyond the fact that we're both female, we have nothing else in common. I'll go this morning. Where is the rental?" There was a bit of curiosity in her eyes, as if she hoped Jamie had driven to wherever she'd spent the night.

"It's in my driveway. Probably smells of Mischa."

"How the hell did you get her into the car by yourself?"

"I didn't." Though one doughnut contained more than enough calories for one day's breakfast, Jamie fished out another and took a bite, mumbling through it. "Actually, Russ Calloway was working at the Petrovskis'. He helped."

Eyes wide-open, Lys stared at her. "He just happens to 'find' the nail strip behind your tire, and then he's 'working' in your neighborhood at the same time Mischa gets poisoned? You don't think that's a little too coincidental?"

"No. I don't."

"Jamie, he hates you. He's avoided you for three years, but now, when things start going wrong, suddenly he's there every time you turn around? Come on. So you used to be in love with him. That was years ago. He's not the same guy anymore."

She'd been in love with a man whom she'd thought loved her back. He'd *never* been that guy, Jamie thought morosely. She'd been wrong about him then. Could she be wrong now?

No. Certain things were just inarguable facts. Grass was green, water was wet and Russ was *not* the kind of guy who'd stalk a woman. Even if he did hate her.

Rather than argue with Lys, she simply said nothing.

Rolling her eyes, Lys got to her feet, chose a doughnut from the box and headed for the door. "I'll go through the messages and the e-mail, then pick up the rental and head for Augusta. The county bar's monthly dinner is tonight at the country club. I assume you'll want to skip that." She glanced over her shoulder into the outer office, then said, voice dripping sarcasm, "Maricci's here."

"That's Detective Maricci to you, Paxton."

With another roll of her eyes, Lys went to her desk. Tommy came inside and closed the door. He wore snug-fitting jeans and a blue polo shirt embroidered with the Copper Lake Police Department seal. "So you survived the night."

"Did you think I wouldn't?" Jamie asked dryly.

"It occurred to me that one of you might kill the other. I'd've put my money on you strangling him, though. Anything new I should know about?"

"We had a quiet uneventful night."

"Yeah, so did I. I usually do when I get called out in the middle of a date."

"Sorry my stalker interfered with your social life."

He shrugged magnanimously. "Who needs a social life? I know a number of people who get by just fine without one. You, Russ…"

Jamie gave him a surprised look as she rose from her desk. "I have a social life."

He snorted. "When's the last time you went out? And Robbie and Lys don't count. Robbie's like your best girl-friend, and Lys is freaky."

"Don't call her that." She swung open the heavy vault door and gestured to the strip of wood on top of a file cabinet.

Tommy made notes on an adhesive evidence seal, scooped the strip into a paper bag using a napkin from the desk, then sealed the fold with the label. "We'll need to get fingerprints from you and Lys to rule you out. I got Russ's this morning." He looked back at her. "So? Last date?"

"I don't remember."

"Since me?"

"Maybe not." She and Tommy had gone out to dinner once. They'd had a nice time, he'd kissed her good night, and they'd decided to be friends.

"I know I broke your heart, but you're too young and pretty to live life alone."

She imitated his snort. "Sorry to disappoint you, but my heart is intact." More or less. More than six years ago, maybe a little less than twenty-four hours ago.

"Listen." That quickly Tommy turned serious. "The only prints on the note from last night were Russ's. We haven't gotten anything on the flowers or the candy, but we're looking. I checked on the Davises. They're both still in prison. Between them, they've had maybe three visitors since they went in. My gut says this doesn't involve them."

"So that leaves someone local."

"Anyone ask you out that you turned down?"

Because she liked the closeness and security of the vault too much for her own comfort, Jamie returned to her desk. "A number of guys, but no one who cared enough to try to change my mind."

"Make a list for me, will you?"

She pulled a notepad and pen from her desk drawer and began writing. She hated pointing a finger at men who were very likely innocent, hated the doubts and the wariness and the suspicion. But not as much as she hated the fear.

It was a short list—six names. Tommy scanned it, then folded it and stuck it in his hip pocket. "Okay, so we know who likes you. Who doesn't like you?"

Russ. But she wouldn't say it out loud. *Wouldn't.*

"Besides the obvious," Tommy added grimly. "Have you defended anybody here in town who's gone to jail?"

She shook her head. "I don't take major criminal cases. Just misdemeanors."

"Anyone get a raw deal in a civil case?" Again, he added, "Besides the obvious."

"I'm not comfortable discussing my clients," she said stiffly.

"You weren't comfortable taking your dog to the vet last night, either."

"I don't have any ideas. Honestly. I've hardly gotten used to the idea that I've got a stalker. I can't begin to think who it could be."

Tommy studied her a moment, then nodded. "Okay. Someone will come over to take your prints. Other than that, stay alert. Let me know if anything comes up. Here's my cell phone number." He flipped a card onto her desk. It spun three hundred and sixty degrees in midair and landed, right side up, in the middle of the desk pad. With a grin and a wink, he left.

"Hey, Paxton," she heard from the outer office. "We need your prints. Don't leave town till we get them."

Friends fingerprinted, potential dates investigated…how had her life come to this?

Chapter 5

It was 5:55 p.m. when Russ's cell phone rang. He slid it from his waistband and flipped it open. "Calloway."

"It's Jamie. Lys is gone, so whenever you're ready…" She sounded tired. It had been a longer day than usual, and probably a tougher one. Having the cops come by, asking a lot of questions and taking your fingerprints wasn't anyone's idea of fun, not even when it was Tommy.

"I'll meet you at the back door in ten minutes." He hung up before she could say anything else and walked through the building until he located his foreman. "I'm heading out. If you need anything, you can reach me on the cell or at home."

Ken Martin's eyes widened. "You're going home? It's not even six o'clock. I can't remember the last time you quit work before six o'clock."

"That's because you're a slacker who thinks ten-hour days are long enough. I'll see you Monday."

The condos were going up on the west side of the river, each with a view of the water, downtown and River's Edge. They snaked along the riverbank, backing up to tennis courts and a golf course, and would be modern and high-tech inside while looking on the outside as if they'd been there a hundred years.

Sometimes he felt as if he'd been working on them a hundred years. He was glad to be leaving, glad to be going home.

And it didn't have a damn thing to do with his houseguest. He hadn't given her a thought all day. Well, except when Tommy had caught up with him this morning. And when he'd seen Lys driving the convertible. And when he'd taken a break for lunch at the deli. And when he'd stopped by River's Edge... Hell and damnation.

He drove into downtown and turned into the alley behind Jamie's office. Before he had a chance to get out, the rear door to the building opened and she came out, locked up, then headed his way.

There wasn't anything deliberate about the way she moved—it was just her usual walk—but there *was* something about it, something feminine, something... He didn't want to say the word, didn't want to even think it in connection with Jamie, but the sway of her hips, the flex of muscle, the faint movement of her breasts...

Sexy.

She climbed into the truck, settled her purse on the seat and the briefcase on the floor, then fastened her seat belt. Her only greeting was a hesitant smile. His was a curt nod.

He turned around and pulled back onto the street, but instead of heading toward home, he went east. When she glanced his way, he said, "We're going by Yancy's. He said Mischa could go home."

Surprise crossed her face. "You don't mind?"

Could having a ninety-pound dog in his house be any more distracting than having Jamie there? He couldn't imagine it.

Mischa was ecstatic about seeing Jamie, dragging Yancy along by the leash, lunging at her owner, who'd had the sense to brace herself against the counter. The dog wiggled and shivered all over while Jamie cooed to her, then, greeting finished, Mischa headed for the door.

"Here, Russ, make yourself useful," Yancy said, handing the looped end of the leash to him. "Walk her around the grass a bit."

Scowling, Russ took the leash, then opened the door. Mischa didn't seem to know any commands. She jerked him here and there as she sniffed along the grass before finding a good spot under a tree to relieve herself. That done, she turned abruptly to look at him, as if she'd just realized she was in the company of a stranger. Her dark eyes narrowed and the patch of hair between her shoulders bristled. A low growl rumbled up from inside her, ending quickly when Jamie and Yancy came out of the clinic. Mischa ran to Jamie, and Russ gladly surrendered the leash to her, then took the twenty-pound bag of dog food Yancy offered and tossed it into the truck bed.

The dog made the cab seem a lot more crowded. She sat on the seat between him and Jamie, panting excitedly, breaking off on occasion to look at Russ and display her teeth. She didn't growl again, though, until Russ reached out to adjust the air conditioner.

"Mischa! Bad girl." Jamie gave her collar a tug. "She never gets aggressive with anyone. She's just a big baby."

As if to prove it, Mischa dropped to her side, laid her head in Jamie's lap and stretched, her huge feet pushing hard against his leg. Wearing a wolfish grin as Jamie scratched her, she looked at him and curled her lip back from her teeth.

Great. He was spending the weekend with Satan and the hound of Satan. This ought to be fun.

They were halfway home when the dog went to sleep, her snores sounding remarkably like Robbie's, just louder. Russ glanced across her to Jamie. "What did Yancy say about the drug?"

"It was a sedative, commonly used, the dosage calculated for her size."

"So the intent was to scare you, not to harm her."

She nodded grimly.

"The guy wrote her name on the note. Who knows her?"

"My friends, my neighbors. I take her for walks through the neighborhood and down by the river pretty regularly, and we see the same people. Everyone at Dr. Yates's office knows her." She shrugged. "A lot of people."

"And anyone who's been watching you at home." The houses on her street sat two hundred feet back from the curb, and there were plenty of trees and bushes where someone could take cover. What kind of sick bastard hid in the dark and watched a woman alone?

The same kind who drugged a dog just to scare its owner.

He slowed to make a turn from one logging road to another. "I saw Lys driving your car today. Where has it been?"

"In a garage in Augusta. Something with the transmission."

Not something a stalker could have done. Just bad luck and coincidence.

Still scratching the dog's neck, Jamie asked, "Could we not talk about this right now? It gets a little overwhelming."

"Yeah, sure."

They were silent the rest of the way home.

After the dog ran around the yard, doing a frenzied sniff-and-piss job, they went inside. Mischa trotted ahead, checking out everything along the way. She sniffed along the sofa, one of the chairs, then paid meticulous attention to the chair where Russ usually sat. Tongue out, she climbed into it, turned a couple of times, then dropped down.

"Mischa," Jamie started to scold, but the dog closed her eyes and breathed loudly, mimicking her own snores. "I'm sorry. I made a mistake in letting her on the furniture in the beginning. She likes to be comfortable, and I'm a bad disciplinarian."

Russ stifled a snort. Choosing that chair had nothing to do with comfort. The dog had claimed it because it was his, and as long as she was sitting in it, he couldn't.

Could have been worse. She could have peed on it.

"It's okay," he said, laying his cell phone and the gun rug on the island. "I'm going to take a shower, then I'll fix dinner."

He went to his room and into the bathroom, closing the door behind him. The privacy didn't make him forget that there was someone else in his house. That she was probably headed for the guest room, where she would probably take off those clothes, maybe let down her hair and put on something more casual. He'd vote for the skimpy pajamas, even if bedtime was three or four hours away.

Not that he cared as he turned on the shower to hot. No matter what she wore, she was still Jamie. Ex-friend and scum-sucking lawyer. She was still Melinda's partner in crime.

And none of that changed the fact that she was still pretty. Still sexy. That he still remembered the good times they'd had back in school.

The sex between them had been the best of those good times.

Until Melinda. Meeting her had knocked him on his ass. Six years later he still regretted it.

He kept the water hot enough to steam and scrubbed off the day's work and sweat. He didn't want to think about

Melinda, or all the sex he hadn't had since the divorce, or how good all the sex he *had* had with Jamie had been. He didn't want to think about Jamie, either, but since she was in his house, that seemed unavoidable.

He'd dried off and pulled on boxers when the phone beside the bed rang. Caller ID showed Robbie's cell, so he picked up, bracing the phone between his ear and shoulder while stepping into a clean pair of jeans. "Hey, bubba, how's the fishing?"

"Worth coming down here for. How're things there?"

"Okay."

Robbie waited a moment, then said, "Aw, come on. Mischa got drugged, you saved the day and took Satan home with you, and all you have to say is 'okay?'"

The back of Russ's neck prickled with the nickname. Yeah, he'd resented Jamie like hell, but maybe he should have kept it to himself. Right, and then one day he would have exploded. "How do you know I brought her here?"

"Tommy told me."

"Huh. He told us not to tell anyone."

"I'm not just 'anyone.' I'm the most important guy in Jamie's life."

That made Russ's neck prickle, too. Most people in town assumed Robbie and Jamie were secretly sleeping together, the kind of no-strings-attached affair that would end when someone better came along for one of them. Russ had never thought that, though. Robbie being friends with his enemy was one thing. Sleeping with her, especially when Russ had slept with her first, was something way different.

But Robbie had never actually said they were platonic. All his flaws aside, he rarely discussed the women in his life. The last time he'd been indiscreet, it had been a combination of way too much booze and the rowdy atmosphere of a strip club, and he'd learned from the experience.

"So how's it going?"

Russ stubbornly repeated the same answer. "Okay."

Robbie muttered a profanity. "Has Tommy found out anything?"

"Sounds like you know as much as we do. He interviewed me. He called it talking, but it was an interview." How often had he been in contact with Jamie, had he known that apricot roses were her favorite, had he remembered that she had a fondness for liqueur-filled chocolates—that sort of stuff. No, Russ hadn't known about the roses or the chocolates. Truth was, he didn't remember much about her likes and dislikes, other than the fact that she would never go to his favorite restaurant with him. He could have eaten Mexican five nights a week, but she'd refused to touch it.

He'd slept with her for more than six months. He should remember more than the facts that she didn't like Mexican food, that she smelled good and that the sex was great.

He would bet she remembered more.

He would bet that she'd cared more.

"So how are you two getting along?"

There was a sly quality to Robbie's voice, but Russ knew how to deal with that. "Okay."

"Damn, bubba... Don't you be mean to her."

Russ's first instinct was to deny that he was ever *mean* to anyone. But when he was angry, he talked to his brother. Robbie had heard every ugly name, every insult and curse a dozen times over. He *had* been mean. Justifiably, but still... "If you're so worried about her, cut your trip short, come home and babysit her yourself."

"I can do that."

Cut a fishing trip short for a platonic friend? Not Robbie. Not any Calloway worthy of the name.

His neck twitchy again, Russ rubbed his hand over it. "Yeah, sure. I'll believe that when I see it. Listen, I've got to get dinner started. If anything comes up, I'll call you."

"Yeah. Tell Jamie I called."

If they *were* more than just friends, wouldn't he want to talk to her, to see for himself that she was all right? Maybe. Maybe not. Russ didn't offer to call her to the phone. He just muttered that he would pass on the message and hung up.

When he went into the kitchen, Jamie was sitting at the island, a bottle of water in front of her. She'd changed clothes, though he'd have to find an excuse to walk around the island to see her outfit. She hadn't let her hair down, though. He'd always liked it down. She'd liked it out of the way.

One more thing he'd remembered. He hadn't been totally self-centered in their months together.

"Can I help with dinner?" she asked as he opened both refrigerator and freezer to see what was available.

"I don't know. You like spaghetti?"

"Sure."

He pulled a container of sauce from the freezer, then a hunk of mozzarella from the refrigerator. "You can grate that. Grater's in the middle drawer there." Sure, he could have handed it to her, but then she'd have no reason to move away from the counter.

She slid to her feet and walked into the kitchen. Her orange top ended about the same place where khaki shorts started. They were cuffed, pressed and creased, and about five inches too long for his tastes. Her feet were bare, and her toe nails were painted scarlet. Jamie washed her hands, located the grater, a knife and a bowl to grate into, then returned to the barstool. Finally he peeled the lid off the freezer dish, stuck the sauce in the microwave to thaw and placed a pot of water on the stove to heat.

"Robbie called," he said after salting the water and adding a blob of olive oil.

"How's the fishing?"

"Worth going down there for."

She snorted. "Robbie thinks a bad day fishing is better than a good day doing anything else."

"Except having sex."

Jamie's grating paused before starting again. "I wouldn't know about that part."

"You've never slept with him?" The words came out before he realized it and brought a flush of heat to his neck.

The hunk of cheese stilled over the grater again. He stared: the cheese creamy-white, her pale slender fingers holding it delicately, the pinkish-tan nails the only spot of color. Her fingers tensed, then eased, and slowly began moving the cheese back and forth again.

"No, I never have," she said, sounding almost normal. Then her voice darkened. "One Calloway was enough for me."

He raised his gaze to her face then. Her forehead was lined, her mouth thinned, and she was concentrating as if getting the cheese into perfect shreds was of utmost importance. What she was really concentrating on, though, was not looking at him. Because she was lying? Or because she wasn't?

"He was interested and you weren't?" he asked.

"Neither of us was interested. We're friends. That's all we've ever been."

"We were friends, too, but we still slept together."

Finally she laid the cheese down, pushed the bowl away and rested her arms on the counter. "Is that what you think, Russ? That we were just friends with benefits?"

He shrugged.

"I've got news for you. You took me to dinner, to movies and concerts and home to spend the weekend with your family. I slept over at your house three or four or five times a week. Half my clothes stayed at your house. In the real world, that's called dating. You know, girlfriend-boyfriend, serious relationship, maybe moving toward something permanent. I don't sleep with friends. I don't just use whoever happens to be handy until someone better comes along. I'm not that shallow or insensitive."

"And I am?"

Her only response was a shrug.

Robbie was the shallow, insensitive one. Well, half the time he was; the other half, he pretended he was. Not Russ. He'd liked Jamie a lot, but there hadn't been a chance of anything permanent between them. After six and a half months together, he'd felt the same way he had when they'd started: like friends.

"I didn't use you," he disagreed. "I didn't lie to you. I didn't mislead you. We were friends—"

"Did you sleep with all your friends?"

"Of course not."

"You let me believe that there was something between us, something special. Something *serious.* I was in a relationship, and you—" her tone turned scornful "—were just having sex."

Water boiling on the stove gave him an excuse to turn away. He stirred the sauce and reset the microwave, then added handfuls of spaghetti to the pot. Something *serious,* she said. Just last night he'd told her that he'd never dated anyone seriously until Melinda—including her—and she'd walked away.

He'd deliberately said hurtful things to her before, something he wasn't proud of, but he hadn't meant to hurt her last night. He'd simply stated the truth. He'd never felt anything for any woman compared to what he'd felt for Melinda.

And he'd never thought about what any woman besides Melinda might have felt. Had Jamie cared about him? Had she thought they had a future together? Could she have thought he loved her—or, worse, that she'd loved him?

But it hadn't been that kind of affair. They'd been *friends.* Everyone had known it, except, apparently, her.

Everyone had treated them as a unit. If they invited Jamie out, it was assumed he would go, too. It was never just him or just her, but Russ-and-Jamie. After that first weekend when he'd brought her home with him, even his mother had expected her for every visit. She'd included Jamie in holiday and birthday celebrations. She'd even offered to let them share a room in her house.

Because she'd thought they were a couple. She'd thought Jamie was his girlfriend, maybe the one he'd marry. She had even made a few comments in that direction that he'd dismissed because everyone knew they were just friends.

With benefits.

Jeez, he really was the shallow and insensitive one.

"I'm sorry," he said at last. "I didn't…"

He didn't finish the statement, Jamie noticed. That was all right. She could supply several endings. He hadn't understood the difference between her perception and their reality six years ago. He hadn't known how much she cared. Hadn't thought she was important enough to care about.

She finished shredding the cheese. After rinsing the grater, she stuck it in the dishwasher, then leaned against the counter at the end of the island, a safe distance from Russ. The air was perfumed with the scents of tomato, garlic, onion and pasta, and he looked so domestic, stirring, chopping, doctoring salad mix into an appealing display of greens and fresh veggies.

There was something amazingly sexy about a man who knew his way around a kitchen.

Opting for a change of conversation, one that might stop her from thinking about Russ and sexy, she remarked, "I'm guessing you didn't learn to cook from Melinda."

He grimaced. "She was a worse cook than you."

So he'd noticed *something* six years ago while he wasn't loving, wanting or needing her. Not even the microwave had been her friend back then. She'd lived on take-out, delivery and sweets.

"Do you ever see her?"

He cast a sidelong glance her way. "No."

"Hear from her? Hear about her?"

"No. She screwed around on me. She left me. She lied to and about me, and she took half of everything I owned. Why in hell would I want to stay in touch with her?"

Because he'd loved her. And he'd only liked Jamie. As a friend. With benefits.

Yeah, yeah, life isn't fair. Get over it.

Giving herself a mental shake, she pushed away from the counter, located silverware and took a handful of paper napkins from a wooden holder on the island, then started toward the dining table.

"We can eat out on the deck," Russ said.

Following his suggestion, she carried the items outside instead. The deck stretched the length of the house, with doors opening into the living room, the dining room and what she presumed was Russ's bedroom. On the other side of the railing, azaleas formed a hedge, then a patch of yard led thirty feet to the banks of Holigan Creek. The furniture was wood—a table weathered silver, slat-backed chairs with thick cushions in green-and-white stripes—and a set of wind chimes hung from the eaves, tinkling softly in the breeze.

Jamie anchored the napkins under the silverware on the table, then walked to the steps. The creek marked the east edge of the yard. To the north and south, the woods formed a natural barrier. A lot of trees, heavy undergrowth, plenty of places to hide. Would Mischa alert on someone back there? Probably not. She was a city dog. She was accustomed to having people nearby.

Would Russ?

Probably, she thought with a wry smile. He *wasn't* accustomed to having people nearby. At least, not at home.

She turned to look at the third set of doors. Definitely Russ's bedroom. Without walking up and pressing her face to the glass, she couldn't see much beyond the massive bed to the left of the door—dark wood, white linens, a bloodred comforter. Jamie knew that bed well. Mahogany, rice carvings on the four posters, the patina of a two-hundred-year-old finish. She'd slept in it many times, had made love in it even more.

Did Russ remember that? Was he ever haunted by the ghosts of all the "friends" who'd slept there with him? Had they understood the rules better than she? Had she been the only one foolish enough to think she mattered?

She'd been twenty-four years old and had graduated from college with honors. She'd dated a lot, had even been in love a time or two. She would have described herself as experienced. Nobody's fool. Only Russ's.

Russ came out with two plates of spaghetti and steaming sauce, then returned for the salads. She brought the drinks and the cheese, then eyed Mischa. "You coming?"

The dog yawned, then snuggled deeper into the chair.

"Behave." With that warning, she closed the door, then sat

down across from Russ, moved her fork to her plate and
spread her napkin in her lap.

"Does she know the meaning of that word?" he asked dryly.

"She knows. She just doesn't care."

"You could train her."

"We've lived together three years with me the only one
getting trained, and that's fine with both of us."

"You going to raise your kids like that when you have them?"

Though the question, so carelessly asked, hit a nerve deep
inside her, she hid it as she sprinkled cheese over the pasta.
"I don't know if I'll have kids."

"Don't you want at least a couple?"

She did, and he knew it. Four was a good number, they'd
agreed. She had three sisters; he had three brothers. He'd
wanted sons. She preferred a mix. She'd wanted his kids. He
hadn't wanted hers, she knew now.

"Call me old-fashioned, but I need a husband to have kids.
Since I don't know anyone whose genes I would be remotely
interested in sharing with my children, that puts a kink in things."

"There are a lot of single guys in town. Tommy."

"Didn't work." She tasted the spaghetti. "Mmm, this is good."

His eyes narrowed and something she couldn't identify
flashed through them. "You went out with Tommy?"

She wondered for a moment what it was. Curiosity? Annoyance? It couldn't have been anything more. Nothing of
substance like possessiveness or jealousy. A person had to
care to feel those emotions.

"Just once. I've been out with everybody once." At least,
it felt that way. Once was usually all it took to know that the
chemistry wasn't there. They might be handsome, sexy,
charming guys, but whatever she was looking for, they didn't
have it. "What about you? Don't you date?"

"I don't have time."

"Your boss must be a real slave driver."

His gaze narrowed again and just the corners of his mouth turned up in a sarcastic impression of a smile.

She wanted to press on, to ask when his last date was, which "friend" he'd used for sex since the divorce, but because she *wanted* to know, she refused to let herself ask. Instead, she stuck with the subject of his work. "Does it bother your family that you chose construction over practicing law?"

He shrugged. "Half the law degrees in the family are used for nothing but wall decoration. Granddad was probably a little disappointed, but Mom never cared."

"All Sara wanted was for you to be happy. And your work makes you happy even if your marriage and divorce didn't."

His brows drew together in a scowl. "The marriage is over, and I'm fine with the divorce."

"Yeah. You work all the time, you live out here alone in the middle of nowhere—" she gestured to the wilderness around them with her fork "—you don't date and you do God knows what for sex. Sure, you're the textbook definition of *fine.*"

"You work all the time, you live alone in the middle of town, you don't go out with anyone more than once and you do God knows what for sex. At least I have the divorce from hell as an excuse. What's yours?"

She took a bite of gooey cheese, slightly sweet sauce and perfectly cooked spaghetti, savored every flavor of it, then washed it down with cold water before simply replying, "You."

His mouth thinned, the muscles in his jaw tightening, but he didn't argue, didn't apologize. Instead, he changed the subject. "When you left Macon, why did you come to Copper Lake?"

Easy question. She'd answered it a dozen times, asked by her parents, her sisters, her associates at the law firm, her

friends. *I want to make a new start. I've always intended to
go out on my own. I've got friends there. It's a great little town
that can use another good attorney.* "Robbie said it would
lower his long-distance bill."

"Yeah, I'm sure Robbie's phone bill was a concern."

She smiled at his dry comment. "I know you have trouble
grasping the concept, but most people like to stay in touch
with their friends."

"Robbie keeps in touch with every friend he ever had. He
still talks to the girl who sat across the aisle from him in kin-
dergarten, and she's lived in California for twenty years."

She believed that. "And you consider catching a glimpse
of someone driving past contact enough."

"Sometimes too much," he muttered.

Jamie figured he was referring to her in the past three
years, when she'd finally come to mean something to him.

"So why Copper Lake?"

"I liked what I knew of the town and the people. It was far
enough from Macon that it seemed safe, but I could still get
back there quickly if I needed to. It appealed to me." And it
had felt *right*. The minute Robbie had made the suggestion,
she'd pictured the town—the square, the lovely old buildings,
the river—and herself in it, belonging. The trauma of the
attack had left her feeling so out of place in Macon, in her
office, at home, even in her parents' home where she'd grown
up. She'd needed desperately to belong somewhere again.

"Why did you take Melinda's case? Were you that pissed
off with me?"

She left her chair, going to sit on the top step that led to
the grass and the creek. In the quiet evening, insects buzzed
along the water's surface, and a fish occasionally popped up
before splashing back and sending ripples to the banks. "I was

never pissed off. I was hurt. You'd broken my heart and you didn't care. Didn't even realize it, I know now." She shook her head regretfully. "God, you were clueless. And so was I. I knew you could be dense, but I had no idea just how thick-headed you really were."

After a moment, there was a creak, then bare feet on wood. He sat down a short distance to her right, his pop in one hand, her bottled water in the other. "Don't worry about my ego," he said wryly.

"You Calloways have way more than enough of that." She accepted the water and took a long drink while eying him peripherally. His T-shirt and jeans, per usual, were snug-fitting and well-worn. The jeans had a hole in one knee and a two-inch rip in the other leg that had frayed into a mass of soft thread. He smelled of soap and shampoo and sunshine-fresh laundry detergent. He'd shaved while he was in the shower, his jaw smooth with just a tiny nick on his adam's apple. He was a brave man, putting a razor to his throat while the Queen of the Damned was in his house.

"Melinda needed a lawyer," she said at last. "I needed a client. I was new, bumming office space off Robbie, looking for some billable hours. That first year, I took every single case that came my way. I couldn't afford to be choosy. Someone was going to represent her. Someone was going to get paid for it. I figured it might as well be me. Robbie said you'd understand that it was just business."

For a time Russ stared across the yard. She couldn't tell whether he was seeing the creek or the woods beyond, or three years into the past. After a time, though, he raised his pop, took a deep swallow, then said, "Robbie says a lot of things."

"You could have hired me yourself."

He looked at her, and she could tell that the thought had

never crossed his mind. He was a lawyer himself. So was his brother and half of his extended family.

After a minute, he shrugged. "Yeah, well, if I ever find myself considering getting married again, I've got dibs on you for the divorce."

The idea of him marrying another woman, falling in love with another woman, stung deep inside, but Jamie hid it behind a smile. "You've got to get out of this house and off the job sites to meet someone first."

"Nah. I prefer things the way they are."

"Don't you ever get lonely?" She expected him to brush off the question, or to make some flippant response or even turn it back on her. He didn't.

"Lonely beats miserable every time. Trust me. I know."

Chapter 6

About ten seconds after that last comment that told way more than Russ had meant to say, Mischa let herself out the door, trotted over and forced her way between them. As soon as she'd wiggled into the space, she turned her back to Jamie, put all four feet against him and pushed hard until he was against the railing.

"I don't think your dog likes me." Sitting next to Jamie and smelling her faint scents was a hell of a lot better place to be than next to Mischa, smelling her not-faint-enough dog scent and catching all-too-frequent glimpses of her bared teeth.

"Mischa loves everybody. She's just not used to having a man around."

And she wasn't making any effort to get used to it. "Does she always open the door herself?"

"Only when there's something on the other side that she wants a lot. That's one of the reasons I keep the outside doors at home locked all the time. Otherwise, she'd be letting herself out every time she saw a squirrel."

Mischa's ears pricked, and she scanned the area intently before laying her head down again.

"So she doesn't let you know when there's an intruder, but you get fair warning on every squirrel."

Jamie smiled. "It's a good thing I bought her for companionship and not protection."

She was pretty when she smiled. It brightened her whole face, made her eyes sparkle and eased the lines of tension. For just that moment, she looked as if everything was right in her world. There was no stalker, no danger, no threat to her spoiled dog or herself. She wasn't being forced to look over her shoulder or worry. She just looked pretty. Happy. As if life held promise.

How long had it been since he'd felt that way? Longer than three years. Maybe closer to six. He couldn't remember exactly when he'd realized there were problems with Melinda. The two and a half months they'd dated had been pretty damn good. Of course, he'd lived in Athens and she'd been in Charlotte, so they'd seen each other only on weekends. The first year of their marriage had been good, too. He was building their house along with his business. Money wasn't a problem; Melinda hadn't had to work. Everyone in town had accepted her as if she'd been born there. She'd shopped and lunched and shown her appreciation every night.

But gradually the appreciation diminished until it wasn't even a memory. She'd spent the money but complained about the time he spent earning it. She'd wanted more than he and Copper Lake had to offer. She was unhappy and determined to share the feeling with him.

Then somewhere along there, the affairs had started. She'd stopped loving him, and no matter how hard he'd tried, he'd stopped loving her, too. Divorce had been inevitable. Given the woman Melinda was, the nastiness of it had been inevitable, as well.

No matter who she'd hired to represent her.

"I understand Mitch's wife is pregnant."

He glanced Jamie's way, just enough to catch a blur of colors. "Yeah. He says he's living in Hormone Hell—but not when she's within striking distance."

"When is the baby due?"

"October."

"Sara must be thrilled."

"Aw, hell, yeah. She started talking about grandbabies around the time each of us graduated from college. But Mitch's first marriage ended in divorce, and so did mine, and Rick took his sweet time about getting married."

"I'm lucky," Jamie said. "My sisters have provided my parents with eleven grandchildren. The pressure's off me."

"I don't think it's supposed to work that way. Mom's response to Jessica's pregnancy was to remind the rest of us that she's not getting any younger and neither are we."

Her gaze turned on him. He could feel its heat, its weight. "Do you still want kids?"

He liked kids. When the extended family got together, he was the one who played football, baseball or soccer with them, who took them on hikes or fishing or berry-picking in the summer heat. It had always been an assumption, on his part as well as his mother's: he would grow up, get married, have kids, do the dad thing. Virtually every Calloway did it, some more successfully than others.

But did he *want* kids? Truthfully, yeah. He wanted to make

Sara a grandmother several times over. Wanted to be the kind of father he'd never had, the kind Mitch would be, and Rick and eventually Robbie.

But instead of telling Jamie that, he shrugged and parroted her earlier response. "I'd need a wife to have kids, and since I don't know anyone whose genes I would be interested in sharing with my children…"

She didn't say anything to that. In fact, for a long time she did nothing but stare out into the deepening dusk, lazily scratching Mischa's belly. Occasionally her hand stilled, and the dog pawed at her until she started again, but she didn't glance his way, didn't seem to even notice that he was still there.

After a time, he crumpled his pop can and pushed himself to his feet. Mischa's head jerked around at the sudden movement, as if she'd also forgotten he was there, and a growl sounded low in her throat.

"Shh, Mischa," Jamie chided. "He didn't mean to scare you."

Oh, yeah, the mutt *looked* scared, he thought dryly as he moved to the table, gathering dishes. He cleared the table and went inside to the sink.

A moment later, Jamie came to the door. "Go on, Mischa. Go pee on something." Half a heartbeat later, she murmured, "Not that."

Russ took the necessary steps to look out the French door. Mischa had obeyed Jamie. She was standing at the top of the steps, urinating on the spot where he'd sat. He shook his head and flatly said, "I really don't think she likes me."

"I'm sorry," Jamie said, but she kind of hiccupped when she said it and then, despite her best efforts, a laugh slipped out.

And though Russ didn't find anything particularly

amusing about getting pissed on figuratively if not literally, he laughed, too.

For the first time in a long time.

On Saturday morning, Jamie awoke to a dark room, Mischa's body solid and warm against her back, virtually no light seeping in around the blinds. It must be the wee hours, she thought, until she brought the numbers on the bedside clock into focus. Seven-fifteen. Then she recognized the sound of rain beating against the roof.

Slipping from the bed, she padded to the nearest window and peeked out between the slats. The sky was practically night dark, and the rain poured in a steady deluge. It overflowed the gutters, puddled in the yard and flowed along in the creek at a merry pace.

She sighed softly. She didn't mind rain as a rule, but Mischa hated to get her feet wet. The good news was that Jamie wouldn't have to hose down the deck this morning. The bad news was that she would have to force Mischa out the door to do her business, then deal with wet doggy when she came in.

Leaving the dog asleep on the bed, she went to the bathroom next door for a quick shower. She'd just put on panties and bra and was reaching for the sundress she'd hung on the back of the door when a distant voice sounded.

"James! You want to come out here?" Russ's voice sounded equal parts demand and caution.

She hastily undid the buttons, yanked the dress off the hanger and wrapped it around her, then began fastening the buttons from the bottom up as she hurried down the hall and into the living room. She picked up a low hum as soon as she turned the corner but didn't realize that it was a snarl until she saw Russ, backed into the corner where the kitchen counters met, and Mischa a few feet away, head lowered, rump in the air, tail quivering excitedly.

She was stunned. Sweet Mischa, who would expose her belly to total strangers in the hopes of getting a scratch, was bristling all over. Russ looked more annoyed than concerned, but he had the good sense to remain calm and still.

Jamie moved between them and pointed at the dog. "Mischa, *bad girl.*"

Mischa looked at her, those big brown eyes so innocent, then ended the snarl, yawned, stretched and regally walked around the island into the dining room.

"I'm so sorry," Jamie said, turning to face Russ. "She's never acted this way before. I don't know…"

He was looking at her, but he wasn't listening. And he wasn't actually looking at her face. His gaze had settled lower, on the buttons she'd forgotten the moment she'd seen Mischa. The cotton print gapped open across her breasts, and since the dress fitted snugly when done up properly, it was quite a gap. Her bra was no more revealing than a swimsuit top, but it *felt* more so. It was lingerie, not meant to be seen by just anyone.

Not that Russ was just *anyone.*

She was standing too close to him, her position dictated by Mischa's. He wasn't wearing a shirt, just faded denim shorts that rode low on his hips, and heat radiated from him. His lids were lowered, and when he swallowed, she saw the lump in his throat, felt a similar lump in her chest, spreading and tightening, making a deep breath hard to come by.

She half wished he would touch her—it had been so long since anyone had touched her, even longer since he had—and was half afraid he would. No matter that he'd broken her heart and resented her like hell since the divorce, she would dissolve in a puddle of need if he stroked so much as a fingertip along the swell of her breast or the lace of her bra.

"Do you always match your underwear to your clothes?" His voice was hoarse and raspy and made her nerves tighten.

Unable to remember what she wore, she glanced down. Her dress was a summer print, white and aqua flowers on a salmon background, her bra a shade or two darker than the aqua. "Coincidence," she replied, sounding no stronger than him.

"Hmm." Soft sound. Sexy.

Then his gaze shifted and everything about him changed. He went still, and his muscles tightened, his body radiating tension instead of heat. "Jesus, Jamie."

He'd seen the scar that sliced across the top of her right breast. It was hidden by most of her bras, but not this one, with its lower-cut cups. It was two inches long, a neat zigzag created from an ugly wound.

Flushed with heat—arousal, not embarrassment—she took a few steps back as she raised shaky hands to finish up the buttons. "You know that saying, the first cut is the deepest? The first one hurt so much that I didn't really feel the other three."

"Was that…?"

She nodded. "There was one on my throat—" she touched it, a thin line that people rarely noticed "—and the other two are on my ribs."

"You're lucky to be alive."

Smiling shakily, she went to the refrigerator to get a bottle of water. "My fortune. Your misfortune."

"Don't say that!" His voice was loud, sharp. Its unexpected anger startled Jamie and, across the room in her new favorite chair, Mischa looked up warily. "I never wanted— I'd never wish—"

Guilt flashed through her. She knew he wasn't the kind of

person to wish harm to anyone. Wasn't that why she was here—because she could trust him? Because the only threat he represented was to her heart, not her life?

Now she was the one at a loss for words. "I didn't mean—" She touched his hand, wrapping her fingers around his. "I'm sorry. That was uncalled for. Sometimes it's just easier to joke."

Apology made, she squeezed his hand, then released it and would have walked away, but he didn't let go. She stared at their hands—large and small, strong and delicate, brown and callused, pale and soft. He did heavy labor with his hands every day, while she rarely did anything that posed a risk to her manicure. He could protect with those hands, could keep her safe, could make her weak, could bring her awesome satisfaction. He could hold her there or push her away, and because she really wanted to be held, she prayed he would push her away.

He didn't. His thumb stroked across the pulse on her wrist, and its beat doubled. Such a simple action for such an outrageous reaction. She thought her heart was thundering until the lights flickered around them, then went out, followed instantly by a flash of brilliant lightning. As the thunder rumbled away, she realized her heart *was* thundering. Her body had grown warm, from the tips of her still-damp hair to her bare toes, and for a moment she fancied she could feel steam rising off her in waves.

Without the kitchen lights, they stood in murky shadow. The air around them was still, undisturbed by the usual sounds like the refrigerator or the central air cycling on and off, and it felt heavy, alive with energy, awaiting the next clap of thunder, the next bolt of lightning.

Both came simultaneously, blinding, a deafening *cra-ack* as if a nearby tree had fallen victim to the strike. Involuntarily

Jamie moved a step closer to Russ; his fingers tightened comfortingly around hers and pulled slightly, barely perceptibly. Then he kissed her, and when he kissed her, it was as if a storm had been unleashed inside her. Her heart pounded, her breathing became labored, her blood rushed, her nerve endings sizzled and crackled.

It was a familiar kiss—greedy, coffee-flavored, Russ—and it danced through her, its usual effects intensified by the storm, their physical isolation, her hunger and need and loneliness and old love, interrupted love. She couldn't have avoided responding to it to save her life. Couldn't have stopped herself from taking a step forward, couldn't have kept her hands from raising to his shoulders or her arms from entwining around his neck.

Couldn't have pushed him away to save her life.

Thank God for Mischa.

Whining like the baby she was, the dog wound herself around Jamie's legs, stepped between her and Russ and pushed them a few inches apart. With the next round of thunder and lightning, she increased from a whine to a pitiful whimper and started climbing her way up Jamie's body until she had no choice but to break the kiss. Satisfied that she had Jamie's attention, Mischa gave a mournful bark, dropped to the floor and trotted to the French door.

Jamie couldn't tear her gaze from Russ's face. She felt exactly the way he looked: dazed, aroused, surprised, dismayed. "I usually have to take her out on the leash when it's raining," she murmured.

"I'll take her."

"I can."

"I'll take her," he repeated. But for a moment, until Mischa barked again, he didn't move, didn't stop staring at her. After

the bark, he abruptly strode to the table, picking up the leash
there, hooking it to Mischa's collar, then dragging her out the
door with him.

Jamie went to watch them. Russ was soaked by the time
they reached the steps, his hair flat against his head, his shorts
turning a darker shade of faded. Mischa looked back at her
as if hoping for a reprieve, then hung her head against the
torrent of rain and followed him down the steps into the wa-
terlogged grass.

Suddenly Jamie's knees went weak and she sank into the
nearest dining chair. That kiss… She'd never imagined that
they might be friends again, had never in her wildest dreams
fantasized that he might kiss her again. If she'd had any socks
on, he would have knocked them off. As it was, her toes were
still curled.

Thank God for Mischa.

She would *not* fall for Russ again. Wouldn't be his friend
and occasional bed partner. Wouldn't invest her emotion and
time in another one-sided relationship. Wouldn't risk her heart
again without some assurance that he was risking his, too.
Since the only person Russ held in lower regard than her was
his ex-wife, that didn't seem likely.

No more kisses. No even thinking about sex. They could
be friends, maybe, but without benefits.

A knock at the glass door startled her. She looked up to find
Russ and Mischa, soaked to the skin. "Grab some towels from
my bathroom," he said through the few inches of open door
space, keeping the leash wrapped tightly around his hand as
Mischa tried to drag him inside, "and meet us at the front door.
You can dry her off on the porch."

She nodded and went through the kitchen into his bedroom,
then the master bath. It was by far the best room in the house:

big, with skylights, intricate tile work, a large Jacuzzi tub, a glassed-in shower with multiple showerheads and a stone countertop. What a great place to get ready for work or to relax after work.

Or to set a seduction.

Grimacing, she took an armload of thick towels from the armoire that occupied most of one wall, then went to the front door. Russ and Mischa were waiting on the shelter of the porch. He dried himself with one towel while she used the others to get Mischa as dry as possible. The instant she finished, the dog gave a vigorous shake, splattering raindrops from deep inside her coat everywhere.

"About that kiss," Jamie began as she rubbed the dog with the damp towel one more time.

Russ gave her a flat stare. "What kiss?"

The one that made my hair sweat and steamed the polish right off my toe nails, she wanted to reply. But sure. If he wanted to pretend it hadn't happened, she could go along. Better than discussing it to death, right?

The power was back on when they went inside. She fed Mischa, then found a box of cereal and milk for her own breakfast while Russ changed into dry clothes. He was scowling when he returned to fix himself a cup of coffee and a toaster pastry, then settled in the other leather chair with his laptop.

When the phone rang, it seemed so out of place that it startled her. Russ didn't flinch, though, or rise from his chair to answer. Instead, after two rings the answering machine clicked on.

"Russell, it's your mother. Don't forget that dinner is at seven tonight. Rick and Amanda are on their way, so don't try to weasel out. I'm sure Robbie told you that bringing a date wouldn't displease me at all. I hear that Ginny Pearce's daughter is visiting from Montgomery. Didn't you go out with her in school? She's not married, you know, and prettier than ever. Think about her, will you? I don't expect a call back, but I do expect to see you at seven. Be careful, babe. I love you."

Jamie felt a sudden twinge of homesickness. That was exactly the kind of message her mother used to leave for her. Janine Munroe had been better informed about the available men in Macon than Jamie ever was. For thirty-five years and counting, she'd had a happy marriage and wanted the same for all four of her daughters. Since the stabbing, she didn't pressure Jamie the way she had before, but she surely wouldn't be displeased if her third daughter fell in love with someone who loved her back.

She rinsed her dishes, then went to sit on the sofa, tucking her feet beneath her. "You're not planning on weaseling out because of me, are you?"

Russ didn't even glance her way. "You can't stay here alone."

"Of course I can. No one knows I'm here. How could I be any safer?" He didn't answer that because he had no answer. She would have gone on even if he had. "I'm thinking I shouldn't stay here at all."

That did make him look at her. Correction: scowl at her. "You're not going back to your house, not when Tommy's no closer to finding this guy."

No, she didn't want to go home and stay by herself while the mystery guy was still running around. She was a weenie, but she wasn't stupid. And she really didn't want to go to a motel. But there was one alternative they hadn't considered. "Actually, I was thinking about Robbie's condo. It's a gated community. You can't get in without the security guard clearing you. It's got an alarm system, with a panic button that sounds in the security office, and Tommy lives only two blocks away."

His expression was blank, but he didn't argue with her. He knew the River Crossing condos were secure; *he'd* built them. Robbie's fishing trip was no secret. No one would expect her to suddenly move in, and even if people did figure it out, no one would be able to get to her.

After a moment, he turned his attention back to the computer. "We'll ask Tommy later."

"I don't need Tommy's permission." She paused, then politely added, "I don't need your permission, either. I have the key to Robbie's place and the code to the alarm."

"You need a ride from me to get there."

She was about to inform him that she could manage on her own. Lys would be happy to pick her up...if her low-slung little car could handle the dirt roads with all this rain. If Jamie could manage to give her halfway decent directions, which she couldn't. Hadn't she commented to Russ that all those intersections looked the same? And he'd said something smart, like *not if you know what you're looking for.* She didn't, and neither would Lys.

Tommy would give her a ride. If she told him where she was going. If he agreed that it was a good idea. If he gave his permission.

Maybe she could call Sara. Man, the questions that would raise. And Sara was a mother. If Russ told her it was safer for Jamie to stay where she was, Sara would believe him and refuse to help.

She was a prisoner, Jamie realized, and she didn't like the feeling.

"Maybe we could call Tommy now," she said, careful to keep her voice even.

Again, Russ didn't look up from the computer. "It's Saturday. Tommy stays out late on Friday, sleeps in late on

Saturday. You wake him before eleven, he's not going to be happy, especially if he's not alone."

It was a fair bet if he wasn't alone that the woman wouldn't wake up denying whatever had happened, she thought with a scowl. Of course, sleeping with Tommy wasn't stupid or risky, unless she had a husband tucked away somewhere. Kissing Russ *was* stupid and risky and could so easily lead to stupider and riskier stuff that she would regret deeply once it was over.

Then she glanced at him. But damned if she wouldn't enjoy it tremendously before it was over.

A few minutes after eleven, Russ set the laptop aside, went to the French doors and stretched as he gazed out. The rain showed no sign of moving on; a check of the weather online had shown a system stalled over the region. The creek had risen a few inches, but was still a good foot from flooding. He'd seen it come out of its banks a few times, but he wasn't worried about it.

Jamie had finally gotten a book from the shelves, read for a while, then dozed off on the couch. The hellhound had slept, too, her snores damn near hypnotic. He'd managed to finish the bid he was submitting next week for the restoration of an antebellum home twenty miles south of Copper Lake, but if he'd stayed in that chair five minutes more, he'd have been asleep, too.

He and Jamie and the demon dog all asleep together in the same room. Six years ago he would have joined her on the couch. Better yet, he would have undone the buttons on that dress and awakened her slowly, with his mouth and his hands, and they would have moved into the bedroom for a little play before snoozing. They'd spent a lot of rainy days together in that bed. A lot of sunny ones, too. And one hell of a lot of steamy nights.

If the dog had waited just two minutes to decide she needed to go out, odds were damn good that they would have wound up there this morning. He hadn't kissed a woman, held a woman, gotten so close that he could feel the heat and softness and desire coming off her in waves, in longer than he wanted to recall. One glimpse of Jamie's breasts, one whiff of her subtle, sexy perfume, and he'd wanted, damn it, wanted sex, wanted steam, wanted *her*. They'd always been good together, always satisfied each other.

He'd been unsatisfied for so damn long.

Her moving into Robbie's was for the best. She would be as safe there as she was here, and Russ would be safer, too. If he was ready to have sex again—and apparently he was—he could find someone else, someone he didn't have a history with. Someone he hadn't hurt before and couldn't hurt again.

His mom had mentioned her friend Ginny's daughter. Vicki Pearce had been a year behind Russ in school, a cheerleader, homecoming queen, and unofficially The Girl Most Likely To do whatever a guy wanted. He could call her, take her to dinner, make Sara happy and, unless Vicki had done a one-eighty, probably make himself happy.

While Jamie stayed alone at Robbie's.

With a glance to make sure she was still asleep, Russ went into the bedroom and called Tommy from the phone there. Tommy was awake, but just barely, and there was someone with him. Female. Husky-voiced.

Russ sat on the bed, stuffing pillows behind his back. "Hey, Jamie wants to go stay at Robbie's condo. I think it's a good idea. What about you?"

There was a moment's silence, then, "What did you do to her?"

"Nothing." *Liar.* The kiss had come out of nowhere. He

hadn't been thinking about it, hadn't been wanting it. He'd just suddenly *done* it.

And she'd kissed him back. Put her arms around him. Clung to him.

"So she's been fine there for two nights, and now suddenly she wants to go stay by herself in town where it's a lot more likely her stalker can find her? And you didn't do anything?"

With his free hand, Russ rubbed the spot between his eyes where a headache was forming. "Yeah, exactly. So should I take her or make her stay here?"

Tommy was silent, no doubt weighing the options. He knew the pros of Robbie's condo, including the fact that he could get there in under two minutes in an emergency and that onsite security could do it even quicker. The biggest advantage to Russ's house—the isolation—was also its biggest disadvantage in an emergency.

"You guys aren't hitting it off, huh?"

"We're getting along fine." For a few minutes that morning, *too* fine.

"Yeah, sure. That's why she's looking to leave and you're looking to let her." Tommy didn't bother to hide his yawn. "Okay. Tell her I'll come get her this afternoon. I want to look around the condo when she goes."

Russ was about to volunteer to deliver her himself, but he cut off the offer. Tommy was the cop. This was his case, his responsibility. All Russ had owed Jamie was a safe place for a few days, and he'd given her that. No one expected more. "Call before you come," he said shortly.

"I will. Don't want to give you an excuse to shoot me."

"Man, if I were going to do that, I'd've done it years ago. Later." Russ hung up, then gazed at the phone. He could call Vicki Pearce now. She'd made clear the last time he'd seen her that she would like to spend some time with him. He hadn't been in the mood then, but things had changed. He could look her up in the phone book, or call his mother and ask for the number. Sara would be thrilled, and Vicki would enjoy dinner with the family, and if she was still The Girl Most Likely To…

He tried to imagine him and her, together in this bed, but the picture wouldn't form. He could put himself there, of course, and with a woman, but instead of Vicki's white-blond hair, this woman had brown hair that fell past her shoulders whenever she let it out of the clips and bands. She had a light dust of freckles across her nose and cheeks, eyes the color of an autumn sky and a mouth made for kissing.

And a scar marring the soft, delicate skin of her breast.

The memory was as effective on his arousal as a blast of ice water. A man had tried to kill her. *His* son had committed a crime, and he'd wanted to punish her for it by taking her life. What kind of lunatic reasoning was that?

It made about as much sense as his own behavior, he was forced to admit. It was Melinda who'd screwed him over, Melinda who'd made his life hell. Yet he'd taken his anger out on Jamie, because Melinda had left town, because Jamie had been his friend, because he'd thought she owed him better than that.

He'd dated her, slept with her, had—but denied—a serious relationship with her. He'd dropped her without a second thought when he met Melinda, had broken her heart and not had a clue, yet he'd thought she owed him because of their friendship. He was a dumb, arrogant bastard.

He wasn't going to call Vicki Pearce. Wasn't going to ask her out for the sole purpose of seducing her. Wasn't going to use her when his mind was on someone else.

He might be a slow learner, but he did eventually learn.

Returning to the kitchen, he laid out the items necessary for lunch on the island. Mischa raised her head to watch, then eased to the floor, stretched and sauntered around the island. He watched her warily, occasionally slipping a piece of sliced ham or bread to her as he assembled three fat sandwiches, buttered the outside of the bread and put them on the grill to brown.

The sandwiches were sizzling, and the dog was deciding that anyone who provided treats couldn't be all bad when Jamie stirred on the couch. The dress moved first, the bright fabric shifting with her, then her legs straightened and her arms raised in a taut stretch. Slowly she pushed herself up on one elbow, facing him over the back of the couch. Strands of hair had come free and fell over her face. She shoved them back, released the clip and shook her hair loose, then sniffed appreciatively. "Grilled bread," she said with a smile, her voice husky from sleep.

"Grilled ham, cheese, pickle, onion and olive sandwiches with spicy mustard and mayo," he corrected.

"They smell wonderful." She stood and stretched again, the movement pulling the hem of her dress almost indecently high. With her hair down and mussed, her feet bare and a soft, hazy look on her face, she looked vulnerable…and sexy as hell.

If inviting her to stay here hadn't been the worst idea in his life, letting her leave might qualify.

She retrieved the book from where it had fallen among the cushions, set it on the end table, then came into the kitchen. Without being asked, she took out plates and napkins and filled glasses with ice. He watched her pop the top on a soda can and pour it into one glass, then do the same with the second, careful not to let the fizz overflow, and he resisted the urge to comb his fingers through her hair, to smooth the out-of-place strands. To remind himself how it felt. Soft. Silky.

"What do you normally do on a Saturday?"

It took him a moment to realize she'd asked him a question and rein in his thoughts so he could answer. "Clean house if it needs it. Catch up on laundry and paperwork. Go fishing or hunting." What he didn't do was spend it with people. While a certain amount of time alone was good, too much was just pathetic. His mom had been telling him for months that he needed to get out, but he'd insisted he was good.

No need to tell Sara that he'd finally seen how right she was.

After checking the sandwiches, he took a container of potato salad from the refrigerator and set it on the island next to the plates. Obligingly Jamie added a serving spoon and forks to the dishes.

"I clean house and do laundry, too," she volunteered. "And I run errands and buy groceries, which usually amounts to a twenty-pound bag of dog food, treats for Mischa and for me and a stack of frozen entrées. If Lys didn't provide me with doughnuts and/or pizza for breakfast most mornings, I would probably start to look like those little stiff cardboard boxes."

To keep himself from studying all the ways she *didn't* look like a stiff little cardboard box, he asked, "Why did you hire Lys?"

"She had secretarial experience, she's a paralegal, she's nice and she was willing to work for what I could pay. Why wouldn't I hire her?"

"Because she's a freak."

"Why do you and Tommy insist on calling her that? She's a nice, smart, pretty woman who's just a little…"

"Freaky."

"Different."

"Different word, same meaning." He dished up one sandwich on the first plate, two on the second, then set them aside to cool a little before he sliced them in half. "Lys has been weird for as long as I can remember. She always went out of her way to be different. She listened to weird music, read weird books, did the whole living-dead thing with her clothes and makeup."

"She was in training to work with the Queen of the Damned," Jamie pointed out.

Russ grimaced, but didn't apologize for the nickname. "She never seemed to like anyone a whole lot, and she's always had a special place in her cold heart for Calloways. I don't know if she just hates us in general or on principle, but she hates us."

After he sliced the sandwiches diagonally, he spooned potato salad onto the plate with two halves, then handed it to Jamie before scooping out his own salad.

"You Calloways make an easy target," Jamie said thoughtfully as she carried her plate and drink to the dining table. "At one time you owned the whole damn county. Your family still owns or controls probably half the businesses and four-fifths of the money in town. When you have generation after generation working their entire lives for Calloways and watching you guys prosper while they just get by, it's only natural to have some resentment."

She sat at the side of the table. He slid into the chair on the end and bumped knees with her. "You make us sound like some sort of evil land barons, getting rich off the blood, sweat and tears of the working class."

"In a world of haves and have-nots, no one would argue that the Calloways are definitely among the haves."

He scowled at her, but he wasn't really annoyed. She wasn't telling him anything he hadn't already heard or figured out on his own. "Some of us work for what we have."

"I know. And some of you never do a worthwhile thing in your lives."

"So Lys dislikes us because my great-great-great-grand-daddy had some money when he came to this country and he used it to make more money."

Jamie grinned. "I don't have a clue why Lys dislikes you. Truth is, your family is a subject we tend to avoid except when it comes to Robbie."

Mention of Robbie reminded Russ of the afternoon's plans, and the muscles in his jaw tightened a notch. "I called Tommy while you were asleep. He said he'll come out and pick you up later today. He'll take you to Robbie's."

She grew serious, too. Because he'd reminded her that she had a stalker? Or was there a chance that she'd changed her mind about leaving? "Okay," she said quietly, then she smiled, but there was something strained about it. "Nice of Robbie to go out of town at just the time I need a place to stay."

"Yeah, tell him that. I'll bet he'd be happy to extend his vacation until he's fished the ocean dry."

"Only a fool would bet against Robbie and fishing." Again with the strained smile. "And I'm no fool."

Chapter 7

It was still raining hard when Tommy arrived at Russ's house in his SUV. He parked as close to the garage as he could so Russ could load Jamie's bags without getting them too wet, then grimaced when Russ whistled and Mischa leaped in the rear door. "Aw, man, I didn't realize you had the mutt. I would've brought my department car if I'd known."

Mischa rested her front feet on the console and leaned forward to nuzzle Tommy's jaw. He rewarded her with a scratch.

Jamie stood beneath the roof overhang in the small space protected from the rain and faced Russ. "Well...thanks."

He nodded.

"I really appreciate..." She shrugged, and he nodded again. Since he had nothing to say, she bobbed her head once, too, then darted into the rain and into the dry doggy-scented SUV. "Sit, Mischa," she said absently as she fastened her seat belt, and the dog did. Russ went into the garage as Tommy started to back up. The door lowered, blocking him from sight, and she gave a small sigh.

Naturally Tommy heard it. "Is that relief or regret?"

"Mind your own business, Tommy."

"You're my case. You are my business."

"My stalker's your business."

"Every tiny little aspect of your life is my business."

"Have you learned anything?"

Tommy grinned. "Sorry, darlin'. It's the weekend. I'm off. Unless this guy does something new, I'm not gonna do anything more than maybe think about him until Monday."

Jamie fell silent, gazing out the window. For dirt, the road was in amazingly good shape after all the rain. Years of use by heavy logging trucks had compacted it until it was like rock. Mud was rare, erosion rarer.

Tommy turned on the stereo after a few minutes, and the music of Carrie Underwood accompanied them the rest of the way into town. As the turnoff for her street appeared ahead, Jamie finally spoke. "I'd like to stop at my house and pick up some clothes and my car."

"You can use Robbie's car if you need to go out. He said you know where the spare keys are."

"Robbie's 1957 Corvette? That's not going to draw attention to me, is it?" she asked drily. "I'd rather have my own car. If I got a scratch on the 'vette, he'd never forgive me."

"Nah. He'd use it as an excuse to do a whole new paint job."

"I'd rather have my car," she repeated. "I don't plan on going anywhere before Monday. I just want it available in case…" Of an emergency. "And I need clothes. I'm not wearing Robbie's."

"Yeah, sure, okay." He slowed, flipped on the signal and turned onto Walton Way.

The neighborhood seemed a little closer, a little darker, because of the rain. Sodden branches dipped lower to the ground. No one was working in the yard or walking a dog. The houses were closed up, outside lights on in the middle of the afternoon.

Jamie suppressed a shudder as Tommy pulled into her driveway.

"Will Mischa stay?" he asked.

"If you're fast enough. But I should put her in my car."

"She can ride over with me. We'll follow you to make sure no one's following you."

They left the truck and jogged through the rain to the stoop. Inside the house, Jamie flipped the light switch, but nothing happened. "Every house on the street has power but mine," she grumbled.

"The storm probably blew the transformer that feeds this end of the street. Get your stuff. I'm gonna look around."

She went upstairs to her bedroom and hastily gathered enough clothes and shoes for three or four days. Her makeup and toiletries were already in Tommy's truck, and she had enough earrings, hair clips and scrunchies to last the whole summer. Staying alone at Robbie's, she'd have no use for the bathrobe hanging on the back of the closet door. The only other thing she wanted was her pillow. She grabbed the garment bag in one hand, the pillow in the other, and hurried downstairs.

Tommy was coming down the hall from the back of the house. "Everything looks the same as it did Thursday. No break-in, no obvious attempt."

She swallowed hard as she took a slicker from the hall closet. "If he knows I'm not staying here right now, would he come back?"

"Maybe. The idea is to let you know how easily he can gain access. Wouldn't it freak you out to know he'd been in here, touching your stuff, maybe lying in your bed, going through your clothes?"

She looked at the garment bag and shuddered again. If she thought the stalker had been in her house, she honestly didn't know if she could live there again. It was her home, her safe haven, and that was such a violation. "I'm burning the sheets on my bed and buying all new underwear. Just in case."

Tommy took the clothes, she wrapped the pillow in the slicker, and after locking up, they made a dash to their vehicles. "I'll be right behind you," he called before he opened the truck door, shoved Mischa aside, then climbed inside.

Jamie's car started on the first try. It smelled faintly of Lys's perfume and even more faintly of the garage. She switched the wipers to high and drove at a slower-than-normal speed through the neighborhood.

Robbie's condo was on the south edge of town, between the river and the old paper mill that was the center of Copper Lake's museum complex. She turned off the main road onto a narrower, two-lane street that followed the curves of the river. Tommy had been forced to stop for oncoming traffic, so she slowed even more, her gaze shifting between the road ahead and the SUV still waiting to turn.

She hated the nerves. It was the middle of a Saturday afternoon, and she was in the middle of a completely respectable neighborhood in a safe little town. There was no reason for the fine hairs on her nape to be standing on end, no reason for her fingers to be gripping the steering wheel so tightly.

Then, suddenly, there was. The pickup came out of nowhere, screeching around a corner and appearing in Jamie's rearview mirror. The driver was traveling too fast; the wheels slipped and the truck skidded sideways before gaining traction again.

"Oh, God," Jamie whispered as the truck filled her mirror. All she could see of the driver was a shape—dark clothes, dark hair or a hat. Her hands knotted on the wheel as she rounded a curve, the pickup only inches off her bumper. There was a short straightaway, a few hundred yards, and the driver suddenly whipped into the other lane, gunned the engine and drew even with her car.

It was just some stupid kid who didn't know better than to play around on wet streets, she thought with relief. He was going to pass her, probably laughing about the scare he'd given her.

She braked, leaving him plenty of room to move back into the lane before the next curve, but he slowed, too, then abruptly jerked the wheel to the right. Metal ground against metal. Unprepared for the move, Jamie was flung to the side before her seat belt locked, stopping her, and her hands automatically jerked the steering wheel to the right, as well.

The car bounced violently as it left the roadway. Murmuring squeaky prayers, she fought to control it, but another crashing blow from the pickup was more than she could handle. She slammed on the brakes and the car spun crazily, skidding sideways across the opposite lane, bouncing across the water-filled ditch before coming to a jarring stop.

Mud from the ditch covered her windshield. The wipers were stalled midswipe, and her head was hurting like a son of a bitch. Jamie raised one hand to her left temple, expecting to find blood, but it came away dry. She'd cracked it against the window, she guessed, but not hard enough to break the skin. Just hard enough to make even shallow breathing hurt.

Tires squealed, and for an instant, she tensed, wondering if the pickup had returned. But through the mud, she recognized Tommy's SUV. It took her a moment to find the button to roll down the window a few inches.

"Jeez, Jamie, are you okay?"

She started to nod, but pain stopped her. "Y-yeah, I think so."

"I called it in. Stay in the car and lock the doors. I'm gonna see if I can catch this bastard."

She rolled the window up again, let her head sink back and closed her eyes, concentrating on not moving, not thinking, not being too terrified. Maybe it wasn't the stalker, wasn't connected to him in any way. Maybe it had just been a bizarre coincidence, some stupid kid playing stupid games. The stalker couldn't have followed them from her house or Tommy would have noticed him. He couldn't have known to find her on this road. She couldn't even remember the last time she'd been to Robbie's. A month ago? He couldn't have found her here.

But in her gut, she knew he had. It was no coincidence, no stupid kid. Somehow he'd known where she would be.

But only Tommy knew. And Russ. And she knew it hadn't been Tommy.

Moving her head gingerly, she straightened, then located her purse in the floor. She dug out her cell phone and the business card Russ had given her, then punched in his home number.

The answering machine picked up, the message short and to the point. "This is Russ. Leave a message."

"Hey, Russ." *Please be home, please be home.* "It's Jamie. I, uh, I just got run off Forsythe Road about a half mile south of Carolina Avenue. Tommy's gone after the guy, and I'm waiting… I think my car's totaled, b-but I'm all right. I hit my head really hard. But I think—"

There was a click, a change in the sound of the line. "Jamie? What the hell happened?"

She was so relieved to hear his voice that she felt as if she were dissolving. "I don't know. This pickup...it just hit me. I, uh, I don't—" She broke off, tears filling her eyes, her hands starting to tremble. "The—the police are coming now."

"I'm on my way." The line went dead before she could say anything else.

Sirens wailing, first a police car, then an ambulance, pulled to the shoulder on the opposite side of the road. The officer jumped out, followed by the paramedics, and she fumbled with the door lock.

The officer asked questions about the pickup, the paramedics about her head, her vision, her pain. They hustled her from the car to the back of the ambulance where it was dry and well-lit, and they gave her a blanket to combat her shivers while they examined her.

The paramedics recommended a ride to the emergency room, and that made her shudder even more. She'd been in the back of an ambulance once, on an emergency run to the hospital. The prospect raised old memories, old fears, but she nodded meekly and let them strap her onto the gurney.

A moment later the big vehicle began moving, and she closed her eyes. The pain in her head was sharp and strong enough to make her regret having lunch a few hours ago. A sick headache, her mom used to call this kind of ache, and it did make her feel sick all over, exacerbated by her uncontrollable shaking.

The stalker had wanted to hurt her, maybe even kill her. Or, more likely, he'd wanted to remind her that she was vulnerable, wanted to toy with her and keep her scared until he made his final move. Harlan Davis had been much more straightforward about his desire to punish her. He'd decided to kill her, and he'd acted on that decision. No threats, no warning, no terrorizing.

This lunatic wanted her scared, and he'd succeeded. She was more scared than she'd ever been in her life. She wanted to find someplace safe, curl up in a ball and not come out until Tommy had caught the guy.

And the only place she could think of that was truly safe wasn't a place at all but a person.

The paramedics delivered her to the emergency room staff, who put her in a room, dressed her in a cotton gown and repeated the basic exams. She was huddled under a pile of blankets, thinking that she could survive this if she could just stop shaking, when the curtain was jerked back and Russ walked in. And just like that, the chills were gone, the shudders stopped. Just like that, she knew she was safe.

Dear God, she was in trouble.

His scowl seemed etched into his features, and his jaw was taut as he came to the side of the gurney. He took her chin in hand, his touch surprisingly gentle, and turned her face so he could see the left side. She didn't know how long it would take the bruising to appear, but it was already swollen and tender. He stared a long time, then flatly said, "You're going back to the house with me."

She nodded.

"Tommy wasn't able to catch the guy. Never even got close enough to get a tag number or any kind of description besides a small red Ford pickup, older model."

"With my car's black paint on the right side, I imagine." She breathed and found her lungs filled a little easier. "My car looked totaled."

The corner of his mouth quirked. "It didn't have any personality anyway. Now you can get a real one."

"I liked that one," she protested.

The semismile faded. "It doesn't matter. You're not going anywhere by yourself until this guy's caught."

"How are they going to catch him?" she asked. "He ran me off the road right in front of Tommy. He was riding my bumper, but I can't give you a description of him. It was raining, I was scared…"

"Tommy will figure it out."

The curtain opened again with a *whoosh,* and the nurse returned with a doctor. Russ released Jamie and moved around the head of the bed, out of her sight. She missed his touch, missed his solid presence right beside her, but she knew he was still there. She could sense him, could *feel* him.

God, she was in *so* much trouble.

The exam room had one small window that looked out over the employee parking lot. Russ stared out a long time—while the doctor poked and questioned Jamie, while the nurse started an IV, a lab tech drew blood and Radiology took her for X rays and a CT scan. He stared, waited and wondered who the hell had done this to her.

How did you find a mystery man when you had no place to start? No idea where the flowers had come from, no way to narrow down which of the countless sales of liqueur-filled chocolates had been delivered to her, no clue who had slipped Mischa a sedative. At least the red pickup was something concrete, even if it was like looking for a needle in a haystack.

Jamie was still in Radiology when Tommy came in. His hair was wet and water dripped off his jacket. "She okay?"

"I think so. They're doing a CT scan."

"I was half a freakin' mile behind her. I got hung up in traffic turning onto Forsythe. Half a freakin' mile, and this guy came off one of the side streets and *boom.* Like he was waiting for her."

"Only you and I knew where she was going."

"I know, and I swear to God, I didn't tell anyone."

Russ believed him. Tommy was one of the few people he trusted as much as his brothers. "He must have followed her from her house."

Tommy shook his head. "I was looking, and I didn't see anybody, but maybe he saw us leave and guessed where we were heading. Maybe he knows her that well. So she can't stay at Robbie's now."

"She's going back home with me."

Rummaging through the cabinets, Tommy located a towel to dry his hair and face, then grinned. "Nothing like a little near-death experience to work out your troubles, huh?"

"We don't have any troubles."

"A few days ago, you hated her."

Russ couldn't argue that he'd resented the hell out of her. But a little time with her, a little conversation, a whole lot of thinking… "I was…"

"Acting juvenile? Hell, yeah. Me and Robbie wondered how long it would take you to realize it. He was betting on seven years or more." Tommy tossed the towel in the hamper. "Hey, you'd better call your mom and let her know you won't be there tonight."

Russ wasn't surprised that he knew about the family dinner. Hell, he wouldn't be surprised if he was invited. Tommy had eaten as many meals at their table growing up as at his own. "I don't suppose you'd call and tell her you arrested me."

"Yeah, right. Sara'd have my badge, and then you'd have to give me a job, and I'd have to work too hard. Tell her the truth. You're taking a beautiful woman home to spend the night with you. She'll be thrilled."

She would be—and double-thrilled if she knew it was Jamie and thought they'd be sharing the same bed.

There was a squeak of wheels in the hallway an instant

before the curtain was pulled back. A pretty young girl maneuvered the gurney back into the room, smiled politely at Russ and more appreciatively at Tommy, then left.

Jamie was as pale as the sheet she lay on, her eyes closed, even her freckles fading out. Color was starting to appear on her left temple and at the corner of her eye, sickly shades made all the more stark by her pallor.

Tommy moved to the side of the gurney and picked up her hand. "How're you feeling?"

"Like I got run off the road and smacked my head. Is Mischa okay?"

"She's fine. She's at the station with the dispatcher, getting a lot of scratching and pizza."

"She's loving that." She smiled faintly as she opened her eyes. "Did Russ leave?"

"Nah. You know how those Calloways are. You can't get rid of 'em no matter what you do."

Russ finally moved away from the window, stepping up to the other side of the gurney. Before he could say anything, though, the tail of the curtain whipped into the air and Lys burst into the room.

"Jamie, oh my God, I just found out—" Her gaze shifted to Tommy, then to Russ, and she stabbed one unnaturally dark fingernail in his direction. "What the hell is he doing here? Did he do this to her? Why isn't he under arrest? Do you think just because you're a Calloway, you can get away—"

"Lys." Jamie raised one unsteady hand. "I'm fine. You didn't need to come out in the rain. I'll be out of here before long."

Lys's eyes, heavily rimmed with dark makeup, moved again from Russ to Tommy to Jamie. "Why didn't someone call me? I'm your emergency contact. I should have been the first person they called. Why didn't they—"

"They didn't call anyone," Jamie interrupted, her tone weary but gentle. "Tommy witnessed the accident, and I called Russ. I told the nurse not to call anyone else."

It was like watching a balloon deflate, Russ thought. Lys actually got smaller. All the bristling emotion disappeared, leaving her pale and vulnerable and hurt, and for a moment he forgot that he didn't like her, that she was freaky and hated everyone in his family for nothing more than an accident of birth. For a moment he felt sorry for her, because he knew how it felt to not be wanted.

"But, Jamie, I'm your emergency contact," she said in a thin voice. "You should have called me."

"I'm sorry." Jamie stretched out her hand, and after a moment, Lys moved forward to take it. "I didn't think...I didn't want to worry you."

She didn't think; she'd reacted. And she'd called *him.* The action said a lot—that she trusted him, that she felt safe with him, that she'd wanted him—and it affected Russ in ways he didn't want to acknowledge.

"But why would you call *him?*" Lys pressed on. "He hates you. He says such ugly things about you. He'd probably be happy if this creep killed you. Why on earth—" Suddenly her eyes opened wide, and her jaw dropped. "Oh my God, you've been staying with him since the attack on Mischa! No one would ever think— No one would ever believe— This was your idea, wasn't it?" she demanded of Tommy.

Tommy snorted. "This doesn't concern you, Paxton."

"Doesn't concern me? She's my boss and my best friend! Of course it concerns me!" Clasping Jamie's hand in both of hers, she insisted, "You can't go back there. Come home with me. You'll be safe there. You know you can trust me, Jamie."

"And you know I'm not going to put your life in danger,

too." Gently Jamie freed her hand. "I appreciate the offer. It means more than I can say. But I couldn't bear it if something happened to you because of me."

"Don't worry about me. I can take care of myself, and I can take care of you, too. Come home with me, Jamie. You're safe with me."

"I'm safe with Russ."

"You don't know that."

"Yes. I do." Jamie spoke quietly, with such conviction, that even Lys couldn't argue.

What had he done to deserve that kind of faith? He'd treated her badly for three years. He *had* said ugly things about her. And yet she was utterly convinced that she was safe with him. It was humbling.

The silence in the cubicle was sharp, expectant. Lys drew a breath to argue further, but before she could say a word, the nurse came in. "Okay, folks, you're gonna have to take this party somewhere else because we're getting Miss Jamie ready to blow this joint. Come on now, out." She made shooing motions with both hands, and they obeyed, moving to the E.R. waiting room.

There Lys rounded on Tommy. "This is incredibly stupid even for you. Her life is in danger, and you send her to stay with *him?* How do you know he's not the one behind all these incidents? He damn near lived with her. He knew she liked those particular chocolates and those roses. She caught him putting that strip of wood behind her tire, and he just happened to be across the street the night Mischa got poisoned. Who knew she would even be out today besides him and you? And you're letting her go with him again?"

Tommy rocked back on his heels, looking as if he had all the time in the world to debate Lys. His tone was even and bland when he said, "You're right. No one else knew she was going to be out. So how did you find out she was here?"

Lys hesitated a moment too long, her gaze darting away, then back. "It's a small town. Word gets around."

Russ looked in the direction she had and saw that they were being watched by the woman behind the check-in desk. She was about the same age as Lys, her hair fake copper-red, her clothes all black like Lys's, a stud piercing her lower lip. It gave her the look of a perpetual pout. "Still friends with Nina?"

Lys blushed. "I don't— She knows I'm Jamie's best friend. She knew I'd want to be here."

"Seems like that's violating patient confidentiality or something like that," Tommy commented. "Seems like it's probably a firing offense."

"Don't get her in trouble, please," Lys blurted out. "There's not another person in town she would have done that for."

"There's Jamie," Tommy said with a nod, making no promises about Nina. "Russ, why don't you pull your truck up to the door? Paxton, go home. If anything comes up, Jamie will call you."

Tommy making an effort to be nice to freaky Lys. That was as good a time as any to make an exit, Russ decided. He dug his keys from his pocket as he crossed the lobby, stepped outside into the protection of the covered entrance, then dashed across the lot to the truck. The rain had kept the temperature below normal all day, and the fact that there had been so damn much of it somehow made it seem even cooler.

By the time he drove back to the entrance, Jamie was waiting with Tommy and the same pretty girl who'd returned her from Radiology. She looked small in the wheelchair. Fragile. Her face was lined with pain; her fingers tightly gripped the discharge orders and a prescription. If the bastard who'd done this could see her now, would he leave her alone? Would it satisfy whatever sick need drove him?

Probably not. He *was* sick. He wanted her for himself, no matter what lengths he had to go to.

Tommy helped her into the truck and gave his own instructions: an officer in a marked unit would meet them at the pharmacy, then follow them to the police station to pick up Mischa, then home. Tommy was going along for the ride, too, but he would hang back, the better to identify anyone paying undue attention to them.

"It seems so cloak-and-dagger," Jamie said with a taut smile as they finally left the parking lot.

"You do whatever it takes to stay safe."

She acknowledged him with a nod but didn't speak, and he let the silence grow until they were sitting at the pharmacy drive-through window, when he finally faced her. "Should I remember that you like orange roses?"

"Apricot," she corrected before meeting his gaze. Besides tired and achy, she looked amused, her mouth forming half a smile before thinning again. "Not really. You gave them to me for my birthday. It was just a fluke. For whatever reason, the florist had them in stock, just a dozen. You were in a hurry, and they were all ready to go, so you bought them."

He remembered giving her flowers a couple of times. Sara had said more than once—with a degree of cynicism, he now knew—that you could never go wrong with flowers or diamonds. His father had had a habit of coming home from his frequent business trips with both.

But Russ hadn't recalled the kind of flowers or the color.

Now he would remember apricot roses as long as he lived.

As they left the pharmacy, a Copper Lake police car, with the Petrovskis' son Pete behind the wheel, pulled into traffic behind them. They picked up Mischa, who bared her teeth at Russ only a couple times all the way home. There he settled Jamie on the couch, gave her water to take a pain pill, then brought in the luggage he'd carried out only four hours earlier.

"I'd feel better if I thought that mutt might alert on something besides squirrels," Tommy said quietly where he waited on the porch.

"No one ever comes out here."

"No one's ever had a reason. I know you have guns. You keeping them handy?"

"Yeah." But not as handy as he would now.

"You know, shooting a person's not the same as shooting a deer."

That was the kind of comment Rick would make if he knew what was going on, or Mitch. His brothers' influence was everywhere. "Yeah, the deer doesn't shoot back."

"It could be someone you know."

Someone he knew, someone he considered a friend, someone related to him—not farfetched since about half the county was. He couldn't imagine anyone he knew drugging Mischa or forcing Jamie off the road. But people could appear perfectly normal while hiding the worst of secrets.

"If the guy comes here, it's not going to be a social call," he said, glancing down the hall where Jamie was now lying on the couch. Mischa sat on the floor in front of her, and Jamie's fingers were buried in the fur between the dog's shoulders. "I've never shot at a person, and I hope to God I never do. But if I have to…" He'd been handling guns since he was a kid. He didn't carry a weapon as part of his job, like Rick, Mitch and Tommy, but he was as good a shot as any of them.

And if he had no choice, he could live with the consequences.

Tommy walked to the steps. "You know how to reach me if you need anything. Keep your eyes open." With that, he went out into the rain and, a moment later, backed out of the driveway. Another moment, and his taillights disappeared around the curve.

Everything was quiet. A line from an old movie popped into his head: *Too quiet.* But he didn't think in this case, there was such a thing as too quiet. He went inside, locked up, unzipped the .45 from the rug and laid it on the kitchen island. In his bedroom, he opened the gun safe and removed a .40, leaving it on the night stand.

Back in the living room, he stood behind the couch, looking at Jamie. She lay on her right side, her hands pressed together beneath her cheek. The left side of her face had turned an array of ugly colors, creating a pretty awful contrast to her orange-and-blue dress. Her breathing was easy, steady, and she didn't wake when he shook out the afghan from the back of the couch and laid it over her. She just gave a little sigh, snuggled closer to the back cushions of the sofa and slept on.

"Let's make a deal, Mischa," he said, drawing the dog's gaze to him. "You call Mom and explain to her why I'm weaseling out of dinner, and I'll sit here and watch Jamie."

The dog blinked, then rested her chin on the sofa cushion. She looked worried. So he and the demon dog had one thing in common.

Reluctantly he went to the phone and dialed Sara's number. As soon as she recognized his hello, she said, "Oh, no, you don't, Russell Wayne. You are not skipping dinner tonight. Your brother and sister-in-law have driven all the way from Atlanta just to see the family, and Robbie's out of town, and you think you're going to cancel? And for what? So you can sit home all alone? That's not healthy. You're a young man. You've got your whole life ahead of you. You can't just give up—"

"I'm not alone."

That stopped Sara. He could practically hear the little gears spinning in her brain as she made the huge leap from him not being alone to being with a woman to falling in love and getting married again and living happily ever after.

"Why don't you bring her with you?" she finally asked.

"That's not a good idea."

"Why? Do you think she would be uncomfortable having dinner with us? Do you think we would have a problem with her?" Her voice sharpened. "Oh, Lord, Russ, it's not Melinda, is it?"

The idea was so ridiculous that he laughed.

"Well, I'm happy I can amuse you," Sara said sarcastically, but he knew she was smiling. It became even more apparent when she went on. "I haven't heard you laugh in longer than I can remember. I've missed it."

"I know." She worried about all her sons, but she'd worried most about him. "Tell Rick and Amanda I'll catch up with them next time they're in town."

"You'll catch up with me long before that. I want to know everything."

"Mom, I haven't told you everything since I was sixteen and going out with Hailey Armstrong. You'd be shocked."

"You didn't invent sex, sweetheart," she said drily. "You haven't done anything that hasn't been done millions of times before. If you want to try to out shock me, I'll win, hands-down. I know you prefer to think that your father and I had sex only three times, but that's far from the truth—"

"Mom, you're my mother. No talk about your sex life or mine." His gaze went automatically to Jamie. His sex life had been nonexistent for so long that he'd stopped even missing it. Not true anymore. One kiss out of the blue, and he wanted more. Hurt with wanting it.

With wanting her.

Now he just had to decide if he could risk doing anything about it. Not for his own sake, but for hers. He'd hurt her once before. Damned if he wanted to do it again.

Chapter 8

Night had fallen by the time Jamie awoke. Despite the fuzziness courtesy of the pain pill, she had instant recall of the afternoon's events and shuddered, then winced at the resulting pain.

But it was okay. She was back at Russ's house. She was safe.

And hungry, she realized as she caught the scents of spices on the stove. And in dire need of a bathroom.

She pushed the afghan back and slowly sat up. The sky was dark, rain still fell, and there was no sign of Russ or Mischa. He'd probably forced her outside before she exploded.

Jamie eased to her feet, then went to the bathroom, examining her face in the mirror before taking care of business. She didn't look too scary. By Monday she should be able to cover the worst of it with makeup, and at least this time she could put a better spin on the cause: *I was in a car wreck.*

There was just no way to spin *I was attacked by an angry man with a knife* so it sounded better.

After washing her hands and brushing her teeth, she went into the bedroom next door. The bags she'd left with were neatly stacked beside the bed; the garment bag she'd picked up at her house that afternoon hung on a hook on the closet door.

She'd changed into shorts and a T-shirt and finger-combed her hair when the front door opened. A moment later the scratch of Mischa's nails tracked her progress through the foyer and the living room and into the kitchen. A quiet command—"Down, Mischa"—indicated Russ had followed her.

She was removing what was left of her makeup when he spoke again, this time from the hallway. "James?"

"Yeah." Gingerly she eased the makeup pad along the edges of the bruise as he came to the bedroom door.

"How do you feel?"

"Better." She grimaced in place of a smile. "I know. I look like hell."

"You're still beautiful. At least, on one side. On both sides soon enough. Dinner's about ready. Do you feel like eating?"

"I do." She watched him go, then shook her head. Such a careless compliment—the best kind. As if it was so obvious that saying it wasn't necessary.

When she got to the dining room, two places were set, each with a bowl of steaming pasta *fagioli* and a plate of salad. She took a bite of the soup—macaroni, ground beef, tomatoes, beans and peppers in a not-too-spicy broth—and sighed appreciatively. "Oh, that's good."

After a few more bites, she put the spoon down and gazed at him. His hair was damp from the recent trip out with Mischa, and his jaw was stubbled with a day's growth of beard. There were stress lines bracketing his eyes and mouth, and the look in his eyes was dark, troubled. Worried.

"Thank you," she said quietly. "For fixing dinner, for

letting me stay here, for taking care of Mischa, for coming when I called this afternoon."

"Did you think I wouldn't?"

She thought back to that moment in the car. She had called him to prove to herself that he was home, that it hadn't been him in the red pickup, that he hadn't raced into town after she and Tommy left and found a good place to ambush her.

But there'd been more to it than that. The instant she'd heard his voice, she'd *known* everything would be okay, that calling him was right in a way that had nothing to do with proving his innocence. He was the only person she'd wanted to call, the only one she'd wanted to see, the only one she'd needed.

"I don't know that I even thought about whether you'd go to the hospital. I just needed to hear your voice." Her cheeks flushed, but he didn't scoff or sneer at her.

In fact, he almost smiled. "If you hadn't called, I would have been pissed."

She'd needed him, and he'd needed her to need him. The knowledge filled her with warmth and eased the dull pain that throbbed in her head. Or maybe it was the food that did it, or the residual effects of the medication.

"Call Lys after dinner, will you?"

Jamie stared at him in surprise. He was asking her to call freaky Lys? Wanting her to keep Lys updated?

Her stare made him scowl. "She's worried, and her feelings were hurt that you didn't call her this afternoon."

She was embarrassed to admit that Lys hadn't crossed her mind even once until she'd walked into Jamie's room. Lys was her best friend; she'd been there for Jamie through a lot. But it wasn't Lys she'd wanted when she was hurting and afraid. It wasn't Lys who made her feel comfortable sitting in a room with a lot of uncovered windows looking out on the night.

Oh, God, she was such a stereotypical bad friend—the kind who got a boyfriend and forgot that her girlfriends existed until he dumped her and she needed them again.

Except Russ wasn't her boyfriend. He was…she didn't know what to call him.

Maybe her future.

Maybe just another broken heart.

But if he broke her heart again, at least she would know what to expect. She was walking into it with her eyes wide-open. She wouldn't be able to blame anyone but herself.

"I'll call her," she agreed, then changed the subject. "I'm sorry you missed dinner with your brother and his wife."

He shrugged. "It's not like we never see them. They come to Copper Lake about every other weekend."

"I understand she's a college teacher." She'd heard more from Robbie about Mitch's wife than Rick's. It seemed there was some history between him and Amanda Calloway, something about a broken heart when they were teenagers. Amanda's, Jamie was pretty sure. Robbie didn't keep one woman around long enough to risk his heart.

"She is now." Russ's grin was rare, and all the more enticing for it. "When they met, she was an exotic dancer." Then, as if that might not be clear enough, he added, "A stripper."

"Your brother, the GBI agent, married a stripper."

"He did. She quit not long after they met. I never got to see her dance except at their wedding reception and she kept all her clothes on. Robbie said she was damn good."

He sounded so regretful that she laughed, then winced when it made her head throb. "So that would explain the black eye and swollen nose Robbie got last fall while in Atlanta and wouldn't talk about."

"It's a better story than yours. Though Rick wasn't trying

to kill Robbie." His gaze settled on her bruises, and his jaw tightened. "I should have kept you here."

"You thought it was safe to leave. So did I. So did Tommy, and he's paid to know this stuff."

"But I knew…"

"Knew what?"

His mouth quirked, but didn't quite manage a smile. "That letting you go was a bad idea."

Her fingers tightened around her spoon as she scooped another mouthful of soup, but this time she didn't taste it. What she would give if he meant that in a different context, if he was talking about the end of their romance six years ago. But he hadn't let her go then; he'd done the leaving, and for another woman. If he had any regrets about that, they were probably just the general gee-I-could've-handled-that-better type.

She shrugged. "We thought it would be okay. Live and learn. No lasting harm done."

"Except to your car. I'll help you find a better one."

The idea that when this was over, he would still be around was an appealing one. Still, she managed a wary look. "You Calloway boys don't like anything made after 1975."

"Yeah. So?"

"Old cars need work. I don't know the difference between a carburetor and a muffler, and I don't want to add my own personal mechanic to my budget."

"There are ways to pay a mechanic that don't involve spending a dime."

Again her nerves tightened. There wasn't a hint of innuendo in his voice, and his expression was as innocent as was possible for a thirty-two-year-old man, but deep inside, she knew there was more to the words than a simple statement. Suggestion. Implication.

"Really," she said, her throat constricted. "Too bad I didn't know that before I paid the garage in Augusta three hundred and fifty dollars to fix the car that's now totaled."

"I'd've given you a deal."

"Except you were still hating me."

Abruptly he left the table, carrying his dishes to the sink and rinsing them. When he returned, he looked serious and intense and amazingly handsome. "I didn't hate you. I was pissed off. You were an easy target."

"I guess so. You, Harlan Davis, this guy…"

"I would never physically hurt you, Jamie."

She smiled faintly. "I know. I wouldn't be here if I thought otherwise."

"Lys thinks—"

"She's just concerned. If my life changes, so does hers. She likes the status quo. And she's only heard the bad stuff about you from me. She knows how much losing you hurt. She doesn't know…" Jamie broke off. *How good having you was.* But the truth was, she'd never really had him. She'd just thought she did.

But he was looking at her now as if that could change. Maybe had changed. As if they could be friends and lovers and maybe even more. *The one* for each other.

At least for a while.

She swallowed hard, then reached across the table, her fingertips grazing the back of his hand. "About that kiss this morning…"

He didn't deny it, didn't ask, *What kiss?* He just waited for her to go on.

"It was really nice."

"Nice." His brows arched. "Don't worry about my ego. I hear I have way more than enough of that."

"But it *was* nice."

"When a man kisses a woman, he doesn't want to hear that it's 'nice.' That's like saying, 'Oh, the sex was fine.' *Nice* and *fine* aren't compliments."

"This morning you wanted to pretend that it didn't even happen."

He rolled his hand over, wrapping his fingers around hers. "I knew it happened. Jeez, you think I went out in the rain with the mutt for fun? I knew I shouldn't have done it. I knew it was out of line." His voice grew huskier, more intimate. "I know it was a hell of a lot more than 'nice.' I was there, remember? I was the one you wrapped your arms around. I was the one you were kissing back. I was the one you were clinging to. Until Mischa interrupted."

Thank God for Mischa, she'd thought at the time. Right now the dog was snoozing in Russ's chair and wasn't showing the slightest inclination to get up. Thank God for that, too, because unless she was very wrong, Russ was going to kiss her again.

She wasn't wrong at all.

He stood slowly, tugging her hand, pulling her to her feet. "This can wait until you feel better," he murmured, his free hand coming close to, but not touching, her face.

"I feel fine."

Then he did touch her, just the tips of his fingers, grazing barely there across her cheek. "'Fine,' as in 'nice'?"

"'Fine' as in 'no pain.'" It was true. The medicine, the sleep, the food, the desire—whatever the reason, she was feeling no pain. Just heat. Hunger. Anticipation.

The very first time he'd kissed her, they'd known each other for two hours. Fifteen minutes later, they'd been in her bed.

The last time he'd kissed her, prior to this morning, he'd been leaving on a spring-break trip that she'd talked him into, then she'd gotten sick and been forced to cancel. Go without me, she'd encouraged him. *Have fun.*

He had. He'd met Melinda his first day in Daytona Beach. A few hours later, he'd been in bed with her.

That goodbye kiss hadn't even been a real kiss. She'd been sick; he'd pressed his mouth to her forehead before leaving.

This promised to be one hell of a kiss.

His mouth touched her right temple, fluttered at the corner of her eye and brushed slowly across her ear, his tongue delicately touching once, twice. He kissed her cheek, her jaw, insubstantial kisses, then reached her mouth, chaste, sweet, an innocent touch. When she felt his tongue between her lips, something inside her tightened, sending tiny shivers through her at the same time her blood started pumping hotter, harder.

He didn't take her mouth, though, but left a line of damp kisses along her jaw, down her throat to the pulse that pounded there, over the thin scar that few people noticed. Her muscles were quivering, her fingers curling over the waistband of his jeans for support.

"I wish you hadn't taken off the dress," he murmured against the skin revealed by the rounded neck of her shirt.

"I'll put it back on."

"I'll take it off next time."

"Russ…" One syllable, soft sounds, all plea.

He chuckled as he straightened, his hands settling on her hips, pulling her snug against his arousal. "Jamie. What do you want?"

She managed to catch her breath long enough to say, "Surprise me."

"Yeah, like you're going to be surprised if I carry you off to bed. What do you want?"

She'd forgotten he could be playful. Forceful. Demanding.

Selfish. Generous. Greedy. Gentle enough to bring tears to her eyes. Sweet enough to make her ache.

"I want you to kiss me," she replied.

"Is that all?"

"It's a start."

He quit toying with her then and brought his mouth to hers, his tongue thrusting inside. Blindly he maneuvered her back, and blindly she let him, feeling a barstool bump her legs after three steps. She eased onto it, knees apart, and he moved between her legs, rubbing his erection against her soft heat.

So damn long. The thought echoed through Russ's head as he tried to damn near absorb everything about Jamie into himself. So long since he'd held a woman. So long since he'd wanted to. So long since the last real kiss, since the last serious touch, since he'd felt the lust and the need. So long since he'd wanted to be intimate, to make himself vulnerable, since he'd felt anything besides anger and bitterness and resentment. So damn long.

His hands were used to textures—wood, concrete, stone, brick, tools, drywall, mortar, mud—but *these* textures were all new. The silk of Jamie's hair, gliding over his fingers. The fineness of her skin. The softness of her shirt. The rougher cotton of her shorts. The warmth of her middle. The scratch of the lace on her bra. The pebbled hardness of her nipple.

She smelled of shampoo, perfume and a sweet, tempting fragrance all her own. Fresh and clean and feminine. Womanly. Sexy. The scent stirred faint memories. So did her shiver when he nipped her lower lip and her soft gasp, swallowed by his own mouth, when he slid his hands beneath the flimsy bra, his fingers finding her nipples. She liked sex, she'd told him years ago, and she particularly liked sex with *him.*

He had particularly liked it with her. He'd liked everything with her. She'd been one of his best friends. But he didn't want friendship now. He wanted to possess her, wanted her to possess him. He wanted to crawl deep inside her. To protect her. To keep her safe and close and his.

Finally he ended the kiss, but he didn't step away from the cradle of her hips. For a long time, he stared at her, and she stared back, her expression dazed, wanting, soft. Offering her an out was the hardest thing he'd done in the past few hours— though not the hardest all day. Walking into the emergency room, not knowing what he'd find; hearing her voice on the phone, shaken and tearful; walking away from that morning's kiss—those had all been harder.

"You can change your mind."

She stared back at him, then a little smile curved her mouth. "I could," she agreed. "But I'd regret it." She slid to her feet, forcing him to back away, then caught his hand and walked around the island.

He followed her into the bedroom. At the door, she let go of him and walked ahead to the bed, folding back the rumpled comforter he'd carelessly tossed on that morning. There was something about the way she moved that was so damn hot, and it was totally natural. She didn't know she was turning him on just by bending to smooth the sheets, or that he could get a hard-on—as if he didn't already have one—just by watching her walk around to the other side of the bed.

She turned, looked at him leaning against the door frame and mimicked the position against one of the bedposts. "You can change your mind, too."

He pushed away from the door and walked to her, shaking his head all the way. *Regret* didn't begin to describe how he would feel if he stopped now.

When he reached her, she straightened, pulled his T-shirt

from his jeans and tugged it over his head, then dropped it to the floor. Her gaze skimmed across his chest, followed by her fingers, then her mouth, and he groaned aloud. He pulled off her shirt, careful of the bruises on her face, and she fumbled with his belt, then his zipper, finally shoving his jeans and boxers out of the way. He'd left his shoes at the front door when he'd come inside with Mischa, making it easier to kick off the last of his clothes while she removed her shorts.

He was naked, hard and hot. She wore a skimpy bra and skimpier panties and was incredibly hot. Her skin was pale gold all over, soft and smooth except for the scars—the one he'd already seen on her breast, another on her ribcage on the right, the third on the left. Lightly tracing each one with his fingertip, he wondered if she had any similar emotional scars from his own pigheaded bitterness. Wondered if he could make right all he'd done wrong.

They'd have a long time to find out.

She moved, a sinuous sensual flexing of muscles, and the bra fell away. Hooked her fingers in the elastic band of the panties and pushed them down until a little shimmy sent them to the floor as well.

And he quit wondering, quit regretting, quit thinking at all.

He laid her back on the bed and followed her down, tangling his hands in her hair, kissing her, rubbing against her, sliding between her legs and inside her with one long, easy thrust. Always good, always *home*.

For a moment, he didn't move, just savoring the tight, familiar feel of her, remembering all the times they'd been like this before, regretting all the times they hadn't. Then her body tensed around his and she moved her hips in a teasing, tortur-ous thrust and she kissed him, her tongue stabbing inside his mouth, and he couldn't help it. He had to move, to taste her, to fill her, to stroke in and out, long, easy, hard.

It didn't last long. After three years alone, keeping women at a distance, too lonely to admit, he didn't expect it to. The second time was much slower, at least until the end, when their skin was slick with sweat and his nerves were on fire, his muscles burning, his lungs too tight to manage a breath, his heart pounding as if it might explode.

Instead, he exploded inside her, everything going dark and roaring, and he had one moment of clear thought—*no condom*—and didn't care. Would have done it anyway if the thought had occurred to him earlier. Intended to do it again.

For a time the only sound in the room was their harsh breathing, and he could hear the thud of his heart with every beat. Gradually it slowed, and their breathing returned to normal and the sweat cooled on their skin except where their bodies were still touching. He lay on his back, one arm beneath his head—the pillows had slid off the bed—and the other holding Jamie close. Her left hand rested across his ribs, and her left leg draped over his hips.

Rain dripped outside. In the next room leather creaked as Mischa resettled in the chair, and the grandfather clock in the foyer chimed. He didn't know the time and didn't care. It had been one hell of a long day, and for the first time all day, he felt good.

For the first time in years, he felt satisfied. Any more satisfied, and it would kill him.

He looked at Jamie in the dim light, his gaze falling first on the bruises. "Are you okay?"

Eyes closed, she smiled. "I'm fine. As in postorgasmic, holy-cats-you-curled-my-toes, fabulous, fantastic, fine. How about you?"

He rolled onto his side to face her. "You ever go someplace you've never been, or at least not in a long time, and you walk in and instantly you feel like you belong?"

She looked at him. "I felt that way about Copper Lake when I moved here."

That was how he felt—as if he'd come home. Even though he'd never left. Who ever would have believed that Satan, Queen of the Damned, the bloodsucker, could make him feel that way?

As if she'd read his thoughts, she sobered. "I'm sorry I took Melinda's case."

Two words that he hadn't even realized he wanted to hear until she'd said them. *I'm sorry.* She probably hadn't offered them earlier because he hadn't been ready to hear them.

And now he was. Funny how quickly things could change. *Nothing like a little near-death experience to work out your troubles,* Tommy had said. But, yeah, he was ready to move on. To quit licking his wounds, to quit letting the failure of his marriage dictate the rest of his life.

He parroted back her own words. "She needed a lawyer. You needed a client. It was business."

She smiled ruefully. "That wasn't my first divorce. I knew as well as anyone that divorce isn't business. It's damn personal. I shouldn't have expected you to understand. I should have told Melinda I couldn't help her."

"I would have been pissed no matter who represented her. Well, unless it was Robbie. I would have kicked his ass and then gotten over it."

"Is that how you Calloway boys solve your problems with each other?"

"As often as not. What do you and your sisters do? Talk it out? Compromise?"

"Of course. We're mature adults."

He shifted so her left leg was over his waist and his growing erection was nudging against her curls. "Are you saying that I'm not mature?"

"You *are* a man," she pointed out, moving against him before wrapping her fingers around his length and guiding him into place. He thrust against her, filling her despite the awkward position.

"I'm glad you noticed." He eased her onto her back, rose above her and sank into her more deeply. Completely.

She gave a soft sigh, then murmured, "So am I. Damned glad."

Jamie was a well and truly satisfied woman.

She lay in Russ's bed, the sheet tucked under her arms, only one dim lamp on, listening to his even breathing and the sound of the rain splashing in the night. She wasn't particularly tired; she just lacked the energy to move. At all. Unless he found the energy to make love one more time…

Just call me greedy, she thought with a smug smile.

Russ reached over to the nightstand, then rolled back, cordless phone in hand. "Call Lys."

She squinted at the display. "It's almost eleven o'clock."

"Will she be in bed?"

"Probably not. She's young. She doesn't need much sleep."

He snorted. "You're what? Four whole years older than her?"

"It's not the years. It's the mileage."

He quirked his brows, but she would bet he agreed with her. They'd both had three years of hard roads. Please, God, let the worst of it be behind them.

As she dialed the number, he rolled to his feet, grabbed his boxers and sauntered from the room.

Lys answered on the first ring, her tone anxious. "Jamie? Is everything okay?"

Guilt washed over her again. She should have called Lys as soon as she woke up from her pain-pill-induced nap, should have talked to her longer at the hospital, should have been a more considerate friend. Okay, so her life had gone to hell in the past few days. That was no reason to exclude her best friend.

"Everything's fine, really. I took some medicine when I got home, then slept for a while. I'm a bit battered, but I'm great."

"You mean, when you got to *his* house."

Jamie blinked a moment, then realized that she'd referred to Russ's house as *home*. In a few short days, it had come to feel that way. *He'd* come to feel that way. "You know what I mean."

There was a moment's silence, then, "I just don't understand it, Jamie. What's going on? Why are you staying with him? Why would he even let you? He's been mad as hell at you for three years, and you've avoided him for three years, and suddenly it's just all in the past? You're going to his house? You're trusting him with your life? You're acting like nothing ever happened?"

From the kitchen, Jamie heard the refrigerator closing, the water in the sink running, the clatter of after-dinner cleanup, accompanied by Russ's low voice as he talked to Mischa. No doubt, she'd roused herself as soon as he entered the kitchen. The prospect of a handout was always good to get her moving.

Jamie would rather be in there herself than having this conversation. "It's complicated, Lys. You just have to trust me. I know what I'm doing."

"Do you? Really? He could be your stalker, Jamie."

"Come on. You've known him and his family all your life. I know you're not fond of him, but honestly, can you imagine any man in the world less likely to stalk a woman than Russ Calloway?"

Lys's answer was grudgingly given. "Probably not. He's kind of cute, he has a nice body, a good business and a lot of family money. Women would have been lined up for a chance at him after the divorce if Melinda hadn't chewed him up so bad."

Jamie was surprised. That was probably the nicest thing Lys had ever said about any Calloway.

"So…" A teasing note came into Lys's voice. "With all this forced proximity, are there any sparks still smoldering?"

Though they'd confided a lot in each other over the years, Jamie didn't want to tell Lys about any of her time with Russ—talking, fixing a meal together, sharing the silence, kissing, making love. It was still so new, so intimate. "It's hard to say," she hedged.

"No, it's not. Is he still being ugly to you? Has he talked to you without calling you Satan? Has he tried to touch you or kiss you?"

Jamie was silent so long that Lys squealed. "Oh my God, Jamie, he has! Did you let him? Did you kiss him back? Was it fantastic? As good as you remembered?"

She glanced at the open doorway before replying. "Better."

"Oh my God." Lys took a long, unsteady breath. "Okay. You know I don't like him. You know I think this is a really bad idea. But if you like him, I'll make nice. Those will be my last negative comments, I promise. Just…take it slow, Jamie. Make sure he's not just using you this time. Don't let him hurt you."

"I'll be careful." But it was already too late. If her stalker was caught the next morning and she went home, and Russ chose to have nothing more to do with her, she would be hurt. Not brokenhearted. But close.

"I don't know what I'd do without you, Lys," she said, emotion creeping into her voice.

Lys's voice sounded a little clogged, too. "Yeah, I've heard that before. You'd get along. No one's indispensable."

"You are. You're the best."

"Now you're getting mushy. Take a pain pill. Go to sleep. Alone."

"Aw, that's no fun."

"Hey, I don't want to be the only one sleeping alone. I'll see you Monday morning."

"I'll be there." After hanging up, she stood, found Russ's discarded T-shirt and pulled it on, sniffing his scent on it as she went into the kitchen. He was starting the dishwasher and straightened as she came in. He'd put on the boxers, cleaned away all the remains of dinner and given Mischa her usual three scoops of dog food. "Everything okay with Lys?"

"Yeah. She's just feeling a little…"

"Threatened?"

"Yeah." She leaned against the counter and watched as he washed his hands. "It sounds silly, but when I was a kid…Chelsea Smith and I had been best friends since fourth grade. We did everything together—took the same classes at the same school, went to the same church, worked part-time at the same store. We were inseparable until our sophomore year, when she started dating David Martin. Suddenly, all the stuff she'd been doing with me she started doing with him. She hardly had any time for me, and when she did, all she talked about was him. I hated it. I felt so left out and abandoned. I'd lost my best friend. He broke up with her our junior year, but things were never the same for us."

He dried his hands, then hung the towel on the rack. "Lys isn't a high-school sophomore."

"No, but she's young."

"So you'll still do things with her once this guy's caught, and you'll see her at work until then. Nothing has to change."

A chill danced along her spine, but she tried to ignore it. Was he saying that once she was safe again, life would go back to the way it had been before? In every way? She wanted to quash her questions, put his remark out of her head, but she knew herself too well. The uncertainty would nag at her until it drove her nuts. "What do you mean?"

He turned off the kitchen lights before glancing at her. "Lys will still be your best friend. I don't need every minute of your time. Just some of it." He picked up Mischa's leash and snapped his fingers, and the dog lumbered to her feet, stretched, then trotted to him. After hooking the leash onto her collar, he straightened, his forehead wrinkled into a frown. "Unless this—" he gestured to her, then himself "—is just a temporary thing. You know, full-service protection."

Resisting the urge to smile at the dark note that had entered his voice, she solemnly shook her head.

He held her gaze a moment, even though Mischa was pulling hard for the door, then nodded. "Grab some towels and meet us around front, will you?"

She moved to the French door to watch them—Mischa taking her steps carefully as if where she stepped could keep the rain from soaking her, Russ barefooted and in boxers coaxing her along. She waited until they had disappeared into the night to go to the bathroom, waited until she was within its privacy to give a little twirl of delight. He still wanted to see her when this was over! He wasn't going to break her heart.

Yet.

She got two towels for Mischa, one for Russ, and was waiting at the front door when they came onto the porch. She dried the dog and he dried himself, sliding out of the sodden boxers, knotting the towel around his waist.

When they were done, he gathered the towels and boxers in one hand, then slid his other arm around her. "You look tired."

She was, she realized. Despite her nap that morning. Despite her other nap that afternoon. "It's been a busy day."

"Go on to bed. I'm going to put some towels in the washer, then I'll be in."

"Mischa likes to sleep with me," she warned.

He looked at the dog, and the dog looked back, tongue hanging out, looking as innocent as a ninety-pound dog could until she pulled her lips back to show her teeth for an instant. "We'll have to negotiate that, won't we, girl?" he said, giving Mischa a light swat as he passed her.

She raised her bushy tail and trotted after him.

Jamie made sure the door was locked, shut off the lights in the foyer, then detoured to the guest room for her pillow. Russ liked her dog. He liked *her*.

Damned if that wasn't worth having a stalker.

Chapter 9

Russ woke early Monday morning, Jamie's body warm against his, Mischa's snores soft from her bed near the glass door. For the first time in more than three years, he wasn't happy to see Monday arrive. The job had been his salvation when his marriage headed south, and it was the only thing that had kept him going through the divorce and the months after. But he hadn't even given it a thought since completing that bid on Saturday morning.

He and Jamie had stayed in all day Sunday. Her bruises had been more vivid, and she'd had a few aches in her ribs and neck. They'd watched TV, dozed, talked, had very nice, very gentle sex.

He grinned faintly. *Nice* could be a compliment, after all.

He eased from the bed, tucking the covers around Jamie as she resettled, then closed the door behind him on the way to the kitchen. The timer on the coffeemaker cycled on as he took the milk from the refrigerator. By the time the coffee was ready, he'd fixed himself a bowl of cereal and some toast, and Mischa had started thumping her tail against the bedroom door. He let her out, gave her a piece of toast, then sat down at the island to eat. Before he'd taken two bites, the phone rang.

It was Tommy. "How's she doing?"

"She's fine." Definitely a compliment.

"What's the plan for today?"

"She's going to the office." He hadn't tried to talk her out of it when they'd discussed it the day before. She couldn't put her entire life on hold; she had clients, cases, court dates. It was important to her to maintain some semblance of normalcy. "So is Rafe, one of the guys that works for me." He had clients, too, and deadlines and meetings. He could chuck it all to become Jamie's shadow, but Rafe seemed a better choice. Russ knew he could trust him, and the mere sight of Rafe wouldn't set Lys off, while having to face Russ for eight or nine hours would probably make her homicidal.

"He gonna stick with her all day?"

"Yeah, until I pick her up this evening."

"Good. We found the red truck. It was taken from a house about five miles east of town and abandoned on a country road a couple miles south."

"So the stalker can hot-wire an engine." Russ could. So could his brothers and Tommy. But it wasn't a really common skill these days.

"No. The guy who owned it kept the keys in it. Made it easier to find them when he wanted to go somewhere." Tommy sounded disgusted. "His name is Brent Johnson. You know him?"

"No."

"He was six or eight years behind us in school, and about all he's done since then is get high, get drunk and get laid. He has a really sweet marijuana patch growing out behind his house."

Mischa rubbed against Russ's leg, whining, and he absently slipped her the rest of the toast. "Doesn't sound like he could be the guy."

Tommy snorted. "Rolling a joint is about the extent of his planning abilities. We're looking at his friends, though. There were no fingerprints on the steering wheel or door handle, not even his. The keys were still in it when the deputy came across it just sitting at the side of the road. That's how ol' Brent found out it was gone. He hadn't even missed it. And with all the rain, there was no way to tell if another vehicle had been there waiting or if the guy had taken off on foot. Nothing but mud."

"Anything else new?"

"We're working."

That was an old Robbie-and-Tommy evasive tactic that translated to not accomplishing anything.

"Tell Jamie I'll swing by the office a couple times, just to look in on her."

"Okay. I'll see you." Russ finished his cereal, gave Mischa her breakfast, then stuck two more slices of bread into the toaster. He was buttering one piece when there was a soft rustle behind him, then a delicate hand reached past him and scooped up the toast.

"Yum, I love honey-buttered toast," Jamie murmured. She took a small bite, chewed it politely, then swallowed before offering it back to him.

"Keep it. I'll fix more." After dropping in two more slices, he finished buttering the other, then watched her fix her cereal. She'd taken to wearing one of his T-shirts both as pajamas and robe, and it made her look so girly. With her hair down and mussed, her eyes hazy from just awaking, her body still soft and warm from the covers, she could lure him back into bed with nothing more than a look, and she probably knew it, because she kept *not* giving him the look.

She slid onto the stool where Russ had sat. "What news did Tommy have?"

"What makes you think it was Tommy?"

"Someone calls to chat before six a.m.? He's the only one I know besides you who gets up that early, at least Monday through Friday. He jogs out for doughnuts and cigarettes before work."

Russ scowled at her as he brought two saucers with toast to join her. "I don't think even Robbie knows that about Tommy."

"I'm a lawyer and usually a good friend. I listen when people talk." She smiled smugly. "And though it had slipped your mind, I'm a good lover, too."

"I never forgot that." Not even when he was stupid-in-love with Melinda. He'd figured Jamie was making some other guy really happy. It was only fair, after all. But instead she'd been missing him.

What would have happened if he'd skipped that spring-break trip and stayed with her instead? If he had never met Melinda, never royally screwed up his life? Would he have made the effort to continue seeing Jamie after he'd graduated and returned home? Would he have fallen in love with her along the way?

Probably not. *Things happen when they're supposed to happen,* his mother said. Rick hadn't been ready to settle down until last year because he hadn't met Amanda. Ditto for Mitch and Jessica. And when it was Russ's and Robbie's turns, Sara fully believed it would happen. Though she wasn't averse to helping them along if she could.

After polishing off his toast and the last half of hers, he

asked, "You know a guy named Brent Johnson? Lives in the county and likes his weed a little too much?"

"The name's not familiar. Why?"

He repeated Tommy's information to her. When he finished, she shook her head. "I prefer clients who haven't voluntarily made themselves stupider than they already were and who don't pay me with drug money."

"His friends probably knew he left the keys in the pickup. Maybe one of them borrowed it, knowing he wouldn't realize it was gone."

Her expression turned serious. "Maybe."

He bumped his shoulder against hers. "You want to stay home today, we can. You call Lys, I'll call my office, and we'll go back to bed."

She looked seriously tempted for a whole five seconds, then purposefully shook her head. "I'm not going into hiding any more than I've already been. I'll be safe in the office with Lys, and with your crew across the street, and with Tommy dropping in."

"And with Rafe sitting there."

She nodded. "I don't suppose Rafe is about as tall as you, with shoulders about as broad, and about as muscular, with dark hair and a pair of jeans with a rip right underneath his truly impressive butt. Because if he is, you will have won Lys over to the dark side."

"I don't ever look at Rafe's butt, so I can't say about the jeans, but the rest of it…yeah. He's gonna have to sit all day with Lys ogling him? Poor guy."

"Lys won't ogle *all* day." Jamie slid to her feet, deliberately brushing against him and sparking little electrical shocks all over. "She has to blink sometime."

Her fingers were the last part of her to slip away from him, brushing lightly across his belly, not even coming near his arousal but affecting it just the same. She knew it, too, if that sexy smile and the sashay of her hips were anything to judge by.

Nearby Mischa was snoring again, though she hadn't been outside yet. His coffee was getting cold in its cup, and it was past time for him to be shaving and dressing and getting ready for the day.

But he was the boss. He hadn't gone to work late and unprepared even once in the past five years. If Jamie wasn't a good reason to start, such a thing didn't exist.

"Sleep a while, Mischa," he murmured as he headed around the island. "We're going back to bed."

Jamie and Russ were just approaching the edge of town when his cell phone rang. He pulled it from his pocket, flipped it open and mostly listened to the conversation, his jaw tightening. "We'll be right there," he said tersely before hanging up.

She took a breath, bracing herself. Obviously something had happened: her house vandalized, her office targeted, maybe even—*please, God, no*—Lys.

"It's not Lys," he said as if he'd heard her prayer. "Someone did a little painting at the condo project across the river. Tommy wants us to come by."

She had seen the condos only at a distance, but knew several people who'd already bought in. They were going to be luxury places that reminded her of her last visit to Charleston, and the multihued houses on Rainbow Row.

He drove past the square, then turned right on Carolina and crossed the river. The street leading into the project wound through a grove of live oak trees, moss dangling from their branches, before passing through a gate and branching off to various buildings. Tommy's SUV, along with a police car, was

parked in front of the clubhouse straight ahead, with several
pickups belonging to Calloway Construction.

The first message was painted in white across the brick face
of the clubhouse. It lined the walls inside in red, orange and
black, dripped down the windows, sprayed across the fireplace. It was scrawled across the concrete floor and visible
from the clubhouse patio on six of the seven buildings.

Stay away from her.
Stay away from her.
Stay away from her.

And just in case there was any confusion regarding who
the message was for or who it was about, on the largest wall
inside the common area were two photographs torn from a
newspaper, Jamie's tacked to the drywall, Russ's held there
by a hunting knife stuck between the eyes.

Dear God.

Jamie swayed, feeling sick, and Russ slid his arm around
her waist. Tension vibrated through him as he guided her
back outside, where only the one threat could be seen.

"You don't have security at your sites at night?" Tommy
asked.

"Some of them. It depends on where we are on the job.
Once fixtures and appliances have started going in, yeah.
They tend to grow feet and walk away if we don't. And usually
the site foreman and I both drive by a couple times on
weekends just to check things out."

But he hadn't been able to do that this weekend because
he'd been babysitting Jamie. It was probably a good thing he
hadn't, because he might have surprised the stalker. That knife
might have wound up in his chest instead of his photograph.
Just the thought made her hug herself tightly.

"Who knows you're staying with him?" Tommy asked.

She breathed for steadiness. "You, Robbie, Lys. A number of people at the hospital saw me leaving with him Saturday and probably guessed."

"Maybe it's time for us to move you elsewhere."

"No." Russ's voice was sharp, angry. "She's staying where she is."

"This bastard's threatening you now."

"I don't give a damn. She's not going off somewhere else to keep *me* safe."

Jamie freed one hand to touch his arm. "Russ—"

He wrapped his fingers tightly around hers, but didn't look at her. "No. Absolutely not."

He looked so grim, so foreboding that she didn't argue with him. After he'd calmed down, then she would reason with him. *She* was the one this guy was after; if she was gone, he would forget Russ. She could run, she could hide on her own. She could handle that. But if Russ got hurt, if, God forbid, he died because of her, she would never survive.

Apparently, *later* seemed a better time to Tommy, too, because he abruptly changed the subject. "We know how the stalker found you Saturday. Our evidence guys were going over your car at the garage, and they found a Global Positioning System transmitter. He knew where you were from the minute you left your driveway."

That was even creepier than just being followed. What did this guy want from her that would justify the trouble and expense of high-tech stalking? "Will that help you find him?"

Tommy shook his head, then indicated Russ and himself. "We use GPSs when we go hunting. Fishermen use 'em. Hikers. Delivery services. Probably every soldier who's been to Iraq or Afghanistan has one. They're relatively cheap and easy to find."

"How did he get access to my car?" she asked numbly.

"He only needed a minute. Parked outside the office, in your driveway, in the grocery store lot… He could have done it the same night he drugged the dog, or it could have been the first thing he did, before the note or the candy. There's no way to know."

She stared at the message. At least the damage inside was minimal; the drywall hadn't yet been painted, the glass could be cleaned, and carpet or tile would cover the words on the floor. But the brick…even she knew paint was difficult to clean from brick, and there were seven threats, all in bright white against dusty-red.

One threat. Not against her, but Russ. The knife in the photograph was impossible to misinterpret. He'd tried to do the right thing by offering her a place to stay, and in return, she'd brought danger into his life.

Suddenly shuddering, she pulled free of him, went to his truck and climbed in. She was huddling there, unable to tear her gaze from the words on the wall, when he finished talking with Tommy and joined her.

For a moment, he sat motionless, his right hand clenching his keys, then he breathed loudly and stuck the key in the ignition. "It's not a big deal."

What she intended as a snort came out choked, closer to a sob. "He's *threatening* you."

"Yeah. Well. It's not gonna get him anywhere." He backed out, then accelerated, tires spinning before finding traction.

"He feels threatened by you. He knows I'm staying with you. He knows I—" *used to love you. Maybe do again. Maybe never stopped.* "I care about you. If he can't get me away from you, then he's got to get rid of you."

Russ stared ahead, his jaw clenched so tightly that he might as well have been carved from stone. "I'm not going any-where, and neither are you." After rolling through a stop sign and onto Carolina Boulevard, he scowled at her. "Don't give me any bull about leaving me for my own good. I can take care of myself. I know the risks and I'm willing to take them. You can't win this argument, James, so don't waste your breath."

Conceding he was right—at least about wasting her breath—she fell silent, staring out the window. But on every brick storefront they passed, every expanse of glass, she saw the words again. *Stay away from her.* She saw the photograph and the knife.

He parked in the tiny lot behind the building, went inside with her and searched every corner of the office. He was standing at the window staring out when a knock sounded at the door. His muscles visibly tightened just as Jamie's own before he spun and strode into the outer office.

It was Rafe, and he was, indeed, the guy with the impressive butt. He wore jeans, a T-shirt and work boots that had seen better days. His muscles had muscles, and he carried a gym bag filled with magazines and, she surmised from the look Russ gave it, the arch of his brow and Rafe's answering nod, a weapon.

Russ introduced them, talked for a few minutes in the outer office with Rafe, then returned to Jamie's office and hugged her. "I'll check back."

The independent woman inside her—the one who thought her leaving for his own good was still the best idea—should have protested, saying, *No, it's not necessary.* The real Jamie, though, just hugged him tighter, her face hidden against his shirt, and murmured, "I appreciate it."

After holding her a moment longer, he kissed her, hard and quick, then left. Jamie walked to the doorway of the outer office, where Rafe had made himself comfortable with the latest issue of *Newsweek*. "Can I get you coffee?"

"No, thanks."

Just as well. Lys always made the coffee, and Jamie didn't feel like reading instructions just now.

She nervously crossed her arms over her chest. "I've never had a bodyguard before."

Rafe grinned. "Sure, you have. At least, for the last couple days."

"Do you do this sort of thing often?" As far as she knew, he was a carpenter or framer or something, not the kind of guy who first came to mind when you thought *protection*.

"Nah. But I spent two years in Iraq, and I was a cop in Atlanta for a while."

And now he worked in construction. No doubt, there was an interesting story behind that, but she didn't have a chance to ask as Lys swept into the office. Buds in her ears, she was singing along to a song Jamie didn't know and balancing her bag, a pizza box and a doughnut box. She made it halfway across the room without noticing Rafe, skidding to a stop when finally she did. The instant she recognized him, her face flamed red and her mouth dropped open, but no words came out.

"Lys, this is Rafe. He's going to spend the day with us."

He nodded politely, then went back to reading.

"H-hey." Lys started walking again with stuttering steps, reaching Jamie before darting another look at him, then mouthing, "Is that—?" She tilted her head toward River's Edge. When Jamie nodded, she rolled her eyes. Wow.

"How do you feel?" she asked aloud, her gaze locking on the bruises.

"I'm fine. There's been another incident, though." Going

to sit behind her desk, Jamie quietly told her about the vandalism, the message and the photographs.

Lys's color paled to match her stark-white dress. "Oh my God, Jamie," she murmured. "You're not going to continue staying with Russ, are you?"

"I don't know." Hard words to say. There was no place on earth she would rather be than with Russ, but not if it meant directing the stalker's anger at him. She wanted to be safe, but even more she wanted him safe.

"Wow. I'm not even going to ask you to come to my house. No offense, I love you dearly, but I don't want this guy trashing my place or me. Maybe you should leave town for a few days."

"I thought about that." Vaguely, in the small part of her mind that had still been functioning normally on the drive over from the condos. "I don't know where I'd go. Not to Macon. Not anyplace someone might expect me to go."

Lys opened the doughnut box and took out a glazed one, then resettled in the client chair. After she'd savored the first few bites, she said, "I have an idea. My grandfather has a little place up on Lake Oconee. It's nothing fancy, but no one would ever think to look there."

"I'll think about it." She didn't need fancy. All she needed was to know that she and Russ were both safe. Then she glanced at the calendar open on her desk. "Who am I kidding? I can't leave town now. I've got appointments and hearings all this week."

"You could get someone to fill in on what's important and reschedule everything else. It's an emergency, Jamie." Lys picked another doughnut. "Trust me—the other lawyers and the judges don't want you showing up if there's a chance this crazy perv will show up, too."

She'd had to reschedule her whole life once before because

of an emergency. That time she'd been in the hospital recovering from a murder attempt. Would it come to that again?

A glance into the reception area at Rafe made her feel a little braver. Not if she, Russ, Tommy and Rafe could help it.

"I'll talk to Russ," Jamie said, and she saw Lys's eyes start the slightest roll upward. "If he agrees, and Tommy does, I'll go somewhere for a few days, but I think it'd be best if none of you knows where."

"But, Jamie—" The ringing phone made Lys break off to check her watch. "Jeez, ten seconds past nine o'clock."

The second line also rang.

"Do these people *sit* on the phone?" Lys muttered, snatching up the receiver. "Jamie Munroe's office, please hold." After repeating the greeting on the second line, she fixed her frown on Jamie. "We'll finish discussing this during our break."

"You discuss. I'm going to be watching the hot guys there." Jamie pointed to River's Edge, already buzzing with activity. Before long, Russ would show up over there, and either before or after, or both if she was lucky, he'd show up here again, too.

Lys snorted. "You watch them. I'm gonna watch the hot guy sitting five feet from my desk. I'll be lucky if I even remember how to answer the phone." Taking a drink and one last doughnut, she walked to the door, singing tunelessly, "There is a God, and She likes me."

Jamie looked at the cold pizza, still untouched, then moved the box from her desk. "I hope God likes me, too," she whispered. Because if she got Russ back just to lose him by dying, she was going to be haunting someone for a long, long time.

The morning passed slowly. By lunch she had a headache and a nagging burn in her stomach. Hunger, she hoped, though nerves seemed more likely. Lys went to pick up lunch, and Jamie finished the notes on her eleven o'clock appointment.

She went to the file room to pull a folder and flipped the switch, but the light didn't come on.

Scowling, she went on in, leaving the heavy door open, found the right drawer and was bent over trying to read the handwritten labels when a soft noise sounded in the outer office, followed a moment later by the faint disturbance in the air that meant the front door had been opened or closed. She didn't have another appointment until two o'clock, so she figured either Lys had been quick with lunch, Tommy was making another stop or Russ had finally found time to drop by.

"I'll be right out," she called. As she straightened, she caught a glimpse of movement, a dark flash, something swinging through the air, then pain exploded through her head. She pitched forward, trying to catch herself, but the blow had caught her already off-balance, sending her crashing into another oak cabinet.

The pain washed over her in waves; it was the last thing she remembered.

It was one of those curious moments when, like turning a switch, everything went quiet. Conversation lulled, the saws and sanders and grinders all went silent, the hammering stopped, and even traffic noise on the streets died down. It was as if the entire small area of the universe that surrounded River's Edge had been put on hold, just for an instant.

Then the scream came.

It was shrill, piercing, worthy of a Hollywood horror movie, and it raised the hairs on the back of Russ's neck. Like everyone else on the crew, he turned reflexively toward the noise, coming from the sidewalk across the street. Unlike the others, he dropped the blueprints he'd been rolling, took the steps in a leap and raced across the lawn and across the street.

People on the street were staring toward the source of the screams—*Help her, oh, God, someone please help!*—and Sophy Marchand, whose shop was in the building next door to Jamie's, was hurrying along the sidewalk, cell phone in hand.

Lys's eyes were huge, her face whiter than Russ had ever seen. Her whole body was shaking, and there was a bright smear of red across her white dress. Blood.

Dear God. Heart pounding, he gave her a shove toward Sophy and said, "Call 911. Tell 'em to get Tommy over here *now.*"

"An—and an—an ambulance. T-t-two," Lys added hoarsely.

Sophy nodded, already dialing, as she wrapped one arm around Lys's waist and guided her away, murmuring softly to her.

Muscles knotted, his chest so tight he could hardly breathe, Russ skidded around the corner and into Jamie's outer office. Rafe lay motionless on the floor, as if he'd just slid out of the chair to the floor and decided to stay. There was no blood, no sign of a wound of any kind.

The scene in the file room was the opposite. A lot of blood, covering Jamie's face, matting her hair, seeping into the carpet.

"Oh, Jesus, Jamie." Russ knelt beside her, afraid to touch her, afraid he might hurt her. The wound was still bleeding, so she was alive, thank God. She just had to stay that way. "It's gonna be okay, babe. Help's coming. You're okay."

He risked picking up her hand, the skin soft and warm, and her fingers tightened fractionally around his. She made a low sound, part whimper, part moan, then went still again.

Pounding feet sounded in the corridor; a moment later a number of cops, including Tommy, rushed into the office, with the paramedics behind them. Reluctantly Russ released Jamie's hand—once again her grip tightened before going slack—and moved out of the file room.

"Get out of my crime scene," Tommy said grimly, giving him a push toward the door. "Come on outside. I need to find out what happened from freaky Lys."

"Don't call her that," Russ said numbly as he obeyed. It felt wrong to be walking away from Jamie, but there was nothing he could do for her at the moment. But damned if it wasn't the last time he was going to be away from her in the foreseeable future.

More paramedics were working on Rafe, who looked like he was sound asleep. They'd rolled him over and there was still no sign of an injury. "What do you want to bet they find the same drug in him that was in Mischa?" Russ muttered as they skirted them, then went out the door.

There was a crowd gathered outside now. Pete Petrovski stood guard at the door, keeping them back, and another officer was directing traffic around the emergency vehicles blocking the street. Russ ignored them all, including ogling members of his own crew, and looked to the right for Lys.

She was sitting on the front steps of Sophy's shop, huddled and trembling as if she were naked in a snowstorm. The blood—*Jamie's* blood—was a stark contrast to her white dress.

As they turned up the walk, Sophy gave Lys a comforting pat on the arm, then went inside the shop.

"What the hell happened?" Tommy demanded.

Lys flinched, then raised her gaze to Russ, her dark eyes glazed over. "Is she going to be okay?"

"Yes." He had no clue how bad the wound was. He just knew that yes was the only answer he could live with. She *had* to be all right. His life depended on it.

If his answer brought Lys any comfort, it didn't show. She looked away, fixing her attention on the flashing lights of the nearest ambulance, slowly shaking her head. "She asked me to drop some papers off at the courthouse and to go to the post office, then pick up lunch from that new place across the river. But it was crowded. New places always are. And she had an appointment, and I'd already been gone about thirty minutes, so I didn't wait. I came back to see if she wanted a sandwich from Ellie's instead and I found Rafe and—and then Jamie, and there was so much blood…"

She covered her face with both hands, shudders racking her. Russ was tempted to lay his hand on her shoulder. After all, she was Jamie's best friend. They were going to have to make peace with each other for her sake if nothing else. But if he reached out, his own hand would be shaking, and he preferred to keep it under control while he could.

"Did Jamie have any appointments while you were gone?" Tommy asked.

Lys shook her head.

"Did you lock the door when you left?"

"No. We never do during office hours if either of us is there."

"Did you notice anything odd when you came back?"

"Yeah. The big, strong bodyguard lying unconscious on the floor," Lys snapped, but her irritation disappeared as quickly as it had come. "No. The lights were on, and the music was playing in Jamie's office. She always turned it off when people came in. The old guy next door had moved his car into my parking space, but he does that every time I have a closer space than him. Everything was fine. Normal."

Except that Jamie had been surprised by her stalker in her own file room. It took a certain kind of lowlife bastard to attack a woman from behind.

"Did Rafe go to lunch before you left?" Tommy asked.

"No. He hadn't left that chair except to get up and walk around the office a few times."

"Did he eat anything? Drink anything?" Russ asked.

Lys shrugged. "He brought some bottles of sports drink with him."

"I'll have 'em checked." Tommy's gaze shifted back down the street, and he gestured. "They're bringing them out. You two going to the hospital?"

"Yes." Russ and Lys answered together, then he grudgingly asked, "You want a ride?"

"No. I'll take my car." Just as grudgingly, she added, "But thanks."

It was only a couple miles to the hospital. Nagged by the same dread he'd felt Saturday magnified a hundred times, Russ grabbed the nearest parking spot, then strode across the lot and into the emergency department.

The staff kept him waiting while they examined Jamie and Rafe. Lys arrived fifteen minutes after him and claimed a spot of wall nearby. She'd changed clothes, wearing all black now, still unnaturally pale. Not only could she scream like a horror movie chick, she could pass as one of the undead in the same movie.

Minutes dragged by, too many to count, while his gaze remained locked on the doorway that separated waiting room from treatment area. If he didn't hear something soon—

"Are you going to hurt her again?"

Lys's question surprised him. She'd been so silent that he'd practically forgotten she was there. "I would never—"

"Maybe you'd never physically hurt her, but you broke her heart. Do you think that didn't hurt? She loved you. She thought you loved her back. She thought you were going to marry her, and instead you married Melinda."

She loved you. He'd been too young and stupid to appreciate that at the time. There had never been any shortage of women in his life. The women he hadn't attracted on his own had been drawn by the family fortune or the family name, and he'd been too stupid to care about that, either.

He was smarter now. He knew how hard love was to come by. He knew how rare a woman like Jamie was. He just needed the chance to show her.

"What happens between Jamie and me—" He broke off. He'd been about to say, *is between Jamie and me*. But Lys did have a legitimate interest. If Robbie announced that he was getting involved once again with the woman who'd turned him into a mean, angry and, thank God, short-term drunk when he was twenty, Russ would damn well be interested.

He settled for saying, "I'm not going to hurt her. And I'm not going to let anyone else hurt her."

Predictably, Lys didn't look convinced. "This is her second visit to the emergency room in three days."

"Yeah. It's also her last time out of my sight."

"For how long?"

"As long as it takes." He shrugged. "The rest of our lives."

Lys opened her mouth, but at that moment the door Russ had been watching so intently opened and a woman in scrubs came out and straight to him. It was Cate Calloway, doctor and cousin by marriage.

"Hey, Russ, you here with Jamie? She's gonna be fine. She's got a couple of spectacular knots on her head, a mild concussion and one hell of a headache. I wanted to admit her overnight for observation, but she says she's going home. With you. Is that right?"

"It's the only way she's leaving the hospital."

Cate gave him a curious look. "So the rumors are true. You're having a thing with the woman you used to call Satan. We gonna be welcoming her to the family soon?"

"Probably." He couldn't miss Lys's look. She might be making an effort to bury the hatchet, but as the old joke went, she would probably prefer to bury it in his head. "Can we see her?"

"Yeah, come on." Cate led the way to the door, where she typed in a code, then held it open for them. "We're waiting for a couple test results before we let her go. The nurse will give you discharge directions. You need to keep a close watch on her and get her back here if anything seems odd. And for God's sake, don't let anyone hit her in the head again. She's running out of places that aren't bruised, split open or swollen."

Jamie was in the same exam room as before, head turned to one side, eyes closed, looking even more ragged. There was a livid knot across her forehead, swabbed and sutured, and another on the back of her head, with matching sutures.

"Hey, James."

She opened her eyes and smiled just a little before it turned to a wince. "Hey," she whispered.

"Man, the lengths some people will go to to avoid Monday in the office." Gently he took her hand, then crouched beside the bed so they were on eye level. "You're okay."

"Yeah. How's Rafe?"

Russ felt guilty; he'd pretty much forgotten about Rafe. "In better shape than you. I'll ask Cate the next time she comes by. She'd like to keep you overnight."

Jamie's fingers tightened around his. "I hate being in the hospital. I just want to go home."

"All right. We'll do that." He raised his free hand to touch the only part of her face where he was pretty sure it wouldn't hurt, stroking his fingers along her jaw. "Lys is here."

Jamie's gaze shifted to the left, but she couldn't see without turning her head. Rising, Russ released her hand, then traded places with Lys. "Are you okay?"

Lys's smile quavered. "I'm fine. The guy was gone before I got back."

"Thank God. They shaved my hair." Jamie raised one unsteady hand toward the back of her head, thought better of it and lowered it again.

"It'll grow back. Until it does, we'll buy you a big, floppy, Southern belle hat with ribbons trailing everywhere."

"Eww," Jamie responded, and they both laughed weakly. "I'll see if I can get a Calloway Construction ball cap."

"Yeah, well, sleeping with the owner's got to be good for something."

Russ leaned against the opposite wall, watching them. Despite Jamie's claims, he'd never thought of Lys as friend material. She'd always been so weird, deliberately standing out instead of trying to fit in, and lately all her energy had been directed at persuading Jamie she was better off with her instead of Russ.

But now, the way Lys looked at her…

Tommy came in a moment later, asking Jamie questions that she had no answers for. What she did know was sketchy: she'd been in the file room, she'd heard a thud, then the front door had opened or closed. No help at all, she reluctantly admitted.

In the silence that followed, Cate returned. Rafe had been admitted; blood tests showed a powerful sedative in his system—the same sedative, as Russ had guessed, that had been given to Mischa. They would keep him until the effects had worn off.

Jamie looked troubled. "This is my fault. If he hadn't been there—"

Russ stopped her. "I was the one who asked him to stay.

He was the one who agreed. The only one who bears any fault in this is the bastard who drugged him."

"You're sure he didn't eat anything while he was in the office?" Tommy directed the question to Lys, who shook her head. "And the only thing he drank was what he brought with him. So the drug was either in one of the bottles, or he was injected with it."

Russ moved to stare out the window. The bastard had just waltzed in, taken out a two-hundred-pound ex-soldier–ex-cop and tried to kill Jamie, with people all over the place, with *him* just across the street. And then he'd walked out the door, along the sidewalk to his vehicle, calm and cool, drawing no attention to himself.

Russ should have prevented it. He shouldn't have let Jamie go to work, shouldn't have counted on one guy, no matter how formidable, to protect her. When she'd talked that morning about leaving, he should have agreed, should have taken her out of town himself.

He should have done a better job watching over her.

Finally Cate laid the chart aside. "Well, Jamie, if you're sure you don't want to spend the night with us, we'll get rid of these guys and get you dressed and out of here."

"I'm sure."

Russ squeezed her hand as he followed Tommy out the door and back down to the waiting room. Looking more serious than usual, Tommy went to a deserted spot, then faced him. "I didn't want to say anything to Jamie just yet, but there was another note. He left it on her desk."

Russ had glanced at her desk only long enough to see that she wasn't sitting there. He had a vague memory of papers and files, nothing more. "What did it say?"

"'Get rid of him.'"

Stay away from her. Get rid of him. "Bossy bastard, isn't he?" he asked with a grim smile.

After a moment, they both spoke at the same time. "About my suggestion— Maybe moving her—"

Tommy broke off, and Russ went on. "Maybe moving her is a good idea."

"Where would you go?"

Russ shrugged. Between them, his aunts and uncles had probably a dozen vacation homes, from the Georgia coast to Vail. Any of them would be happy to give him the keys for a while. Or they could go to some touristy place and rent a cottage under a fake name, or move from motel to motel, or take a road trip. They could get lost in a city, the bigger, the better.

"I'll figure something out. Right now—" His gaze moved to the security door as it opened. A kid in scrubs pushed Jamie through in a wheelchair. Lys was behind them, clutching a handful of papers. "She's in no shape to travel." She was pale, slumped in the chair, one hand pressed to her right temple as if trying to ease an ache there.

Tommy turned to look, too. "Yeah. If he keeps cracking her skull, the son of a bitch's going to kill her whether he means to or not. I wish I could assign a couple guys to watch her."

But he couldn't. Private security wasn't the police department's job. Jamie's private security was Russ's job.

"I'll get someone." And he was going to move her. She might be too weak for a long journey, but the place he had in mind was only a mile or so south of his house. It had never been part of Granddad's logging operation, so there was only the one road in.

And he wasn't telling anyone, not even Tommy.

Damned if he was going to let anything happen to her again.

Chapter 10

On the unending ride home, Jamie's head throbbed, a bruise formed on her shoulder, and the acid in her stomach had reached boiling point. She wanted bed and food in that order, so it was with relief that she recognized the last crossroad before reaching Russ's house.

He'd been on the cell phone for a while, but she felt so crappy that she hadn't even listened. Now, as they rounded the last curve and the house came into sight, she roused herself to summon the energy to walk inside and to the bedroom.

Russ had different plans. He laid his hand over hers when she started to unfasten the seat belt. "We're not staying here. I just came to get some clothes and Mischa."

The idea of sitting upright for even another mile was enough to make her head throb in new places. "Where are we going?"

"Rick's house. It's not far. Wait here and I'll get what we need."

She was so woozy that she knew she'd lost track of time. It seemed only a moment before he returned with suitcases that he put in the back, a moment after that with two handfuls of plastic sacks filled with groceries, once more with Mischa and her dog food.

The dog jumped into the truck, sniffed curiously around Jamie, then sat down and gently nuzzled her. Jamie wrapped her arm around her; that was the extent of her energy.

Back over the hard-packed road, onto the highway heading into town, then onto another dirt road. This one was less traveled, bumpier, and it increased her discomfort to the point that she thought she might cry, when she *never* cried from physical pain. Not when she'd been stabbed, not when she'd been run off the road. Her tears were saved for emotional pain, like getting her heart broken.

Or, she added with a glance at Russ, getting it put back together.

Finally, they reached Holigan Creek and the house that, like Russ's, sat on the bank. It was a log cabin, smaller than his, but charming just the same. It faced south, with a wrap-around porch that offered views of the creek to the east. He pulled into the garage, shut off the engine and waited until the door was closed again before he got out.

He helped her inside, through a large family room-kitchen with sleeping space in a loft overhead, past a guest room and into the master suite. She barely noticed the colors—burnished yellow, khaki and rust—as he settled her on the bed.

"Crackers?"

She nodded once and regretted it.

He made several trips back to the garage, and before long, she was stripped down to her panties, wearing one of his

T-shirts and munching from a sleeve of saltine crackers, feeling marginally better.

Russ put away the groceries, their clothes and toiletries, then fixed a couple of ham sandwiches and brought them, with water and chips, into the bedroom. She made room for him to sit beside her, then took a cautious bite of her sandwich. "You're very good at pampering."

He grinned. "I expect the same next time I get thumped on the head."

"There's been a first time?"

"Hell, yeah. Rick and Robbie have probably done it twelve or fifteen times, and one time at work, I fell off a scaffolding and pitched headfirst onto a stack of drywall. Broke the top sheet of the drywall. Just gave me a bit of a headache."

She smiled faintly, then it faded. "What did Tommy tell you when you went out to the waiting room with him?"

His gaze steady, he told her about the note. It was ominous enough on its own, but the implied threat—*or I will*—made her blood run cold. "Lys's grandfather has a place at Lake Oconee."

She expected an argument, but it didn't come. "My family's got places all over. Or we could just see the U.S.A. in my Chevrolet. But first you need some time to rest."

"You don't have to go with me."

"Yes, I do."

Her smile was thin and regretful. "Because he's targeting you now."

Russ finished off his sandwich, then picked up the other half of hers. "He's not getting to you again unless he kills me first."

"I don't want your death on my conscience."

He studied her while he chewed, then drained half his water in one swallow. His grin came back slowly, broad and sexy enough to stir a tingle of desire deep inside her. "I've got plans for you and me, James, and they don't include dying an untimely death."

"What—" She cleared her throat, but her voice was still husky. "What kind of plans?"

"Long-term."

"Friends with benefits?"

"Friends, I hope. It's no fun living with someone you don't like. But more than that."

She ate a little of her sandwich while considering that. The warmth in his voice and his gaze was going a long way to ease her discomfort. "I hope, too," she murmured before taking another bite.

She dozed off and on through the afternoon and into the evening. Sometimes when she awoke, Russ was sitting in a chair nearby, reading or staring out the window or just watching her. Once she caught a glimpse of him outside, tossing a chewed-up tennis ball for Mischa to fetch. A couple of times he was on his cell phone in the next room, his voice a distant rumble, familiar, comforting.

The glowing numbers on the nightstand clock showed 10:43 p.m. when she finally got up and went into the connecting bathroom before padding into the kitchen for what she needed next: a cold drink and Russ.

He was standing at the long peninsula that separated the kitchen from the family room, staring fixedly into the distance, looking worried. Lord knew, she came with plenty of things to trouble him. Her stalker. The vandalism to his job site. The threat against him. The ongoing upheaval in his life.

He didn't notice her until she slid onto a stool opposite him. "Hey," she said softly.

His gaze moved over her, pausing on her forehead. Even if a look in the bathroom mirror hadn't told her that she looked pretty bad, she would guess it from the way his eyes narrowed and his jaw tightened. Anger entered his expression, followed by determination and something else, something softer, warmer, sweeter. It made her blood hot and her knees weak, and instantly everything felt better.

He gestured toward the cooktop beside him. "How about some soup?"

She sniffed the redolent air, decided she was hungry and nodded. As if glad of something to do, he filled a bowl from the pot, got silverware, a glass of ice and a bottle of water and opened a new sleeve of crackers, then set everything in front of her. Standing back, arms folded across his chest, he leaned against the counter and watched until she'd finished all but a few bites of the soup.

"What's on your mind?" she asked as she pushed the bowl a few inches away.

"You. What happened."

"Have you heard anything about Rafe?"

"He's awake. Fine. Pissed he let his guard down."

"It wasn't his fault."

"No," Russ agreed. Once again he busied himself, rinsing the bowl, putting away the crackers, storing the leftover soup in the refrigerator. She didn't offer her help, aware he wouldn't accept it and, truly, not sure how much help she could be. Her head was still hurting, and just about every expression she made, she'd discovered, tugged on the stitches across her forehead.

"Hey, James." His back was to her, his voice muffled. "When did you start eating Mexican food?"

Curious question, even more curious tone. Too casual. She tried to sound just casual. "I don't eat Mexican. Not since I was ten and threw up in the middle of La Cantina at my sister's birthday party. Considering the number of times you tried to get me to eat it in school, and the number of times I refused, I'd think you'd remember."

Though there was a lot he hadn't remembered about the two of them together, because he hadn't been serious about her. In the past few days that knowledge had lost most of its power. Only a faint twinge of regret stirred inside her.

"I do remember. I was just so damn worried about you that it took a while…" He faced her then, lines of tension marking the corners of his mouth, looking as if what he had to say was unpleasant. "Lys told Tommy and me that she was gone to get lunch when you were attacked. She said you wanted it from the new restaurant across the river."

Jamie thought back to that morning. The doctor had told her not to worry if her memory of the events just before the assault was fuzzy or missing altogether. It was common in a head injury, and since she'd gotten conked twice that day—once by her assailant, once when she fell—and was already concussed from the car accident, it was even expected in her case. "I don't remember. I might have."

"The condos are just one of our projects on the west side. We've got four houses going up in the new subdivision down-river, so I spend a lot of time over there. There's not much commercial development yet—a couple convenience stores, a movie rental place, a fast-food drive-through…and the new restaurant. Taquito Tacos."

Maybe it was all the knocks to the head she'd taken; maybe it was stress or fuzziness from sleeping most of the afternoon and evening, but it took a moment for his words to sink in. When they did, she felt a moment's queasiness, as if dinner might reappear.

"She said you *asked* for Mexican food for lunch. Why would she say that?"

"She must have misunderstood. Or maybe she asked if I wanted to try the new place, thinking I knew what it was, and not knowing, I said yes." Both were plausible excuses. Except for the fact that Lys rarely got anything wrong, and while Jamie could clearly remember asking her to go to the post office and the courthouse and to pick up lunch while she was out, she couldn't for the life of her recall a discussion of where to get the food. She often left the choice to Lys, who knew her favorites at every restaurant in town.

"Have you ever told her you don't like Mexican food?" Russ asked quietly.

Jamie wished she could give the same answer as before: *I don't remember.* But she did. Lys had been aghast at the idea of anyone who didn't find great pleasure in queso, salsa, fajitas and carne asada. She'd even tried to entice Jamie to Tia Maria's with the promise of the best margaritas in three counties.

"Yes," she said softly, hating the answer, hating what she was thinking, what he was clearly thinking. "Maybe…maybe she…" She was such a bad friend because she couldn't come up with a single excuse that wasn't flimsy. There was only one reason for Lys to lie: she didn't want anyone to know where she'd been or what she'd done. Why? What was she hiding? Was she somehow involved with Jamie's stalker? Was she protecting him or—Jamie felt crappy for even thinking it—helping him?

She shied away from the idea. Lys was her best friend. She would never help anyone who threatened Jamie. *Never.* The idea was too ridiculous to consider.

"There's got to be some explanation," she said, her face warming while her core turned cold.

"Like what? She confused you with her other best friend?" He didn't have to spell it out: Lys's life wasn't exactly overflowing with friends. In fact, outside of the occasional date or family events, her social life was pretty much time spent with Jamie.

Russ pressed on. "Does she know you like those roses?"

Again, she wished she could say *I don't remember.* Again, she couldn't. "She—she's ordered them online for me a couple times."

"And the chocolates?"

She nodded bleakly.

"She had access to your car. She was there the night you should have gotten a flat. She knows Mischa and would have no trouble feeding her something laced with sedatives. She knows our history and knows that we're back together. She feels threatened by me. You said so yourself."

"Yes, but…she's my *friend.* She can't be a stalker. My stalker is supposed to be a guy." She knew it was a silly thing to say. Stalkers came in all types. But it was more common for men to stalk women, or vice versa, than for a woman to stalk another woman. That just added a little extra to the creep factor.

"All a stalker has to be is obsessed."

"And you think Lys is obsessed with me?"

He rested his elbows on the counter, bringing him much closer. "Today at the hospital, when you were talking to her, the way she looked at you…I knew that look, but I didn't recognize it, then Tommy came in, and Cate. It wasn't until I was watching you sleep a while ago that I knew. She was looking at you the way I do. Like…like she's in love with you."

Jamie stilled in the act of reaching for her glass, her hand utterly motionless. Had he just said that he was in love with her? She wanted to ask him to repeat it in a more straightforward fashion, wanted to tell him that she loved him again, too, that maybe deep inside she'd never stopped. But he looked so damn grim and this wasn't exactly the conversation where she wanted to lay bare her most tender feelings.

"Of course she loves me," she said in a halfhearted protest. "She's my best friend. Best friends love each other."

"Not love, James. *In* love. You know the difference as well as I do."

"But…she's not…I'm not…I'd never…" Jamie stared at the counter. Other people could have known about the flowers and the chocolates; though Lys didn't have many friends, Jamie did. And anyone could have planted the GPS on her car; it sat outside her office all day and her house all night. And Mischa was a friendly dog; the only person she'd ever disliked on meeting was Russ, and she'd changed her mind about him soon enough. Offer her food, and she would be your new best buddy.

But who besides Lys had known that Jamie would go back to the office after her trip to Augusta last Wednesday? Who had known that nothing-special rental car had taken the place of her convertible? Who had come around the corner mere moments after Jamie's tire would have gone flat, if Russ hadn't interfered? Lys had said she'd gone to pick up a pizza—the woman who had Luigi's on speed dial for delivery.

Who had known today that Rafe would remain in the office with Jamie when Lys went out? What were the odds that the stalker had coincidentally come prepared for a second victim even though he'd waited until the only other person usually in the office was gone?

Her shoulders sagging, Jamie covered her face with her hands, winced and lowered them again. "I tell her I love her, that I don't know what I'd do without her, that meeting her was my lucky day, but I mean it as a *friend*. Why would she think…?"

"She's not thinking. She's obsessing."

"But she dates guys!"

"And she's in love with you."

Jamie shivered, and Russ came around the end of the counter to gather her into his arms. She leaned against him, absorbing his warmth, his strength, wishing he could somehow make this whole mess go away.

But it was this mess that had brought them back together.

She clung to him a while before finally murmuring, "We should tell Tommy."

"Yeah." But Russ made no move to release her.

"If we're wrong, she'll be so hurt that I suspected her."

"We'll find a way to apologize."

After a few minutes, he let go, picked up his cell phone from the coffee table and came back to stand beside her. She could hear the faint ringing, then Tommy's voice, pretty alert considering the hour. She couldn't make out his words, and Russ's responses were terse, offering no information: *Good. Really? Yeah.*

Then the meat: "That's not the only thing she lied about." He repeated his and Jamie's suspicions, while she clung to the fading hope that it was all just a horrible misunderstanding. How could she have been so wrong about Lys? How could she have become friends with a woman who could do the things Lys had apparently done? Why hadn't she known?

Finally Russ hung up. Instead of relating the conversation to her immediately, he slid the phone into his pocket, then picked up Jamie.

"I can walk," she said, her protest too feeble by far. She liked being in his arms. She'd never felt safer.

As they passed through the family room, he gave a short whistle and Mischa, stretched out on the couch, jumped to her feet and followed them into the bedroom. He settled Jamie in bed, folded the comforter in fourths, tossed it into a corner for Mischa, then stripped off his clothes and joined her. He laid his cell phone on the night table, next to one of his pistols, and gathered her into his arms.

"Rafe's been awake off and on this evening, but kind of woozy. He's finally clearheaded enough for Tommy to question him."

Jamie knew from his tone that she wasn't going to like what he had to say. She wanted to stick her fingers in her ears, clap her hands over his mouth or kiss him into silence, but she remained stiff and still and waited.

"Lys told us that Rafe hadn't eaten or drunk anything except the stuff he brought with him. She *didn't* tell us that she got him a cup of ice before she left on her errands. He poured the bottled stuff into it, drank it, and the next thing he knew, he was waking up in the hospital. And when the evidence guys searched the office, they didn't find the cup."

Her heart sank.

"You said you heard a thud in the outer office, then the door opening or closing. Tommy thinks Lys was hanging out in the hall, waiting for the drug to take effect. When Rafe fell from the chair, she came in and—and attacked you." His muscles tightened with the last words, and he wrapped his arm a little tighter around her.

"So she hit me, left the note on my desk and got rid of the cup she'd given Rafe. Then she came back and 'found' me, got a bit of my blood on her for effect and ran out screaming."

"Yeah. And remember Brent Johnson? The guy who owned the truck that ran you off the road? Tommy's been checking him out. Three guesses who he used to date."

Guilt was giving way to anger. Maybe she was finding it too easy to place blame on Lys; maybe a true friend would insist on proof. But a true friend wouldn't poison her dog. A true friend wouldn't terrorize her, wouldn't try to hurt her, maybe even kill her. A true friend wouldn't threaten the man she loved or the stranger who was doing nothing but keeping an eye on her.

But Jamie had *always* believed Lys was a true friend. She'd always trusted her, had faith in her. And *this* was what she'd gotten in return.

"Is Tommy going to question her?" she asked, her voice small and quiet.

"He was on his way there when we hung up."

As if on cue, the cell phone rang and Russ grabbed it. It was a short conversation, and he ended it looking even grimmer. "She's not home. They're checking for her car around town."

"Should we go someplace else?"

"No. I've got guys watching the road and the house, people who work security for the family. We're okay here for the night."

For the night. That was all they could hope for right now— to survive the night. And then they would get through tomorrow and tomorrow night, and sooner or later, Tommy would find Lys.

Sooner or later, this nightmare would be over.

Ordinarily Russ was out of bed before sunrise, ready to get to work and face the day, but the previous day had been far from ordinary. Though he and Jamie had stopped talking after he'd reassured her that they were safe, neither of them had fallen asleep for a long time. Once he'd drifted off, he hadn't changed position, and his body was protesting.

Jamie was using his left arm for a pillow, so he raised his right hand to his face, rubbing his eyes, then scratching across the bristle on his jaw. He looked at her, at the dark sutures and the rainbow of colors that marked half her face, and everything in him stiffened all over again. The desire to shake Lys like a junkyard dog with a rag doll clenched his free fingers into a fist before he pushed it to the back of his mind.

He glanced around, needing a moment to realize he wasn't in his bed, another moment to remember where he was. The clock said 5:25 a.m. Everything was quiet, Jamie's breathing slow and soft, Mischa's deep and rumbling. He wasn't sure if he'd just awakened, or if something had disturbed his sleep.

Then he heard it—a discordant hum coming from somewhere on the floor. He eased away from Jamie and slid out of bed, then located her purse where he'd dropped it the day before. The hum stopped, then started again within seconds. He turned back the flap that closed the purse and located her cell phone inside, set to vibrate instead of ring. The screen showed a number, no name. He flipped it open on his way out of the bedroom and said hello.

"Russ, it's Lys. I need to talk to Jamie right away!"

The anger returned, but he kept it tautly under control. "She's asleep, and I don't want to wake her."

"But it's an emergency!"

"Tell me."

There was silence for a moment, broken by the sound of a car passing at her end. "Okay. I guess… Yeah. I mean, you two are together, right?"

"Right," he agreed with more force than was necessary. He'd already told her at the hospital that he was going to watch out for Jamie for the rest of their lives. That had probably goaded her into whatever plan she was putting in motion now.

Probably a plan to get him out of her way.

"Okay. I went out for my usual run this morning, and when I came by the office, I glanced in the window, and—" Her voice began trembling. From fear, he would have guessed twenty-four hours ago. Excitement, he knew now. "Everything's been trashed—the files, the furniture, the pictures on the wall. It's a mess. She's got to get down here. All of our clients' confidential records…"

After the past eighteen hours, the last thing Jamie needed was to see her office in shambles. However, it was too good a chance to catch Lys to turn down. "Okay," he said. "We'll be there soon as we can."

Returning to the bedroom, he woke Jamie and told her about the call as they dressed. Once they were both decent and Mischa had been let out, they were on their way.

"I didn't know freaky Lys was a runner," he commented as he negotiated the night-dark road.

"Five miles every weekday, seven to ten on weekends. She's really serious about it."

"Apparently, she's really serious about a lot of things." He checked his cell phone, saw it had no signal, then turned his attention back to the road. About halfway to the highway, they passed two armed guards, sitting on the tailgate of a Calloway truck, rifles in one hand, cigarettes in the other. Around the last curve before the highway, they reached the other two guards, similarly occupied. Both men raised a hand in greeting when they recognized Russ's truck.

As soon as he turned onto the road, the cell's signal strength went to maximum. He called Tommy, expecting to drag him out of bed or maybe catch him in the middle of his morning run, but Tommy was wide-awake and wasn't out of breath. There was a lot of noise in the background—shouts, the slow wail of a siren winding down, some sort of crackling.

"I've been trying to reach you," Tommy said.

"There's a dead zone on the road out here. What's up?"

"Someone set Jamie's house on fire. It's fully involved. Don't think they're gonna be able to save anything. And about a minute ago they got a call to another fire, this one on Calhoun Street. Lys's duplex. *Damn.*" Tommy's last word was followed by a crash so loud that Jamie, across the seat, flinched.

Russ could imagine the scene: fire trucks and police cars, their lights flashing in the dawn, neighbors standing around in robes or hastily thrown-on clothes, flames devouring everything in their path, brick and mortar collapsing into rubble.

But Jamie was safe. That was all that mattered.

"Lys called," Russ said shortly. "Said Jamie's office has been trashed and she wants Jamie to come in."

"So you go in to check it out, get surprised by the stalker, one or both of you get killed, and Lys discovers your bodies later this morning."

"Sounds about right. We're just coming into town. Why don't we meet someplace?"

"What? You don't want to face her alone?" Tommy teased.

"I'm not a cop," Russ retorted. "I'm not paid to deal with nutcases."

"I hear some of those people you build houses for can get pretty psycho. Meet me at the doughnut shop. I'm on my way." The sound of a gunning engine confirmed that an instant before the line went dead.

Russ set the phone on the seat beside him, then glanced at Jamie. He wasn't good at gently breaking news to anyone. When he'd returned from spring break that last year of law school, his first stop had been Jamie's apartment. She'd been looking pretty ragged from her bout of illness, and he'd said hello, how do you feel, then blurted out the words. *I met a girl, and we're getting married the week after graduation.*

Now he was just as blunt. "She set your house on fire."

Jamie's eyes widened, and she jerked around to look to the right. The sky had lightened enough to show plumes of dark smoke rising in the west, with occasional glimpses of a yellowish glow through the trees. Mouth open, she looked back at him, trying to speak but unable to put a thought together. "But— She— Why?"

"She set her house on fire, too. And what do you want to bet that she plans to burn the office, too, with me in it?"

Jamie's shoulders sagged, and suddenly she looked very tired, very fragile. Russ wanted to keep driving through the town and on into the day. He wanted to pull over and put his arms around her and hold her until she was strong again, to protect her from any more hurt or betrayal. But he made the turn for the doughnut shop, pulling into the parking lot where Tommy's SUV and three marked units were waiting.

Five minutes later, Jamie, still shaken and pale, got into Tommy's vehicle with him. Russ left the parking lot first, driving the few blocks downtown, turning at the square, taking the next right and parking in front of Jamie's building. Tommy and his officers stayed around the corner, out of sight.

Russ's palms were sweaty as he got out, touched Tommy's two-way radio in his pocket, locked in the transmit position, and crossed the sidewalk. His heart was beating a little too fast, his breaths coming a little shallow. Was this how Rick and Mitch felt when they started a new undercover assignment or found themselves face-to-face with the bad guys? They might thrive on the adrenaline rush, but not Russ. He just wanted life to go back to dull and boring. Just him and Jamie doing ordinary things—working, making love, making a home and a family.

He went inside the building, down the hall, then turned into the office. The first thing he noticed was the faint whiff of gasoline. He'd guessed right about one thing.

There was no sign of Lys immediately, but her words had certainly been true. The furniture had been tossed about, the cushions slashed open. Damaged books littered the floor, and the contents of the desk drawers had been dumped. The computer lay in pieces, and great gouges marked the walls. Even the carpet had been sliced in a fit of rage.

A noise came from Jamie's office—a soft pant—and he slowly, cautiously walked that way. The gasoline odor was stronger there; from the doorway, he saw the spout of a five-gallon can showing behind the overturned desk. The damage was the same as outside. Large sections of carpet were hidden under piles of paper from the file room, and Jamie's law degree lay in pieces around the room. Even the potted plant that had stood in the corner was destroyed, yanked from its pot, leaves stripped off.

Behind the desk, next to the gas can, stood Lys. She wore black jeans and a black T-shirt, and her hair was disheveled, her normally pale face red with exertion. Her eyes were glittering with excitement, anticipation, fury, and *he* was her target.

"Where's Jamie?" she demanded.

"She's still pretty weak. I left her at home." He wished he could have. If he could have let her rest, come out and dealt with this, then gone home to tell her that it was all over… But how could he have left her when there was a chance Lys was just trying to lure him away so *she* could get to her?

He moved a few steps farther into the room. "You usually jog in black jeans and a black shirt before dawn?" he asked mildly. "It's a wonder someone hasn't run you down." A pity, too. He waited a moment before he flatly stated, "She's in love with me, you know."

She shook her head so vehemently that the ends of her hair

slapped her cheeks. "No. She's just emotional. Infatuated. She loves *me*. She said so."

He shook his head, too, slower, more emphatically. "She's been in love with me a long time. What she feels for you is friendship. That's all she'll ever feel for you."

Now her entire body was shaking. "No. No, she just thinks... It's this whole rescuer-victim thing. It wasn't supposed to work out this way. You weren't supposed to screw things up."

"You're the one who screwed things up. You stalked her. You drugged her dog. You scared her."

"It wasn't like that! I was—I was flirting with her. The note, the candy, the roses...they were just sweet little gifts. Having a secret admirer is fun, it's sexy. It's nothing to be scared of!"

Russ took a step and glass crunched beneath his feet. He glanced down and saw a photograph of Jamie with her family. It had been taken at a sister's wedding, and Jamie looked so happy. So carefree. "You *drugged* her dog."

Lys's expression turned mutinous. "She was watching you, thinking about you, remembering... I saw the look on her face. I knew she thought she still cared about you. She didn't, of course. She was just confused. Besides, Mischa was never at risk. It was just a sedative. I made sure the dose was right for her size."

"You put the tack strip under her tire."

Lys shrugged jerkily. "A flat. No big deal. It wasn't even her car. And it was a good plan. She would back out, her tire would go flat, and I'd come around the corner, headed home with her favorite pizza. Then you showed up and ruined it. You ruined everything. I was on my way to her house the next night to help her take Mischa to the vet, but you were there. When

Tommy suggested she stay someplace else, she was supposed to come to *my* house, but you had already persuaded her to go home with you. You ruined it all!"

What was her plan now? He would have bet on a sneak attack—both times she'd caught Jamie off-guard. Given his size and the fact that he was inherently stronger than her, waiting behind the door with a baseball bat seemed more her style.

Then she moved, pulling a pistol from beneath her T-shirt, pointing it at him, her hand shaking violently. Jesus. Was this how Rick and Mitch felt when they knew odds were good they could die in the next few minutes? Probably not. If they ever got as scared as he was at that moment, they'd turn in their badges and take up fishing for a living.

He swallowed hard and forced a breath into his lungs. He didn't want to die here. He had too many reasons to live, starting and ending with Jamie. He'd wasted too much time being pissed off and hurt, and he wanted to make up for that. He wanted to die at a ripe old age with Jamie holding his hand.

He swallowed again. "Tommy knows it's you, Lys. He'll never let you get away with killing me, and Jamie will never forgive you for it."

Her agitation increased. "It doesn't matter now. Don't you see? Nothing matters now because of you! We had a chance. I know we did! And then you…"

From the corner of his eye, he gauged the distance between him and the door. Five, maybe six feet back and to his right. Whether he could make it would depend on how good a shot she was. The way she was trembling should count to his advantage, but the only thing worse than a competent person with a gun, Granddad used to say, was an incompetent one.

Where the hell was Tommy? Surely they'd heard enough by

now. It was past time for them to come busting into the room, but he hadn't heard even a whisper of sound from outside.

"You won't even have her friendship anymore, Lys," he said, easing one step closer to the door.

"I know," she said softly. "But you won't have her, either. And she'll be sorry. She'll regret the choices she made. She'll realize that I really was the best thing that ever happened to her. She tells me that, you know. That she loves me. That meeting me was her lucky day."

Her face screwed up and tears filled her eyes. "She lies. She loves you, she doesn't know what she would do without you—she's lying. She says the same things to me, and she didn't mean them. She never meant them." Angrily, she wiped her free hand across her face, and the other hand, the one with the gun, grew steadier. "She'll be sorry when we're dead."

Russ swallowed hard again. So much for using threat of arrest to sway her. He took another step back, but the crunch of glass underfoot brought her attention to what he was doing. She cocked the hammer on the pistol, leveled it square on his chest and snarled, "Stay where you are. Don't move—"

The gunshot was deafening in the confines of the office. For an instant, everything about him froze—no breath, no thought, no emotion—as he watched Lys's body jerk backward, thrown against the wall by the force of the blast. An instant later Tommy stepped into the room, his weapon in hand, and said quietly, "Funny. That's what I was about to say. You all right?"

Russ nodded. It would be a surprise if he made it outside without his legs giving way under him, but he was okay. He wasn't going to die, not today at least. Jamie was safe and waiting for him outside— No, she was shaking off the cop who tried to stop her at the door. Tears glittered in her eyes as she wrenched free, then hurtled across the room, throwing herself into his arms.

His legs weren't as weak as he thought. He caught her without staggering back more than a step or two and held her tightly, his face buried in her hair.

After a moment, she forced his head back, her hands cupped to his cheeks, and stared into his face. "Oh my God, Russ! She was going to kill you, and I'd never even told you I love you. I was so—" She swallowed. "Are you all right?"

Lys had been shot. Jamie's house and office had been destroyed. Her life was still in chaos, and as long as her life was, so was his. There would be statements to give, cleanups to start, all the hassles that came with vandalism and arson and attempted murder and criminal trials.

But he was alive, and the woman he loved had just said she loved him back. The rest of it paled to insignificance in the face of that.

"I'm better than all right," he told her, gently touching the uninjured side of her face. "I'm damn fine."

She smiled faintly. "And that's good?"

He smiled, too. "You and me together, James, for the rest of our lives…that's as good as it gets."

Epilogue

Jamie gazed at the ruins of her house, still smoldering in the morning light. She couldn't imagine the belonging that could have survived such heat. Everything—brick, concrete, steel—lay in a careless tumble, and sooty odor filled the air.

She sighed, and Russ, standing behind her, tightened his arms around her middle. "I know a great builder. He can replace this with anything your heart desires."

Her heart desired a lot, and in the past twenty-four hours, she'd gotten a lot. Russ was alive and well, Lys was under guard in the hospital, and the danger was past. Better, Russ had told her he loved her. Wanted her. Wanted babies with her. Yep, that was as good as it got.

Smiling, she turned in his arms to face him. "Actually, I've got my eye on a house north of town. Two years old, tough to find, but worth the effort."

"I know the place. It's not for sale."

"Oh, I don't want to buy it. I just want to share it."

His grin was charming. "There are some stiff requirements—marriage, a family, the rest of our lives."

"I think I can meet those." She moved so close that his breath was warm on her skin and murmured, "I have a stiff requirement or two of my own."

Right there, where anyone could see, he slid his hands to her hips and pulled her snug against him. "My requirements aren't negotiable. They're hard and fast."

"Funny. So are mine." She brushed her mouth across his. "And slow and easy, and always, always fine."

He kissed her, making her breath catch and her head spin, making everything right. Six years ago she had dreamed of so much with this man, and then he'd gone off and fallen in love with someone else, married someone else. But things happened in their own time, and six years ago hadn't been their time. They'd needed to grow, to each become the person the other couldn't live without.

Ending the kiss, he gazed at her for a time, his expression intense, then smiled. "Let's go home, James."

She let him lead her toward the truck, where she glanced back at the rubble of her house. They'd survived their trial by fire. She didn't expect everything to be easy from now on.

But she damn sure expected it to be fine.

* * * * *

*Mills & Boon® Intrigue brings you
a sneak preview of...*

Delores Fossen's Security Blanket

*Quinn "Lucky" Bacelli thought saving Marin Sheppard
would be the end of their dalliance. But then she asked
him for protection from her domineering parents. And
to pretend to be the father of her infant son...*

Don't miss this thrilling first story in the new
TEXAS PATERNITY: BOOTS AND BOOTIES
*mini-series available next month from
Mills & Boon® Intrigue.*

Security Blanket
by
Delores Fossen

The man was watching her.

Marin Sheppard was sure of it.

He wasn't staring, exactly. In fact, he hadn't even looked at her, though he'd been seated directly across from her in the lounge car of the train for the past fifteen minutes. He seemed to focus his attention on the wintry Texas landscape that zipped past the window. But several times Marin had met his gaze in the reflection of the glass.

Yes, he was watching her.

That kicked up her heart rate a couple of notches. A too-familiar nauseating tightness started to knot Marin's stomach.

Was it starting all over again?

Was he watching her, hoping that she'd lead him to her brother, Dexter? Or was this yet another attempt by her parents to insinuate themselves into her life?

It'd been over eight months since the last time this happened. A former "business associate" of her brother who was riled that he'd paid for a "product" that Dexter hadn't delivered. The man had followed her around Fort Worth for days. He hadn't been subtle about it, either, and that had made him seem all the more menacing. And she hadn't given birth to Noah yet then.

The stakes were so much higher now.

Marin hugged her sleeping son closer to her chest. He smelled like baby shampoo and the rice cereal he'd had for lunch. She brushed a kiss on his forehead and rocked gently. Not so much for him—Noah was sound asleep and might stay that way for the remaining hour of the trip to San Antonio. No, the rocking, the kiss and the snug embrace were more for her benefit, to help steady her nerves.

And it worked.

"Cute kid," she heard someone say. The man across from her. Who else? There were no other travelers in this particular section of the lounge car.

Marin lifted her gaze. Met his again. But this time it wasn't through the buffer of the glass, and she clearly saw his eyes, a blend of silver and smoke, framed with indecently long, dark eyelashes.

She studied him a moment, trying to decide if she knew him. He was on the lanky side. Midnight-colored hair. High cheekbones. A classically chiseled male jaw.

The only thing that saved him from being a total pretty boy was the one-inch scar angled across his right eyebrow, thin but noticeable. Not a precise surgeon's cut, a jagged, angry mark left from an old injury. It conjured images of barroom brawls, tattooed bikers and bashed beer bottles. Not that Marin had firsthand knowledge of such things.

But she would bet that he did.

He wore jeans that fit as if they'd been tailor-made for him, a dark blue pullover shirt that hugged his chest and a black leather bomber jacket. And snakeskin boots—specifically diamondback rattlesnake. Pricey and conspicuous footwear.

No, she didn't know him. Marin was certain she would have remembered him—a realization that bothered her because he was hot, and she was sorry she'd noticed.

He tipped his head toward Noah. "I meant your baby," he clarified. "Cute kid."

"Thank you." She looked away from the man, hoping it was the end of their brief conversation.

It wasn't.

"He's what...seven, eight months old?"

"Eight," she provided.

"He reminds me a little of my nephew," the man continued. "It must be hard, traveling alone with a baby."

That brought Marin's attention racing across the car. What had provoked that remark? She searched his face and his eyes almost frantically, trying to figure out if it was some sort of veiled threat.

He held up his hands, and a nervous laugh sounded from deep within his chest. "Sorry. Didn't mean to alarm you. It's just I noticed you're wearing a medical alert bracelet."

Marin glanced down at her left wrist. The almond-shaped metal disc was peeking out from the cuff of her sleeve. With its classic caduceus symbol engraved in crimson, it was like his boots—impossible to miss.

"I'm epileptic," she said.

"Oh." Concern dripped from the word.

"Don't worry," she countered. "I keep my seizures under control with meds. I haven't had one in over five years."

She immediately wondered why in the name of heaven she'd volunteered that personal information. Her medical history wasn't any of his business; it was a sore spot she didn't want to discuss.

"Is your epilepsy the reason you took the train?" he asked. "I mean, instead of driving?"

Marin frowned at him. "I thought the train would make the trip easier for my son."

He nodded, apparently satisfied with her answer to his intrusive question. When his attention strayed back in the general direction of her bracelet, Marin followed his gaze. Down to her hand. All the way to her bare ring finger.

Even though her former fiancé, Randall Davidson, had asked her to marry him, he'd never given her an engagement ring. It'd been an empty, bare gesture. A thought that riled her even now. Randall's betrayal had cut her to the bone.

Shifting Noah into the crook of her arm, she reached down to collect her diaper bag. "I think I'll go for a little walk and stretch my legs."

And change seats, she silently added.

Judging from the passengers she'd seen get on and off, the train wasn't crowded, so moving into coach seating shouldn't be a problem. In fact, she should have done it sooner.

"I'm sorry," he said. "I made you uncomfortable with my questions."

His words stopped her because they were sincere. Or at least he sounded that way. Of course, she'd been wrong before. It would take another lifetime or two for her to trust her instincts.

And that was the reason she reached for the bag again.

"Stay, *please*," he insisted. "It'll be easier for me to move." He got up, headed for the exit and then stopped, turning back around to face her. "I was hitting on you."

Marin blinked. "You…what?"

"Hitting on you," he clarified.

Oh.

That took her a few moments to process.

"Really?" Marin asked, sounding far more surprised than she wanted.

He chuckled, something low, husky and male. Something that trickled through her like expensive warm whiskey. "Really." But then, the lightheartedness faded from his eyes, and his jaw muscles started to stir. "I shouldn't have done it. Sorry."

Again, he seemed sincere. So maybe he wasn't watching her after all. Well, not for surveillance any way. Maybe he was watching her because she was a woman. Odd, that she'd forgotten all about basic human attraction and lust.

"You don't have to leave," Marin let him know. Because she suddenly didn't know what to do with her fidgety hands, she ran her fingers through Noah's dark blond curls. "Besides, it won't be long before we're in San Antonio."

He nodded, and it had an air of thankfulness to it. "I'm Quinn Bacelli. Most people though just call me Lucky."

She almost gave him a fake name. Old habits. But it was the truth that came out of her mouth. "Marin Sheppard."

He smiled. It was no doubt a lethal weapon in his arsenal of ways to get women to fall at his feet. Or into his bed. It bothered Marin to realize that she wasn't immune to it.

Good grief. Hadn't her time with Randall taught her anything?

"Well, Marin Sheppard," he said, taking his seat again. "No more hitting on you. Promise."

Good. She mentally repeated that several times, and then wondered why she felt mildly disappointed.

Noah stirred, sucked at a nonexistent bottle and then gave a pouty whimper when he realized it wasn't there. His eyelids fluttered open, and he blinked, focused and looked up at Marin with accusing blue-green eyes that were identical to her own. He made another whimper, probably to let her know that he wasn't pleased about having his nap interrupted.

Her son shifted and wriggled until he was in a sitting position in her lap, and the new surroundings immediately caught his attention. What was left of his whimpering expression evaporated. He examined his puppy socks, the window, the floor, the ceiling and the ruby-red exit sign. Even her garnet heart necklace. Then, his attention landed on the man seated across from him.

Noah grinned at him.

The man grinned back. "Did you have a good nap, buddy?"

Noah babbled a cordial response, something the two males must have understood, because they shared another smile.

Marin looked at Quinn "Lucky" Bacelli. Then, at her son. Their smiles seemed to freeze in place.

There was no warning.

A deafening blast ripped through the car.

One moment Marin was sitting on the seat with her son cradled in her arms, and the next she was flying across the narrow space right at Lucky.

Everything moved fast. So fast. And yet it happened in slow motion, too. It seemed part of some nightmarish dream where everything was tearing apart at the seams.

Debris spewed through the air. The diaper bag, the magazine she'd been reading, the very walls themselves. All of it, along with Noah and her.

Something slammed into her back and the left side of her head. It knocked the breath from her. The pain was instant—searing—and it sliced right through her, blurring her vision.

She and Noah landed in Lucky's arms, propelled against him. But he softened the fall. He turned, immediately, pushing them down against the seat and crawling over them so he could shelter them with his body.

INTRIGUE

Coming next month

2-IN-1 ANTHOLOGY

SECURITY BLANKET by Delores Fossen

Lucky thought saving Marin would be the end of their affair. But when she asks him to pretend to be the father of her infant son, it's an offer he can't refuse…

HIS 7-DAY FIANCÉE by Gail Barrett

When Amanda is held at gunpoint in his casino it's up to Luke to protect her – by pretending to be her fiancé! Yet could their fake engagement put them in danger too?

2-IN-1 ANTHOLOGY

THE BODYGUARD'S PROMISE by Carla Cassidy

Clay West isn't happy about his latest bodyguard assignment, protecting a Hollywood child star from an unknown menace… until he meets the tiny starlet's sexy mum!

THE MISSING MILLIONAIRE by Dani Sinclair

Harrison's shocked to discover beautiful Jamie's his new bodyguard. And Jamie's ready to risk everything to protect him – even losing her heart.

SINGLE TITLE

THE VAMPIRE'S QUEST by Vivi Anna

Nocturne™

Vampire Kellen has come to the city of Nouveau Monde to save himself. But fiery Sophie is about to cause him even more trouble!

On sale 18th December 2009

Available at WHSmith, Tesco, ASDA, Eason and all good bookshops.
For full Mills & Boon range including eBooks visit
www.millsandboon.co.uk

INTRIGUE

Coming next month

2-IN-1 ANTHOLOGY

HIS BEST FRIEND'S BABY by Mallory Kane

When ex-air-force man Matt's dead best friend's tiny son goes missing he is determined to save the child. But he didn't expect his attraction to widow Aimee.

THE NIGHT SERPENT by Anna Leonard

Lily is an ordinary girl. Until she's caught up in a murder investigation led by Special Agent Jon Patrick and learns she is being stalked by the Night Serpent.

SINGLE TITLE

MATCHMAKING WITH A MISSION
by BJ Daniels

McKenna can't keep her mind off brooding bad boy Nate. He's come back to town to bury his past – but McKenna is determined to get him back at the ranch by her side.

SINGLE TITLE

CAVANAUGH HEAT
by Marie Ferrarella

It's been years since top cop Brian Cavanaugh has seen his former partner Lila, but he's surprised to discover their chemistry is as hot as ever!

On sale 1ˢᵗ January 2010

Available at WHSmith, Tesco, ASDA, Eason and all good bookshops.
For full Mills & Boon range including eBooks visit
www.millsandboon.co.uk

millsandboon.co.uk Community

Join Us!

The Community is the perfect place to meet and chat to kindred spirits who love books and reading as much as you do, but it's also the place to:

- **Get the inside scoop from authors about their latest books**
- **Learn how to write a romance book with advice from our editors**
- **Help us to continue publishing the best in women's fiction**
- **Share your thoughts on the books we publish**
- **Befriend other users**

Forums: Interact with each other as well as authors, editors and a whole host of other users worldwide.

Blogs: Every registered community member has their own blog to tell the world what they're up to and what's on their mind.

Book Challenge: We're aiming to read 5,000 books and have joined forces with The Reading Agency in our inaugural Book Challenge.

Profile Page: Showcase yourself and keep a record of your recent community activity.

Social Networking: We've added buttons at the end of every post to share via digg, Facebook, Google, Yahoo, technorati and de.licio.us.

www.millsandboon.co.uk

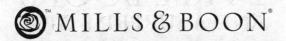

2 FREE BOOKS
AND A SURPRISE GIFT

We would like to take this opportunity to thank you for reading this Mills & Boon® book by offering you the chance to take TWO more specially selected books from the Intrigue series absolutely FREE! We're also making this offer to introduce you to the benefits of the Mills & Boon® Book Club™—

- **FREE home delivery**
- **FREE gifts and competitions**
- **FREE monthly Newsletter**
- **Exclusive Mills & Boon Book Club offers**
- **Books available before they're in the shops**

Accepting these FREE books and gift places you under no obligation to buy, you may cancel at any time, even after receiving your free books. Simply complete your details below and return the entire page to the address below. You don't even need a stamp!

YES Please send me 2 free Intrigue books and a surprise gift. I understand that unless you hear from me, I will receive 5 superb new stories every month, including two 2-in-1 books priced at £4.99 each and a single book priced at £3.19, postage and packing free. I am under no obligation to purchase any books and may cancel my subscription at any time. The free books and gift will be mine to keep in any case.

Ms/Mrs/Miss/Mr _____ Initials _____

_____

Surname _____

Address _____

_____

_____ Postcode _____

Send this whole page to: Mills & Boon Book Club, Free Book Offer, FREEPOST NAT 10298, Richmond, TW9 1BR